the
MIDNIGHT
WATCH

the
MIDNIGHT
WATCH

A NOVEL OF THE *TITANIC* AND THE *CALIFORNIAN*

DAVID DYER

St. Martin's Press ⧉ New York

THE MIDNIGHT WATCH. Copyright © 2016 by David Dyer. All rights reserved. Printed in the United States of America. For information, address St. Martin's Press, 175 Fifth Avenue, New York, N.Y. 10010.

www.stmartins.com

Library of Congress Cataloging-in-Publication Data

Names: Dyer, David, 1966– author.
Title: The midnight watch : a novel of the Titanic and the Californian / David Dyer.
Description: First U.S. edition. | New York : St. Martin's Press, 2016. | "First published in Australia by Penguin Group (Australia)"—Title page verso.
Identifiers: LCCN 2015044975| ISBN 9781250080936 (hardcover) | ISBN 9781466893085 (e-book)
Subjects: LCSH: Titanic (Steamship)—Fiction. | Californian (Ship)— Fiction. | Shipwrecks—North Atlantic Ocean—Fiction. | GSAFD: Historical fiction.
Classification: LCC PR9619.4.D94 M53 2016 | DDC 823/.92—dc23
LC record available at http://lccn.loc.gov/2015044975

Our books may be purchased in bulk for promotional, educational, or business use. Please contact your local bookseller or the Macmillan Corporate and Premium Sales Department at 1-800-221-7945, extension 5442, or by e-mail at MacmillanSpecialMarkets@macmillan.com.

First published in Australia by Penguin Australia Pty Ltd

First U.S. Edition: April 2016

10   9   8   7   6   5   4   3   2   1

FOR MY MOTHER AND FATHER

'Consider the subtleness of the sea; how its most dreaded creatures glide under water, unapparent for the most part, and treacherously hidden beneath the loveliest tints of azure.'

HERMAN MELVILLE

Contents

the
MIDNIGHT
WATCH

Part One

CHAPTER I

In the early years of the twentieth century my father heard that there was good money to be made in Venezuela. He had reliable information – from a Spaniard who knew a cattle-herder who knew the Venezuelan president personally – that more oil seeps had been discovered and that further concessions would soon be granted. Although I was living in Boston and had profitable work as a journalist, I agreed to go with him. His plan was to explore the seeps, obtain concessions and sell them on. 'A year's work to make a fortune,' he said. He also said my wife Olive and two young children could come too. It would be perfectly safe.

But it was not safe. A month after our arrival my baby son got a fever and a week later he was dead. He was four months old.

On the morning that he died, the local women came to help my wife dress his tiny body and rub red powder into his cheeks. They placed him gently among flowers and candles. Olive would not let me touch the baby: I had killed him by bringing him here, I had no more rights over him. He stayed where he was for the whole day, and then another. I was not allowed to bury him.

On the third day, I took Harriet, our six-year-old daughter, to my father's temporary office – a ramshackle building on stilts a few miles north, along the shore of a swampy, sulphurous asphalt lake. I planned to keep her busy and show her that life went on. We visited nearby seeps, unpacked equipment and spoke to local workers. At dusk we watched lightning dance among the vapours of the lake. The effect was dramatic and unearthly; Harriet squealed and clapped her hands. I was pleased. I wanted her to see that the spark that was no longer in her brother existed elsewhere, that there was energy all around.

But when we arrived home we saw that the family chickens had been slaughtered in their pens. They lay in the mud featherless and mutilated. Harriet – who had tended these birds, given them names and collected their eggs – slipped her quivering hand into mine.

As we climbed the stairs we heard rhythmic clapping and the singing of songs in Spanish. I held Harriet's hand tight and opened the door. The mosquito nets had been removed from the windows and candles placed on the sills. A makeshift altar of taller candles had been built on the floor, around which local women – half a dozen or so, all dressed in white – sat on boxes. When they saw us they sang and clapped louder, rocking back and forth.

In the centre of the room, on the floor near the altar, sat my wife. Perhaps she had drunk liquor, because she did not seem to notice us.

Harriet began to cry. At first I did not know why, but then I saw. Her mother was holding thin hemp strings that ran up to the ceiling through a crude system of blocks and pulleys. I followed the strings upwards and there, suspended from the central beam, was the body of my son. He too was dressed in white, and was covered in feathers. Bird wings, still bloody, were attached to his shoulders and they opened and closed as my wife pulled the strings.

A woman came to Harriet, dabbed at her tears with a rag and said, in faltering English, 'No tears, no tears – tears wet the wings of the angel, he cannot fly to heaven.' The woman turned to me: my son was an *innocente*, she said, an angel baby. His place in heaven was certain, and there could be no greater happiness. No one must cry. The other women clapped and sang. '*Nada de lagrimas. Nada de lagrimas.*' Olive joined in the clapping, applauding the dead little body creaking on its contraption of strings and pulleys.

It took only seconds for me to pull it all down. The women screamed; I felt one beating me hard on my back. I ignored them and held the tiny corpse in my arms. At first I was repulsed by this grotesque parody of my son – even after I tore away the feathers and bloodied wings, its strange, deadweight stiffness appalled me. But as I looked into the face I became mesmerised. His eyes were open and he peered out into the world with an unfocused stare, just as he had when he was born, seeming to see everything but nothing: so physically present but so absent too. There is something strange and profound in the gaze of the newly born and the newly dead. They seem able to see two worlds at once.

Olive tried to retrieve the baby from me but I pushed her away. She slapped me hard across the face and said she would not let me take him from her a second time. There was hot blood in my cheeks and stinging tears in my eyes, but my wife's face was blank and dry. Not then or ever after did I see her cry for our poor son.

'There is a better way,' I said, turning from her and carrying the small body outside to be washed by the rain.

I buried him on top of a green and gentle hill overlooking the lake. Harriet stood with me as I did so and said a quick prayer of goodbye. A week later we returned to Boston. Olive refused to speak to me about our son, but I showed her some brief sketches I'd made of him in words: the way his tiny fingers had curled tightly shut when she tickled his palm with her breath, how he was soothed by the smell of orange skins.

Over the following months I wrote of our son's life in more detail. I began, even, to extend it a little by envisaging his future. I published a small portrait of him in a Boston magazine in which he grew into a young boy who raced automobiles. Olive read my work, but she never forgave me. I might be able to convey something of a likeness of our son, she said, but I would never be able to show how much she had loved him. That was something beyond words.

In time I began to write about others who had died – at first, people I'd known personally, but then strangers too. I began to specialise in floods, fires and catastrophes. At the *Boston American*, where I worked, I became known as the Body Man. If there was a disaster, they would call me. I wrote about the sinking of the *General Slocum*, the Terra Cotta train wreck, the Great Chelsea Fire, and more. When I tried to report on commerce or politics, my writing lacked – well, the *life* of my body stories. The city editor said I should stick to what I did best, and so 'follow the bodies' became my motto.

But I want to say at the outset that I was never a ghoul. I respected the dead. I always sought out the truth of how they had died, and when I wrote about them I thought always of my own son and how much I loved him. I wanted to give the poor mangled bodies of this world a voice. I wanted to make them live again. My writing was an act of justice.

In 1911 I happened to be in New York when the Triangle Shirtwaist factory caught fire, killing nearly a hundred and fifty people, most of them young immigrant women. I saw the Asch Building ablaze at Washington Place and watched the girls jumping from the ninth and tenth floors. I saw five girls leap together from a window, their hair and dresses on fire. I saw another girl hang as long as she could from the brick sill until the flames touched her hands and she let go. I watched another stand at a window, throw out her pocket book, hat and coat, and step out into the cool evening air as calmly as if she were boarding a train.

When the bodies were taken to a ramshackle pier adjacent to the Bellevue Hospital I followed them. They were lined up in neat double rows, either side of the long dock, some in open boxes, others simply laid on the bare planking. I walked up and down. I said sorry on behalf of my country to those poor girls, who stared back at me in open-eyed surprise, and I took notes. In the following weeks, I found out the truth of what happened to them. I told the world how Max Blanck, the factory's owner, had climbed a ladder to a building next door and left them to die. I brought the girls to life as best I could, publishing stories in Boston, New York and London. Like a courtroom sketch artist, I tried to capture their likenesses in a few finely observed strokes – a phrase here, a sentence there. It worked. People read my little portraits and felt the injustice of it all. They said such a thing must never happen again. At the *Boston American* the city editor passed a note to his juniors: 'If there are bodies, call Steadman.'

So when my telephone rang at two o'clock one Monday morning just over a year later, I knew it would be my newspaper and I knew there would be bodies. I wasn't disappointed. The duty editor told me an extraordinary thing: the new *Titanic* had struck ice and been seriously damaged. People may have been killed in the collision. The station at Cape Race had heard the ship calling for help. The duty editor assured me he was perfectly serious; it was not a joke.

I dressed quickly and walked the mile and a half from my apartment to the *Boston American* office. The streets were deserted. There was no moon and shreds of cold mist drifted in from the harbour like floating cobwebs. I could smell saltwater. In downtown Boston the North Atlantic always felt close and alive, but at this hour it seemed especially so. I thought about the *Titanic* out there somewhere, her bow crushed, crewmen caught in the mangled steel. I began to plan how I might get aboard when the ship limped into port.

When I arrived at the Washington Street office, Krupp, the city editor, was already there, shouting at newsboys and dictating cablegrams. Tickers clattered and telephone bells rang. As soon as he saw me Krupp told me to go downstairs and get hold of someone from White Star in New York on the long-distance line – preferably Philip Franklin himself. But the line was overloaded. The operator could not get me through. I tried instead to call Dan Byrne, my friend at Dow Jones, and then the Associated Press, but the lines were busy.

'Never mind about the telephone then,' Krupp said, interweaving his fingers so that his hands looked like a mechanical bird trying to take flight. 'Go down there, to New York, on the first train, and get it all from Franklin direct. There are bodies here, John, I can smell 'em.' He laughed at his own joke.

A couple of hours later, as streaks of pale grey began to lie along the horizon and a feeble crescent moon showed itself in the eastern sky, I boarded the train out of Boston for New York. Something told me that Krupp was right: there was a good body story for me here. I felt a tingling energy in my fingers, as though they were already beginning to write it.

CHAPTER 2

Herbert Stone tapped his teeth with his fingers as if playing a small piano. He had come from his cabin to the port side of the promenade deck to take his afternoon sun sights, and been surprised to see three large, flat-topped icebergs a mile or so away across the still ocean. They were magnificent things, with lofty cliffs catching the yellows and pinks of early sunset, but Stone was worried. Only last year the *Columbia* had struck ice off Cape Race and smashed up her hull plates, and this year even more bergs had come sweeping south into the shipping lanes. There would be many more up ahead.

He lifted his sextant, put in place its shades and took two altitudes of the low sun. He then stepped into the chartroom, a small space squeezed between the captain's cabin on one side and a bare steel bulkhead on the other, and began to work up his sights. Someone had marked on the chart the ice reported by wireless over past days, and most of it lay to the west, directly across their track. When he plotted the ship's position he saw that the ice was only about seven hours' steaming away. They would likely meet it during his watch later that night.

Stone walked back to the ship's rail and looked again towards the south. The three icebergs had drifted astern but he could still see them, stately and tall and brilliantly lit. But he knew not all icebergs were like this. Some were low and grey, and tonight there would be no moon. He wondered how, during the dark hours of the midnight watch, he would able to see them.

The SS *Californian* was an ordinary ship, but that's what Herbert Stone liked most about her. The glamorous new liners of White Star or Cunard were not for him; this modest vessel was good enough. She was middle-aged, middle-sized, and carried commonplace cargoes. Sometimes she also carried passengers – in nineteen old-style, oak-panelled state-rooms – but there had been no bookings for this trip. Instead she had loaded in London textiles, chemicals, machine parts, clothing and general goods, and waiting for her in Boston were a hundred thousand bushels of wheat and corn, a thousand bales of cotton, fifteen hundred tons of Santo Domingo sugar, and other assorted cargoes.

Stone had learned during his training that ships could be spiteful, dangerous things. They could part a mooring rope so that its broken end whoop-whooped through the air like a giant scythe, or take a man's arm off by dragging him into a winch drum, or break his back by sending him sprawling down a cargo hold. But the *Californian* had done none of these. She was gentle and benign. She had four strong steel masts, and a single slender funnel that glowed salmon-pink and glossy black when the sun shone on it. She rode easy in the Atlantic swells, found her way through the thickest fogs, and her derricks never dropped their cargo. She was a vessel at ease with herself – unpretentious, steady and solid.

Stone was proud to be her second officer and each day he tried to serve his ship as best he could. He was responsible for the navigation charts, making sure they were correct and up to date, and had charge of the twelve-till-four watch. From midday until four o'clock in the afternoon, and from midnight until four o'clock in the morning, he stood watch on the bridge and had command of the ship. The twelve-till-four shift at night was properly called the middle watch, but most sailors knew it as the midnight watch and Stone liked the name: it gave a touch of magic to those four dark hours when the captain and crew slept below and he alone kept them safe.

The midnight watch required vigilance, so he tried always to get some good sleep beforehand. While other officers might visit the saloon after dinner to play cards with the off-duty engineers, or even have a shot of whisky, Stone would retire to his cabin. By eight o'clock he'd be in bed reading, and by nine he would be asleep. That gave him almost three hours' sleep before his watch began.

But on this cold Sunday night, halfway between London and Boston, he found himself still awake at nine-thirty. He was thinking about the icebergs he'd seen. The lively bounce and throb of his bunk told him that the ship was still steaming at full speed. He thought the captain might have slowed down as darkness fell, given there was ice about, and he was worried they might keep up full speed for the whole night. Stone pictured the men crowded into cramped living quarters low in the ship's bow – the bosun, the carpenter, the able-bodied seamen, the greasers, trimmers, firemen and donkeymen – lying in their bunks with less than half an inch of steel between their sleeping heads and the black Atlantic hissing past outside.

He flicked on his reading light and took up his book again – *Moby-Dick*, a gift from his mother. The novel soothed him. He thought no more about icebergs but instead imagined Starbuck aloft, scanning the horizon, handsome in his excellent-fitting skin, radiant with courage and much loved by a noble captain.

In the wireless room Cyril Evans, a bespectacled twenty-year-old with black hair pasted flat to his head with machine oil, was at work at his equipment. He loved the new technology. He'd been a star pupil at the Marconi school in London, mastering quickly the dash-dot sequences of Morse code, learning the rhythm first of each letter and then of complete words and sentences. Nowadays he even dreamt in the code.

Evans had been happy to be appointed to the *Californian* when her wireless set was installed on the previous voyage, but life on board soon became difficult. Captain Lord, on their first meeting, looked at him as if he were part of the machinery, a box with wires and dials, and had referred to the equipment as 'an instrument for tittle-tattle and gossip'. The wireless room doubled as Cyril's sleeping quarters, and within this confined space he worked from seven o'clock in the morning until eleven o'clock at night, seven days a week. Whenever he walked on the open deck, sailors laughed at his thin arms and thick glasses. During a lifeboat drill he had been assigned the role of panicking passenger, and when the seamen asked him to sit in the stern and look pretty, and then to put on a lady's hat and cry for help, he tried to join in the fun, but at the end of it all he was humiliated.

He learned quickly that he was just the Marconi man and had to look after himself, but he was not entirely alone. Charlie Groves, the third officer, loved the wireless equipment too, and spoke kindly to him, and Evans made friends with Jimmy Gibson, the apprentice officer, who was the same age he was and had also once been the panicking passenger. 'Don't worry, Sparks,' Gibson told him. 'We all have our turn.'

Evans was grateful for this encouragement, but he hoped for more than graduation from his role in lifeboat drills. He had grander ambitions. He hoped he might one day be a hero, like Jack Binns, the wireless man on the White Star's *Republic*, who only three years earlier had brought ships racing to the rescue when his own vessel had been rammed in thick fog off New York. It was Jack and his Morse key, not the sailors, who had saved all the passengers.

And this quiet Sunday night, he thought, might just be his opportunity, because a little before half past ten the deck beneath his feet became suddenly still and the usual rattle of his cabin door stopped. Something odd was happening with the ship. Evans took off his headphones and waited. Seconds later the deck began to come to life again, slowly at first, but then building up to a pounding, spasmodic thumping. It was not the usual rhythm: it was more irregular and violent. The ship's engine, he realised, was going astern. He ran from his cabin to the deck outside and leaned over the port rail. The cold shocked him but he stayed where he was, waiting for his eyes to adjust to the darkness. Sounds drifted to him from the bridge above – the bell of the engine telegraph, the captain's voice calling, 'Hard a-port,' a seaman calling back the orders. Evans looked forward along the ship's side, but could see nothing. Then he heard a low, crunching, grinding sound from below and saw large chunks of ice sliding beside the hull, riding up in high arcs, snagging rivet heads and leaving neat white scars on the black steel. He gripped the rail tighter.

Now the ship was turning sharply and slowing. As the ice moved astern it was sucked into the thrashing turbulence beneath the stern overhang. One large chunk, Evans thought, would be enough to wreck the propeller or the rudder and leave them all stranded. But moments later he heard the order 'Stop engine' from the bridge. The deck became still again, the sucking turbulence ceased and the *Californian* drifted onwards in silence. Soon she was back in clear water and the ice passing below slowed and thinned until one small, flat piece, winking in the reflected light of a porthole, nudged against the hull and stayed there.

The ship had stopped. Evans wondered whether she was damaged. There might be water rushing in below, and there was only one place to be if there was: at his key. He walked back to his cabin, rubbed his hands to warm them and sat at his desk. If the captain came, Evans would be ready to send out a CQD.

But nobody came. The ship did not begin to list; he heard no sounds of sailors preparing the lifeboats on the deck outside. Everything was silent and still. He sat at his equipment listening to messages until just before eleven o'clock, then he put down his headphones, took off his shoes and picked up his magazine. He was standing at his bunk when the door opened and the captain himself stepped in.

Captain Lord was a tall man and he was forced to stoop a little in the cabin. Evans waited as he surveyed the wireless set, reaching out to touch each component in turn – the Morse key, the headphones, the transformer, the magnetic detector.

'We have run into some field ice,' the captain said at last. 'We turned around and got out of it, but now we have stopped for the night. You might want to use your instrument to let nearby ships know – in case one of them comes crunching up into it.' He placed on the desk a piece of paper. 'Our position,' he said, and walked out.

Evans sat back down at his desk, switched on the transmitter, put on his headphones and began tapping at his key. 'CQ all ships CQ all ships this is MWH we are stopped and surrounded by ice —' But he did not finish. A reply came instantly and with such power that he winced with pain and lifted his phones from his ears. Even then he could still hear the code sputtering through loud and fast: 'This is MGY shut up shut up shut up keep out I am busy I am working Cape Race you are jamming me.'

Very well. Enough was enough. He had earned his pay for the day. He hung up his headphones, turned off the transmitter and lay on his bunk with his magazine. At midnight, third officer Charlie Groves would come in after his watch to get the day's news and practise his Morse. Evans looked forward to his friend's visits, but in less than five minutes the magazine fell to his chest and he was asleep.

In the final half-hour of the evening watch, standing on the *Californian*'s cold, open bridge, Charlie Groves was watching the lights of a ship that had appeared about ten miles away, coming up from the southeast. He had reported her to the captain below – a passenger steamer, he'd said, heading west – and the captain told him to keep an eye on her.

As he watched, the ship's lights grew steadily brighter until, at twenty to midnight, most of them seemed suddenly to go out, and the ship appeared to stop. 'Now, that is strange,' Groves said to himself, bringing his binoculars to his eyes. When he worked for P&O he had known ships to turn off deck lights late in the evening to send passengers to bed, but it was never as dramatic and abrupt as what he'd just seen. He studied the ship carefully through his lenses but all he could see were her faint steaming lights – white lights, and perhaps a hint of red.

He was about to walk down to the chartroom to report again to the captain, but as he turned towards the stairs he saw there was no need: Captain Lord had come up to the bridge and was standing quietly at the starboard rail.

'Is that the ship you reported to me?' the captain asked, looking south.

'Yes, Captain,' Groves said, 'although she's stopped now.'

'She doesn't look like a passenger steamer. She's not carrying enough light.'

'She *was* carrying a lot of light,' Groves replied, 'but she's put them out.'

'She's probably a tramp steamer,' the captain said. 'Stopped for the ice, just like us.'

Groves agreed: the lights did now look like those of a small steamer. But he knew what he had seen. A blaze of light. A passenger ship steaming at full speed. In any event, it didn't much matter – passenger ship, tramp steamer or Mississippi showboat, in a few minutes his watch would be over and he would be in a warm cabin below.

In the *Californian*'s engine room, Ernie Gill, the newly promoted assistant donkeyman, neared the end of his own watch. He was working on a pump with the fourth engineer – there was something wrong with a valve, and the pump kicked and jumped like a rabid dog. Gill grunted and cursed, his thin flannel overalls damp with sweat. He dropped his spanner. The fourth engineer called him a fool.

Gill was pleased that in his new role he no longer had to shovel and rake coal, but the fourth engineer was taking advantage of him by giving him these extra jobs. So when his watch was at last over he walked aft along the main deck sullen and sulking. The fourth engineer had no right to talk to him in that manner. No right at all. And he shouldn't be working so hard on a Sunday night anyway. He thought about making a complaint to the chief engineer.

It was painfully cold. In the distance he saw the lights of a ship, but lights in the dark were no concern of his. He hurried to the washroom and then to his cabin, where he undressed and lay in his bunk. But he could not sleep. The ice was grinding away at the hull right next to his head and it sounded like a barrel bumping along a road. He got up, threw a thick coat over his pyjamas and went on deck to smoke a cigarette. The captain had told him many times not to smoke on the open deck, but tonight he didn't care.

The first thing Herbert Stone noticed when the standby quartermaster woke him for the midnight watch was just how calm everything was. There was no pitch, no roll, and no throb of the engine. For ten days the ship had rocked him back and forth like a baby, and her engine had lulled him with its rhythmic heartbeat. Now there was nothing. Never before, not even in port, had he felt the ship to be so silent and still.

Stone was tired and moved slowly. By the time he got up, used the washroom and dressed himself he was running late. It was already after midnight. The third officer would be waiting. He hurried along the alleyway to the chartroom to read the captain's night orders before heading up to the bridge. But when he reached the doorway he was surprised to see Captain Lord himself leaning over the chart table, working with his dividers and parallel rulers. Having brought the lamp low over the table, he stood in a golden circle of light.

Stone waited silently. The captain was carrying out his task delicately and precisely. He seemed to stand at the very centre of things, surrounded by light, a high priest performing a sacred ritual. The polished brass leaves of his cap glittered, and beneath its glossy black rim Stone could see his focused, intense eyes. Captain Lord would introduce himself to people by saying, 'I'm Lord – Lord of the *Californian*,' but Stone knew that he was lord of so much more. He was one of Leyland's very best, having been appointed captain at the age of twenty-eight – unheard of! – and was on the way up. He was now thirty-four, but seemed to Stone like an old man of the sea, wise and inscrutable.

'We have stopped because of the ice,' the captain said to him, without looking up from the chart. 'I'm not going to try to find a way through it until daylight. We will drift until then. We will keep up steam for the engine, but you shouldn't need it. Now come and look at this.' He turned from the chart table and walked past Stone into the cross-alleyway.

Stone followed him outside to the starboard rail of the boat deck. The cold shocked him and he pulled on his gloves. The captain never wore gloves; he grasped the hard steel of the rail with bare hands.

Stone stared into the darkness, waiting for his eyes to adjust. There was no swell and no wind and no horizon. The sea was dead flat and solid black. He understood now why the ship was so still.

'Can you see her?' the captain asked, pointing into the night.

A tiny cluster of lights slowly showed itself, suspended between the stars and the ocean.

'A small steamer,' the captain said. 'She has stopped, just like us.'

Stone was already late for his watch but the captain did not yet dismiss him. He stood waiting. The captain's close presence made him think of Captain Ahab and Starbuck standing at the rail of the *Pequod*, looking for Ahab's great white whale. 'Close!' Ahab says. 'Stand close to me.' But Stone heard no such words from his captain, and saw no vengeful whale on the horizon. He saw only the lights of the distant ship: placid, silent and perfectly still.

'Tonight's watch will be an easy one for you,' the captain said, dismissing him at last, 'with nothing much to do.'

It was ten minutes past midnight when Stone finally walked

up the steep stairs to the upper navigating bridge – a broad, open platform running the full width of the ship atop the amidships accommodation block. It had no walls or ceiling; the only protection from the elements was afforded by a chest-high steel bulkhead at the forward end, designed to deflect upwards the steady wind caused by the ship's movement. There was a fully enclosed, steam-heated lower bridge directly beneath the upper and accessible from the chartroom, but it was never used. 'A warm bridge means a sleeping officer,' claimed Captain Lord. So Stone and his fellow officers stood on the open upper bridge, no matter what the weather, and shielded themselves as best they could.

On this bitterly cold night the heavy, still air soaked through to the skin as if it were liquid. Charlie Groves was standing just abaft the ship's steering compass, rubbing his gloved hands together and hopping from one foot to the other. His open, round face, lit from beneath by the soft glow of the compass card, seemed disembodied, floating free in the darkness.

'Sorry I'm late, old chap,' Stone said. 'The captain was talking to me.'

'Oh yes, I know,' Groves replied. 'The captain likes his chitchat.'

Stone gave a short laugh as he took the bridge binoculars from Groves and looped their lanyard around his neck. He thought Groves would want to hurry off to the warmth below, but the third officer lingered awhile. He seemed to want to talk.

'The captain was on the bridge with me,' Groves said at last, 'when we ran into the ice. It was low slushy stuff – we didn't see it until we'd got right into it. I thought we'd be trapped, but the captain whipped us around and we got out of it all right. He knows how to handle a ship.'

'Yes,' said Stone. 'He does at that.'

There must have been something in his tone, because Groves

turned to him with a sympathetic smile. 'He *is* a good skipper, you know. Just give him a little more time. A few more trips and he'll loosen up with you.'

'Thank you,' Stone said. He knew that most second officers would not take advice from a third, but he and Charlie Groves were the same age, and besides, Stone liked him. Groves had been educated at a school in Cambridge but was no snob. Stone had never heard him put on airs and graces. Groves once worked for P&O but had left because he couldn't stand the passengers. Tramp steamers were more his style. He was the sort of man, Stone thought, for whom the world was a playground. One day, Groves said, he would fly in an aeroplane. But for now he was learning all he could about the *Californian*'s new wireless installation, and often gave Stone little speeches about wavelengths and frequencies and self-sustaining electromagnetic fields. He'd befriended Cyril Evans and would hurry down to the wireless cabin each night after his watch.

'So now we're stopped for the night,' Stone said.

'Yes. Until dawn.'

Stone looked through the binoculars at the lights in the south that the captain had pointed out to him. He could see a white masthead light and a smudge of others behind. He could not tell how far away the ship was. Her lights grew neither brighter nor darker, but remained perfectly steady.

'She came up from the southeast,' Groves explained. 'Stopped about half an hour ago. She's a big passenger ship – had lots of lights on at first, but she seemed to put them out when she stopped.'

Stone let the binoculars hang on their lanyard and looked at the ship with his naked eye. She was not going to cause him any trouble. He told Groves his eyes were in and he was happy to take over.

'Very good,' Groves said. 'Enjoy yourself.'

Stone watched the third officer disappear down the bridge stairs and then stared into the darkness. He could hear the distant hiss of a steam condenser, and fragments of conversation drifting up through an engine room vent, but otherwise the *Californian* was silent and still. The North Atlantic was a flat calm stretching ahead into an engulfing moonless blackness and the air was absolutely clear and sharp, seeming somehow to focus the light of the stars into cold, hard points of blue-white. The ship's bow was pointing back towards England, and in the eastern sky he could see more stars rising slowly from the ocean, throwing little threads of silver across the water.

He walked to the rear bridge rail. Somewhere out there, Groves had said, was the icefield. Stone couldn't see it now, but he could hear its low, grinding whisper – it felt close and alive. Then, slowly, just beyond the ship's stern, he began to make it out: a cold and feeble light, as if the ice had somehow caught and stored up starlight. It was so faint, so delicate and so elusive that he could see it only with the sensitivity of his peripheral vision. When he stared directly at it, it vanished into darkness. There was a smell too, equally insubstantial, a clammy glacial odour that faded to nothing the more he breathed it in.

No wonder they'd run into the ice at full speed. The captain would have been expecting icebergs, great towering things with straight edges and clear outlines, like the bergs they'd passed that afternoon, not this low shapeless ice that you could barely see.

Stone shivered. The stillness pressed in on him. The ice seemed to suck everything from the world – the waves, the wind, light, warmth – everything.

Charlie Groves hurried aft along the boat deck to the wireless room, but when he knocked on the door there was no answer. He walked in anyway. The room smelled of cigarette ash and shirts that had been worn for too long, but it was warm. The light was on and Evans was snoring lightly in his bunk with an open magazine across his chest.

'You awake, Sparks?'

Evans muttered something and rolled over towards the bulkhead.

'There's a big ship stopped on our starboard beam,' said Groves, sitting at the desk. 'Have you been speaking to her?'

Evans grunted and pulled a pillow tight over his head. His magazine slipped to the floor.

Groves looked at the boxes and wires and dials in front of him. Science at its best, he had always thought, was indistinguishable from magic, and each component before him performed its own special trick – the condenser, the key, the headphones, the transformer, the magnetic detector. He placed the earphones on his head and took up a pencil and notepad. He had been practising and could easily pick up three words out of four.

But now the headphones were silent. There was none of the usual *dit-dah-dit* of Morse code. The third officer gave them a quick jiggle and turned the volume control through its full sweep. He waited a minute, perhaps two, but no sound came.

It was half an hour past midnight. Evans was snoring more deeply now, and Groves decided it was time for him, too, to go to bed. He placed the headphones back on the desk, switched off the light and walked out of the room.

Herbert Stone had been standing his watch for ten minutes or so when James Gibson arrived on the bridge with two mugs of coffee. The twenty-year-old apprentice had been rummaging around in the chief officer's store for a new rotator for the ship's patent log.

'The old one was caught in the ice,' Gibson explained, 'and torn away. The captain asked me to rig a new one but I couldn't find one in the store.'

A sudden high-pitched squeal made Stone jump. It was the whistle stopper in the speaking tube leading to the captain's cabin. It squealed again as he walked forward to the tube, pulled out the stopper and put his ear to the opening. The captain's voice was muffled and distant. 'That ship,' the captain said, 'has she come any closer?'

'No, Captain. She hasn't moved.'

'Very well. I'm going to lie down in the chartroom. Call me if you need me.'

'Yes, good night, Captain.' Stone replaced the stopper and took up a position next to Gibson at the forward bridge rail.

'There's something odd about that ship,' Gibson said, looking through binoculars towards the south. 'Her lights are strange – see, there's a glare on her afterdeck.'

Stone took the binoculars. Gibson was right: there was a smudge of light behind the masthead light.

'There's something flickering, too,' Gibson continued. 'Do you see that? I think she's trying to Morse us.' He walked to the electric Morse lamp key and began signalling. The lamp, mounted high on the deckhouse abaft the bridge, threw its rhythmic light out into the darkness. Stone watched for a reply from the other ship, but couldn't make out distinct letters. Long-short-long-short: a C, perhaps? Now a D? But he soon lost the flickering among the glare of other indistinct lights. Gibson flashed the Morse lamp for a few moments longer, then gave up. No matter; they could try again later.

In the meantime, Stone was glad to have the apprentice's company. Stone had been helping him with his studies over the past weeks by showing him how to use a sextant and how to plot position lines.

Lately Stone had begun to talk of more personal things – his recent wedding, his childhood in Devon, and even the problems he'd been having with the captain. So when Gibson went below to look again for a rotator, Stone held his coffee mug tight to warm his hands, and felt more alone than usual. He thought of his wife, at home in her sunlit garden with her hyacinths and tulips and daffodils, which only made the darkness and cold press in closer. He stood at the starboard rail and waited. A single stroke on the bridge bell told him it was half past twelve. Time was going slowly.

It would be an easy watch, the captain had said. Perhaps, thought Stone, looking down at the black water below, but even on a stopped ship on a calm sea the midnight watch was the hardest of all. Sailors sometimes called it the graveyard watch, because it was said that during its four lonely hours the spirits of drowned men could be seen rising from the surface of the sea, quiet as mist. It was also the watch during which good men, with everything to live for, had been known to throw themselves over the side into the depths. Perhaps they saw mermaids beckoning them, or perhaps the vastness of the ocean and sky made their loneliness unbearable, or perhaps their will was overwhelmed by a momentary curiosity, or a momentary insanity. Whatever the reason, Stone knew that the shock of entering the water would bring any man out of his reverie, so that in full and sane consciousness he would watch his ship steam away until it slipped forever out of sight. Stone thought that must be the most profound loneliness the universe could devise. 'Alone,' he whispered to himself, 'alone. All, all alone, alone on a wide, wide sea.'

But when he lifted his head and glanced towards the south, he was reminded that he was not, after all, entirely alone. The other ship was still there, suspended in the darkness, placid and quiet. There were no souls of dead men flying up to heaven, just her steady faint lights, hanging there, keeping him company while he sipped the last of his coffee and waited for Gibson to return.

Then, just above the other ship, he saw something unusual: a small white light climbing into the air. Stone wasn't quite sure at first what it was. It rose slowly, higher and higher, until it burst silently into a delicate shower of stars. For a short time, while the upward streak was still visible and the star cluster drifted slowly downward, it looked like a fragile white flower – perfectly white, clear and startling against the blackness of the void.

CHAPTER 3

Penn Station soared above me. Although it was only midmorning, I had been drinking on the train and the building confused me. The floor was acres of concrete but embedded in it were twinkling glass bricks. Everywhere there was indestructible granite but it was baby pink in colour. There were colonnades of giant Corinthian columns but the ironwork was as frivolous as dainty lace. Why all this contrast? My eyes hurt; I felt an incipient headache. It was time for another drink.

I went to my favourite hotel off Christopher Street and headed straight to the back bar, known for opening early. I hadn't been here for a year, but nothing had changed. The room was closed in and gloomy and the air glowed dull red. Two prostitutes leaned against a giant papier-mâché horse, which was as tall as a man and stood on floor panels of red glass lit from beneath. I laughed. The horse reminded me of Boston's Watch and Ward Society, trying to stamp out the warm red glow of vice wherever it was seen. I tipped my hat at the prostitutes and ordered two bourbon highballs from a pretty waitress.

I sat in a corner and spent an hour or so reading the morning editions I had bought at the station. Great scareheads proclaimed the dramatic accident at sea: the Allan Line's *Virginian* had relayed to Cape Race that the *Titanic* had struck an iceberg and was calling for help. The embarrassment at White Star, it was said, was equally dramatic. There were some very famous Americans on board the ship.

My headache worsened. I had never much liked New York. If you took a deep breath in Boston you could smell the sharp, clear air of revolution, of new thinking, but all I ever smelled in New York was melodrama and money. The city's newspapers were filled with action, indignation and thrills, but they had no nuance and no heart. I ordered another highball, rubbed my temples and read no more.

By midday my headache began to ease and I set out downtown. The weather was growing warm. I could smell fried fish and horse manure. Wagons trundled by with potatoes, carrots and onions left over from the Monday morning markets. I drifted east along Fourth Street, past Washington Square, and for old time's sake I took a detour to the monumental brown-brick and terracotta edifice of the ten-storey Asch Building.

In the year or so since the fire, the upper brickwork had been scrubbed of the soot that had streaked upwards from the windows like clownish eyelashes, and the interiors had been refurbished and replaced. From where I stood I could not see them, but I knew that new young immigrant girls now worked at the sewing machines, the braiders and corders, the seamers and binders. 'Welcome to America,' I whispered to them. I hoped they were safe. I was not religious – I had abandoned my Catholicism as a child – but I did make the sign of the cross, and I did pause to remember.

On Broadway I hailed a hansom, and by Canal Street the traffic had thickened. Our horse grew fractious and lively. Two young women drove by too close in a shiny automobile, veering from side to side and shouting suffragette slogans through a megaphone. The horse shied alarmingly; the women laughed, and I did too. One of them reminded me of my daughter Harriet, just turned seventeen, who romped and leapt through life with the same energy as these young drivers. The encounter made me think two things: that I must visit Harriet as soon as I returned to Boston, and that this century, whether it be wonderful or horrible, was going to belong to the women.

We passed Wall Street. Broadway became narrow and gloomy. The great stone edifices of ten- and twenty-storey buildings blocked the light. People spilled from the sidewalks into the roadway and we were forced to slow. As we neared the end of Broadway, trolley cars were backed up and automobiles crept along in low gear. I paid for the cab and pushed my way south on foot. Soon enough I was at Bowling Green Park, an oval of lawn fenced in by a tall iron grille. At its western edge was the towering facade of number 9, Broadway – the offices of J.P. Morgan's International Mercantile Marine, owners of the White Star Line.

It was a strange sight. Squeezed around the park's perimeter and along its interior pathways was a great crowd of people. Men in small black bowlers and women in great hats of every colour surged along the sidewalks; people emerging from the subway stairs had nowhere to go; mounted policeman tried to use the flanks of their horses to keep people off the roadway. They shouted at anyone who reached out a hand to pat a horse. The bells of trolley cars sounded incessantly. Automobile horns blared. Two men were taking photographs of the scene with Box Brownie cameras.

So this, I thought, is what happens when you put the best of New York society onto a boat and run it into an iceberg.

On the western side of Broadway a large portion of the crowd had formed itself into an amorphous queue, three or four people abreast, which led to the wide brick and granite steps of number 9. Two policemen stood at the top of the stairs, guarding the enormous revolving door of polished brass and glass. The door was flanked by twin granite columns etched with the names of J.P. Morgan's shipping companies: the American Line, the Atlantic Transport Line, the Dominion Line, the Red Star Line, the Leyland Line and – there, at the bottom, his most famous acquisition of all – the White Star Line.

Morgan, I thought, must be embarrassed. He was a man who bought shipping lines and railroads as if they were curios and trinkets, but now the most perfect of all his prizes was adrift in the North Atlantic with half of New York aboard. It was as if he had invited friends for cocktails at his magnificent white-marble library and then set the place alight. It was worse than embarrassing. It was bad manners.

I pushed my way up the stairs and presented my card to a policeman with a tired face who let me through. I entered a hallway crowded with people. Cablegram boys in green blazers rushed in and out and men pressed themselves against walls to allow women to pass. Reporters smoked cigarettes and whispered names to each other. To my left, in the cavernous passenger office, young men guided people into queues marked with soft burgundy ropes on brass stands. Behind counters, White Star staff answered questions, and behind them, still others sat at desks talking on telephones.

A White Star page, his chest puffed with importance beneath a blue tunic, directed me to the freight office, where Mr Franklin would come down shortly to speak. 'He comes down every hour,' the boy said.

The freight office was smaller than the passenger office and filled with the smoke of too many cigarettes and the heat of too many steam radiators. As soon as I pushed inwards I bumped into Dan Byrne of the Dow Jones service, a boisterous man with a florid face and dubious morals whom I knew from the *Republic* collision and the Triangle fire. He had been in the freight office all morning. He held me by the arm and told me some very interesting things: that Franklin had been on the telephones since two a.m.; that the young Vincent Astor had been in tears of worry about his father; that frumpy Mrs Guggenheim had been up to see Franklin personally to demand news of her husband. Morgan, I learned, was in France, but his fretful son had gone upstairs and not come down again. Even the President of the United States had been calling: his friend Archie Butt was aboard. As was Bruce Ismay: President of the International Mercantile Marine, Chairman of the White Star Line, and Franklin's boss.

'My god,' I said. 'Poor Franklin. Who *isn't* on that boat?'

There was a commotion: a desk was moved, people stood aside, a door opened and closed, and there, suddenly, as if appearing from nowhere, was the man himself. I thought he would stand behind the desk but instead, in two quick strides, he stood upon it. The pressmen shouted questions and surged closer and a table was knocked over. A man fell against a wall clock and dislodged its brass pendulum. It seemed for a moment that Franklin too might be knocked down.

'Gentlemen, please,' he said, coughing in the thick smoke. 'Some patience.'

One or two reporters called for silence and others suggested that respect be shown. In a moment or so the room became still.

Philip Albright Small Franklin towered above us all. He looked monumental, as if he were a statue of himself, as if he were already immortal. In the press he was known as the tycoon of American shipping – when it came to the North Atlantic he was John Pierpont Morgan's man. I had met him several times: when the *Cedric* was overdue and thought sunk, during the drama of the *Republic* collision, and in the days after the Triangle fire, when I learned that he had cried with grief and donated money to the dead girls' families. He was toastmaster to the White Star's billion-dollar passenger list, but he was a good man too. He was fatter than the previous year, I saw, but there was still a magical lightness about his being. He was known to climb ladders and leap gaps. Nothing scared him. When an Atlantic Transport ship ran aground one night in New York Harbor, he dashed out to the vessel himself in a tug, making tea for the passengers and supervising their rescue. His head was shiny-bald and his eyes were strikingly intense. They commanded attention. People who saw them thought, Here is a man who gets things done.

'Everybody on the *Titanic*,' he told the assembled group, 'is safe. The ship is diverting to Halifax.'

It pains me to admit it, but I was dismayed. No bodies. That meant no story for me.

'I have made arrangements,' Franklin continued, 'with the New Haven railroad to send a special train to Halifax to meet the passengers. The train will consist of twenty-eight sleepers, two diners, and coaches sufficient for seven hundred and ten people. That, you will appreciate, is enough for the entire first and second class of the ship. I have been speaking to the Canadian government over the long-distance telephone. They will do everything they can to help us. We plan to – we *will* – get our passengers to New York just as soon as possible.'

Franklin undertook to answer questions.

No, he did not have any more information about damage to the *Titanic*; his understanding was that it was slight and the ship was making her way to Halifax under her own steam. If not, she would be towed. He was planning to charter a tug to send out to her if necessary. No, he had not heard directly from Mr Ismay, he was relying on dispatches from the Allan Line in Montreal. He read out a message he had received from their Boston office: 'The Allan Line, Montreal, confirms the report that the *Virginian*, *Parisian* and *Carpathia* are in attendance.' Franklin was waiting for an update from Captain Haddock of the *Olympic*, the *Titanic*'s sister ship, which was nearing the scene.

So, I thought, definitely no bodies then. The *Boston American* would send down Bumpton. He would write a dashing, racing tale of rescue and adventure – a good New York story. I needed another drink. But before I let go of the story for good there was a puzzle I wanted to solve. There was something about what Franklin had said that didn't quite make sense.

'Mr Franklin,' I asked, 'you said you are talking to the *Olympic* and other stations. But have you heard directly from the *Titanic*?'

'No,' Franklin replied, with some exasperation. 'But I am not worried at all about that, I am not worried about that.'

'But Mr Franklin – and I'm sorry if you've already answered this – do you know why her signals would stop so abruptly?'

'I am told that there are any number of possible reasons – atmospheric conditions, or damage to the wireless apparatus, or anything at all.'

That *is* odd, I thought. I had in mind the *Republic* accident of three years before: a ship rammed and slowly sinking, a wireless room in tatters, a Marconi boy scared out of his wits, a freezing North Atlantic fog pressing in thick and heavy – and yet all the while an unending stream of Morse code had poured from the ship, calling for help, guiding ships to the rescue. If the wireless had worked then, under such conditions, why not now, on a calm clear Atlantic?

I don't know whether it was the bourbon, or the vision of Bumpton's eager face arriving at Penn Station, or simple puzzlement that made me put my next question, but it came flying out into the room before I realised I'd asked it. It seemed independent of me, as if it had its own form and presence.

'Might it be because the *Titanic* has sunk?'

People gasped. Franklin looked at me. He did not seem angry; his face was expressionless, waxlike, as if he'd been expecting the question. The thick smoke in the room softened the shine of his brow.

'Let me tell you this,' he said, his words low and measured. 'I am absolutely confident that the *Titanic* is safe. Perfectly safe. It is inconceivable that she would have met with any serious accident without our being notified. In any event, the ship is unsinkable. Her bulkheads will keep her afloat indefinitely, so there's no danger to the passengers. That much I do know.'

I was watching his face carefully, trying to read it. There was something strange about it.

'She is unsinkable,' Franklin said again, more to himself than the reporters. 'Her bulkheads, her bulkheads . . .'

He stepped down from the desk, turned and walked out the door. The pressmen followed, rushing to their offices and telephones.

I am not a rusher. I strolled from the building and found a saloon near Battery Park. I sat alone in a corner and tried to think. I could already see what sort of story this was becoming: a rerun of the *Republic* accident. A damaged ship, a spotty boy at his wireless key calling for help, a brave rescue at sea. A good story, no doubt, but it had been done before, and my own paper would not want me to write it. Bumpton was the adventure man. 'His pen,' the city editor had told me, 'has a sensitivity to the narrative arc of adventure which yours does not. And his verbs are more active.'

I doodled in my notebook, experimenting with some headline phrases: *Titanic*'s danger over. Steamer hit iceberg late last night.

Hours of anxiety at last relieved. 'This afternoon,' I then wrote, 'Mr Franklin expressed his utmost confidence in the new liner *Titanic*.' Too dry, I thought. I tried adding some Bumpton-like verbs. 'The *Titanic* is limping towards Halifax. Mr Franklin has commanded a special train to race north on the New Haven line to collect her passengers.' Limp. Command. Race. But still my copy was no good. Perhaps the city editor was right. My pen was just not suited to thrilling adventure.

I found a telegraph office and wired my newspaper – 'No bodies no story' – and then caught a cab back to the station. As soon as I stepped into the vast brightness of the main concourse I saw on a nearby newsstand the late edition of *The Evening Sun*, proclaiming in inch-high letters: ALL SAVED FROM *TITANIC* AFTER COLLISION.

What a shame, I thought, before I could stop myself.

CHAPTER 4

Cyril Evans was woken by the glare of his cabin light. Stewart, the chief officer, stood in the doorframe, his hand on the light switch.

'You'd better get up,' said the chief. 'A ship has been firing rockets. You'd better see whether anything is the matter.'

'What time is it?' Evans asked, blinking his eyes and swinging his legs from his bunk.

'A quarter to six.'

The chief had brought cold air into the cabin with him. Evans stood up, yawning and shivering. He pulled on trousers and a coat over his pyjamas and sat at his equipment, trying to make sense of what the chief had said. A ship firing rockets?

There was silence in his headphones. For a moment he was puzzled, but then he saw: the magnetic detector had wound down. He rotated its handle a few times until its ebonite discs began to whirr. The chief officer stood by him, perfectly still, waiting. George Stewart was an odd man, Evans thought, with his droopy moustache and glassy eyes.

He hardly ever said a word; you just never knew what he was thinking.

Evans switched on his transmitter and sent out a general stations call: 'All ships, this is MWH.' His headphones instantly crackled with pulses. He took up his pencil and wrote out the letters as they came: 'Say old man, do you know the *Titanic* has struck an iceberg and is sinking 41 46 N 50 14 W?'

He tapped his Morse key as quickly as he could. 'Thanks old man but did you say *Titanic*?'

The reply came at once. 'Yes *Titanic*. Tell your captain.'

Evans took off his headphones and turned wide-eyed to the chief and held out to him the slip of paper. Stewart read the message and, strangely calm, asked him whether he was sure. Evans said he was. 'I was just talking to her,' he added, 'last night. I can't believe it. I was just talking to her.'

The chief officer frowned a little and turned away. 'Never mind about all that,' he said as he walked from the room with the message held tightly in his hand.

Evans replaced his headphones and began tapping the key as fast as he could. In a few moments, he knew, he would feel the deck beneath his feet jump and leap as the ship's engine went full speed ahead, and soon after he would see the great liner, flashing her lights and hoisting her flags in gratitude. Her signals had been very strong the night before, so she must be close.

But the deck remained still, and a minute or so later the chief was back in the room. 'The captain wants an official message,' he said, 'captain to captain. He doesn't want to go on a wild goose chase.'

Evans was surprised. He had already confirmed the *Titanic*'s position and thought they should be making full steam for her – right now. But he took to his key again, listened carefully through his headphones, and soon had a message written out in his very best lettering on an official Marconigram form. '*Titanic* struck berg, wants assistance urgent. Ship sinking, passengers in boats. Her position: Lat 41.46 Long 50.14. Signed: Gambol, Master, *Virginian*.' He stamped it with his rubber *Californian* stamp.

The chief thanked him and once again left the room.

Evans' headphones now crackled with Morse – from the *Mount Temple*, the *Frankfurt*, the *Baltic*, the *Virginian*, the *Birma*. He worked each ship one by one, getting what details he could, and telling anyone who listened about how close his own ship was to the sinking liner. 'I had MGY very loud last night,' he sent. His Morse key had never tapped so fast. The stale cabin air became acrid with ozone from the transmitter's spark. 'What happened to her? When did she hit? Was she in the icefield? How close are you? We are closer! Do you see us? We are a four-master with a salmon pink funnel. We are very near her.' He kept sending until a message came in from Mr Balfour, a travelling Marconi inspector on the *Baltic*: 'Stand by and keep out. You are jamming. We are trying to hear *Carpathia*. Balfour, Inspector.'

Evans paused. He did not want Mr Balfour to report him to the company, but he also knew the rules: closer ships had precedence over distant ones. And his ship was certainly closer than the *Baltic*. He had every right to find out what was happening.

He took off his headphones and began to hunt for his operator's manual. But when he heard the ring of the telegraph bell from the bridge above, and then felt at last the thump of the ship's engine, he could hold off no longer. He replaced his headphones and began to send again. 'We are steaming full speed now,' he tapped out to anyone who would listen. He waited for indignation from the *Baltic*, but instead heard the faint signal of the *Titanic*'s giant sister, *Olympic*, steaming east out of New York. She called repeatedly, '*Titanic*? *Titanic*? This is *Olympic*. Please reply.' Then he heard a message, sent via the Cape Race shore station, direct to the *Titanic*'s captain himself: 'To Smith: Anxiously awaiting information and probable disposition of passengers. Signed: Franklin, White Star New York.' He listened for a reply from the *Titanic*, but there was none. He heard, too, the Associated Press calling the Allan Line's *Virginian* via Cape Race: 'Do you have any more information about *Titanic*? New York most anxious.'

The whole world was listening and Evans was right there, on the spot.

He was thinking about what message to send next when the door of his cabin opened and Jim Gibson burst in. He was barefoot and clad only in his dressing gown, beneath which, Evans glimpsed, he was naked. Evans lifted the headphones from his ears.

'Sparks!' Gibson said, burying his hands in his gown pockets to keep them warm. 'The chief officer just told me. The *Titanic*! Do you have her?'

Evans smiled. His friend might be good at boat drill and might one day be an officer, but he could not understand Morse, and that was what mattered now. 'I can't hear the *Titanic*,' he said, 'but I have the *Mount Temple*, the *Baltic*, the *Olympic* – and even the Vice President of White Star in New York.'

Gibson lowered his tone, as if to emphasise the special importance of his own information. 'I saw her rockets, you know. I saw them.'

Evans looked at his friend. He didn't know whether to believe him. He thought the chief officer had seen the rockets, and that that was why he'd come down to wake him. 'Really?'

'Really,' said Gibson. 'With my own eyes. The second officer saw them, too.' He turned and ran from the room as quickly as he'd come in.

Evans chewed the end of his pencil until it splintered. It tasted bitter in his mouth. He put down his headphones. He was puzzled once more. He knew that Gibson stood the midnight watch with the second officer, but that watch had finished many hours ago. So if Gibson and the second officer did see rockets, why was the *Californian* only just now speeding to the rescue?

Herbert Stone did not understand. He thought it a strange sort of joke. But the chief officer was insistent. 'The *Titanic* is sinking up ahead. You'd better get up and get dressed,' he said, pulling open the curtain to let in the light. 'You'll be needed in the boats.'

The chief disappeared into the alleyway. Stone got to his feet, half asleep and trying to think, to remember, to make sense of things. The deck pounded, the whole cabin rattled and shook. He drew back his top lip and tapped his teeth hard. He could think only of white rockets.

Now Charlie Groves stood in the doorframe, doing up the buttons of his shirt, his cheeks pink. His words came out so fast Stone could hardly follow them: 'passengers in boats', 'unbelievable', 'the unsinkable ship', 'an iceberg'. Stone interrupted him. 'I saw her rockets,' he said abruptly. 'During my watch. I saw her rockets.'

Groves fell silent. He stopped doing up his buttons.

'Yes, old chap, I saw her rockets,' Stone continued. 'Just after you handed over the watch.' He glanced briefly at the third officer, who had become very still, and then added, 'I told him,' as if the words were nothing, an afterthought. But he knew already, in the deepest part of his being, that they were the most important words of all. *I told him.*

'Who?' asked Groves, his eyes narrowing. 'Who did you tell?'

'The captain.'

Groves paused. Stone could see that he was surprised.

'When?' Groves asked.

'During my watch. As they were being fired.'

'And what did he do?'

'He stayed in the chartroom.'

The third officer stood waiting, as if he expected more. But Stone could think of nothing more to say. He stood up and began hunting about for his clothes. 'Anyway,' he said, laying out his uniform, 'you'd better hurry up. The chief said we'll be needed in the boats.' Groves stepped back across the alleyway to his own cabin and Stone dressed as quickly as he could.

A moment later he was on the bridge. Things were very different from the calm black stillness of the midnight watch. Everything now was action and movement and light. The sun had risen and the deck bounced hard with the ship's engine at full speed. There were lookouts everywhere, on the bridge wing, on the focsle, and Stone could even see a man swinging high in a coal basket hoisted aloft.

There was ice all around. A vast, low, lumpy field extending many miles north and south rose and fell gently in the morning swell, and everywhere there were icebergs. Some were trapped in the unyielding slush of the field, others floated free at the edges. Stone could see at least thirty or forty of them, standing tall like the majestic giants of some magical world, radiant and silent. They made him uneasy; they seemed to be watching him, waiting for his next move.

The ship was steaming west across the icefield through narrow channels, and at the fore part of the bridge Captain Lord stood in full uniform with the chief officer, facing into the wind. The captain seemed again to be at the centre of things, to be illuminated by a special authority. From his upright, unwavering figure a power seemed to radiate. Men reported to him one after the other – the chief engineer, the chief steward, the bosun – and Stone marvelled at his quick thinking and clear commands. The captain ordered the uncovering and swinging out of the lifeboats, the rigging of ladders, the piling up of lifejackets, the opening of valves to steam winches. For every man there was an action, for every problem an answer.

Stone thought Captain Lord would have a solution for him, too, but when he walked up and reported himself ready for duty, the captain turned a dismissive eye to him and said only that he should stand by. So Stone walked to the aft end of the bridge, where he waited and watched.

The ship pushed on through the ice. In some places it was no more than a thin slush; in others it thickened to a lumpy, greedy mass that sucked at the hull and made for slow going. The captain looked as much aft as forward. Whenever large chunks drifted towards the propeller or rudder he called, 'Dead slow,' or, 'Stop.' Stone knew what he was thinking: that no matter what, he must not disable his ship. Thousands of lives might depend upon him.

Soon the *Californian* steamed into clear blue water to the west of the icefield and turned south. The morning had a glory to it. The sun had driven away any hint of mist or haze and the distant horizon was vividly clear. The water hissed and frothed below the bridge as the ship steamed at full speed.

When a cry of 'Ship dead ahead!' came from the man aloft in the coal basket, Stone thought it must be the *Titanic* at last. But the captain, looking through binoculars, called out, 'One funnel!' and as the *Californian* drew nearer, Stone could see that the ship was a mid-sized passenger steamer. Minutes later, at six bells – seven o'clock in the morning – Captain Lord rang 'Stop' on the telegraph and announced that they were at the *Titanic*'s SOS position.

Stone watched as the captain and chief officer searched the horizon with their binoculars. He saw that on the main deck engineers, stewards and seamen were looking too. But there was only the nearby ship, rolling gently in the low swell, her single funnel glowing yellow in the sunlight.

A pervasive stillness settled over the *Californian*. The deck work was complete. Pilot ladders had been rigged, the lifeboats had been swung outboard and secured by their bowsing tackles, lifejackets and lifebuoys had been piled fore and aft ready to be cast into the sea. Halyards clicked against the slowly rocking masts like the ticking of a clock. The sun rose higher, the calm blue water glittered, and the ice began to glow.

Where, Stone wondered, was the *Titanic*?

Now Cyril Evans appeared at the top of the bridge stairs, with trousers over his pyjamas and a pullover that was back-to-front and inside-out. He was wearing slippers. He stood for a moment and then announced, 'The *Titanic* has sunk. Not sinking – *sunk*. I have it confirmed from the *Carpathia*. She is picking up her lifeboats right now.'

Captain Lord seemed to Stone to be made of iron; he did not flinch. For some time he said nothing whatsoever, then he turned to Evans. 'Go to your cabin,' he said, 'and put on your uniform. A ship's bridge is no place for a man in slippers.'

Before Stone had time to think, the third officer was on the bridge, running and shouting and pointing towards the icefield, his large square jaw thrust forward. On the other side of the field, a ship had drifted into view from behind two icebergs. She was a passenger steamer with a slender red funnel and four masts, perhaps five or six miles away. Groves was crying out, 'See? She has her flag at half-mast!' and Stone saw that it was true. He saw, too, that the ship was using her derricks to recover empty lifeboats from the ocean.

The ship must be the *Carpathia*, he thought, and, more importantly, she was on the other side of the icefield – the side from which they had just come, in the very position in which Stone had seen a ship firing rockets during the night. The *Californian*, he realised, had come too far west: they had steamed through the icefield for nothing.

The captain found his voice. 'Full ahead!' he called to the man on telegraph, readjusting his cap on his head, and resecuring the buttons on his blazer. 'Steer for that steamer,' he ordered.

Slowly the ship's head came around to the northeast, and began to push back through the ice.

Stone felt a tightness in his chest and he wanted to cry out. The *Titanic* had sunk and he had seen her rockets. He could hardly speak; he could not think what to do next. He felt that he wasn't in the world any more, that things were passing before him as if on a screen, out of reach.

In half an hour they were at the *Carpathia*. She was a pretty ship, with a gleaming white accommodation and a funnel standing proud and tall in the red and black livery of Cunard. Stone could see people crowding on the decks, staring across the water at him. A derrick was lifting a lifeboat onto the foredeck where perhaps a dozen boats were already stacked. On the bridge, the captain waved his right hand above his head and an officer walked to the rear of the bridge to hoist a signal pennant up the jumper halyard. They were about to semaphore.

Stone heard Captain Lord ask the chief officer to stand by with the flags, and the third officer to run up an answering pennant and read off the *Carpathia*'s replies. The *Carpathia*'s officer took up the bright yellow and red flags and began signalling.

'D!' called Groves, then 'o' and then 'y-o-u.'

Do you . . . Stone watched the outstretched arms adopt their odd angles, and mouthed the letters silently to himself as Groves called them: 'h-a-v-e a-n-y s-u-r-v-i-v-o-r-s a-b-o-a-r-d?'

The sun rose higher. The water lapped gently at the sides of the ship. Stone knew at once what that question meant: the *Carpathia* did not have all of the *Titanic's* people aboard. He took a step closer to his captain. How many were the dead? he wondered.

'What shall I say, Captain?' asked the chief officer, the flags fluttering in his hands.

Captain Lord spoke quietly. 'Tell them no,' he said, 'and . . . ask them . . .' He faltered.

Ask them how many, Stone thought. How many were they?

'Ask them what is the matter.'

The chief officer moved his flags quickly – 'What is the matter?' – and again Groves called the reply. '*Titanic* sank here 2.20 a.m.'

Six hours ago, thought Stone. During the midnight watch.

The signalling from the *Carpathia* continued. 'We have picked up all her boats and survivors.'

There was a pause. Stone looked at the signalling officer on the *Carpathia* through his binoculars. He was holding both flags straight up, the left at a slight angle, indicating that he was about to signal numbers. Stone knew they would be *his* numbers – his and his captain's. Captain Lord was, he knew, like him, waiting for them. Once they came they would be theirs forever.

The sun grew smaller and more intense as it climbed the sky. It poured such a torrent of white light onto the bridge that it seemed to wash the colour from things. There was no subtlety of shading; the scene appeared to Stone at a uniform saturation, like an overexposed photograph. Even the black pitch between the planks at Stone's feet glistened as if wet with light. Under the black rim of his cap, Captain Lord was squinting. Stone thought of *Moby-Dick*. 'Oh, my Captain! my Captain!' he said to himself. 'Away with me! Let us fly these deadly waters!'

At last the numbers came. 'One,' he heard Groves call. Then, 'Five.'

Fifteen? Could it be only fifteen?

Groves called, 'Zero.'

One hundred and fifty, then.

Raising his hand to shield his eyes, Stone waited for the signal that letters were to follow, but instead the officer held his arms perfectly still – one flag pointing straight up, and the other pointing down and to the right. It was unmistakable, and the bright image of it burned itself into Stone's mind. It was another zero, and Groves called it, calmly, firmly. And then the letters l-o-s-t.

Captain Lord spoke. 'Was the zero signalled twice, Mr Groves?'

'Yes, Captain. He repeated it.'

'Very well.'

The light bore down on Herbert Stone. He thought, for some reason, of his first day at sea, and the narrow, stinking pump room into which he had been sent to clean the bilges, and the caustic sludge that had scalded his hands. He wished he were there again now. At least it had been dark; there was not this burning, unforgiving light. He took a step backwards, looking for some shade. There was none – not even the flimsy bridge awning cast shadow. Light filled every corner.

On the starboard bridge wing he saw the captain standing alone, erect and still, pulling his cap tighter on his head, lest it be blown off by the wind. 'I told him,' Stone whispered to himself. '*I told him.*'

CHAPTER 5

Harry Houdini stared at me. His hair was parted in the middle above a high forehead that told me he was intensely clever – so clever he was most likely insane. In a few weeks, I knew, he was going to lock himself in a packing crate with two hundred pounds of lead and have himself thrown into the East River from a tugboat. He blazed with a fearsome intelligence; he seemed to know that life could only be tasted in its most concentrated form at its boundary with death. But there was something about his face that was pained. This man, I thought, was a prisoner of his own brilliance, his own incessant thoughts. His was a brain that never stopped. Every packing crate, steel box and vault he escaped was an enactment in the outer world of an escape he could never achieve in the inner. His mind was a straitjacket. Behind those eyes, that furrowed brow, that non-compromising intensity, was someone trying to get out.

A man's own soul can be the very worst sort of prison, I supposed.

At least, that was how I read the face in the framed photograph above my table as I drank my beer, waited for my train and thought about things. I am good at reading faces. 'Show me a face and I'll give you a story' was my promise, and I almost always got it right. Often I could sum one up in a single word. For Harry Houdini, the handcuff king: *trapped*. For my wife, all those years ago in Venezuela: *empty*. For my daughter, who waited for me in Boston: *life*.

But what word for Philip Albright Small Franklin, Vice President of the International Mercantile Marine? I drank a straight bourbon chaser, closed my eyes and conjured his face as I'd seen it in the freight office. I saw one thing very clearly: pride. Pride in his company, in his staff, in his ships, and especially in the *Titanic*. Or even more than pride – love, perhaps. But there was something else, too. His face began to appear before me in the finest detail, and I could see now the slight tightening of the lips, the almost imperceptible pulsing of the eyelids, the strange quiver of the tongue, the sweat that showed itself as a smooth sheen rather than collecting in drops. Shapes emerged, colours clarified, and I knew what I was seeing. I had another word for Philip Franklin: *fear*.

Philip Franklin, that great empire of a man, the tycoon of American shipping, was afraid.

'Waiting for a hooker?'

Dan Byrne slid into the chair next to mine. He wore the same stale overcoat he'd been wearing when I was in New York a year ago. He was smoking a cigarette and he exhaled the smoke directly into my face.

'No,' I said. 'I've just had one.'

Byrne smiled. 'Congratulations.'

'Thank you,' I said. 'Your mother was in fine form, as always.'

Byrne gave a violent, snorting laugh and dropped his cigarette. He picked it up, snubbed it out, and lit another. 'I've come to get you,' he said. 'You're leaving too soon. Everybody's rushing down to number 9.

Franklin's about to say something big.'

I finished off my bourbon. 'Something big?'

'That's the rumour,' Byrne said.

I stood up and breathed deeply, trying to sharpen my thinking. Byrne helped me steady myself as we left the station saloon and wandered south. Broadway was clogged with automobiles. Women, I could see, had come straight from the opera to White Star in black and silver furs. Police lurched perilously on horseback and a gasoline dynamo had been placed in the middle of Bowling Green Park to electrify a temporary instalment of large light globes. Police standing guard made announcements through megaphones: there was no access to the White Star offices at the current time; information was available at Times Square on the *New York Times* bulletin boards.

'I've heard,' Byrne said in my ear, 'that there are more than four thousand people up there.'

This, I thought, was turning out to be quite a story.

Byrne's maxim was 'Lie to police whenever there is chaos', so we told the policemen at the great revolving door that we were Mr Burlingham and Mr Underwood – Mr Franklin's lawyers, no less – whom he had called upon urgently. No, we did not have our cards because we had come direct from our restaurant. The police seemed not to believe us, but they let us in anyway. Perhaps they had their own maxim: 'Whenever there is chaos, let in the press.'

The passenger and general offices of the International Mercantile Marine were even more crowded than they had been in the afternoon. The radiator cocks were fully open and the rooms were stuffy and hot. Women standing in queues fanned themselves with theatre programs. A rack of hooks had come free of a hallway wall and coats lay in a heap like a giant dead animal. In the freight office reporters jostled for space. They had become dishevelled, unruly and impatient. Deadlines for the next morning's editions loomed but nobody could file – not if 'something big' was in the wind.

'Follow me,' I said to Byrne as I walked past the freight office to the elevators at the end of the hallway. I pushed on an adjacent door and we slipped into a stairwell. In a moment we were in the second-floor general offices. It was after seven o'clock but there were people everywhere: telephonists, stenographers, bookkeepers, clerks. We walked straight to Philip Franklin's office, a large room separated from the general offices by frosted glass. Two cable boys stood waiting outside the door, fiddling with their caps. We knocked and a voice from inside invited us to enter.

The office was enormous. Franklin sat at a great mahogany desk, flanked on either side by two men I recognised as Frederick Ridgeway, Head of Steamships, and Frederick Toppin, Assistant to the Vice President. Toppin saw at once that we were press and demanded we leave. He walked towards us, placing himself between us and Franklin's desk, as if he thought we might try to lunge at the man. But Franklin called him back. 'Wait,' he said. 'Just wait.' His face was drawn, his eyes red. 'Let them stay. In fact, go down and get the others – tell them that I will see them here, in this office.'

Toppin set off on his errand, and as we waited for him to return I thought about all that I had read of Franklin – of his beginnings as an eager office boy in Baltimore, his rapid rise to become the 'ablest shipping executive on the Atlantic seaboard', his 'positive genius in the handling of difficult situations', his unwavering loyalty to John Pierpont Morgan in that man's battle against Cunard and quest to dominate the North Atlantic. On the wall behind Franklin were hung perhaps twenty photographs of IMM ships, in neat rows in gilded frames, each with a small brass name plaque – Atlantic Line ships, Leyland Line ships, Dominion Line ships, and others. To the far right were the White Star ships: the *Baltic*, the *Cedric*, the *Majestic*, the *Olympic*. As I looked at Franklin sitting at his desk, framed by these photographs, I knew what the 'something big' was. I knew it absolutely. I was staggered by its immensity and took a step backwards. Byrne propped me up.

I knew, too, why Franklin wanted the press to come to his office for the announcement. When he said what he had to say he wanted to be backed by his precious ships, like a man surrounded by his family.

I noticed for the first time that he was holding in his hand a Marconigram. He stretched it tight between his hands, perhaps to keep it steady, perhaps to help him focus when the time came to read it. I could see a pattern of tiny printed words in blue ink. The fragile yellow paper seemed about to tear.

'Mr Steadman, isn't it?' Franklin said softly, looking up at me with tired eyes as we waited for his assistant to return.

'Yes.'

'You were here for the *Cedric*?'

'Yes. And the *Republic*.'

'And the Triangle fire, too?'

'Yes.'

'It affected us all, you know. The fire. All those girls. What you wrote.'

'Thank you,' I said.

'What you found out, I mean.' Franklin looked away, as if troubled by his memories. 'It affected us – here. We take great care . . .' He gave a gentle nod of his head towards the office outside, to the office girls, the clerks. But I knew he meant more than that: he meant his ships. He took great care with his ships. He was telling me he was no Max Blanck.

There was noise and bustle. Toppin reappeared and ushered in the reporters, yelling orders, trying to control them. There were men from Associated Press, Reuters, *The New York Times*, the *New York Tribune*, *The Evening Sun*, and others. There must have been at least twenty men in the room. One knocked over an Egyptian statuette that cluttered to the floor and broke into two pieces, and another slipped on a pile of papers. Many tapped the ash from their cigarettes directly onto the carpet. The reporters were excited; they smelled of body odour and damp wool.

'Gentlemen,' Franklin said in a low voice without getting up. 'With the greatest sadness, I am going to read to you a message I have from Captain Haddock of the *Olympic*, the *Titanic*'s sister ship. It is, you understand, a confirmed message.' There was instant silence. The reporters in the room lifted their pencils to their notebooks.

Franklin began to read in a flat, clear voice. '"Six-thirty a.m. *Carpathia* reached *Titanic*'s position at daybreak. Found boats and wreckage only. *Titanic* had foundered about 2.20 a.m. —' He did not have a chance to finish. Five or six men rushed from the room. That the *Titanic* had sunk was enough for them. Franklin waited, and then began again. '"The *Titanic* had foundered about 2.20 a.m. in 41 degrees 46 minutes north, 50 degrees 14 minutes west. All her boats accounted for. About 675 souls saved, crew and passengers, latter nearly all women and children. Leyland Line SS *Californian* remaining and searching position of disaster. *Carpathia* returning to New York with survivors. Please inform Cunard. Signed, Captain Haddock, *Olympic*."'

Franklin looked up. 'That is the message. I do not have a list of those who have been saved. I am trying to get that just as soon as possible.' He gave a quick nod to invite questions.

'Has Mr Astor been saved?'

'I do not have a list of those who have been saved,' repeated Franklin.

'Mr Guggenheim?'

'I do not have a list —'

'What of Major Butt? Have you spoken to the President?'

'I have not spoken to the President.'

'But what about Mr Ismay?'

'I have not heard from Mr Ismay.'

The questioning continued. Franklin seemed distant and disconnected. One reporter asked whether he might see the *Olympic* Marconigram for himself. It was then I noticed that Franklin had not let it go. It was still taut between his hands, perfectly steady.

Franklin refused. It was the only copy he had; he would keep it, but he would read it again if the reporter liked. The reporter, with his pencil poised, said that he would be grateful.

Franklin began to read again but as he did so his voice cracked, then broke. His eyes watered, so that drops fell onto the yellow paper of the Marconigram and spread in little lily pads of blue ink. When he reached the words 'latter nearly all women and children', he could not go on. He wept freely and openly, as if some force, suppressed for too long, had finally broken free. Great heaving sobs shook his frame and there was an immensity about him, as if he were crying not just for the many hundreds of people who had died on his ship, but for all America, and all Great Britain.

No one in the room spoke. I watched Franklin's face, transfixed. I saw something reborn, something washed clean, something breathtakingly honest. In one word, I saw courage: the courage to face the world anew, courage to stare down the truth. 'The *Titanic*,' he said at last, his sobs subsiding, 'has gone.'

The remaining reporters, their own eyes wet, straggled away. Byrne whispered to me that it was time for us to leave, too. But before we did I had a question.

'Mr Franklin,' I asked, 'the cablegram you read says the Leyland ship *Californian* is searching the position of the disaster. Does that mean that there might yet be other survivors?'

Franklin stared at me: such deep blue eyes. 'No,' he said. 'The only survivors are on the *Carpathia*. This we know.'

'So the *Californian* is searching for the dead?'

'Yes.'

'Where is she bound?'

Franklin looked to Ridgeway, Head of Steamships, standing to his right.

'Boston,' said Ridgeway.

'Thank you,' I said.

Byrne and I left the room, and the IMM offices, and walked out once more into the cold Manhattan evening. I held Byrne by the shoulders and thanked him. When I told him I was going to the train station he was puzzled: why not stay in Manhattan to get the survivors' stories when they arrived?

'I will leave the survivors to you,' I said. 'I'm going home to the bodies.' I turned and began my slow walk north along Broadway.

CHAPTER 6

'To Lord: I am taking the survivors to New York. Please stay in the vicinity and pick up any bodies. Rostron.'

Cyril Evans held the message tight in his small, dirty hands. Pick up *bodies*? This was an important message – direct from the captain of the *Carpathia* to the captain of his own ship – but he did not rush it to the bridge. It was not what he had expected. For a moment he sat at his desk and thought.

It had been the morning of his life. These hours and minutes had been the reason he'd studied so hard at the Marconi school. The *Californian* had been closest to the scene of the rescue, and in the cacophony of crisscrossing signals, all on the same frequency, operators were obliged to listen to him first. 'We are at the *Carpathia* now,' he tapped out to the world the moment his ship arrived at the scene. 'I can see her taking up the boats. She is only a mile away. *Titanic* foundered about two a.m.' Evans had wound the magnetic detector as tight as it would go; he had tapped at his Morse key with frantic energy.

Inspector Balfour on the nearby *Baltic* asked him again to keep quiet and keep out, but this time Evans kept going. He had precedence. He took scribbled notes of what has happening, hoping that when the *Californian* arrived in Boston the newspapers would ask him all about it. This was his chance to become a hero, just like Jack Binns.

But then this message about picking up bodies. It gave him pause. He did not know what notes to make. No one would want to hear about bodies. As he smoothed the yellow Marconi paper, smudging its pencilled letters, he began to imagine them coming aboard, hauled up at the end of a hook by the ship's derricks, wet and bloated, to be laid out on the foredeck hatches. Would the captain then bury them at sea? No, he thought, it would be pointless to pull them up only to send them back again. But how would they be stored? Would the rich, perhaps, be laid out in the empty passenger cabins, amid the satinwood and teak and woollen quilts? And the poor lie on ice on the rough wooden pallets of the 'tween decks? Jack Binns had never spoken of cargo hooks or refrigeration, or faces twisted in death.

Evans wanted to screw up the Marconigram and throw it into the sea. But he knew he must not. He put on his coat and took it up to the bridge.

Herbert Stone knew something of what it was like to drown – or at least to gasp for air and to suffocate. Once, as a young boy, he had tried to please his father by taking hay to their cattle. But he was forgetful and left a gate open, so that a calf escaped and drowned in a bog. As punishment, his father took him into his workroom, a small space cluttered with splintered wood and tools and animal skins, and struck him hard across the face. Blood rose hot in Herbert's cheeks and tears burned his eyes. When he could not stop his sobs, his father stuffed his mouth with a turpentine-soaked rag, whispering in his ear as he did so, 'What are you? A *girl*?' Mucus bubbled and blocked his nose; he was not able to breathe. He struggled and tried to cry out, but his father held the rag even tighter in his mouth so that he 'would know how the drowned calf felt'. Herbert punched and struck with his arms but he could not break free and he thought he must die. But at last he made himself still and quiet, and, desperate for air, locked his wide unblinking eyes onto his father's. In his mind he begged his father to stop. He imagined the word 'sorry' passing from him to his father. He concentrated; he willed the word through. And at last the rag was removed. As he gulped in air – cool, soothing, wonderful air – his father enfolded him in his arms and rocked him gently. 'My dear, dear son,' his father said. 'See? You're a good boy, really.'

Years later, as a junior apprentice, he had been forced to share a cabin with a senior boy who was fierce and cruel. Between them they were assigned only one bucket of wash water per day. The senior boy would use it first then pass it on to Herbert. One day, before passing on the bucket, the older boy urinated in it. Herbert refused to take it. In an instant his arms were pinned behind his back and his head forced deep into the filthy water. He writhed and panicked, but the more he struggled, the more tightly his head was held down. His chest tried to draw in air, but he fought it, keeping his mouth firmly shut. And then, just as he had in his father's workroom, he willed himself to be still. He waited, with his head in the bucket, perfectly still, until at last he was pulled free.

When Stone told these things to the third officer, standing with him at the rail as their ship searched for the dead, Groves said, 'But you know, none of the people from the *Titanic* will have drowned.'

Stone turned to him. 'What do you mean?'

'On P&O ships there were always enough lifejackets for everyone, and if there was any sort of emergency, the first thing they said was "Put on your lifejackets!" And you can't drown with a lifejacket on so they will have died of the cold.' Stone wished Groves would stop talking, but the young man went on. 'Hypothermia,' he said, 'is what they call it. I learned all about it. Did you know, water sucks heat from your body thirty times faster than air? But they say it's not such a bad way to die. After a while you just feel a bit tired, then you stop shivering, and by the end you feel quite warm. Then you fall asleep.'

Stone stared at him. The third officer, he realised, was trying to comfort him, to offer some small twig of consolation. Don't worry about the fifteen hundred who died, he was saying, because they did not gasp desperately for air, but quietly fell asleep. Stone wondered whether the third officer knew just how tiny and withered that twig was.

But either way, frozen or drowned, where were the bodies?

In the water around him, Stone could see none. He could see the pretty *Carpathia*, less than a mile away, her white accommodation glittering and flashing in the sun, and her passengers lining the rails and waving at him as if they were daytrippers on a picnic steamer. He could see, in the vibrantly blue water between the rescue ship and his own, some debris: a piece of rope, an oar, a lifejacket, a woman's shawl spreading silently on the water. Closer inboard was a small lifeboat whose canvas sides had collapsed so that the frigid water lapped freely over a sodden suitcase jammed between the thwarts. So little wreckage, he thought, for such a large ship.

'Probably,' said Cyril Evans, who had appeared briefly by his side and seemed to be reading his thoughts, 'everything was taken down by the suction.'

When the *Carpathia* steamed off to the west and the semaphore flags had been put away, Captain Lord ordered full ahead on the engine. Stone heard the chief officer talking to the bosun about grappling hooks and derrick booms. The second officer was not asked to do anything. Nobody came near him; he stood alone at the aft end of the bridge, out of the way, while the captain stood on the starboard bridge wing and stared straight ahead into the hardening morning light. Captain Lord's bridge coat looked oddly square and stiff. He seemed almost to be part of the ship's structure. Stone wanted to speak to him – about the rockets, about what to say and do about them – but now was not the time.

He held tight to the rail and observed the water below, which had begun to hiss and spit as the ship picked up speed. The wind rose, rattling the bridge awnings, and the sea became choppy, with streaks of white froth scudding along low-lying crests. When the captain stepped inboard to speak to the chief officer, Stone heard only scraps of what was said – that the bodies might have been carried south by the Labrador Current, or west by the wind, that it was impossible to know where they were.

There was a cry from the third officer, who stood on the port bridge wing looking through binoculars to the south. He was gesturing to an iceberg in the middle distance, perhaps three or four miles away. It glowed white and rose to grand and sparkling pinnacles, but Groves was pointing downwards, towards dark shapes on a lower shelf of the berg, close to the sea. The shapes could not be clearly made out; they were indistinct dark patches. They might be dirt, Stone thought, or rock. But then, as he watched, the shapes moved.

'Hard a-starboard!' the captain called to the quartermaster. The ship's bow swung round to the south. The captain rang the telegraph twice forward to its stops, and the smoke at the funnel thickened and billowed as the *Californian* thrashed through the water. But as three miles became two, and then one, and the ship came to a stop near the iceberg, her bow drifting gently around to lie broadside to it, the chief officer said aloud what Stone could plainly see.

'Seals,' Stewart said. 'They're seals.'

The large black creatures lay on the ice, their skin glistening in the sun, their grotesque bodies slippery and fat. They clapped their fins as if applauding, and lifted their heads to emit strange chattering snorts. It seemed to Stone that they were laughing at him. Then, as if responding to an invisible cue, they slid one by one from the ice shelf into the sea.

Perhaps the captain felt the sting of their laughter too, because he rang the telegraph for full ahead and ordered the quartermaster to steer due west for Boston. Their search for bodies was over.

In the wireless room, Cyril Evans chewed hard on the knuckle of his forefinger. He had no messages to send. Other operators had messages to send from their captains, but not him. And his ship was right there, on the scene.

He heard the *Carpathia*'s captain talking to the *Baltic*: 'To Commander, *Baltic*. The *Titanic* has gone down with all hands, as far as we know, with the exception of 20 boatloads, which we have picked up. Number not accurately fixed yet. We cannot see any more boats about at all. Rostron.' Then, a little later: 'To Commander, *Baltic*. Am proceeding for Halifax or New York full speed. You had better proceed to Liverpool. Have about 800 passengers aboard. Rostron.' The *Baltic*'s captain made his replies, other ships called the *Carpathia* and were answered, the ether crackled. Evans listened but sent nothing. No one was talking to him.

He began to hear Cape Race working a new ship amid the clatter – distant, distorted, barely audible, but slowly growing in strength. It was the *Olympic*, the *Titanic*'s giant twin sister, steaming at full speed from the southwest. She would soon be in range, but for now all he could hear was Cape Race talking to her. 'To Wireless Operator, *Olympic*: We will pay you liberally for story of rescue of *Titanic*'s passengers, any length possible for you to send, earliest possible moment. Mention prominent persons. *The World.*' He could not hear a reply but he did hear, beneath the crisscrossing and interfering signals of closer stations, another intriguing message from Cape Race, this time to a passenger of the *Titanic*: 'To Mr W.T. Stead, *Titanic*. We will pay you one dollar per word for your story of this deplorable catastrophe. Please respond at earliest opportunity. *The New York Times.*' Evans was not sure he had heard right but then the message came through again, and there it was, most definitely – *one dollar per word.* He scratched out some quick calculations. Mr Marconi paid him four pounds per month. That was about twenty dollars. He could easily send ten words per minute. So he could earn one month's pay in two minutes. 'Cyril Evans was the only Marconi man on his ship,' he scratched in his notepad, 'and he was the first to hear of the disaster.' There. Twenty words. One month's wages.

He tried to call up the *Olympic* and Cape Race but could get no reply; instead he called up the operator on the *Birma*, who during the morning had become something of a friend. They exchanged messages at speed, but again Balfour on the *Baltic* interrupted him. Evans could hear the shouting anger in the staccato speed of Balfour's letters. 'Stand by stand by! Keep out! You have been told to keep out and stand by. Signed: Balfour.' Evans gripped his key tight. Balfour might be an inspector, but Evans had *precedence.* He tried again to send to the *Birma*, but again the *Baltic* signal came in, loud and persistent. 'Stand by or you will be reported. Signed: Balfour.' Evans threw off his headphones and went below to the steward's washroom to splash icy water on his face. He splashed again. He was being treated poorly, and he felt the injustice of it.

Back in the wireless room, he replaced his headphones and waited. When at last he heard the faint signals of the *Olympic*, working other ships, asking questions, seeking information about her lost sister, he held back no more. He took off his headphones so that he would hear nothing from Balfour and sent at his best speed: '*Californian* to *Olympic*. We were the second boat on the scene of disaster. All we could see there were some boxes and coats and a few empty boats and what looked like oil on the water. When we were near the *Carpathia* he would not answer me, though I kept calling on him, as I wanted the position. He kept talking to Balfour on the *Baltic*. The latter says he is going to report me for jamming. But we were the nearer boat to the *Carpathia*.' That explained everything, Evans thought, taking up his headphones once more. At first there was silence, but then he heard the distant *Olympic* again, still faint but uninterrupted. 'Don't worry, we will take note of the fact that in cases of distress nearer ships should have precedence.' Evans smiled to himself. He had the mighty *Olympic* herself on his side. That ought to silence Balfour on the *Baltic*.

Evans relaxed. He imagined himself explaining the Marconi rules to reporters standing in the sunshine on the Boston pier, gathered around him as eager children might surround their schoolteacher. He would wait while they pencilled the word 'precedence' in their notebooks. 'Mr Evans,' they would write, 'the Marconi man who went to bed only because he had been told to shut up and keep out by the *Titanic*, became a reluctant hero the next morning when he did all he could to carry out the duties of the nearest ship.' Evans leaned back from his key and allowed the vision to build and clarify before him – the angle of the reporters' hats, the smell of clamshells on the pier, the taste of the bean and cod soup they would buy for him.

But then something happened that chilled his imaginings and choked his flow of words. His friend on the *Birma* was again in his earphones, calling him, bringing him back from Boston to the icy Atlantic. 'Were you the nearest ship to the *Titanic*?' the operator asked, and even as Evans tapped back, 'Yes, the nearest,' his fingers began to tighten on the key.

'Nearer than the *Carpathia*?'

'Yes.'

'Did your ship see the *Titanic*?'

Evans had not forgotten, during the frantic events of the morning, what the apprentice Gibson had told him at dawn. 'We saw her rockets, you know. We saw them with our own eyes.' And all morning he had wanted to send: 'We saw her. We saw the *Titanic* sinking.' Even Mr Balfour would have been awed into silence by such a message. And its words would surely be worth more than a dollar apiece to *The World* and *The New York Times* – they would be worth ten times as much. People would forget Jack Binns and the *Republic*. They would know only Cyril Evans and the *Californian*, the ship that watched the *Titanic* sink.

But he had not sent out Gibson's words. When he thought of them again – 'We saw her rockets, you know' – they frightened him. He did not understand them and he could not think through their implications. If his own ship had been close enough to see, why did the *Carpathia* get there first?

Now his friend on the *Birma* was asking him directly, 'Did your ship see the *Titanic*?' He sensed the rhythm of 'yes' in his hand; he felt the tiny ripple of muscle in the forefinger that would send it. It would take but an instant, and the rest would follow in a few seconds more: 'We saw her distress rockets.' But he did not send them. His left hand slid over to clasp tightly his right and he sat still, head hanging low, waiting, wondering, thinking of the captain and Mr Stone. Why had they not gone to the *Titanic* during the midnight watch? There must be a reason, but he could not think of it.

As he lifted his head he sensed, in the floor, ceiling and walls around him, the shame of it. 'No,' he sent at last to his friend on the *Birma*. 'We did not see the *Titanic*.' It was the first time, he reflected, that he had ever used his key to send a falsehood out into the world.

Herbert Stone waited in the stuffy chartroom, where there was a faint smell of turpentine. He sat down on the settee but then stood up again. He took his cap off, he put it on again. He read and reread the notices on the noticeboard.

He reminded himself that he had come to sea to be tested and strengthened, just as Starbuck and Captain Ahab had been by their great white whale. But had *this* been his test? This strange black night? This bright morning, with the white sun beating down mercilessly on him? Those semaphore flags, fluttering and waving and telling him that fifteen hundred people had died? He had seen the way the chief officer looked at him, and even Charlie Groves stood distant, as if fearful of catching a disease, or of being asked to share some part of the responsibility for all those people.

He waited ten minutes, then twenty, then thirty. When the captain at last entered the room he walked past Stone without stopping and stepped into his cabin. The chief officer followed and took up a position just outside the door, as if standing guard. Stone noticed just how thin Stewart was, how gaunt his face, how rock-like his strength. He imagined, for a moment, that the chief might strike him. But the chief only said, 'You had better go in,' and Stone, clutching his cap tightly, walked past him and through the doorway. The chief closed the door behind him.

Stone had never been in the captain's cabin before. 'No one is allowed in here,' he had once heard Lord say to the chief officer, 'except the steward to clean it.' Well, it was clean, but it was small and windowless and dark too. The steel hatch of the skylight was dogged shut with a locking lever that had been painted over with black paint. The electric light was switched off. An oil lamp on the captain's narrow fold-down desk cast a flickering, fragile glow.

Captain Lord turned and pulled a chair out from beneath his desk. It was a large chair, too big for the cabin, with a steel seat and thick, bolted crossbars for a back. He angled it awkwardly into the tight space between desk, bunk and door. Stone felt trapped. The white walls pressed in on him. He could smell the soap the captain used and the starch of his shirt.

The captain gestured for him to sit and Stone perched on the far end of the bunk, placing his cap next to him. Captain Lord took out a pipe, slowly packed its bowl with tobacco, and lit it. He drew a long breath and ejected smoke in a thin, continuous stream that rose and curled back on itself in little delicate eddies. The air became thick. Stone felt he could hardly breathe.

'Now, Mr Stone,' the captain said, looking at him, 'you had better tell me just exactly what happened during your watch last night.'

Herbert Stone had wanted to be a schoolteacher. Nothing had moved his adolescent soul as much as the grand themes of Shakespeare and the magical lyricism of Coleridge, and he thought he might make a career of teaching others to love literature just as he did. But his beer-bloated father disagreed. Schoolteaching was no ambition for a son of his. Schoolteaching was for women. Herbert was weak, his father said, and prone to tears. He needed to be made a man. He would go to sea.

His mother did not want him to go. She worried that the sea would surely drown him. A reader of American literature, she bought him his own beautiful, leather-bound edition of *Moby-Dick*, hoping that he might find at sea something of that novel's vast skies and close friendships. If he was to drown, then at least let him do so nobly, standing side by side with a captain who might place a hand upon his shoulder and say, 'Close! Stand close to me, Herbert.'

But young Herbert soon learned that life on real ships was not at all as it was in *Moby-Dick*. The age of steam had come, so there was no climbing to windswept heights or swinging through tapestries of ropes and sails, no flying in great canvas hallways of air. Instead, when he stepped aboard his first ship, a small tramp steamer, a chief officer with a cruel mouth and stinking breath led him to the door of the pump room and told him to get below and clean its bilges. As he went obediently down the narrow rusting ladder – down and down until the sky was no more than a postage stamp of light thirty feet above his head – his visions of himself on the bridge vanished into the dim future, and for days he trawled through the acidic sludge with ungloved hands until they were red raw. He slipped and fumbled in the putrid iron-scale and grease, and alone in the darkness, with no father to scold him, he let his tears mingle freely with the grimy water.

Still, he persisted. He tried to make his father proud. He discovered that he slept in a cabin, not a bedroom; that he scrubbed the deck, not the floor; that the photograph of his mother was hung on a bulkhead, not a wall. He painted decks and spliced ropes. He studied ship stability and learned his chartwork as well as any apprentice. He mastered the arcane art of the sextant. When he turned nineteen he concluded that he had seen the worst the sea could do, and nothing it had done was so very bad or fearful. He wrote his mother not to worry. He did not think the sea would ever drown him.

When he passed his examinations and completed his indentures his mother bought him a special soft brush to keep clean the gold stripes of his officer epaulettes. He obtained a berth as a third officer, and then as second on the *Californian*. When the captain shook his hand and said, 'I'm Lord – Lord of the *Californian*,' he had seemed to Stone to stand as strong and tall as the ship's towering funnel. 'It is a good ship in a good company,' Stone wrote to his mother, 'and I am happy enough.' But the captain of this new ship never did ask him to stand shoulder to shoulder. He asked instead whether Stone had done his apprenticeship in sail or steam, and when Herbert answered, 'Steam, Captain,' he turned away saying, 'I thought so – steam makes men soft.' After that, Lord said hardly another word to him.

The smell of turpentine and stale smoke. The enclosed space. Stone knew: this was his father's workroom come again. If he wasn't careful, rags would be stuffed in his mouth, tears would come, he might suffocate. He must speak, he must do his best to defy, but he must not struggle. 'I saw her rockets,' he said, 'and I told you.'

He looked straight ahead to the door of the cabin. The ship rolled gently. The captain's bridge blazer swung back and forth on its hook like a pendulum, and the golden cuff braids glowed bright even in the smoky gloom.

Captain Lord leaned back slowly in his chair.

'I whistled down,' Stone hurried on, glancing at the polished silver stopper of the speaking tube near his left hand, 'and then I sent the apprentice, and then I whistled down . . . I whistled down . . .' He faltered. Then, gathering himself, breathing deep, he said simply, 'I told you.'

'Yes, Mr Stone,' said the captain. 'You have said that.' He drew on his pipe. 'Twice.'

Stone sat straight-backed with his hands on his knees. He was trying not to rock back and forth, or tap his teeth with his fingers. Now was the time to be brave, to be honest. It was right to say 'I told you' – twice – and it would be right to say it a third time if he had to, because it was the most important thing of all.

'Let us think about one thing at a time,' the captain said. 'You said "her rockets". Whose rockets do you mean?'

'Hers,' was all Stone could bring himself to say.

'You mean, I think, the steamer I pointed out to you at midnight?'

'Yes.'

'The small steamer?'

Stone closed his eyes, concentrating hard. 'Mr Groves told me it was passenger ship,' he said.

'Never mind about Mr Groves. You saw it. What did you think?'

'I don't know what I thought.'

The tobacco in the captain's pipe pulsed hot red as he puffed. 'Well, did you see a great mass of lights? Did you see rows and rows of deck lights? Did you see anything at all to indicate she was a passenger steamer?'

'No.'

'Well then. Why do you talk to me of passenger steamers?'

'Because Mr Groves —'

'Forget about Mr Groves,' the captain interrupted. 'You know that I saw her myself, Mr Stone? You remember we stood at the rail together, looking at her? She was too dark, much too dark, to be a passenger steamer, let alone the largest steamer in the world. You can never mistake a ship like that, Mr Stone. Never.' The captain's tone was peculiar. Stone did not know whether he was commanding him or pleading with him. The tiny yellow flame of the oil lamp flickered and faltered, as if a ghost had passed. The pipe smoke hung heavy and still.

'Now, you said something about a rocket?'

'Eight rockets,' Stone said. 'I counted them. The apprentice saw some of them too.'

'Never mind about the apprentice.'

Stone stared at the floor. 'Then we saw two or three more later on – at the end of our watch – low, and faint, and further along the horizon, towards the southwest.'

'Further along, you say,' said the captain. 'That means her bearing changed. She was steaming along, then.' He tapped the ash from his pipe into a small china dish. 'You said these . . . rockets were low and faint?'

'The later ones were.'

'Did you hear any explosions?'

Stone shook his head.

'Then they couldn't really have been distress rockets, could they?'

'I don't know. The early ones – the eight – were just white rockets and the later ones were sort of lower.'

'And faint, you said. Low and faint. So they might have been hand flares. Or company signals. Or burning oil rags. Or fishing lights. Or anything.'

Stone was silent. He rubbed his stinging eyes in gentle circles with the palms of his hands.

'Then we are agreed,' the captain said, still tapping ash from his pipe. 'There is nothing whatsoever to worry about. We have a small steamer, close to us, showing flares or company signals, or some such thing, and then steaming away. That is what we have.'

He stopped tapping. Still Stone said nothing.

'Mr Stone?' the captain pressed, holding his pipe perfectly steady. 'Do you agree? That is what we have?'

Stone hesitated. He had another reason in his mind why the ship he saw during the midnight watch looked the way she did. Charlie Groves had suggested it: as she tried to avoid her iceberg, she'd turned towards the north and shown them her dark bow. So Stone had seen only her masthead light, not her blazing deck lights, and that was why she looked like a small steamer. And she had disappeared halfway through his watch not because she'd steamed away, but because she'd sunk. And the rockets he saw later in the watch were low and faint and in a different position because they came from another ship altogether, the distant *Carpathia*, steaming up from the southeast and firing rockets to guide lifeboats to her.

'But Mr Groves,' Stone said, 'thinks they were the *Titanic*'s distress rockets —'

He did not finish his sentence because the captain, in one swift and surprising movement, had thrown his pipe against the back of the cabin door. There was a loud crack as it bounced off and fell to the floor. The captain leaned close. 'As I told you, never mind what Mr Groves thinks.' There was a strange, cold calm to his voice; a deepening, hardening tone. Stone watched the badge of his cap, which he wore even in this private dark room, flicker gold in the frail light of the oil lamp. 'You must try to do yourself justice,' the captain continued. 'You are the second officer. You were in charge of the watch. Now, if you thought you saw distress rockets, would you not have come down and got me out yourself? You would not have stood by and done nothing? Is that what you want me to understand? That you saw distress rockets and stayed on the bridge and did nothing?'

Stone felt his cheeks flush with blood, but he met his captain's gaze as steadily as he could. 'But I *did* do something,' he said. 'I told you.'

'Oh God give me patience,' the captain said. 'We are back where we started.'

In his own cabin, Stone sat at his desk and tried to steady his breathing. Captain Lord would write to the company about him; he would certainly lose his berth and he might never get another. He imagined himself standing before his wife, humiliated, telling her they would have to give up their home and move back to her mother's house. He saw his father, too, scoffing and snorting and spitting at the ground, saying, 'You should have become a schoolmistress after all.'

He took *Moby-Dick* from the shelf and leafed through its pages. As a boy he had not understood all of the novel's strange symbolic prose, but the illustrations had always whispered magical things to him. Now he looked at them again. They were fantastical drawings in black ink. Lines crisscrossed to make light and shade, and images of celestial luminescence emerged from zones of blackness as if drawn in starlight. There was the *Pequod*, her sails full and translucent, all alone on a dark, dark sea; there was shiny black Queequeg hanging from the iron links of an anchor chain; and there was the white whale, bursting forth from the sea into the pure element of air in a great fountain of light, as if the tonnage of its body were born aloft by the light itself. This last picture was called 'The Whale Transcendent'. And there, at the end of the book, was a picture of that same whale with harpoons deep in its flesh, blood pouring out in a torrent of black ink, dragging the captain downwards by a harpoon line caught around his neck like an inverted noose, his mouth and eyes – three black circles – wide open in surprise at death.

But there was one image that caught Stone's imagination most of all. It was a picture of Starbuck, the captain's chief officer and unfailing ally, standing before the mainmast with his head hanging low, his face buried in one hand. His other arm was outstretched, palm forwards, fingers splayed, like Jesus' hand being readied for the cross. Behind him was the great thick spar of the mainmast, half in shadow, half in light, and etched from the black ink of the sky were delicate white streaks, converging upwards, meeting at a point above the frame of the image. Stone had never known whether these glowing white lines were the rigging of the ship or the paths of stars streaking heavenwards. To him it was the most tragic illustration in the book: Starbuck weeping in despair. Stone had always thought he was weeping for Captain Ahab, whom he loved and for whom he would soon give his life. But now, when Stone looked again, he realised that for all these years he had been wrong. Starbuck was not weeping for the captain, he was weeping for the whale itself. He felt sorry for that whale – the innocent whale, 'The Whale Transcendent'.

And yet even though Starbuck cried for the whale, and knew that it was one of the great wronged creatures of the earth, hunted mercilessly by a demonic and vengeful captain, still he lowered his longboat into the sea; still he followed his monomaniacal captain into death. 'Oh what quality of loyalty is that!' Stone whispered to himself.

His thoughts were interrupted by a sharp knock at his cabin door. The chief officer stepped in, holding a cap in his hand. 'This is yours,' Stewart said, placing it on Stone's desk. 'You left it in the captain's cabin.' Stone thanked him, but the chief lingered. He was a small man, with narrow cheeks and a great iron bar of a moustache. He said very little but every word he uttered had a leaden weight. Stone knew he'd once saved the life of a giggling steward by pulling him clear of an untethered derrick block that had come flying through the air like a cannonball. The chief had said only one word, 'Lucky,' and then walked away. He was a man of solid strength and sturdy seamanship and the captain, Stone knew, trusted him absolutely.

'Captain Lord has told me,' the chief said, 'about the small steamer that came up during your watch and showed a flare.'

'Yes,' Stone said. 'The small steamer. A flare.'

Stewart picked up Stone's cap again, turning it slowly in his hands, as if examining a mysterious object. 'Very good,' he said. 'But whatever it was you saw, let me say this: no one knows about it, other than we officers and the wireless boy.'

Stone waited.

'Unless you have told anyone?' the chief asked.

'I have not.'

'Then there is nothing at all to worry about.' The chief used his own shirtsleeve to polish the glossy black visor of Stone's cap and the golden leaves of its emblem. Stone sat still as the chief reached out and placed the cap gently on his head, pulling it snugly down. 'You see? It fits just perfectly,' the chief said. 'You're a good officer, really, loyal and true.'

CHAPTER 7

'You'd better be damned sure there are bodies on that boat.'

I had never liked Krupp. The *Boston American*'s city editor had tufts of reddish hair sprouting from his nose and ears, and his face was as narrow as a rat's. His reporters hated him but he didn't care. Sent up from New York, he was Hearst's man and he was doing Hearst's work here in Boston. He had doubled the paper's circulation in a year or two; on some days it exceeded two hundred thousand. When I once begged a deferral of a deadline so I could be sure of the truth, he told me I was old-fashioned. Journalism wasn't about truth, he said, it was about money: 'Look to where your treasure is; there shall be your heart also.' When I protested that even over at the outrageously yellow *Journal* the men followed Pulitzer's three golden words – 'accuracy, accuracy, accuracy!' – Krupp said I should apply for a job there. I could be accurate and poor. The only three words *he* cared about, he added, red-faced, not bothering to suppress his flatulence, were *cir-cu-lation*.

'There *are* bodies,' I said, trying not to look at him, tired of the battles we had every time we spoke these days. 'I know there are.'

'How do you know?' he asked.

'Franklin told me.'

He gave a quick snort. 'The same Franklin who told you his ship was steaming in glory to Halifax?'

'I'll double-check. I'll confirm it today.'

'You'd better.'

In fact, I had already confirmed it: that very morning I'd heard from the local office of the United Press that the *Californian* was on the scene searching for bodies, and would bring them to Boston. My information, I was confident, was good.

'You know,' Krupp continued, 'I don't know why you didn't stay in New York. It would have been easier.'

'You sent Bumpton.'

'This is a big enough story for two.'

'The bodies are coming here. And they, after all, are why this story matters.'

'You and your bodies! It was fine at first, but now . . . I don't think anyone wants to read about them any more.'

'They will.'

'It's ghoulish.'

I expected nothing more from a man who understood only money. I was never disrespectful to the dead: how could I be, having once gazed on the lifeless body of my own baby son? Krupp seemed to have forgotten my work on the Shirtwaist girls. I gave those girls a voice and returned them to world of the living. Dead bodies are gone too soon in this country. People never look long enough upon a corpse, and whenever they do look they see only a blank nothingness, or otherwise a fearful vision of their own future. I don't see these things – I see a very great richness in the present. It takes courage to look upon the dead. It's not ghoulish.

'And John,' Krupp added, rising behind his desk to let me know I was dismissed, 'try to get some big names this time. Enough of your ordinary-people stories.'

I was about to protest but he held up his hand. 'Just get me a story. A big story. This is it for you, John. This is *it*.'

Minutes later I was on the long-distance telephone to Dan Byrne in Manhattan. His voice was crackly, rising and falling in volume because of some problem with the voltage, but I could hear his excitement. The *Titanic* was definitely on the bottom; Franklin's luxury train to Halifax had been cancelled; there were no survivors other than the seven hundred or so on the *Carpathia*, which was due in New York some time late Thursday. The loss of life was appalling: at least fifteen hundred were dead. The whole city was on edge. Everybody was blaming the British. It was a British ship with a British captain and a British head of the line who had somehow found his way into a lifeboat. There was to be an immediate inquiry into the whole affair by a United States Senate committee. Everyone would be subpoenaed. The President was inconsolable because his dear friend Archie Butt was not on the list of the saved.

'He's sent out two Navy boats,' Byrne said.

'Out where?'

'Out! Out into the Atlantic – to intercept the *Carpathia*, to go to the wreck site if she has to. Anything to find Archie.'

Other famous men were not on the list: John Astor, Ben Guggenheim, Isidor Straus, William Stead, Jack Thayer. It was difficult to believe that such men were dead – on ice in the hold of a nothing steamer tramping its way to my home city. I was right to come to Boston. My editor would get his big names.

But I had to get to them *first*. I had to stake out the territory of my story before others got to it. I needed the *Californian* to reach Boston before the *Carpathia* berthed in New York, and I needed to be first into her icy holds.

I left my office and wandered north along Washington Street. In this part of the city the streets are narrow and crooked, a maze of old cow paths and Indian trails, and the tall granite buildings press in dark and close. But on this Tuesday afternoon in mid-April there seemed to be a certain opening up of spaces around corners that I had forgotten, and new dashes of colour where magnolia and lilac blossoms lay in steamy drains. Spring had come to Boston. The marathon was only days away, swan boats paddled in the Public Garden ponds, and people strolled the streets without their greatcoats.

As I turned down State Street and neared the monolithic India Building of the International Mercantile Marine I saw that, as in New York, a crowd had gathered – men's black bowlers and women's feathered hats bobbed in nervous clumps; pressmen stood together silently smoking cigarettes. Temporary newsstands had been erected on the sidewalks and young boys adjusted cover sheets displaying sombre headlines. TITANIC SINKS, 1500 DIE, said *The Boston Daily Globe*. The *Boston Evening Transcript* had scooped the other papers by publishing a tentative list of the saved, which was being scrutinised by hundreds of the gathered. A FEW MASSACHUSETTS PEOPLE ACCOUNTED FOR was the headline. Boston was bracing itself for its share of the dead.

My own paper was simplest of all: NO HOPE LEFT.

There were no mounted police here to keep control, as there had been in New York. Boston's grief was of the quiet kind. The stoicism of the puritan pilgrims seemed still to hover in these streets.

I pushed my way through the silent crowds to the IMM reception desk. A moment later Jack Thomas, IMM's Boston agent, led me along a narrow hallway to his office at the back of the building.

'I knew you'd come, old boy,' he said, inviting me to sit next to him on a large leather couch. 'I knew you'd come.'

Jack Thomas was fat, much fatter than Franklin, and his body ebbed and flowed next to mine with a wheezy fluidity. He leered at me with tiny eyes set in a puffy face and his breath smelled of the sulphurous blackstrap molasses he ate throughout the day. There were leather boxes stacked against the walls; some of them, I knew, contained illicit photographs stuffed into crumpled envelopes. I knew more than I wished to know about Jack Thomas. Our fathers had been good friends, and some years ago my father asked me to help Jack in relation to an incident involving an Italian sailor, a bowl of fruit and a hidden Brownie camera. It had all been a trap, of course, the sailor turning out to be the son of a member of Watch and Ward's vice brigade. But fate is fickle, and it also turned out that I knew something of that particular member from a story I'd once written about the young prostitutes of North Street. So the Brownie photograph was delivered up, nothing more was said, and Thomas had been very grateful ever since.

'You've been busy?' I asked.

'Oh, the people come and the people go. They want to know whether so-and-so is on the list or isn't on the list. I just show them the *Transcript*. I know nothing more than that. I give them a free copy and send them on their way.'

'That's very generous of you.'

Thomas looked at me with half a smile. 'Well, it *is* a three-cent newspaper, you know. Not the penny trash you peddle.'

'Thank you.'

'You're welcome.'

'This whole thing – it's a terrible tragedy.'

'Oh, come, come. I don't want hysterics from you, John, of all people. These things happen.'

These things happen? I thought of the fifteen hundred dead, and Philip Franklin's heaving sobs of yesterday, the immensity of his shock and grief. This man sitting next to me really was something special.

'I'll tell you what *is* disturbing, though,' Thomas continued. 'Morgan was almost on board. Morgan! New York tells me he changed his mind at the last minute. Can you imagine?'

'Lucky for him.'

'Why yes, and lucky for Ismay too.'

I looked at him, not knowing what he meant.

'Morgan wouldn't have let him slink away in a lifeboat,' Thomas explained. 'Oh no. Absolutely not. He would have made him stand by his side, straight and tall, and Astor, Butt, Guggenheim, too – all of them. "Sorry, old boys," he would have said, "the game is up. We've drawn a bad hand, so you might as well stop your whimpering, Ismay."' Thomas broke into laughter. 'That's what he would have said.'

'So you think Ismay should have died for the company?'

'Of course!' Thomas became suddenly serious, tapping the newspaper on his lap with a violent finger. 'Of course. It is a *catastrophe* for us that he saved himself. There are women missing from this list, you know. *First-class* women! Look —' Thomas thrust the newspaper at me, pointing. 'His is the only name listed under "I". The only one. Ismay. President of the International Mercantile Marine. J.P. Morgan's main man.' Thomas heaved himself to his feet, wheezing and gasping, and helped himself to a spoonful of molasses from a sticky glass jar on his desk. 'This is not good for us, John. Not good. All those American millionaires – Morgan's friends – all dead. You know Senator Smith, down in Washington? He's already turning this into America versus Britain. It's the Tea Party all over again.'

'It was an American ship, really.'

'Yes. But sunk by the British.'

'I'm sure lots of Brits died, too.'

'But not Ismay, not Ismay.'

He ate his molasses. It seemed to calm him. He turned back to me. 'Anyway, John. You're not here because you're worried about our reputation. Why *are* you here?'

I hesitated.

'Come on, John,' Thomas said, rubbing his teeth with a fat thumb. 'Don't be shy. You want something, don't you? Something strange. I know you.'

'I want to be the first to see them – Astor, Butt, Guggenheim – I want to be the first.'

'You mean, their bodies? Their poor frozen bodies?'

'Yes.'

Thomas smiled at me – a great, wide warm smile. 'I should've guessed. You are a sick little man.'

'We all have our . . . oddities, I suppose.' I cast my eyes about the room. All those leather boxes! Thomas raised an eyebrow and I hurried quickly along. 'You know about this ship? The *Californian*?'

'Never seen it. But I know something of her captain. Leyland's youngest, Stanley Lord – very keen, very reliable. He's been a good man for us. But I wouldn't get your hopes up. We haven't heard a thing from him.'

Thomas promised to send a boy to me the moment he had any news, and to make sure I was the first aboard when the ship arrived in Boston early Friday morning. 'For you, John,' he said, 'I'd do anything.'

I rose and left him. Outside, a gloomy dusk had drawn down. The edges of the Custom House Tower had softened and blurred and men were lighting the lamps of their automobiles. I stopped in at a cable office and sent my own message to the *Californian*. It was a simple one that required only a simple answer: 'How many bodies of *Titanic* victims on board – men and women?' I started towards my office but an impulse made me turn about and stroll instead down to Long Wharf. The startled cries of plovers and ospreys rose above the whispering harbour as I headed north along Atlantic Avenue to the tip of the peninsula. At last I reached Constitution Wharf, walking to the very end so that I felt as if I were in the harbour itself.

I stood there to catch my breath, to light a cigarette, and to think. I thought of my wife Olive, and what she would make of all these chivalrous American millionaires, standing aside to let women into the lifeboats. I thought about President Taft, fat and sad and lonely, sending his Navy boats out to find the body of poor Archie, his most loyal friend. I thought of Bumpton, my rival, with his pencil sharpened and his active verbs at the ready, pushing through the crowds of reporters on the Cunard pier in New York, determined to be first to write a Thrilling Tale of Survival. I thought about what the city editor had said: 'This is it for you, John. This is *it*.' I thought about times and speeds and distances and hoped that, with a bit of luck, my ship would come in first, ahead of the *Carpathia*.

But even as I thought these things, and wondered what to do next, the islands of the harbour began to disappear behind veils of mist. I heard the forlorn ringing of the channel buoys, but could no longer see their flashing lights. Curtains of vapour drifted through the masts of ships at the East Boston piers. I was watching the beginnings of a New England fog – a thick, dense grey that would glide in silently from the Atlantic over the coming days. It would envelope us all, causing automobiles to lose their way and babies to cry. But most importantly, it would slow the *Californian*.

I stared out into the gloom and my thoughts became as dismal as the fog.

Across the way were two vessels. One I recognised as the United

States Revenue Cutter *Winnisimmet*: a hundred feet long with a single tall funnel atop a huge Babcock & Wilcox steam boiler and engine. Closer in, beneath the sagging timbers of the pier, was the Chelsea ferry herself, graceful but tired.

As I looked at these vessels, an idea began to form in my mind. It was an audacious idea, quite daring, but if I was lucky it might just work. Follow my heart, the city editor had advised, and there would be my treasure also. I realised I had been thinking of things the wrong way around.

CHAPTER 8

'His pure tight skin was an excellent fit,' Herbert Stone recited to himself as he slowly climbed the stairs at midday to begin his first watch since the disaster. He mouthed the words repeatedly as a sort of prayer, trying to keep at bay as best he could the troubling thoughts that had pressed in on him since his meetings with the captain and the chief officer. 'And closely wrapped up in it, and embalmed with inner health and strength . . . Starbuck seemed prepared to endure for long ages to come, and to endure always . . .' Step by step, word by word, he climbed towards the bridge. 'Inner health and strength, inner health and strength . . .'

When he got to the bridge there was bright air all around and the third officer stood by his side. Groves was still animated: he talked of the great disaster, of the *Carpathia*, which he had been the first to identify as the rescue ship, of the futile search for bodies, of the sparse and pathetic wreckage. 'I still can't believe what's happened,' he said. 'I still can't believe it. That ship of all ships, on her very first voyage.'

The sun was at its zenith, high and white in a cloudless sky, and Stone saw no sign of field ice or bergs, only radiant blue water stretching to a sharp horizon. On the foredeck, crewmen painted handrails and laid out ropes for splicing.

'Course is due west,' said Groves. 'No ships about. The water's warmer – we're in the Gulf Stream. No more ice.'

Stone stood silently watching the seamen at their work. Groves lingered. 'You all right, Second?'

'The captain wants me to write it all down,' Stone said, 'in a letter addressed to him.' He held up a thick pad of writing paper he had brought from his cabin. The cold wind flicked its pages. 'I'm going to work on it during my watch.'

Groves looked back at him wide-eyed, his large open face clear and bright. In the noon sun his brow seemed to shine as white as alabaster; it put Stone in mind of the marble cherubs in his local church, polished smooth by the daily caresses of loving parishioners. There was no dissembling in this man, or judgement either, just a pragmatic openness – an honesty and innocence that seemed to glow from within him with enough radiance to encompass them both.

'What do you think I should write?' Stone asked.

'Just write the truth,' Groves said. 'Write down what you saw.'

Just write the truth. It was the sort of powerful simplicity that had allowed Charlie Groves to bump along with the rich boys at Cambridge even though he himself was poor; that had given him the confidence to laugh openly at P&O passengers and their ridiculous white suits. *Just write the truth.* There was no calculus of morality for Charlie Groves. In his conception the truth was the surest guide to what was right. This was Groves' peculiar gift, Stone supposed – to see simplicity where he himself could see only dense complexities.

First among these complexities was the captain, his face all bronze and angular, telling him he could not have seen distress rockets, and second among them was Starbuck, driven by a loyalty more powerful than Groves' truth.

'But what *did* I see?' Stone asked.

'It was only last night,' Groves said, almost smiling. 'You must remember.'

But Stone wasn't sure what he remembered any more. He had thought of that midnight watch a hundred times since and every time it was different. When he tried to write it down, it changed yet again.

'You saw her rockets,' Groves continued, 'you remember that, at least. You told me about them this morning – "Yes, old chap, I saw her rockets on my watch." That's what you said. It was your very first thought. So you can write that down for starters.'

'But the captain says I *didn't* see her rockets. He says they were too low and faint to be distress rockets.'

'But he was asleep below. You were on the bridge. You saw them. What did you think they were?'

'I called down to the captain about them.'

'And what did he say?'

'He told me to watch her.'

'Anything else?'

'To Morse her.'

'So you watched her and Morsed her.'

'Yes. That's what I did.'

'Then that's what you write.'

Groves spoke as if he were stating a simple solution to a simple problem, but his face had darkened. His eyes disappeared into the shadow of his cap as he leaned forward and his lips were drawn tight between his teeth. He turned away, and Stone sensed exasperation – disgust, even. He suspected Groves was thinking that if he, Groves, had seen the rockets, he would have done more than watch and Morse. Stone had seen him leap into the water from a pier without a moment's thought to rescue a woman's parasol; he would think even less about waking the wireless operator in the middle of the night, or hauling the captain up to the bridge. 'People expect to get woken up on ships,' Groves had once told him. And each night, Stone knew, Groves woke Evans on his way down from his watch just to get the gossip.

The standby quartermaster sounded the first bell of the watch. But still the third officer lingered. He seemed to be building up to something. When at last he spoke, he was tentative and thoughtful.

'We all have to live with this, you know,' he said. 'You're not the only one with this thing on his mind.'

'But you have nothing to trouble yourself with.'

'That's not so. I could have saved everyone.'

Stone looked at him in astonished silence.

'I was in the wireless room,' Groves continued. 'I had the head-phones on. If I'd wound up the detector I would have heard her. She was calling for help by then. Sparks told me this morning that the detector had wound down.' He paused, hanging his head. 'Sparks has shown me before how to wind it. I knew how. I just didn't notice.'

Stone stared hard at him. For Groves there was a straightforward causation: if he had thought to wind up the machinery, he could have saved everyone. But the moral quality of that omission, Stone knew as he nervously clutched his notebook and searched his friend's face for sympathy, was very different from that of his own. Groves had had no hint at all that anything was wrong, but he, Stone, had seen the rockets.

When Groves at last left the bridge, Stone stood alone beneath the great canopy of the sky. There were no longer any men on the foredeck. The derrick booms were stowed, the decks were secured, life on the

Californian had recovered its ordinary rhythm. He leaned against the forward bridge rail, rested his notebook on the steel ledge and began to write.

There was fire in the makeup of donkeyman Ernest Gill. His father was a blacksmith's assistant, and as a child Ernie had played among the glowing forges of Sheffield as freely as other children might play among trees and meadows. He knew from the very beginning that his would be a tough life – every day his father told him so, and said, too, that with all these fires about they would never be far from hell. Ernie was fascinated by the red-hot iron and leaned as close as he dared when his father beat and shaped it with a hammer. 'You see,' his father used to say, 'apply enough heat and anything will bend.'

Ernie liked school. He had ideas, and when he spoke he found that other boys would gather to listen. A teacher taught him the Rule of Three, beginning with Caesar's *Veni, vidi, vici,* which he used in varying forms whenever he could. His mother, a hard little stone of a woman who beat her husband with pebbly fists whenever he drank too much, claimed Ernie was destined for better things than the Sheffield forges, and helped him with his studies as best she could. But she died when he was eleven years old and he left school to earn what money he could. As an adolescent he worked for a glassblower, stoking the furnaces and cleaning away the ash. One day he picked up a flask that he thought had cooled but which in fact was white-hot. His skin sizzled and came away. When his hand finally heeled it was disfigured with unsightly lumps and scars, and never again could he fully open it.

When his father died Ernie moved to Liverpool and got work in the engine rooms of ships. He was a trimmer and then a fireman, shovelling coal into boilers to keep up the steam. He was quick with his devil's claw and slice-bar to rid the fires of ash and clinkers, and he had the hottest, cleanest burn of any fireman. By the time he signed on to the *Californian* he was ready for promotion. He was twenty-seven years old, newly engaged to a girl in Liverpool, and tired of shovelling coal. When, on his third voyage, he was made assistant donkeyman he put on a clean boilersuit to work closely with the gentlemanly engineers and had nothing more to do with coal.

His new position, and the whiteness of his overalls, gave him a sense that, in his own humble way at least, he had become something of a leader of men. Which was why, early in the afternoon following the sinking of the *Titanic*, he called a special meeting in the focsle. He had seen something very strange during the night, he said, and something needed to be done about it.

The focsle was a private place: it could not be seen from the bridge, and anyone approaching from the 'tween decks could be heard in advance opening and closing bulkhead doors. Gill sat on an upturned crate in an area between the forward stores and the men's bunks, where half-casks and cotton-filled sacks lay about. The men drifted in one by one: the ordinary seamen and able-bodied seamen, the trimmers and firemen, the carpenter and the bosun's mate. They talked among themselves rather than to Gill, but he didn't care. They would listen to him soon enough. His news would shock them all.

He sat tracing the lumps and scars of his right hand with the little finger of his left. The men spoke of the seals they had seen lazing on the iceberg, of the terrible news delivered by the *Carpathia*'s flags, of the futile search for bodies. Some said these must have been drawn down by the suction, others said they had been swept away by currents. Every sailor had become an expert, but they didn't know what he knew.

'We are a ship of shame,' he said when everyone was there, and looked around to see if his words had taken hold. They hadn't. The men continued their talk as if they had not heard him, so he stood up and stepped onto his upturned crate. 'We are a ship of shame,' he said again. 'We saw her rockets and did not go.'

The men looked at him and fell silent. One word had cut through.

'Rockets?' asked a trimmer.

'Rockets,' Gill repeated. 'Distress rockets.'

'Claptrap,' said a seaman.

'It's true. I saw them myself. I went on deck for a smoke after my watch, and that's when I saw them. The second officer couldn't help but see them too. And I know he *did* see them because the apprentice told Sparks that he did, and Sparks told me.'

The men stared at him.

'The skipper was called but he didn't come up. He just lay there and grumped and chewed the second out about it. And that's why I've called this meeting. It isn't right that a man should refuse a ship that calls for help. It isn't right, and something ought to be done about it.'

Gill watched the men closely. Coughin' Kenny spluttered into his cotton wadding, which he held up to the light so the men could see the raspberry-red clots glistening with black dots of coaldust. Brennan, the bosun's mate, surly and sour, mumbled something inaudible. But Fat Ballantyne asked Gill to go on.

'And that's why we didn't find any bodies,' he continued. 'The skipper didn't *want* to find any. He didn't want to be dragging up corpses of people he was too lazy to save when they were living.'

Gill felt a small artery pulsing in his temple and the scar on his hand throbbed. He sensed the power of his words; he saw now that every man was listening. He was triumphant, like a preacher who has just revealed a profound truth of scripture. The men began to ask questions – what the rockets looked like, what colour they were, how far away they seemed. Fat Ballantyne, heaving himself up on his matchstick-thin legs, asked why the captain, when called, did not go up to the bridge.

'I don't know,' said Gill. 'He just didn't, and it isn't right. It brings shame to the ship – it brings shame to us all.' It was time, he sensed, for the Rule of Three. 'He was called, he did nothing, and now it's up to us.' He paused for effect. 'I vote we form a Committee of Protest to go to the captain – a Special Delegation – to go up and tell him that he isn't going to get away with it.' A few men nodded and there were some positive mutterings. He could see they were ready to follow him.

But McGregor, the carpenter, sitting on a small wooden stool, lifted his head and said in a low, measured voice, 'Go up to the captain and lose us all our jobs, you mean.'

Gill had never before heard the carpenter speak a word: McGregor was man who kept to himself, took his soundings and did his woodwork. When he stood he was as tall as Gill was standing on his crate, and his skin was such a deep brown that Gill wondered whether he was an Englishman at all. And now, having found his voice, the carpenter didn't stop. 'The focsle shouldn't be talking so against the captain,' he went on, speaking without seeming to move his lips. 'Nothing good will come of it.' He fixed his eyes on each man and rested them finally on Gill. 'That's what's making this ship shameful – *your* calling this meeting, *your* complaining and chattering. It's mutiny talk – that's what it is, pure and simple. If we were back in sail, you'd be hanging from the yardarm like washing in the breeze.'

'Well, we're not in sail,' said Gill. 'And a *protest* isn't a *mutiny*.'

'It is with this skipper. Say one word against him and he'll have you off articles quicker than you can cry poor. And he might just clap you in irons in the meantime – you and any poor man you talk into coming with you in your Committee of Delegation, or whatever you call it.'

'I'm not scared of the captain.' Gill flung these words out to all the men, but the carpenter blocked them.

'And he isn't scared of you. He's tougher than you are. You go up against him, you'll come off second best. Trust me, I've known him for years.' The carpenter stepped closer, tall and sinewy and strong. Gill could see the topsails of a tattooed tea clipper showing above the low collar of his shirt. 'I don't believe you saw any rockets,' the carpenter went on. 'Our skipper wouldn't ignore a call for help at sea. No man would. I don't know what kind of talk goes on down in the engine room but we don't talk against our ship up here on deck. As I say, if anyone brings shame to this ship it'll be you. So the best you can do is get down off of that rickety crate and stop spouting your nonsense.'

'It isn't nonsense,' said Gill, stiffening and clenching his scarred hand into a fist. 'And you've got no jurisdiction over me. I'm engine room, is what I am. Engine room!'

'Listen to you – *delegation*, *jurisdiction*. Pah!' The carpenter spat on the deck. 'Those are mighty fine words for an orphan boy from Sheffield.'

At that moment, the aft door opened and the bosun stepped into the space. No one had heard him coming. The men were at once a blur of movement: standing, doing up their shirt buttons, taking off their cloth caps and holding them by their side. The bosun was kind, but he was tough and unyielding too. His eyes moved slowly from man to man and then settled on Gill.

'Everything under control here, Mr McGregor?' the bosun asked of the carpenter while looking at Gill.

'Always under control, Mr Bosun,' the carpenter said, turning away and stepping towards his bunk. 'The fireman's helping me with my vocabulary, that's all.'

'Assistant donkeyman!' spat out Gill, as much to the bosun as to the carpenter. And then, apologetically, 'I mean, I'm not a fireman any more ...'

'Well,' said the bosun, 'fireman, donkeyman or candlestick maker, you'd better help open this place up a little – it stinks in here.'

Gill stood down from his crate. He knew he had lost the men. As they pulled on their boots and sou'westers and threw open the forward hatch to let in light and air, they did not look at him. None of them would form a committee with him, or come with him to protest to the captain, or help him right the great wrong that had been done. The carpenter had seen to that.

Herbert Stone often marvelled at the bewitching resonance of his captain's voice. When Lord told of rounding the Horn five times in sail, of meeting Mr Shackleton, of landing a thousand men on the beaches during military manoeuvres, he spoke as an indulgent grandfather might to a loved child. He used words like 'poppycock' and 'balderdash', and seemed always to speak from a position of special knowledge. He even pronounced the name of the *Titanic* in his own particular way, with a strange elongation of the second syllable – *Ti*-tar-*nic*.

So when Lord insisted that it could not have been the *Titanic*'s rockets that Stone saw during his watch, Stone felt compelled to believe him. 'I did not see the *Titanic*,' Stone said to himself. But he was having trouble writing it. The *Titanic* was large, stationary, and had fired rockets, so he knew his letter must say that what he saw was small, moving, and showing signals that were not rockets. He had set these things out clearly enough – 'I judged her to be a small tramp steamer – steaming away to the S.W. I observed a flash of light in the sky' – but then he began to lose his way. He became uncertain. He pressed his pencil hard into the page to make his words dark and bold, but when he read them aloud they seemed timid and ambiguous. He persevered for a day, and then another, and as the ship neared Boston he at last had a draft ready for the captain.

Captain Lord was talking quietly with the chief officer over Thursday luncheon in the dining saloon when Stone drew up a chair and handed him the letter. Stone thought he would read it at once, but instead he carefully folded the two sheets in half and put them in his pocket. He spoke of the weather, of the warming sea temperature, of the possibility of fog ahead. He asked Stone what he thought of these matters and nodded thoughtfully at the answers. The thick velvet curtains swayed with the gentle roll of the ship and the polished silver cutlery rattled softly on the tables. The ship's engine throbbed steadily.

Stone understood. The captain's calm nodding, his upturned palms, his fingers opened slightly towards him, said that everything had been restored. The semaphore flags and their message were forgotten.

'And so,' the captain said, turning to Stewart, 'the crew are working well?'

'They are,' said the chief. 'Very well.'

'They carry out their business on deck in the normal way?'

'They do.'

When, a little later, Stone stood on the bridge and watched the men go about their work he saw that the chief was right. They chipped rust and spliced ropes and seemed carefree and happy. The sun drifted lower ahead of him, the deck pulsed reassuringly beneath his feet, and Boston drew closer.

But not long afterwards, when Cyril Evans came to the bridge looking for the captain, Stone saw a yellow Marconi slip fluttering in the wireless operator's hand and sensed it would bring new worry. He asked if he might see it.

'It's a service message,' said Evans, 'for the captain.'

'Does it refer to the management of the ship?'

'I suppose it does.'

'Then I may see it. I am the officer of the watch.'

Evans seemed unconvinced, but he offered up the message. 'To Captain, *Californian*. Press reports you were near *Titanic* and have remains victims on board. Have you anything to report? Leyland.'

Stone stood for a moment leaning forward into the wind, using its resisting pressure to steady himself. *Press* reports? He'd heard that American reporters would stop at nothing to get a story, but how did they know his ship had been near the *Titanic*? Those four words 'you were near *Titanic*' in Evans' spidery handwriting seemed almost to be an accusation.

'Why does Leyland – why do the *press* – think we have remains on board?' he asked.

Evans was quick with his answer. 'Because the *Carpathia* sent a report to the *Olympic* saying that we were searching for bodies.'

'But we didn't find any.'

'They must have assumed we did.'

Stone thought a little longer. 'The report was sent to the *Olympic* – so how does the press know?'

'There's a United Press man on the *Olympic*. I've heard him sending messages about it – about us having bodies, I mean.'

'You've been listening to this man's messages?'

Evans smiled. 'I listen to *all* the messages. There's only one frequency. You can't avoid it. It's not eavesdropping.'

Stone gave the Marconigram back to Evans and waved him away. He stared ahead. The sun sank towards the horizon as if tired of its own weight, and the North Atlantic heaped up in low, lethargic swells like those of the tropics. Its golden stillness annoyed Stone; its very calm seemed to mock him.

The whole world, then, knew they'd been near the *Titanic*. The press were asking questions. So were the owners of the *Californian*. Stone wondered whether the captain would still tell him that there was nothing whatsoever to worry about.

Later, at twilight, when Stone went to the bridge to take his star sights, Captain Lord was talking to the chief officer at the forward bridge rail. As soon as the captain saw him he took him aside and showed him four Marconigrams. Stone read them carefully. All were inquiries about bodies, but this time they came directly from Boston and New York newspapers. Their tone bordered on the desperate; they begged for information. 'Please rush answers at our expense,' asked one. 'Send collect any news even if slight,' said another. 'Relieve the world's anxiety!'

The most direct message came from the *Boston American*: 'How many bodies of *Titanic* victims on board – men and women?' Stone felt the insult of it on the captain's behalf. The new technology had brought with it new rudeness. No 'Dear sir' or 'Yours sincerely', just 'How many bodies?'

Ahead, the Atlantic was flat and sombre. The pink horizon had given way to turquoise. Stars had begun feebly to show themselves. 'Have you told them,' Stone asked the captain, handing back the messages, 'that we have none on board?'

'I have told them nothing whatsoever,' said the captain. 'I have told Mr Evans to transmit nothing. If you say one word to newspapermen they will demand more. They pounce like animals. They have no honour. No, no one is to speak to them.'

The captain lingered on the bridge as the sky darkened and the stars grew brighter. Stone wondered why. He sensed a subtle change in his mood – a stiffening, a deepening coldness, as if he were preparing to carry out an unpleasant duty.

'I have read your letter,' the captain said.

Stone had been holding his sextant by his side, letting it sway loosely back and forth, but now he slowly returned it to its rosewood box, which sat on a nearby ledge. Then he stared straight ahead and waited.

'In parts,' the captain continued, 'it is satisfactory.'

'But in others . . . ?'

'It is not.'

Stone worried that his nervousness would turn to anger. He had worked for days on that letter. 'But,' he said, very quietly, very deliberately, 'it says just what you said it ought.'

'It does – but then it goes on to say so much more. You start well, but you destroy your good work later.'

Stone resolved to say nothing more; he could not be sure his voice would not quiver or break. But his silence seemed to embolden the captain, who now spoke in a tone that was wholly new.

'I know what you are trying to do, Mr Stone. Please don't think that I don't. I know *exactly* what it is that you seek to do, and all I can say is that it does not become you. It is weak, and it is disloyal.'

Stone had not expected this. He did not speak or move, even as the captain walked away to take up his position again next to the chief officer at the forward part of the bridge. He wanted the captain to sense his unwavering, upright presence, to hear his silent protest. His letter was not weak. It was not disloyal. It was *true*.

The gloom deepened and Stone, thinking upon things, did not at first notice that something strange was happening ahead of him. The boundary between sea and sky had become complex; the varying bands of turquoise had resolved into a single neat line, a stripe which, as darkness fell, was not fading but becoming more distinct. As he watched, the band seemed to broaden. At the same time there was a softening of the ship's steel edges, a blurring caused by something more subtle than the descending darkness. A corona encircled the foremast steaming light; the luminescence radiated outwards through wispy vapour. A moment later, the foremast disappeared altogether. They had steamed into fog – dense, deep and still.

The captain, without turning around, called to him, 'Dead slow ahead, please, Mr Stone,' and Stone walked to the engine telegraph and pulled it gently rearward. The answering clang came and the rhythm of the ship's engine slowly died away. For a few moments he let his hand rest on the handle of the telegraph, feeling in the polished brass the *Californian*'s fading pulse as she groped her way blindly towards Boston.

Hours later, lying in his cabin, Stone could not sleep. The foghorn boomed sorrowfully every minute and the captain's cruel words hounded him. He got up from his bunk. There was something he wanted to do.

He heard seven bells ring down from the bridge: he had half an hour before the midnight watch. It would be his final watch of the voyage – Boston Light must now be only hours away. He dressed warmly and strolled aft along the shelter deck. He wandered down to the poop where he lingered, leaning over the taffrail to gaze into the ship's wake. The black water, visible only by the feeble light of the stern lamp, turned in on itself in gleaming laminar folds as it flowed astern into the fog and darkness. The ship was moving very slowly.

He stepped onto the lowest rung of the rail and leaned out. The rails were slippery. The water passing below mesmerised him. As he stared at it he was reminded of six newborn kittens his father had once put into a cotton bag, thin enough to show the outlines of their tiny wriggling bodies, and thrown into the clear racing waters of the River Dart. For a while the bag floated, bobbing downstream before it became sodden, and Herbert heard squeaking cries as high-pitched as a bird's. He turned away, but his father made him watch. 'Life is hard,' his father said. 'Not every mouth can be fed, not every life can be lived. We best take it from them before they know what they've lost.'

Odd, Stone thought, standing on the taffrail, that he should think of those kittens now, those six little beings squeezed together in that small dark bag – just like the womb they'd come from only minutes before – feeling the mystery of death come upon them. What would it have been like? He felt himself at the edge of strange new thoughts, on the cusp of some exhilarating empathy. He leaned further out. If he slipped he would fall, but he held on tight with one hand and reached with the other to grab the shreds of vapour that seemed to hang close by. But he clutched only at air. The fog was everywhere except where he was. Such was the nature of fog: to seem thickly solid in the distance but invisible close up.

The water slid by smooth and black, and he felt as trapped as the kittens in their death bag on the river.

A single toll of the bell sounded to call the midnight watch, but he did not go. Instead he leaned as far out over the rail as he dared, put his hand into a deep inner pocket of his greatcoat and drew out his copy of *Moby-Dick*. He held it out – this book that his mother had given him, which had made him imagine all the wonders of the sea – and it fell open in the soft light of the stern lamp. For an instant Stone thought he saw the image of Starbuck – radiant, luminescent, his arms outstretched on the cross made of starlight – but he could not be sure, because already the book was falling away from him, tumbling over itself through space. It fell silently into the sea on its spine, and floated calmly on the water, its pages opening slowly outwards. Then it was gone, taken by a downsurge into the darkness below.

He was still at the taffrail when he heard someone nearby humming 'Annie Laurie'. By degrees the sound clarified into words: 'She gived me her promise true, gived me her promise true . . .' He turned inboard but could see no one. Fog drifted in thick shreds between the bollards and capstans; the stern lamp cast only the faintest glow. There was no wind. The ship, it seemed, had slowed further. He walked towards the sound, trying to resolve shadowy shapes in the gloom. 'Her voice is low and sweet, and she's all the world to me.'

But now the singing seemed to be behind him. Another feature of the fog: sound bouncing and leaping so you never knew from whence it came.

He turned. The curved shadow of an air vent split in two and one half moved slowly towards him. A match flared, lighting a face from beneath.

'Evenin', Mr Second,' said Ernie Gill the donkeyman, drawing on his cigarette.

Stone could see a snide smile in the flickering light; he saw a familiarity, a knowledge that frightened him, and when he asked, 'What are you doing here?' he was surprised by the timidity of his own voice.

The donkeyman drew close; his form had a sudden clarity.

'I'd better go up,' Stone said, moving to step around him. 'It's almost midnight.'

But Gill blocked his path. 'What did you just throw over?'

'Nothing.'

'I saw you. You threw a book.'

Stone, wondering just how long Gill had been watching him, remained silent.

'Why?' Gill pressed. 'Why did you throw it away?'

'I'd finished it,' said Stone, but even before his words had vanished into the fog he felt their foolishness.

Gill gave a short, dismissive laugh. 'How did it end?' he asked.

When Stone again did not answer, Gill stepped yet closer. 'Cold tonight, isn't it?' he said, exhaling his smoke into the fog. 'But not as cold as the other night, when I stayed on deck awhile after my watch, thinking about things, looking at the sights . . .'

'What sights?' Stone asked, and at once wished he hadn't.

'Very pretty ones. All bright and pretty.'

Stone tried to push past, and again Gill blocked his path. 'But don't worry,' Gill said, almost in a whisper. 'It's not me you need to be afraid of. It's not *me*.' He turned and vanished back into the murkiness, and as he walked away Stone heard him singing again, his low voice sliding in and around the folds of the fog. 'For Bonnie Annie Laurie, I'd lay me down and die . . .'

Stone arrived on the bridge just as the standby quartermaster rang the eight bells of midnight and pulled the foghorn lanyard. A long, low bass note pulsed out into the night. At the rear of the bridge Groves handed the watch over to him. They were only an hour or so from Boston Light and everyone had an eye out for it, and was listening for its signal. Extra lookouts had been posted; the chief officer and captain had come up. The fog, which had lifted briefly, now set in again thicker than ever. The captain was confident of his dead reckoning, but all were on the alert. They had heard one or two ships pass outward bound but had not seen them.

When Groves left the bridge, Stone stood for a moment, opening his eyes wide to let in every particle of light. Fog surrounded him like a wall. By the glow of the compass binnacle he could make out the shapes of men: the chief officer, the quartermaster, the standby quartermaster, and in the centre, the tall figure of the captain.

As a child, Stone had created pictures of his father using black ink and woodblocks, and this was how the captain appeared to him now: all solid squares and straight edges, black and symmetrical. He stared directly ahead, eyes piercing the fog. He looked like a disembodied spirit floating in the mist.

'Is that you, Mr Stone?' the captain asked without turning.

'Yes, Captain.'

'Move further forward, Mr Stone. We must concentrate. There are thirty islands between us and our berth. We must be vigilant.'

They were relying entirely on dead reckoning. Sheer and savage cliffs were just as likely to be ahead of them as Boston Light. After each sounding of the foghorn the captain held up a hand to command silence, and Stone strained forward to listen for echoes from land, or answering signals from distant ships. The *Californian*'s progress was slow and no one spoke.

For half an hour they heard nothing, but then Stone caught a barely audible note, seemingly dead ahead. Then: a longer note, deep and mournful, like the cry of a whale who'd lost her calf. The *Californian*'s own foghorn sounded again, reverberating, booming, and again there was a soft, distant reply, as insubstantial as the vapour.

But with each repetition the sound grew a little louder.

'Direction, Mr Stewart?'

'Three or four points on the port bow.'

'You, Mr Stone?'

'Dead ahead, I think.'

But when the foghorn next sounded, it seemed to Stone to come from astern. The captain ordered, 'Half ahead,' to get clear of the danger, Stone supposed. He cupped his ears from beneath to shield them from the increasing throb of the engine, closed his eyes and listened hard. When the sound came again it was very close. Stone opened his eyes and stared forward; he could see nothing. He turned his head left and right, closing his eyes again to try to judge the sound's direction. The foghorn seemed to sound in a deeper part of his mind and he had sudden clarity.

'It *is* dead ahead, Captain!' he called.

'Mr Stewart?' There was a distinct urgency in the captain's voice now.

'I agree: dead ahead.'

'Stop engine!'

The foghorn came again, almost as loud as their own now, and Stone could hear the chugging of the other vessel's steam engine. Any moment, he thought, there must be a collision. Instinctively he held onto the bridge rail. Captain Lord called for two short blasts and one long one on the foghorn: 'You are standing into danger.'

A call came from the crow's nest: 'Light fine to port!' And then a second call: 'Light to starboard!'

Stone could see them: two faint white lights growing brighter by the second and moving slowly towards each other. Two small boats, he thought, but then the blackness between the lights slowly resolved itself into a steel hull, and Stone saw one ship, dead ahead, turning fast, her masthead lights drawing together as her angle changed.

The ship disappeared under their bow. Stone braced himself for impact, but the other ship was handled deftly and she darted clear at the last moment, steadying her course as she drifted close down the *Californian*'s starboard side. She was a large ocean tug, more than a hundred feet long, with a tall funnel amidships emitting a stream of glowing sparks and embers. She glided astern, back into the fog, but just before she disappeared she seemed to Stone to be turning again and applying full power. A great burst of flame erupted from her funnel and the pounding of her engine could be heard above the low pulse of their own.

'She's turning,' he called to the captain and chief, who were looking forward. 'She's coming again.'

By slow degrees the tug adopted a course parallel to their own and thrashed her way through the water until she drew abreast, veering recklessly close. The beam of a searchlight swept up and down the *Californian*'s length, and then was switched off and replaced by a softer light on the tug's bridge. The vessel was only yards away; Stone could clearly see the men on her bridge. One lifted a megaphone to his mouth.

'SS *Californian*, SS *Californian*. We are the Revenue Cutter *Winnisimmet* with members of the United States press aboard. They have permission from your owners to board your ship.'

Stone saw his captain's surprise: Lord's mouth was open but no words came. The chief strode to the bridge locker and retrieved the captain's own megaphone, but the captain waved it away. Instead he walked inboard and rang 'Full ahead' on the engine telegraph and told the helmsman to hold steady his course.

The chief lifted the megaphone to his mouth and called, 'Stand clear! Stand clear!' The *Californian* began to draw ahead. Despite the heavy labouring of the cutter's engine she could not keep up. Men scurried about her bridge and her telegraph clanged.

Stone saw another man take hold of the megaphone and call up to them – a thin man with black floppy hair. 'You have a duty to respond,' Stone heard him say. 'I have your owners' permission to board.' As the vessel drifted astern once more his words were drowned out by the pounding din of her engine, but Stone caught fragments – 'the *Boston American*' . . . 'pay good money' . . . 'I have permission.' The man seemed determined. He leaned so far outboard that Stone thought he might try to leap the distance between the two ships. But the gap opened up yard by yard, the mist swirling in turbulent gusts about the vessels. Soon the cutter vanished astern and all that could be heard was the fading chug of her overworked engine. Stone stared aft. What sort of place must Boston be if newspapermen went to such trouble?

When he turned forward again, he saw that something had changed in his captain; there was a quality about the softly lit figure he had not seen before. Perhaps it was the way his cap sat not quite straight, or the way the fog's moisture on his cheeks made him appear to sweat, or the way he seemed to be speaking orders quietly to himself. Stone did not know what he now saw. It might be anger or it might be fear. When Evans brought up a message from the Leyland Line – delayed, he said, because of some problem at the Wellfleet station – the captain seemed hardly to notice. Nor did he seem to remember that his ship was still steaming at full speed through fog towards the rocks and islands of Boston Harbor.

As the fog swirled and eddied, Stone thought of his beloved *Moby-Dick* disappearing into the black water. 'How did it end?' Gill had asked him, and an image now came to him clear and true: Captain Ahab being dragged downwards by the dying whale into the black ink of the ocean.

CHAPTER 9

These were strange times in Boston.

There was so much mud under the bleached white pavers you only had to apply a little pressure for it to come bubbling up through the cracks. I was often splashed: perhaps it was the way I walked, with my weight always at the edge of those dainty white squares, never at the centre.

For us in the dirty business of newspapers it was the time of the great muckraking crusades. Pulitzer and Hearst battled to outdo each other. Pulitzer started it all with *The World* down in New York – with its stories of crimes, scandals and monstrosities – but Hearst had taken things to new heights. Or lows. He would stop at nothing, even instigating a war with Spain to sell more papers. He said to one of his photographers in Cuba, 'You furnish the pictures, I'll furnish the war,' and that's exactly what he did. And when the *New York Journal* published stories of brave American soldiers, circulation rose to a million copies a day.

I never knew why Krupp was sent up from New York, but what I did know was that when he arrived at the *Boston American* he had a score to settle. He wanted to beat New York at their own game and give the *Boston American* the highest readership in the country. This wasn't such a crazy plan: if Mrs Baker Eddy could achieve record circulation in only a few years with her very sober *Christian Science Monitor*, then there was no telling what a man like Krupp could do with a paper like the *American*. I did what I could to help, not with New York-style tales of adventure and manhood, but with touching little stories of the intimate and the domestic, the downtrodden and the destitute, the liars and hypocrites. I wandered the brothels, taverns and jilt shops to talk to pimps and hookers and to catch glimpses of their clients. Sex was like Mr Bell's underground telephone wires: invisible, but connecting everyone. The city had a fascinating hypocrisy, a curious doubleness. Watch and Ward were everywhere, burning books, hunting opium smokers, arresting men for giving away racehorses, but on Charles Street women were known to live with women and channel the spirits of the dead in occult gatherings. The city censor banned a hundred books of 'passion', but Boss Curley was allowed to run his election campaign from prison. Boston Corbett cut off his own penis after staring lustfully at a prostitute, but then roamed North Street yearning for what he'd lost.

At times, I did embrace the sensational and the shocking. I impersonated a madman to expose the brutality of asylums. When a headless, legless, armless torso was found in the East River in New York I travelled south to become part of a joint newspaper-police force searching for more body parts. I devised tricks and stunts. I persuaded my own daughter, at fourteen years old, to pose as a child prostitute. I helped my wife find board and lodging for fugitive suffragette window-smashers. And I pretended to be a grieving Italian father so as to see the burnt bodies of the Shirtwaist girls on the pier in Manhattan.

Such was the spirit of the times. So when, on the morning after the fog rolled into Boston, I walked into Krupp's office and told him I wanted to hire an ocean tug to take me out to the *Californian*, he at once said yes. The papers down in New York were sending boats out to meet the *Carpathia*; he would do the same for the *Californian*. 'But,' he added, 'there had better be bodies on that boat.' It was becoming his refrain.

The adventure seemed like a good idea. Why wait for the *Californian* to come to me? My inspiration to go to her instead was no less a person than the President of the United States himself and his dispatch of the Navy to find Archie Butt.

Things then moved quickly. My newspaper chartered the *Winnisimmet* that very afternoon and I persuaded Jack Thomas to send a Marconigram to the *Californian* authorising me to board. I dug around and found some old oilskins and stiff rubber boots. The next afternoon we steamed out of Boston Harbor and that night we found the *Californian* groping around in the fog a few miles east of Boston Light. So far so good.

But I had not counted on the stubborn defiance of the *Californian*'s captain. He would not let me aboard and instead steamed off at full speed. We chased him but did not reach his ship until it berthed at the East Boston pier just on dawn. I was exhausted and, to be frank, more than a little angry. My grand idea had been a waste of time. But if I acted quickly I could still be the first pressman aboard. I saw a crowd of perhaps a hundred people pressed up against the locked iron gates at the landward end of the pier, and I knew that among them would be newspaper reporters. So I asked the tug master to land me at the seaward end, and he obliged by nudging his craft gently into the wharf fenders. I leapt ashore with my duffle bag and ducked into a longshoreman's shed, where I put on a boiler suit and engineer's cap that I had secreted from the *Winnisimmet*'s engine room. I tucked a clipboard under my arm and a moment later was walking up the *Californian*'s gangway.

'Coal supplies,' I said to the seaman stationed at the top. 'Where's the chief engineer?' The seaman waved me on. I hadn't thought it would be so easy. When I pretended to be a lunatic in the Taunton madhouse, I'd at least needed to forge admission papers.

I wandered aft unhindered. Men went about their business undogging the hatches, running lines to the derrick winches, plugging the scuppers, and the recently painted deck plates shone bright green in the morning sun. No mud under those, I thought.

I opened a steel door and climbed down a ladder. I walked along a lower deck, past strange machine parts lashed to wooden pallets. I tripped over dunnage timbers and old fire hoses. I found refrigerated stores: chilled eggs, frozen milk, meat and bread loaves.

I'm not sure what I expected. I'd heard that ships sometimes carried supplies of ice wrapped in burlap, and imagined that somewhere in these cavernous holds might be a section set aside, dark and cool, with bodies laid out under sheets in neat rows. The *Titanic*'s dead: tidy, numbered, each with a little bag for their possessions. Some would be the richest corpses in the world – John Jacob Astor, Benjamin Guggenheim, Isidor Straus. They might stare up at me with that peculiar gaze, wondering, perhaps, why their money had not been able to save them.

I climbed down another ladder to a yet lower deck, walked its length, and then climbed lower still. Down here the spaces were closed in and dark. I didn't know whether my breathing was rapid because I needed air or because I was becoming tense and anxious.

I looked beneath tarpaulins and searched behind stacks of rubber tyres but found nothing. I decided to start again from the upper decks, and climbing the internal stairwell in the midships accommodation block, I heard an excited commotion. By the time I reached the topmost deck I could make out Bostonian accents, and as I walked further forward they clarified into voices I knew. 'What wreckage did you see?' (Frank, the old drunkard from the *Globe*.) 'Did you see the iceberg?' (Rupert, with the glass eye, from the *Advertiser*.) 'Were you in any danger yourself?' (Sam, the pious Christian with fifteen children to three women, from the *Monitor*.) The questions rolled over each other in a frenetic fugue. I heard not a single answer.

Jack Thomas surprised me by appearing in the alleyway in a white suit, as large and round as if inflated by some pneumatic process. He wheezed and puffed; his face was engorged with blood. 'Old boy!' he said, lurching towards me, fumbling in his pockets for something. 'Where have you been? My god, what is that you're wearing?'

'He didn't let me on, Jack.'

'Don't be peevish, old boy. I sent a Marconigram. What more could I do? At least you're here now.'

'You said I'd be first on board.'

'Come, come. When I couldn't find you I could hardly deny the others, could I? Don't sulk now, you've not missed a thing, and you've me to thank for persuading the captain to say anything at all. Stern fellow, he is – didn't want to speak at first, said he had nothing whatsoever to say. Nothing whatsoever! Until I told him it was his duty to say something. And so he's about to give a little press conference – only one, he said, only one, and absolutely no photographs, but he will tell us all he knows and all he did, and that will be that. It'll make a nice little story for your paper, I should think, a nice little story.'

'But what about the bodies?'

'Sorry, old boy, there are no bodies. I asked him outright and he answered outright. They found none. Not a single one. They didn't even find much wreckage, just a few bits and pieces. He'll tell you all about it. He'll give you a nice little story.'

Jack Thomas was sweating. Perhaps he knew I was done for, and that 'a nice little story' wouldn't save me. He eased himself into an architrave so that I could squeeze past him, then he turned and followed me along the alleyway. 'Straight ahead,' he called. 'Straight through, John. Just push through. Go right to the front. That's it, *push*!'

An open louvred door led into a small room overfilled with men. On one side was a large table, on the other a green settee. There were no windows. A bare electric light bulb gave off a hard glow. Six or seven pressmen shouted, surged and retreated. There was simply not enough space for us all. One reporter stood on the leather settee in his muddy boots. Someone belched.

Then I saw them: four men standing perfectly still, facing the crush, their backs against the bulkhead. They were very clearly Englishmen – tall, stiff and reserved. The tallest of them, the captain, stood at the centre in an immaculate blazer and cap. He had a man either side of him and a third stood partly in shadow behind.

People tell me there's such a thing as love at first sight. I don't know about that. But I do know that there's such a thing as a story at first sight. And there was something about these men – their stillness, perhaps, or maybe their unimpeachable solidarity – that told me at once that something strange had happened on this ship, something more than 'a nice little story'.

At first they reminded me of a Victorian family posing for a photograph, but then I thought of British soldiers mounting a last-ditch defence. The four men gazed into the middle distance and looked at no one in particular. They were a little piece of stoic England here in Boston. Then, as if responding to a secret cue, the captain raised a hand, palm outwards. He seemed somehow to shine with a special light. The pressmen grew silent.

'Gentlemen,' he began, 'I am Lord – Lord of the *Californian* – and I will answer your questions.'

His voice! It was such a surprise – its strange accent and the way it flowed around me like a warm breeze. It made me think, This is a man I would trust with my life.

'But first,' the captain continued, lifting his eyes a little, 'let us say a prayer for those who have been lost in this tragedy.' He asked that every man in the room bow his head. 'Eternal Father, strong to save, whose arm hath bound the restless wave.' It was a hymn we all knew, but Lord did not sing the words, he spoke them in that voice with its own mysterious music. 'Who bids the mighty ocean deep, its own appointed limits keep; Oh, hear us when we cry to Thee, for those in peril on the sea.'

I looked hard at the glazed porcelain of his face, trying to read it. But I could not. I did not know what I was looking at. The officers either side of him were likewise closed off and emotionless. But then I caught something in the man at the back, the man who was almost hidden. He was clearly terrified – his eyes, as large as a woman's, darted left and right, his eyelashes flickered, his jaw twitched – but there was something else there, something less obvious. I stared at him, and for the briefest instant his eyes locked onto mine with a pained intensity, as if he were asking for help, as if he were being held hostage. And in that moment I thought of the photograph I'd seen only days earlier in New York, in the station saloon. I remembered now the word that came to me for Harry Houdini: *trapped*.

This man before me felt trapped. Why?

And then a subtle but odd thing happened. The captain, seeing me studying the officer behind him, shifted very slightly sideways so as to block him from my view. He was protecting him. Again I wondered, Why?

The press conference was about to begin. I got out my pencil and prepared to write down every word Captain Lord said.

'We left London on April 5th and had a comparatively pleasant voyage until about the tenth day out, April 14th, when we ran into such a mass of ice that I deemed it safest to stop the engines and let the vessel stand until the course became clear.'

I wrote down the words verbatim, as quickly as the captain spoke them, using my own shorthand – not a proper stenographical system like Pitman's or Gregg's, but a mixture of words, scrawls and symbols I'd developed over the years. The captain, slightly hunched forward in this low-ceilinged room, spoke clearly and evenly, as if he had memorised his words.

'Scarcely had the boat been brought to a standstill when we received a relayed message from the steamer *Virginian*. The SOS was signalled to C. Evans, the Marconi operator on board our steamer. We knew the danger attending any attempt to steer the vessel through the icefloes, but also knew that no effort should be lost to render what assistance we could. We were about twenty miles away.'

Even though the captain's language was strangely formal – 'C. Evans', 'attending any attempt', 'render assistance' – there was nonetheless some good material here. It would be easy to write Thomas's nice little story – a tragic tale of thwarted heroism. But I had promised a story about bodies, and I was getting nothing exclusive from this captain: my fellow reporters' pencils were just as busy as mine.

Captain Lord described how his ship had pushed through the icefield but arrived just as the *Carpathia* was hoisting the last lifeboat aboard. 'We offered to help, but the captain informed us that he required no assistance.'

I saw Sam Jameson from the *Monitor* write 'tragically, no help needed'. I was losing interest. But then Lord said something that made me look up from my notebook. 'We stood by and watched the proceedings.'

The *proceedings*? His words struck me as so very passive and detached. I saw Jameson put square brackets around them; the other reporters wrote nothing. They wanted this captain to say he had searched the scene frantically, or lowered lifeboats at once, or hung his head in despair. There was no place in their stories for standing by and watching. But I wrote the words down and I underlined them. They seemed to me the most important thing the captain had said so far – there was oddity in their blandness. They put me in mind of pawns in a game of chess, subtly positioned to protect a valuable piece.

'How far away were you?' I asked.

'When?' he responded, his eyes lifting high above our heads as if he were looking at something far away.

'When you were . . . standing by and watching.'

'Oh, *then*. No distance at all. A mile, perhaps.'

The emphasis on 'then' was almost imperceptible, but I had heard it. 'And at other times?' I asked. 'When you got the SOS call, for example? How far then?'

Now there was a distinct hesitation. 'Thirty miles – perhaps more.'

'Thirty? I thought you said twenty before?'

'Thirty.'

I pushed a little harder. 'Do you have the exact latitude and longitude?'

Now his eyes fell. He fixed his gaze on me as if I were an insect that finally needed swatting. A Boston insect – more persistent, and less well mannered, no doubt, than those of England. The officers either side of him seemed hardly to breathe. 'That information,' he said, 'the latitude and longitude, is something of a state secret.'

Latitude and longitude a state secret? Perhaps I had misheard. It made no sense. I pressed him further. 'What do you mean?'

'It will be in my report to the company. You will have to get it from the office.'

I heard Thomas's sugary voice behind me: 'You may give it now, if you wish,' he said.

'I do not have the exact figures for our overnight position – the exact latitude and longitude I cannot give. I shall put them in my report, in the usual way.'

A pencil fell to the floor. It belonged to a thin, bespectacled young man with oily hair – perhaps twenty years old – who loafed against the far wall and whom I hadn't noticed before. The clatter, and the young man's stifled cry, diverted attention from the captain. The reporter from the *Transcript* – the fastest and most astute of us – at once threw questions at the boy. 'Are you the Marconi man? Tell us about the SOS call.' There were instant and overlapping outbursts from others: 'Did you hear from the *Titanic* directly? Can you show us the SOS message?' The boy fidgeted and shuffled forward as if to speak. I tried to read his face: did I see resentment there?

But it was the captain who spoke. 'We received the distress message shortly after dawn. At about 5.30, I would say – yes, about then.'

'Can't the boy answer? There's nothing wrong with his vocal organs, is there?' It was an impertinence that surprised even me. The question came from old Frank of the *Globe*, who I knew drank a gin martini every morning after breakfast, except on Sundays when he drank two:

one for himself and one for the Lord. 'Well?' Frank demanded again. 'Is there anything wrong with the boy? Can't he speak for himself?'

'I will answer your questions,' Lord said, 'on behalf of the ship. That is only proper, as her captain. I said that at the very beginning.'

'Then you need to tell us more. I don't have enough.' Frank held his notebook forward to show its sparse scribblings. 'If you're the only one who can speak, then you must speak more!'

I did admire old Frank. Cobwebs of fine veins laced his cheeks and his left hand quivered with a strange palsy, but he was awed by no one, not even this tall, burnished captain of the British Merchant Marine. In Frank's conception of things, the primary responsibility and duty of people – anyone, everyone – was to give him a good story.

'Tell us about the ice – tell us more about that,' said the reporter from the *Herald*, trying to be helpful.

The captain's words began slowly to flow again – in that exotic accent with its commanding calm. 'Our ship,' he said, and my hand noted down his words as surely as one of Edison's wax rolls, 'bucked her way through continuous icefloes.' He seemed to find his stride. 'I forced my steamer to the limit of safety and all ordinary precautions were abandoned.' He looked to Jack Thomas, who rolled one hand slowly over the other, like a steamer's paddlewheel, as if to say, Keep going – give them more.

'There were icefloes stretching in all directions,' the captain obligingly went on, 'and it was often necessary to slow down the engine to permit the ship to break her way through them without ripping off plates.' The man had thawed a little; he made eye contact with us individually, as if remembering long-ago lessons in public speaking, and began to develop a sense of the dramatic. 'I never in all my marine career saw so much ice!' His words became active and for the first time he spoke of emotion. 'At times, nervous and anxious as we were, we hardly seemed to be moving. We had to dodge the big bergs, skirt the massed field ice and plough through the line of least resistance. For three full hours we turned, twisted, doubled on our course – in short, manoeuvred one way or another – through the winding channels of ice.'

Winding channels of ice! When he tried, it seemed, this captain could be creative. I looked behind me and saw Thomas smiling warmly. The captain was at last doing a good job.

Only a few hours earlier, the *Carpathia* had berthed in New York, watched by forty thousand onlookers. The survivors came ashore in driving rain, and their individual stories – like the tiny flames of candles being lit in a dark cathedral – had begun to illuminate a very great tragedy. Visions flashed upon the consciousness of a nation: first-class men standing on sloping decks in dinner jackets, steerage passengers rushing wildly for the boats, Italians being shot dead by the *Titanic*'s officers, the mighty Captain Smith, his great white beard spreading around him in the black waters, swimming to a lifeboat with a baby in his arms. There were visions of shame, too: when a passenger was asked how Mr Ismay, chairman of the line, had escaped the doomed ship, the passenger simply shrugged and said, 'Well, he got into a lifeboat.'

'I wish I'd been down there,' said old Frank from the *Globe* while we waited to be escorted to the *Californian*'s gangway. 'I'd have shot him. That's what we used to do with yellows back then, you know. Shoot 'em, straight up, no questions.' When Frank spoke this way we never did know who the 'we' were, or when 'back then' was, and no one ever dared ask.

The talk went on. Frank massaged his swollen gums with a dirty finger. Other reporters muttered about being 'down there' – in New York, getting the real stories.

I slipped away. I had no desire to be in New York, and I was not yet ready to leave this ship, which, in her own passive way, intrigued me. I crossed the alleyway to the seaward side of the main deck, where there were no pressmen, and no crewmen either. I climbed the external stairs – narrow, rusty, steep – to the very topmost deck. I knew a little about ships, and there was something very specific and particular I wanted to find on this one.

The bridge, open to the weather, was deserted. There had been drizzle earlier, but now the late morning air sparkled clear and warm. The Bunker Hill Monument seemed strangely tall and close and great clusters of gulls whooped and cried amid the cranes of the nearby docks. The inner harbour, fed by the vibrant waters of the Charles and Mystic rivers, glowed blue and white. Years earlier, when my father had taken me exploring around the islands in an old Maine lobster boat, the harbour was alive with sail; the brown canvas of barques and barges snapped and cracked in the spring winds. But this morning, as I looked out, the harbour was thrashed and pummelled by the power of steam. Everywhere I saw the tall, straight funnels of the steam engines that drove the submerged propellers of tugs, barges and steamers, each taking the most direct route, none caring about the direction of the wind.

It was progress of a sort, I supposed, but I couldn't help feeling nostalgia for those older, lazier days when soft breezes calmed human lives. This modern frenzy of steam-making seemed to bring with it a fevered insanity: I had read in dispatches of a man in Brooklyn who killed his own baby then leapt out a window; of a psychic healer in Dallas – described as 'a holy man of the Punjab' – sent to jail for rubbing his oily palms on women's tumours; of a farmer in Pennsylvania who shot his wife and then forced his nine-year-old grandson to shoot him dead with the same shotgun. And, of course, most insane of all: the *Titanic*, with steam engines the size of office buildings, undone so easily by silent ice. 'And still the horror grows,' declared *The Boston Daily Globe*.

As I stood alone on the sunny bridge of the *Californian* and reflected on all this madness, I could not help but wonder what disorder and chaos might be found beneath the neat decks of this ordinary, sleepy steamer. I brought to my mind the captain's face and tried again to read what I had seen. There were some peculiarities beneath that hard-fired exterior.

Why had he said his ship's position was a state secret?

Why had he silenced the wireless man? Why had none of his officers said a single word?

Why had he first said his ship was twenty miles from the *Titanic* but then later said thirty? Why was he trying to push the *Titanic* further away?

Why, if the captain had received the wireless distress call scarcely after his ship had been brought to a standstill, as he claimed, did he then use the term 'overnight position'? Why was he trying to shrink his overnight hours to nothing? What had happened during those hours?

And I thought, too, about the man standing behind the captain – the man with the pretty face and deep eyes who remained so perfectly still that I wondered what he was trying to conceal with such fixed concentration.

There was a story on this ship. I could smell it.

I looked about. The engine telegraph, compass and ship's wheel, each mounted on steel stands, had been covered in green canvas. A small locker amidships was labelled 'glasses'. It was locked. On the forward bulkhead, beneath a canvas windbreak, was a stoppered speaking tube, and adjacent to this was a card behind glass showing the ship's dimensions, turning circle, stopping distance, and other details. There was also a 'compass deviation' card. It was all very interesting, but it was not what I was looking for.

I walked slowly back and forth. At each end of the bridge an extended awning provided some protection for a small foldout table. I pulled both tables down and stowed them again. Perhaps this was where the officers carried out their navigational calculations. Behind the starboard table, secured to the rear steel wall, I saw a small cupboard. There was a latch, but it was not locked. Inside was a water bottle, a tin tankard full of pencils, and there, resting on a lower shelf, I saw what I wanted: a small notebook, with pages sewn into a soft cover. On the cover were printed the words '*Californian* Scrap Log'.

This, I was sure, would give me some clues as to what had happened. But I was disappointed. About half the log's pages had been torn out, and the remainder were blank, apart from a ruled margin and the word 'date' printed in pencil at the top of each. There was no writing, no clues.

I idly flicked the stubs of the missing pages with my thumb. The pages had been torn out about half an inch from the spine. Then I noticed something odd: one of the stubs had a perfectly straight edge. All the others had been ripped, but this one seemed to have been cut carefully with a knife. I counted back: if one page were used per day, then the cut page represented the 15th of April – the date of the disaster. So whatever had happened on this ship that night, it had warranted removal with surgical precision.

'File your story by three o'clock or don't bother filing at all.'

I received the note at one o'clock from a breathless message boy.

I recognised the rushed yet masterful lettering of Krupp.

I told the boy to come back at half past two – I would have something for him then. But as the wall clock in the Marginal Street saloon neared two o'clock, I still had not put one word on the page. I'd drunk three bourbons to liberate my muse, but nothing came. The more I thought of that enigmatic captain – his inscrutable face, the liquid charm of his voice, the almost hypnotic power he seemed to have over those around him – the fewer words I had. There was something about him that resisted my efforts; it was as if a curtain were drawn around him, behind which I could not see. In the era before Hearst and Pulitzer I would have tried to get at the man by learning something of his past – about his mother and father, his apprenticeship, how he had come to be the Leyland Line's youngest commander. But these days there was no time for such things.

'Hello, old boy!'

I looked up. Jack Thomas had pushed his way into the tavern, red-faced, dabbing at spittle on his lips. 'How did you know I was here?' I asked.

'Oh John, I know how to sniff *you* out.' He heaved himself into a chair and dropped a newspaper onto the table.

'I don't really have time. I've got to file —'

'But that's why I'm here, old boy. I've come to help you out. Read that.'

He pushed the newspaper towards me. It was the morning edition of *The Boston Daily Globe*. STORY OF HEROISM ran the front-page headline in letters an inch high. MAJOR BUTT STOPPED STAMPEDE BY SHOOTING DOWN CRAVENS was the sub-headline. 'The tale of the sinking of the steamship *Titanic*,' the story began, 'is a story of heroism. There were brave men on board that ship . . .'

'See?' said Thomas. 'A story of heroism. I thought, That's the sort of thing you could write. It would certainly help us.'

'You want me to write about Captain Lord shooting people?'

Thomas gave a great laugh; a substance came out of his nose. 'If only he had! That would have been splendid! But no, not shooting – *sacrificing*. Sacrificing the safety of his own ship to help others in the freezing ice. An IMM captain following the very finest traditions of the British Merchant Marine. That sort of thing.'

I slid the newspaper back across the table but Thomas, breathing through closed teeth with a wet, sucking sound, pushed it straight back to me. 'Read on,' he said, pointing at a paragraph with a stubby finger. 'Read it out aloud.'

'"Major Archibald W. Butt,"' I mumbled, bourbon blurring my diction a little, '"the personal aide of President Taft, stood near the starboard gangway for more than two hours assisting women and children into the lifeboats."' I looked up at Thomas. 'That the part you mean?' I asked.

'Yes, yes. Keep going, old boy.' Thomas leaned back to listen.

'"With drawn revolver, Major Butt warned off excited men who tried to leap to the places held for the women and children, and when they would not obey his orders to stand back, he shot them."'

'He shot them!' Thomas gave a little clap.

I read on. It was all rather gripping. '"It was not time for argument, and the President's aide wounded six men before he stopped the stampede to the boats. Every man of them was lost. Major Butt declined to step into a boat himself, and his last hours were devoted to the saving of life. Just before the *Titanic* broke apart and made the dive into the sea, Major Butt leaped overboard and was drowned."' I looked up. 'His last hours were devoted to saving people by shooting them?'

'Not people. Cravens!' Thomas was beaming.

'Who were these cravens?'

'You know who they were.'

'Tell me.'

'Italians.'

'I thought you liked Italians.'

'They're not brave.'

'They're not American, is what you mean.'

'Oh John, don't be so *contrary*.'

'I'm not being contrary.'

Perhaps it was the bourbon, but I felt very sorry for the six men who'd been shot dead by the brave major. I thought it an outrageous crime – to shoot unarmed men in the last desperate moments of their lives. 'Thank God for Major Butt,' I said, raising my glass in tribute.

'Yes indeed!' replied Thomas, raising his in reply.

'But,' I continued after I'd drained my glass, 'surely the biggest craven of all was the head of your own company. And he's no Italian.'

'Exactly, old boy. Exactly. That's why I'm here – asking you to make something of Captain Lord. For every villain there is a hero.'

'But it was Rostron, of the *Carpathia*, who did all the rescuing.'

'Yes, but he's from *Cunard*, old boy. Captain Lord is ours, and at least he tried. He had been very safe, he told me, stopping his ship and turning in for the night —'

'He went to bed?'

'Only after stopping his ship, old boy. If only the *Titanic*'s captain had done the same!'

'Yes,' I said. 'If only.'

'And he had his man on the bridge, of course.'

'Of course.'

'And as soon as he *knew*, he did all he could. You heard him: he risked everything to get there. And you can always add some of your own colour – I know that's what you do – a sailor, perhaps, who was so scared he begged the captain to slow down, a sailor who was *sobbing*, you know, in *terror*, because of the icebergs, but whom Captain Lord strikes away —'

'Like a craven.'

'Yes!'

'With the butt of his pistol?'

'Perfect!'

We both laughed.

'You think Captain Lord was a hero?'

'Of course. A tragic hero, because he didn't get there in time, but a hero nonetheless.'

I paused. Thomas tried to encourage me. 'Don't write it for me, old boy,' he said, 'or even for IMM. Write it for England. Write it for America. Write it in defence of manhood across the world.'

'What do you care of manhood?'

'Whatever do you mean? I am a great fan of manhood.'

'Well – boyhood, perhaps.'

'Let me buy you another drink, John. I can tell you're in one of your moods.'

He was right. I was tired and fractious. I hadn't been sleeping properly. Nor had I seen my daughter since I returned from New York, and without her laughter and energy I soon became dissipated and flat. The tavern seemed airless; there were too few customers and too many dogs. The sawdust smelt of urine. I could hear bar girls, short of tips, arguing in a distant room. And although I liked Thomas, this afternoon, as he sat opposite me trying to get the attention of a waitress, he seemed particularly repulsive. He had rubbed cooking oil into his face to give himself a youthful sheen. His white suit, smeared with coaldust and ink, was too tight. A steamy heat rose from his lap.

But it was the story in the *Globe* that had angered me. In six columns over two pages it described in great detail the deeds of brave men, but I had seen not one word about any of the children who died.

Because by now we knew the numbers. Fifty-eight first-class men had found their way into the lifeboats but fifty-three third-class children had not. It was an almost perfect one-for-one correlation. For almost every rich man who lived a poor child had died. How had this happened on a ship that took nearly three hours to sink in calm water? What sort of tale of heroism was this? Was this the story of America? I remembered the fuss Watch and Ward had made about me using my daughter to pose as a child prostitute on North Street. They bleated and complained and tried to have my story banned, but what had they said about the fat men who'd tried to buy her? Nothing. And what now did they have to say about the dead children of the *Titanic*? Again, nothing. If only those children's little bodies had been in the hold of the *Californian*, I could have written about them and made them live long in Boston's conscience.

'Why should I give you anything?' I asked Thomas. 'You promised me bodies and you didn't deliver. You should go to someone else.'

'You know it's you I come to in times of trouble, John. You've saved me before. Now's your chance to save an entire shipping line. Morgan won't be . . . ungrateful, you know. Write us up a hero, John. We need it. Write us up a hero.'

The new drinks arrived. I couldn't help but smile at my friend. For a man with such dark and depraved secrets, there was something utterly guileless about him. The shine of his face might be grotesque but at least it did shine; I knew too many people whose faces were dark and craggy quagmires. And he was always ready to join me in denouncing Watch and Ward and their sanctimonious, self-righteous moralising; he agreed that life was a thousand times richer than Watch and Ward's frigid conception of it.

'Very well,' I said. 'I'll do what I can. I'll do my best.'

'You promise?'

'For you, Jack, I'd do anything.'

So, as Thomas wobbled off to his next duty as IMM's man in Boston and I ordered another bourbon highball with a lowball chaser, and as the light in the tavern grew yellow and musty, I turned to a new page in my notebook. 'The story of the *Californian*,' I began, 'is a story of heroism. There were brave men on board that ship . . .'

CHAPTER 10

Herbert Stone's mother had taught him always to look carefully at people's eyes and listen carefully to their words. But Captain Lord's eyes were usually hidden in the shadow of his cap, and it seemed, too, that some grinding machine was always at work on his words, so that they came from him like small, hard pebbles. Stone could no more imagine his captain saying 'I'm sad' or 'I'm sorry' than he could imagine him drinking beer or uttering a blasphemy. His face betrayed nothing; Stone only ever saw a stiff blankness.

But on the day following the captain's meeting with the press he seemed different. That morning, a Saturday, the captain asked Stone to join him in the dining saloon, and for once he was not wearing his cap. His eyes were blue and lively; there was an unusual warmth about him.

The captain was sitting at a table covered with newspapers. He gestured to Stone to sit and showed him the headlines of two: LEYLAND LINER RUSHED TO SCENE OF THE *TITANIC* DISASTER BUT FOUND ONLY WRECKAGE, and *CALIFORNIAN*'S RACE TO AID *TITANIC*

TOLD BY CAPTAIN LORD. 'You see?' said the captain. 'Mr Thomas cannot complain that I have not given them what they wanted.'

'No,' said Stone. 'He cannot complain.'

The captain began to read one of the stories aloud. '"It took some mighty good seamanship to pilot the freighter through the narrow winding channels of ice, and although her officers used every effort to keep her going as fast as possible, there were times when circumstance made it necessary for her to proceed at a snail's pace."' The captain paused. 'Very satisfactory, don't you think?' He puffed on his pipe.

Stone agreed: the meeting with the newspapermen of Boston had been a success. The captain's charm – even though of an iron kind, heavy and majestic like an ocean steamer – had been enough to woo the Americans. Their faces shone when they listened to him talk of the *Californian*'s courage and speed. Not one of them had asked about the midnight watch and Stone himself had not had to say anything.

The captain, rummaging through the newspapers, seemed almost thrilled. Only days earlier he'd proclaimed that he would refuse to say one single word to the pressmen. He said they were like animals, that they had no honour. Now Stone stared at him and wondered at the power of flattery. The reporters' praise of the captain's seamanship was all it had taken for him to forgive their muddy footprints in the chartroom, their cigarette butts on the chart table and their impertinence.

In the soft morning light the saloon seemed to fill with the captain's self-satisfaction, with his sense of the justice of it all. Nobody, Stone thought, would ever be able to point a finger at him and say he'd done anything wrong; nobody could ever deny that as soon as the wireless message came through he had gone to the *Titanic* as quickly as possible; nobody could doubt that he had driven his ship hard and shown some 'mighty good seamanship'. For the captain, at least, a wrong in the world had been made right, a tear in the fabric of things had been sewn up, a wound had healed.

Stone watched him gather up the newspapers and fold them as carefully as if they were historic parchment, silently aligning corners and edges. 'The matter is closed,' he said, and perhaps he was right. It had been a difficult Atlantic crossing, with ice, and fog, and diversions from their course, but now the *Californian* was here in Boston, on time, with her men safe and her cargo complete and undamaged. Soon the ship would head back to Liverpool and this whole thing would drift into the past.

On the way back to his cabin, Stone passed by the chartroom. The mud and cigarettes had been cleaned away. The green settee smelled of saddle soap. The chart pencils were arranged in their clips, shortest to longest. The official logbook lay on its back, its large pages lying open as if inviting all to come and read. The steward had done his job well. There was no sign of the mess and dirt of the American pressmen. The chartroom was as clean, in fact, as Stone had ever seen it.

But as Saturday turned into Sunday, and his ship's name slipped quietly out of the newspapers, and the weather grew warmer, Stone found that for him the matter was not quite closed after all.

He sat in his cabin and had little to do but think. 'You spend too long in your room,' his father once said to him, and on the *Californian* Captain Lord had made the same complaint, but this weekend the captain left Stone to himself. In fact no one bothered him, not the chief officer nor the apprentice nor talkative Evans. He was grateful, although he did notice that his friend Charlie Groves kept his distance too, and when they met in alleyways Groves' eyes wandered nervously.

At night he could not sleep. He tried writing to his wife but his words seemed to float away to nothing. 'Things are well in Boston, it is warmer than expected, all the talk is of the great catastrophe.' What else could he say? He turned instead to reworking his letter to the captain, sitting at his desk in a kind of mania, pressing his words hard into the page to make them braver, to make them truer. He tried to picture again what he had seen – those distant lights in a night so black he felt he was adrift in space – and to think again of what he had done: flashing the Morse lamp, talking to Gibson, polishing the lenses of the binoculars. But the important details shifted and vanished like vapour. Was the ship he saw a large ship? Had she moved? How far away was she? 'I don't know what I remember any more,' he'd said to Charlie Groves. And now, during these anxious Boston nights, he became even less certain. He underlined, circled, crossed out. He wrote a second draft and then a third. But each time he came to write down the most important words of all, the words he knew for certain were true, he heard the captain's condemnation of them: 'They are weak and they are disloyal.' So he wrote them instead on a scrap of blotting paper – 'I saw the rockets and I told you' – and then screwed up the blotting paper and threw it away.

His cabin began to press in on him. He felt he was suffocating. When Groves told him he looked tired and should go ashore to get some air, he decided to heed the advice. The captain granted him leave, saying he might take as long as he liked. So, on Monday morning, one week exactly since the disaster, he caught the ferry across the harbour and walked the sparkling streets as if he were a diligent tourist. He clambered up the pretty laneways of Beacon Hill, he marvelled at the great gold dome of the State House, and he visited Paul Revere House where he saw a cardboard display showing the Righteousness of the Revolution. When Americans dipped their hats to him and told him they adored his accent, he smiled awkwardly and thanked them. But as the afternoon wore on and heavy wet air drifted in from the harbour, he realised that to come ashore had been a mistake. At first he had tried not to see the headlines on the newsstands at every corner, had tried not to hear the rasping voices of boys in green uniforms calling out the latest news. But so earnestly did one boy beg him to take a paper that he paid his cent, and then, as if in a trance, he bought another, then another. He took his bundle of papers to the Boston library, where he sifted through them until his fingers were black with newsprint. The *Titanic* survivors had come ashore in New York and every one of them had a story to tell. Above him soared the reading room's great barrel-arched ceiling and twin domes, and although they were filled with light, when he looked up at them he saw again the vast black vault of the sky on the night of the rockets. And he began to hear the pitiful cries of human beings in the black water, flying upwards to a cold and icy heaven, so loud and so many that it seemed the ocean itself was dying.

The papers were brutal; they did not spare his feelings. The *Boston Evening Transcript* listed the names of the passengers one by one, in column after column on its front page, with survivors in bold type. Stone stared silently at the inches of un-bolded names: Abbing, Abelson, Adams, Adams, Adolf, Ahlin ...

Another paper listed the missing Bostonians. Mr Newell, President of the Fourth National Bank of Boston. Mr Futrelle, the famous author. Mrs Omine Honcarek and her two children, who were on their way to join their relatives in Boston. And more, and more. When he looked around the room, the men and women of Boston seemed no longer inclined to dip their hats and smile at him, but instead to be looking at him with hard, judging eyes. They knew what he had done. And what would they think, he wondered, if they knew that only two days ago his captain had sat smiling and chortling at stories in their newspapers about his own heroism and seamanship?

But there was one story worse than all the others, and it appeared in every newspaper. America was having a grand inquiry into the disaster, and everyone who knew anything about it was being called to Washington to appear before it. What if they were to ask the captain to tell his story of racing through the ice? Or worse – and the fear of it made Stone feel sick – what if they were to ask *him*?

He had seen enough newspapers. He hurried from the library and did not wait for the ferry. He took an electric car through the tunnel to the East Boston wharves and within half an hour was back in his cabin. He would try to take the captain at his word: the matter was closed. He need think about it no longer. If a steward brought him a morning paper, he would push it away.

Monday became Tuesday. The ship's derricks banged and groaned under the weight of wheat and corn coming aboard in bulging sacks, and the dust of coaling barges settled on the deck among the spring petals. Groves told him that bad weather was sweeping east from the plains states, but for now Boston was calm: flies buzzed in Stone's cabin and gulls squawked outside in the warm, still air. The fruit in the officers' saloon glowed and ripened. He began, a little, to relax. He saw that the sailing board had been posted at the head of the gangway: the *Californian* would depart for Liverpool on the coming Saturday morning, the 27th of April, a few days away. He thought of home, of his wife bringing him tea and flowers, and lying on his bunk after lunch he slipped at last into a deep sleep.

It was Charlie Groves who woke him, shaking him by the shoulder with one hand and holding a newspaper in the other. It was so close to Stone's face that its pages seemed as large as tablecloths. 'Look,' Groves was saying, 'wake up and look at this.'

Stone sat up, and took a moment to orientate himself. He did not want to read the paper. He wanted to go back to sleep. But something must be wrong, he knew, for Groves to be in his cabin like this, so excited. There was something terrible about the newspaper; it felt to Stone suffocating and overwhelming.

He took the paper from Groves. The front-page headline was so black and bold each word seemed to shake at him like a fist.

SHIP SIGHTED AS *TITANIC* SANK

Beneath it, and in letters only slightly smaller, was the sub-headline: DISTRESS SIGNALS IGNORED, ASSERTS OFFICER BOXHALL.

Stone felt something more than fear – he felt a strange fracturing of himself, as on the morning of the disaster, when he seemed to watch the events from above, from a point outside his body.

He had let the newspaper fall loosely to his lap. Groves snatched it up and read aloud. "'With succor only five miles away, the huge White Star liner *Titanic* slid into her watery grave, carrying with her more than 1500 of her passengers and crew, while an unidentified steamship which might have saved all failed or refused to see the frantic signals flashed to her for aid. Both with rockets and with the Morse electric signal did the young officer hail the stranger.'" There was something frantic about Groves as he read – a breathlessness, a dryness of the mouth, as if it were his own soul at stake.

With rockets and with the Morse electric signal. Stone let the fearful vision of those rockets come back to him. They alone were perfect in his memory. White on black with no greys; little white flowers with delicate stalks and tiny white petals falling silently in the blackness. Odd: it had never occurred to him that just as he had been watching the other ship across the sea, she had been watching him.

Worse than that: she had been calling to him. She had fired those rockets for *him*.

He took the newspaper from Groves and in a moment was in the captain's cabin, holding it up before Lord's large, surprised face.

'You are upset,' the captain said, trying to take the paper from him. 'Sit down and calm yourself. Beware your tendency to panic.'

But Stone no longer cared what Captain Lord had to say. And when he felt the chief officer's grip on his shoulder from behind, he jerked himself free with unexpected strength.

'Captain,' he said, 'they saw us watching them. They fired those rockets for us.' He could not stop himself. 'Now we will have to tell the truth, because they saw us. And they will find us out, no matter what you say.'

CHAPTER 11

I began my story about Lord's heroism in the Marginal Street saloon on Friday afternoon. But I soon stopped. I didn't believe what I was writing. The *Californian* was a story of something, but it wasn't heroism. There was something else at work on that perplexing ship.

So I didn't file. Instead, after half a gallon of beer, I was taken by a bar girl to her home somewhere east along the harbour – a ramshackle place so near the water its walls seemed made of mud. I slept fitfully, plagued by the mournful tolling of buoy bells, and when I awoke early on Saturday morning my friend said I'd been crying in my sleep. My head ached. She gave me a slip of paper with her address on it and asked if I would stay with her again. I said I would, although in the half-light I could see that she was not young.

The fog had come in once more, and as I waited for the ferry little eddies of warm air brought with them the stink of coal and dead fish. I didn't feel well. So I was much relieved when the steamboat at last arrived and by some mysterious means of navigation managed to grope its way to the South Ferry wharf. I ought to have gone straight to my office, but there was something I needed to do first. I walked across the city to a narrow house on Charles Street, nestled beneath Beacon Hill, and knocked hard on the door.

'What do you want?' my wife asked when she opened it. I could see her friend lurking behind her in the parlour, smoking a cigarette.

It was my house – bought with money left to me by my father – but my wife didn't see it that way. These days she had a modern way of thinking and used lawyerly words and phrases that sounded odd falling from her soft lips. She spoke of 'opportunity costs' and 'misrepresentations' and said that if I had disclosed that I was an intemperate drunk and philanderer before she married me she would never have consented to do so. My wife was right about most things, but on this point she had cause and effect around the wrong way. It was *because* our marriage had failed that I embraced bourbon and sought out – well, alternative intimacies. And the failure of our marriage was not my fault, and my wife knew it.

'Hello, Olive,' I said. 'I'm here to see Harriet.'

'She's not here.'

'I can wait,' I said, pushing past her into the parlour. 'I'll take a bath.' My tiny apartment in the fetid air of the Back Bay fens had no plumbing to speak of, and I had 'rights' and 'entitlements' too: at the very least, to use the bathtub from time to time in my own house.

Olive followed me into the parlour, nowadays sparsely furnished with two black sofas. There were no flowers on the tables; instead there were books everywhere. There had once been flowers, of course, in the same way that my wife had once worn shiny silk gloves and bodices with eyelets of gold. Today she wore a plain white dress with a loose, dark green jacket – the colours of the suffragettes – and her hands, I saw, were stained with ink.

'You may stay,' she said, giving me permission I did not need and seating herself at a table. Vivienne, my wife's tall and cadaverous friend, loitered in a corner smoking her cigarette. I had never liked Vivienne. She lived in my house without paying rent and never did me the courtesy of thanking me. She was a radical – a nihilist who hated men and gave speeches at the university while forcing my daughter to stand by and turn the pages. She proclaimed herself a mesmeric healer and asked my wife to help her contact spirits and enchant clients by lighting lamps behind coloured veils. So I was pleased that by the time I returned from my bath she was gone. Olive sat alone at a table among newspapers, books and writing paper. I sat on one of the black sofas. I had scrubbed myself so clean I glowed.

'Where's our daughter?' I asked.

'She is in North Street visiting the Negroes.'

'You allow her to go there unaccompanied?'

'I do.'

'To walk among the Negroes?'

'Yes, and to talk to them. Their suffering is very great.'

'But you don't go with her?'

'She's seventeen. And I have my own work to do.'

'The vote?' I asked.

'Yes,' Olive said, 'the vote. To thinking women, the vote is as important as air. And we're tired of our suffocation.'

'But Vivienne, at least, finds breath enough to give lengthy speeches.'

Olive looked up from her work. 'That has always been your way, John: to mock things that ought not to be mocked. You take nothing seriously.'

'I may mock, but she *hates*.'

'She hates your mocking!'

My wife returned to her writing and I rose to stare out a window. I felt sorry for Olive. In the ten or so years since the death of our son I had never seen her smile. Worse: I had never seen her cry. She worked for The Cause with mechanical ferocity; she took no time for fun or sorrow. She blamed me, of course, for our son's death, and the weight of that blame never lessened.

'What is wrong, my dear?' I asked. 'You seem displeased.'

'I *am* displeased,' she replied quickly, and her reason surprised me. 'This *Titanic* disaster has set us back terribly.' She lifted a newspaper from the table and waved it about. 'We were attacked this morning at our meeting – physically attacked, by a boy throwing fruit – and now there's a call for the New York parade to be cancelled. Anyone would think it was we women who sank that ship.'

'The newspapers have not been helpful?' I asked.

'Don't be cute. Of course they've not been helpful. All this talk of chivalry and heroics – the rich men who did not get into boats, and so on – it's all aimed at *us*. You know that more than anyone.'

'You do not approve of the behaviour of the men that night?'

'I neither approve nor disapprove. I say nothing about it one way or the other. I was not there. But what I do say is that I already hear people ask, Is it to be boats for women or votes for women? Well, if we must choose, then I say to my sisters: Don't get in the boat! But even my sisters have lost their nerve.'

I listened in silence. It was just like my wife to speak so. On this topic she had great passion. 'You,' she went on, rather bitterly, 'in your paper, I suppose, are writing all about these courageous men.'

'As a matter of fact, I am not.'

'But you are writing something?'

'I am – but it's not a story of chivalry.'

I had no chance to explain. The front door slammed and a moment later our daughter burst into the room. She leapt at me with joy as I rose to greet her and almost knocked me over. Her hat fell to the floor, scattering its white and green flowers and releasing a great blur of auburn hair. She embraced me and then held me at arm's length to survey me.

'Papa, you look so tired,' she said. She embraced me again and insisted I sit down. 'Have you and Mama been fighting? She does not look best pleased.'

'Your father has come here to wash himself,' Olive explained.

'Well, he smells like a rose garden!'

Harriet had always had a prodigious energy, but now, as she approached womanhood, she seemed to radiate a solar force. Her intelligence sometimes frightened me; ideas welled up within her like steam in a locomotive. She moved through the world as if there were no power that could stop her. I could not imagine her growing old. As she seated herself next to me – a cascade of colour on the black sofa – I had a vision of something more than youth and beauty: I saw the century opening up and it was something vast and wonderful.

'I have been up on North Street,' she announced proudly, looping an arm through mine.

'Your mother has been telling me. She says you go there to talk to the Negroes.'

'I do. I want to write about people, just like you do.'

'I don't like you going there alone.'

'Oh Papa, no harm will come to *me*.'

'And what if I forbade you to go?'

Harriet laughed. 'I would go anyway. This is a new age, Papa, and girls don't always do what their fathers say.'

I laughed too and held her close. 'Then tell me,' I said, 'what do you learn from the Negroes?'

'How to fight. How to be strong. How they won what we want.'

'And you're ready to fight – to be strong?'

'Yes, Papa. We women are ready.'

'Your mother,' I said, 'has been giving me a little lecture. She says the women on the *Titanic* should not have got into the boats ahead of the men.'

'And she's right. I wouldn't have got into a boat before *you*, Papa. I could easily have made a raft out of deckchairs, or else floated about in the water until I climbed onto an old plank or something. It would have been easy.'

I laughed again, taking her warm hands in mine and pressing them against my chest. Her face glowed white and smooth and pretty. But then, quite suddenly, as I looked at her, I stopped laughing. As if a cloud had passed over the sun, I had a darker vision: I saw her face as the child's face that it still was, and I remembered the fifty-three children who had been left behind on the *Titanic*. Not one of them had made a raft out of deckchairs or climbed onto a plank. I shuddered with the horrible vision of it. I saw Harriet as one of them, crying in that black and icy water, and imagined her hands blue and stiff, reaching skyward to the distant stars.

Our laughing and joking were over. Harriet had fallen quiet and rested her head on my chest. Beyond her I saw Olive looking at me, cold, silent and still. Perhaps she, like me, was remembering our poor baby son crying, his tiny hands opening and closing and his wide eyes begging us to keep him in life.

Later that Saturday afternoon I was berated by Krupp. He huffed and puffed and threatened to blow my house down. 'You got my message,' he said, his nose twitching like a rodent's. 'I told you to file by three o'clock yesterday or not to bother filing at all.'

'Yes, and I chose not to file at all.'

He did not laugh. His face flushed red. 'I meant, don't bother filing *ever*. As in: you're fired.'

'But I've got something. Something better than the others.'

'No, you've got nothing. Bumpton, in New York, has something: he sends us more than we can print. Astor, Guggenheim, Butt – the lot.'

'But everyone has those stories. *The Boston Post*, the *Globe*, the *Transcript* – they have countless columns about rich men's chivalry. There are only so many times we can read of Major Butt and the cravens.' I remembered my wife's complaints. 'People are tired of it. But there's only one *Californian* story – it will be different and it will be ours alone. I promise.'

'Your promises mean nothing.' Krupp thrust out his jaw, chewing his upper lip with his lower teeth, which were crooked and brown. He was angry, but he was thinking too, and that was enough. He wouldn't fire me just yet. He couldn't resist the promise of an exclusive any more than a rat could resist the smell of vanilla bread.

I pressed my advantage. 'I tell you, there is a story on that ship and I will get it. They're hiding something.'

But Krupp hadn't quite finished his resistance. 'What story? They didn't get there in time. They had no bodies. They had no survivors. They have nothing. So, what story?'

'I don't know yet. Perhaps they did find bodies but for some reason didn't pick them up. Or maybe the captain was drunk. Or one of his officers panicked. Or there was a fight on board, or a mutiny. But something happened on that ship – I can tell from their faces.'

'You and your faces. Sometimes a face is just a face.'

'Very well then, there's more than just their faces. One: the captain wouldn't let the wireless man speak. Two: he said his overnight position was a state secret. Three: he first said they were twenty miles away but then later said thirty.'

'An easy mistake.'

'No, it was deliberate. Don't you see? He's trying to push the *Titanic* away. I tell you, he wants to have nothing to do with that ship. In his hour with us he didn't mention her name once. It's as if he can't bring himself to say it. I ask you, why is that?'

Krupp was listening now.

'And,' I continued, 'most important of all, the page for April 15th – the day the *Titanic* sank – was cut from the scrap log with a knife. Other pages were missing too, but they'd just been torn out. Somebody cut that page out, carefully and deliberately, and whoever it was did so for a reason.'

'Well? What was the reason?'

'I don't know yet. *That* will be the story.'

Krupp's huffing and puffing gave way to a tired impatience. 'Go, then,' he said, waving me out of his office with an exaggerated gesture. 'Go and get the story. But I want to see something by day's end Monday. This is it for you, John. This really is *it*!'

On Sunday morning I went to the ship, but was turned back at the gangway by two men who this time were not persuaded by my boilersuit and did not listen to my talk of coal supplies. I telephoned Jack Thomas but he did not take my call. I went in person to his office but his assistant said he wasn't there, even though I could hear his voice bellowing from a distant room. Perhaps, I thought, he was holding a grudge. I had not yet written his Lord-as-hero story. I went back to the ship and asked the men at the gangway to deliver a message to the captain. They refused. Everything had to go through the agent, they said. I said he was unavailable. They said there was nothing they could do.

I retired to the Marginal Street saloon to develop a strategy.

I hoped Thomas would eventually show up. But he did not; instead my waitress doubled up my drinks so that the rest of Sunday became a blur. On Monday morning I was knocked so low by a headache I could hardly move. But Krupp was waiting: I had to produce *something*. So in the early afternoon I made an appointment to use the saloon's silence booth and long-distance telephone. I placed a call to Dan Byrne at Dow Jones in New York. It took half an hour for the connection to be made, but then his voice came through with good volume. My notebook was ready and I wrote down everything he said:

The United States Senate inquiry into the disaster had moved from the Waldorf Astoria hotel in New York to the Senate Office Building in Washington, D.C. The inquiry was being conducted by Senator William Alden Smith, who acted like a bumbling fool but knew exactly how to get what he wanted.

A sensation had been caused when Bruce Ismay had been denounced by Senator Raynor as a coward.

Philip Franklin had had to explain to the senators why he spent a whole day telling the press that the *Titanic* was safe when in fact she was on the bottom. 'During the entire day,' he said, 'we continued to believe the ship unsinkable.'

The *Titanic's* surviving wireless operator, a young man of twenty-two, had been paid a thousand dollars by *The New York Times* for his story – equivalent to four years' salary.

The *Titanic* had sunk in a busy shipping lane, and people were surprised to learn that so many ships had been near her when she went down: the *Mount Temple*, the *Baltic*, the *Birma*, the *Virginian*, the *Carpathia*, the *Olympic*, and others. It seemed that the *Titanic* had been very unlucky that none had reached her in time.

Captain Moore of the *Mount Temple* told newspapers he had wasted time searching the wrong position. In her distress messages the

Titanic gave a position on the western side of the icefield, when in fact she had been east of it.

The *Mackay-Bennett* had been chartered by the White Star Line to go out and find the bodies. There was hope they would find Mr Astor.

These were all interesting points, but Dan Byrne gave me his most significant information just before he rang off. 'By the way,' he said, 'what was the name of that ship – the one you've been chasing for the bodies?'

'The *Californian*.'

'I thought so. Well, the wireless boy on the *Carpathia*, the rescue ship – Cotton, I think his name is, or Cotham, something like that – I talked to him.'

'And?'

'He said that the wireless man on your ship was a nuisance on the morning of the disaster. Kept interrupting. Excitable. Kept saying over and over that he had precedence. Have you spoken to him?'

'No.' I remembered the wireless boy's enforced silence during the captain's meeting with the press.

'Perhaps you ought: my man said he heard yours trying to warn the *Titanic* about ice only half an hour before she hit the iceberg.'

'Half an hour!'

'Yes. The *Titanic* told him to shut up, according to my man.'

I thought hard. The *Californian* had tried to warn the *Titanic*? But the liner had steamed on regardless to her doom? It would be a page one story if it was true.

'You'd better get hold of that wireless boy,' Dan said, the line crackling suddenly with interference.

'Yes,' I replied. 'I'd better.'

Cyril Evans beamed at me like a young boy on Christmas morning. His collar was a startling white; I could smell bleach.

'I am very glad you've come,' he said, 'although I'd rather thought Mr Marconi might come himself.'

'He sends his apologies – and congratulations.'

The young man was unusual-looking. His head was too large, his body too skinny, his hair too black. The light of a brilliant intelligence shone in his eyes, but they were open too wide. They seemed to search about blindly. He struck me as utterly credulous. He had, after all, accepted without question the telegram I'd sent, addressed to the wireless operator, *Californian*: 'Marconi publicity agent wishes meeting to thank you on behalf Marconi. 4 p.m. today Marginal Street saloon.' And here he was. Simple as that. He did not seem to recognise me as one of the press contingent that had bustled about him in the chartroom. My rudimentary disguise – a pair of plain-glass spectacles – had worked.

'I wondered,' the boy said a little nervously, 'if Mr Marconi would want to speak with me in person, like he did with Jack Binns.'

'Jack Binns?' I asked.

Evans tilted his head to one side as he looked closely at me. 'Of the *Republic*,' he said.

'Of course. Mr Binns.'

'The hero.'

'Yes. The hero.' Now I vaguely remembered: Binns was the wireless operator who had called aid to the White Star's *Republic* after it was rammed off New York. Afterwards he travelled the country giving little lectures.

Evans pasted his oily hair to his head with both hands and then looked at me with sudden focus. 'We were the nearest ship, you know. We had precedence.'

'But – certainly you were not closer than the *Carpathia*?'

'Yes we were!' His outburst surprised me. 'We were the *closest*. That's why I had *precedence* under the rules. Mr Balfour said he was going to report me for jamming, but it was my *right* to talk so I could find out what was happening and guide other ships in. Just like Jack Binns.' The boy spoke as if he were unpacking a great storeroom of hurt and indignation. 'I had precedence,' he added one more time. 'Please tell Mr Marconi.'

I thought he might cry. 'Mr Marconi is very proud of you,' I said. This seemed to lift his spirits and there was the hint of a smile. I leaned closer. 'Did you try to warn the *Titanic*?'

This idea – of monumental significance – seemed uninteresting to Evans. 'Yes,' he said, looking at the ceiling. 'At eleven o'clock that night. Just before the accident. I called the operator up and said, "Say, old man, we're stopped and surrounded by ice." He came straight back so loud I had to lift my headphones off. "Shut up, shut up," he said, and "Keep out." He was working Cape Race. You know – sending passenger messages.'

'He told you to shut up?'

'Yes. But it doesn't mean anything. It's just a little way we operators have with each other. We don't take it as an insult or anything like that. I met Jack Phillips once in the Marconi London office. He was very nice to me.'

We sat in respectful silence for a moment. Then the boy began to look around, as if searching for someone more interesting to talk to. 'What did you do,' I gently pressed, 'after he told you to keep out?'

'I took off my 'phones and got into bed, didn't I? I read a magazine and fell asleep. Then Charlie came in – Mr Groves, that is, the third officer – and he tried to have a listen, but he didn't know the detector had wound down. It's a little box,' he said, anticipating my question and using his hands to shape a rectangle in the air, 'with wires spinning around –' here he gave a twirling motion with his forefinger – 'which pick up the signal. So, he heard nothing. If he'd wound it up he would have heard the *Titanic* sending SOS and CQD over and over.'

I paused to think of it. The *Titanic* frantically sending. The *Californian* peacefully stopped, near enough to have precedence, but no longer listening. A girl brought me a drink. A fly buzzed. Through an open door I saw that the afternoon had become clear and blue.

Cyril Evans, his head bowed, was wiping his spectacles with his shirt. 'If somebody had woken me up, I would have heard Phillips, on the *Titanic*. He was kind to me, in London. I would have heard him, and we would have gone down to help him.' He put his spectacles back on – great, thick chunks of glass – and looked up at me. 'But instead,' he added with touching simplicity, 'he drowned.'

The boy's eyes, so large, so round, gave his face a sudden clarity. I saw pain and sorrow: the anguish of a hero denied, a slow-burning indignation that such a tragedy could have happened so close without him being allowed to help. Thin, awkward boys like Cyril Evans, I supposed, did not get many opportunities to prove themselves men; he seemed acutely aware that his chance had slipped away forever.

'So,' I prompted, 'you slept until . . .?'

'The next morning, just before dawn, when the chief officer shook me awake and said there was a ship in trouble, and asked me to find out what was the matter.'

'So you went to your instrument?'

'At once. Within a minute I had the news. We went through the ice to the other side and headed down to her position, but all we saw was the *Mount Temple* searching about. Then we saw the *Carpathia* so we came back through the ice again, but it was too late. She had already taken up all the boats. She steamed off and we stayed behind to look for bodies.'

'Did you see any?'

'None. We steamed around for a while, but all we saw was loose wreckage. A half-sunk boat. Some clothes and lifejackets. That sort of thing.'

Evans paused for a moment, fidgeting nervously. 'Do you think,' he asked, moistening his lips with little darts of his tongue, 'that Mr Marconi would allow me to talk to the newspapers about what happened? About me having precedence and trying to help?'

Something about this boy's open-faced trust, his naïve aspirations and his visceral disappointment, made me regret – just for a moment – my subterfuge. 'You would like to talk to a newspaper?'

'Jack Binns did, and Harry Bride from the *Titanic*, and Cottam from the *Carpathia*, so it seems only fair that I should get to say something, me being the operator who —'

'Had precedence?'

'Yes,' he said slowly. 'The captain says we're not to talk to anyone, but I thought, if Mr Marconi said so . . .'

The boy stopped speaking. He was looking over my shoulder, so I turned in my seat and saw a short, thin man framed by the doorway of the saloon. He wore a great square blazer with golden rings on its cuffs. His mouth was hidden by a large moustache and his eyes by the rim of an officer's cap, but when he stepped further into the room I recognised him as the man who'd stood closest to Captain Lord during the press meeting. He was, I assumed, the captain's senior officer. He did not say anything but Evans stood up quickly and walked over to him. The two spoke quietly for a moment before Evans returned to the table.

'You should have just told me,' he said. 'You didn't have to lie.'

'I'm sorry,' I said simply, taking off my spectacles.

'Which newspaper?' he asked.

'The *Boston American*.'

'You should have just told me.'

He picked up his cap, turned and walked with the officer out of the saloon.

It was late afternoon. I ordered another drink, and then another. I thought about what the wireless operator had told me. Was *this* my story then? A story of spectacular hubris? A story of a small ship trying desperately to warn a mighty liner and being ignored? A story of British overconfidence meeting its just deserts? American readers already had Cowardly Mr Ismay to blame, now I could give them Arrogant Jack Phillips as well.

It was a story, too, with unbearable dramatic irony. The agony! My readers would want to reach desperately into the page and wind up that magnetic detector themselves. How cruel it is, they would think, that fifteen hundred lives should depend on one tiny clockwork mechanism.

And yet still I did not file. There was something about what the wireless boy had said that did not make sense. I read my notes, ordered another bourbon, then read them again. I knew the answer was there somewhere but I could not see it. With a red pencil I circled phrases at random: 'stopped and surrounded by ice'; 'shut up, shut up. Keep out'; 'I went to bed'; 'the detector had wound down'; 'chief woke me in the morning and said a ship was in trouble'; 'in a minute I knew'; 'we came back through the ice' . . . There was something wrong but by now my mind was so addled by drink I could not see what it was.

In the evening my bar-girl friend arrived and we shuffled off to her place. We walked along the harbour's edge on soft grass. She slipped her arm through mine and her face glowed pale in the starlight. I let the red and green lights of channel buoys mesmerise me. I squinted so that the flashing white lights of the cardinal marks danced among my eyelashes. I could not tell how close or far away these lights were;

I felt I could reach out and touch them.

It was later, as I lay in bed listening to my friend's deepening breathing and thinking of those lights across the water, that the answer came to me. I thought about what Dan Byrne had told me, I saw again the senior officer in the door of the saloon, and I understood what was wrong with the wireless boy's story. Suddenly and completely it all made perfect sense.

'The *Californian*,' I said, rather triumphantly the following day, 'saw the *Titanic* sinking and did nothing to help her.'

Krupp pushed himself back in his chair and raised an eyebrow. It was midmorning. The curtains were open; his red hair flamed in the light.

'That is my story,' I continued. 'It's not one of my body stories but it will sell. It will create an outrage.'

Krupp leaned forward. 'Nobody else knows about this?'

'Nobody. It's a scoop.'

My boss sat deep in thought for a moment. 'How do you know that your ship saw the *Titanic*?'

'Yesterday I spoke to the wireless operator. He didn't mean to tell me, but he did – one little phrase gave it away. He'd been asleep all night, he said, with his equipment switched off, but when the chief officer woke him the next morning he asked him to find out what was the matter, because there was *a ship in trouble*.' I paused. My boss looked at me blankly. 'Don't you see?' I continued. 'If the wireless equipment was dead all night how could the chief have known there was a ship in trouble? There's only one way he could have. Somebody on his ship must have *seen* it was in trouble.'

'But how would they know it was in trouble?'

'Rockets,' I said. 'I had thought that perhaps they could tell by a flashing light, or the angle of the lights, or something of that sort – but then this morning, on my way here, I saw this.' I dropped onto his desk the morning edition of *The Boston Herald*. SHIP SIGHTED AS *TITANIC* SANK ran the headline, and I waited a moment for Krupp to read on. 'You see? Mr Boxhall of the *Titanic* has been telling the senators in Washington that he saw a ship in the distance, and that he sent up rockets to call for help.'

Krupp skimmed the rest of the article, sweeping his forefinger from side to side across the page.

'Lots of other *Titanic* survivors have been saying they saw the ship too,' I continued, 'and all America wants to know what ship it was. *But I already know.*'

Krupp rubbed his temples. 'Are you sure?'

'Everything fits. That's why the captain wanted to keep his own ship's position a secret; that's why he tried to push the *Titanic* further away; that's why he didn't let anyone else talk. He was protecting someone – whoever it was who saw the rockets.'

'And that was . . .?'

'The second officer. He looked terrified during the press conference. It's the second officer who keeps watch during the middle of the night on ships, and that's when the rockets would have been fired.'

'But why would this man – this second officer – see rockets and do nothing?'

'Now, that I don't know. Perhaps he'd been drinking, or fell asleep, or mistook them for something else. That's what I need to find out.'

'And could they have got there in time? I mean, if this officer had told the captain?'

'I think so. Both ships were on the same side of the icefield. The *Californian* did push through the icefield the next morning – the

captain was very keen to tell us all about the winding channels of ice –
but I know from Dan Byrne that the CQD position given by the
Titanic was too far west. So the *Californian* pushed through the field
for nothing. The wireless boy told me that they then had to steam *back
through* the icefield to get to the wreck site. But if she'd steamed for the
rockets as they were being fired —'

'Then she would not have been misled by the wrong position.'

'Exactly.' I leaned back a little in my chair. 'She would have gone
straight there. It all fits.' As I say, I felt rather triumphant.

Krupp lit a cigarette. 'Very well,' he said. 'Go back aboard. But
I want the story to run tomorrow. And make sure it's an exclusive.
Stories like this always leak.'

I agreed. I had to move quickly. If I was right – and I knew I was – it
would be a difficult secret to keep. And we needed an exclusive. While
the New York papers told the same tired tales of brave millionaires
shooting cravens and helping women into lifeboats, we would be the
only newspaper in the nation telling a different tale: of a man who
watched it all happen from across the sea and lifted not one finger
to help.

But how to get aboard? Jack Thomas was, at least for the moment,
no longer helping me. I wondered whether I might somehow use my
daughter – ask her to play a prostitute, perhaps, or, safer, a suffragette
collecting money for The Cause. If she could walk alone among
Negroes she could certainly hold her own among sailors, creating just
enough of a diversion for me to get aboard. I braced myself for another
visit to Charles Street, but as things turned out it was unnecessary.
An envelope was brought to me at my desk a short while later, dirty
and torn, and oddly addressed: 'To the Reporter Who Talked to the
Wireless Operator of the *Californian*'. Inside was a short note:

Dear Sir,

Mr Cyril Evans, who you tricked, told me that you write for a newspaper and wanted to know what happened on our Ship. I will tell you what I Saw and All that Happened if you like but I will lose my Berth if I do tell. It is a well-paid Berth so perhaps you could help me with that. If you are interested I will be at the same place you met Mr Evans, at one o'clock this afternoon. This will be your only chance.

Yours truly,
Ernest Gill
Assistant Donkeyman

Half an hour later I was on the ferry, chugging across the harbour once again to the East Boston wharves. The saloon, when I arrived, had drawn its blinds against the afternoon sunshine: inside was dark and humid. Dogs barked and the air stank of horse manure.

I waited. I felt the story close and warm, like a woman's body.

Just after one o'clock, a young man entered. I knew at once it was my informant. He was dressed in a neat brown suit, as if going to church, but there was a hint of coaldust about him. He wore his cloth cap at a jaunty angle; his moustache was thick and straight, his eyes clear and grey. I waved him over and stood to shake his hand. When I heard the strange lilt of his accent, I asked him where he was from. He said Sheffield, although he now lived in Liverpool.

'It isn't right,' he said as we took our seats, 'for the captain to try to hush up what happened.'

'What did happen?' I asked.

'See, that there's the whole point of the matter, isn't it? It's why I'm here, to see if you're interested in knowing just that: what did happen.'

'I am interested.'

'I expect a whole lot of people are interested. But the moment the skipper gets wind of what I've done, I'll lose my berth as sure as I'm sitting here – and it's a good berth too, one of the best I've had – and I'll be on the Boston streets with my dunnage quick as a shot with nowhere to go and no way of getting back home.'

I knew where this was heading, of course, and was prepared for it. I had discussed it with Krupp. We knew what labourers on ships earned: not much more than twenty-five dollars a month. So we would offer him thirty.

'And me with no mother or father to my name, and my lady in Liverpool expecting to be married as soon as I clear the gangway inbound – she said if we aren't getting married, don't bother coming back.'

'Then tell me, what would be a reasonable figure?'

'Well, I hear all sorts of things about Mr Hearst and this and that, and *The New York Times* and Mr Bride of the *Titanic* being paid a thousand dollars for his story.'

I coughed up a little of my drink, then laughed. 'We can't give a thousand dollars. You weren't *on* the *Titanic*, you know. We could perhaps go to fifty.'

'And I could perhaps go to another newspaper, if I had a mind to.'

I eyed him carefully. 'I am sure there are other men on your ship who could tell the story for a great deal less than a thousand dollars.'

The donkeyman met my comment with surprising speed. 'But all they could tell you is what they've been told or what they've heard in the nature of gossip – so-and-so told me this, or so-and-so heard that – but I can tell you what I saw *with my very own eyes*.'

I stared hard at him – at the red flecks in his brown hair, at his focused grey eyes – and tried to read his face. 'Come along, then,' I said.

'Tell me what you saw with your very own eyes and I'll tell you what we can pay with our very own money.'

'All right, then.'

And Ernest Gill, without further ado, told me that with his very own eyes he had seen the *Titanic* firing her rockets. He hadn't known it was the *Titanic* at the time, of course – he'd thought the ship a 'big German' – but he had seen the rockets very plainly. They burst into stars that 'spangled out and drifted down'. He saw them, and the officer on the bridge also saw them, but the *Californian* didn't go to them.

Rockets! I was pleased. I'd been wrong about bodies being aboard, but I was right about the rockets. Provided, of course, this man was telling the truth.

'The men are angry,' Gill went on, 'but they're scared of losing their jobs. We had a meeting and I said we should form a committee of protest and go up to the captain, but they were against it. The carpenter said it was a mutiny and we just best keep our mouths shut. Big tall man he is, the carpenter. Says he's from Liverpool but his skin's browner than a Spaniard's and I don't think he's proper English at all. But I didn't want to cause any trouble. It isn't right, though, and something ought to be done about it.'

Gill paused and I sat for a moment, thinking. The saloon door drifted open. I heard a horse pulling against its reins outside and the distant clatter of freight cars.

'You didn't think to report the rockets to the bridge yourself?'

Again his answer was immediate, and perhaps a shade defensive. 'That isn't my job. Ships in the distance have nothing to do with me. They're for the bridge, and I'd get no thanks for interfering.'

'But you did see them?'

'I did. I swear.'

I continued to watch Gill carefully as he spoke. The sinking of the

Titanic was the story of the century so far, and this man was saying he had watched it happen. If he *was* speaking the truth, his story was worth hundreds of dollars. But was he?

I asked him about his own story – his life, his thoughts, his hopes. He spoke easily, telling me of his childhood amid the glowing forges of Sheffield, the death of his mother and father, and his work as a glassblower's assistant. He opened his right hand as far as it would go, showing me striated pink scars – like the folded flesh of some exotic fruit – where hot glass had burned through to the bone. There were very few nerves in that hand, he said, pressing a fingernail deep into the scars. If he got burned again it would not hurt.

I asked him to stay where he was while I telephoned my office. In ten minutes I returned with a simple but bold plan. We would buy his story. I would, this very afternoon, take down verbatim his detailed statement, and overnight I would have it typed up as an affidavit. Gill would return to the ship, collect his possessions and report to my office tomorrow, Wednesday, 24th April, at noon sharp, where he would swear the affidavit before a notary public. I would then wire the affidavit to Senator Smith in Washington, and Gill would stand by to travel there by train if he were needed – as I expected he would be – to testify before the Senate committee. Gill's affidavit would be published in full in the *Boston American* the following morning. It would cause a sensation.

Most importantly of all, Gill must give his solemn promise not to speak to any other newspaper. For his troubles he would receive five hundred dollars: one hundred in banknotes and the remainder wired to an account of his choosing. With this much money, I thought but did not say, he could invite half of Liverpool to witness his nuptials and buy a gold plaque for the grave of his poor dead mama and papa.

The assistant donkeyman agreed and we shook hands. I had my

scoop. This was better than a body story.

As we prepared to begin our work – Gill to dictate, I to transcribe – I asked him a question. 'Tell me,' I said, 'the officer on the bridge you spoke of, who also saw the rockets, who was he?'

'The second officer.'

As I had thought. 'And his name?'

'Stoney. Mr Stone, I mean.' He gave a quick snigger. 'Or sometimes we call him Old Mattress-back, on account of his close relations with his bunk.'

'Had he fallen asleep, then, when the rockets were fired?'

'Oh no. Stoney loves his bunk, but he'd never sleep on watch.'

'Was he drunk, then?'

Gill shook his head. 'He's sober as they come – just a bit timid is all.'

'Then why didn't he do anything? About the rockets, I mean.'

Gill looked at me for a moment. He seemed puzzled by my question. He drew his eyebrows together in a frown and tilted his head, as might a schoolteacher unsettled by a pupil's unexpected ignorance.

'But he *did* do something. I heard from the apprentice, who stood with him.'

'What did he do?'

Again Gill paused. He seemed to be thinking hard. I wondered whether he was recalibrating the value of his story, now that he knew what I didn't know. But if he had thought about asking for more money, his honour must have reminded him that we already had a deal, because he offered his final piece of information for free. And it was an astounding piece.

'He woke the skipper and told him.'

'The captain was *told*?'

'Three times. The second called down three times. Even sent the apprentice down.'

'Wait just a minute: the captain *knew* about the rockets?'

'Yes.'

'As they were being fired?'

'As they were being fired.'

'Did he come up to the bridge?'

'He stayed below.'

'So he did nothing?'

'Nothing!'

I did not understand. Only a few days I earlier I had seen this captain: a powerful British commander with golden epaulettes, as brave as a soldier, telling us how he had pushed his ship to the limits of safety and endurance, how he had twisted and turned through winding channels of ice in fear of ripping off his hull plates.

'Well, then,' I asked, 'was *he* drunk?'

'No, sir. The skipper's sober too. He's never taken a single drop on a ship, by all accounts. Real proud of it, too.'

'Then . . . why?'

Ernest Gill shrugged his shoulders. 'Maybe he was scared of the ice. Maybe he didn't want to risk the bergs and such. It was a dark night, and freezing too.'

Was my story, then, not one of hubris after all, but dramatic cowardice? I'd been told that Liverpool men were tough, that they had a special sort of courage. Liverpool was, after all, the city from which England sent the ships to build her empire. So was what I had here a very remarkable and unique creature: the Liverpool craven? Had this man left fifteen hundred people to die because he was scared of the dark and cold? If so, how could he go on living? We all commit shameful acts at some time – my life as a drunken journalist had been one long sequence of moral lapses – but this was of a different magnitude altogether. This was worse than Mr Ismay getting into a lifeboat. This would disgrace a nation.

It was the biggest antihero story of all. My wife would be pleased.

All stories have a kernel that has to be cracked, a knot that has to be untied, a lock that has to be opened. Sometimes it's the bodies of the dead that give me the clue I need to unravel a mystery, at other times it's the faces of the living that offer an answer. My problem in this case was that the *Californian* had turned out to be a ship with no bodies, and her captain a man with a face that could not be read. It was a puzzle of the first order. But I intended to solve it, and tomorrow I would have my key: Gill's affidavit. I had taken down his statement and delivered it to our typists. Now I needed to understand something. What – exactly – did rockets fired at sea *mean*?

It was a lovely afternoon. Women wore blossoms in their hats, and coloured bunting from the annual marathon still floated above the sidewalks. I wandered slowly across town to the pilot house at Lewis Wharf. As a boy I'd been brought here by my father, a keen yachtsman, to talk to the mariners and admire the paintings of pilot schooners. There were only two rooms: an anteroom where the men washed and changed, and a large room with writing tables of oak, and shelves and windowsills stacked with sextants, barometers, spyglasses, dividers, compasses, parallel rulers and harbour charts.

'Everyone knows what rockets at sea mean,' said the portly Boston Harbor pilot sitting opposite me on a large red sofa. 'They mean distress.'

'But just so that I understand completely,' I gently pressed, 'what is meant, precisely, by "distress"?'

The pilot raised an eyebrow. He evidently thought it a stupid question, but I wanted his answer. 'Just so I get things exactly right,' I added, pen poised above my notebook.

'Young man, distress means distress. It means: please come to me because I am in trouble. Simple as that.'

'But, you see, that's just my problem. If it *is* that simple, I'm trying to understand why the ship that the *Titanic* saw did not come. There must have been a reason.'

The pilot flattened his great beard to his chest with the palms of both hands, thinking. 'The watch officer on the ship may have been asleep. Or reading a book below decks, or something of that sort, and he just didn't see the rockets.'

'Yes, possibly,' I said. This explanation didn't really help me. Gill had told me the officer – Old Mattress-back – had not only seen the rockets but reported them to his captain. 'But what if he did see them?' I pressed. 'Is there any reason why the captain would not go to the aid of the distressed ship?'

'No. If he saw them, he must go. It is the oldest tradition of the sea.'

'But could the officer perhaps have confused them with a celebration – a display for the passengers?'

The old man looked at me as if I were a deliberately mischievous child. 'In the middle of the night? White rockets are white rockets. They're very distinctive.'

'There's nothing else they could be taken for, then?'

'Well, pyrotechnics are sometimes still used as private night signals – company signals – to show shore stations or passing ships what company a ship comes from.'

'Could white rockets be confused with them?'

'Not really. Company signals are coloured flares or balls or lights displayed in very particular patterns. Distress rockets are fired singly, one at a time. And maritime regulations tell ships not to use any company signal that could be confused with a distress signal.'

'Let me put this to you: if you were a captain, sleeping below decks, and the watch officer called down to tell you rockets were being fired, what would you do?'

'I'd go to the bridge. I'd wake the wireless man. Then raise steam and go for the source of the rockets.'

'But what if there was danger to your own ship?'

'What sort of danger?'

'Ice, for example?'

'No one would thank a captain for sinking his ship, but he must at least try to respond to the rockets. He must do what he can do within the limits of safety.' The old mariner paused. 'We have an example, of course, in this very case.'

I waited, uncertain of his meaning.

'Rostron,' he explained, 'of the *Carpathia*. When he got the message by wireless, he took his ship and his seven hundred passengers at full speed to the *Titanic*, knowing there were icebergs about. It's the law – but more than that, it's a point of honour. No captain would risk the shame of not trying.'

My expert mariner, during this discussion, had been polishing a small brass telescope. Suddenly he lifted it and peered through it at me. 'In New York,' he said, 'everyone is hunting for this mysterious ship seen by the *Titanic*. But you already know, don't you? That's why you're asking these questions. You've found out, haven't you?'

'I have not.'

'Now you're lying.'

I smiled at him.

'Protect your story if you must,' he said, putting down his telescope. 'I expect I'll read all about it soon enough.'

'Perhaps you will. May I use what you've told me?'

'Most certainly,' said the old man as he rose from his sofa. 'But you must let me give you a little word of warning. You really think a man has committed this crime – of not going to the *Titanic*?'

'I do.'

'An American?'

'An Englishman.'

'Then I need to tell you: I think you've made a mistake. You've set your dogs barking up the wrong tree. No English officer would ignore distress rockets. There's something you're missing, something you've got wrong. You must be careful what you publish.'

I thanked him for his warning and took my leave. As I made my way back to my office in the gathering darkness I thought about what the pilot had said: no Englishman would ignore distress rockets. Yet tomorrow Ernest Gill would swear in an affidavit to exactly that, on pain of prison. It was perplexing. It seemed that the more I knew about this story, the less I understood. Each fact pointed to the next in a logical sequence, but, like road signs leading to a cliff edge, their endpoint made no sense. Was Gill lying? I really did not think so. Enhancing the truth, perhaps, or exaggerating it a little. But the nub of what he said, that the officer on the bridge had seen the rockets and told the captain – *that* I believed.

This puzzle became my obsession. Every other aspect of the disaster was subsumed by it: the missing bodies, the lunacy of Major Butt, Astor's chivalry and Ismay's dishonour, my wife's frustration with the suffragettes, Thomas's need for a hero – even my own indignation about the unknown and unsung dead children. All of these things now seemed secondary. None of them would have happened if the rockets had been answered.

Why weren't they? It was a riddle worthy of the sphinx. There was only one man who could answer it, and tomorrow, once I had my affidavit, I would ask that man quietly and directly: Why didn't you go?

But as it happened, I did not have the luxury of waiting until tomorrow. I was back at my desk early Tuesday evening when I heard Krupp calling my name from his office. 'Steadman! *Steadman! STEAD-MAN!*' He did not, as my daughter would have put it, sound best pleased.

'You have this story tied up?' he demanded as soon as the door of his office closed behind me. His face was redder than usual; his eyes seemed to bulge outwards, like a toad's.

'Yes,' I said. I already feared where this was heading.

'So it's an exclusive?'

'Yes.'

'Because we have agreed to pay – what was his name?'

'Gill.'

'Whoever – five hundred dollars?'

'Yes.'

'Which is a great deal of money?'

'Yes.' By now I was distinctly nervous.

'Then why – please do tell me why – is some village newspaper out west running your story on its front page *this very afternoon*?'

I was stunned. 'My story? The *Californian*?'

'The one and the same. I quote,' and here he read from his notes, '"*Californian* refuses aid. Foreman carpenter on board this boat says hundreds might have been saved from the *Titanic*." Do you know anything about this foreman carpenter?'

I vaguely remembered Gill mentioning a carpenter: a big man who accused Gill of mutiny and told the crew to keep their mouths shut. 'He's got dark skin, I think.'

'Dark skin and a big mouth, because he's telling your story to anyone who will listen – for *free*. Listen.' Krupp turned again to his notes. '"This story was told to John Frazer of this town by the foreman carpenter, who is a cousin of Mr Frazer." Lucky Mr Frazer! "It was shortly after the *Californian* had gone by the icefield that the watch saw the rockets which were sent up by the *Titanic* as signals of distress . . . It is said that those on board the *Californian* could see the lights of the *Titanic* very plainly . . ."' Krupp folded his arms across his chest and stared at me. His nose twitched. 'Well?'

I tried to think. I was shocked. 'Where did you get those notes?' I asked.

'The *Clinton Daily Item*. It was read to me over the long-distance line. I wrote down the main parts.'

'I've never heard of it.'

'Nobody has. But they have the story and we have nothing.'

'But it's a small paper, and we have Gill. Tomorrow he will swear his affidavit —'

'Tomorrow is too late. You need to go to the ship *now*. The *Herald* in New York has got hold of this somehow, and the *Post* here, and they're both sending men to the ship *now*. Damn them! So take my notes, throw them at the captain's feet if you have to, and see what he says. But whatever happens, telephone the story back to me *tonight*.'

I left his office, collected my hat, coat and notebook from my desk, and set off into the night. I was angry at the world. It was a rotten piece of luck: a nobody carpenter spills the beans to a cousin in a nowhere town who chats to someone at a two-page rag that no one reads. And then somehow *The New York Herald* and *The Boston Post* find out. If only the carpenter had waited one more day. I'd lost my scoop, and no doubt my job with it.

But as I boarded the ferry once again and headed out into the harbour, I became strangely light-spirited. Boston seen at night from the water has a very special magic. Fine buildings are lit from base to top and the monumental State House stands tall on Beacon Hill, its gilt dome aflame with the electric light of American democracy. It's a sight that always lifts the soul. This is where the East India tea chests were thrown overboard, and the water seems to sparkle with the thrill of it. There's a sense of the new: the colonists, the revolutionaries, the suffragettes. Out here on the water, far from Watch and Ward and Mrs Baker Eddy, Boston seems to be a city of the future. I would make my way in it, somehow. I began to think it might be a good thing finally to be free of the *Boston American* and Krupp's unrelenting quest for *cir-cu-lation*. Something new would come up. It always did.

As the ferry slowed and neared the East Boston wharves, I could see the *Californian*'s pier lit brilliantly by electric lights slung along iron frameworks. The silhouetted hulk of the ship loomed low and dark. Her derricks were swinging wildly, bringing cargo aboard in great canvas slings, and hard, angular shadows played about her upper decks.

Somewhere in all that activity, I knew, was Captain Stanley Lord, preparing to defend himself against the allegations of a disloyal carpenter.

CHAPTER 12

Herbert Stone knew as soon as he saw them that the two men walking down the wharf towards the gangway were reporters. He knew by the way they laughed and sauntered along, sniffing the air as if there might be news in the smell of the gas lamps. It was only a few hours since Stone had read of Mr Boxhall seeing a mystery ship and firing rockets, but the press were here already. Somehow they had found him out.

In a moment they were in the alleyway outside his cabin. He heard the chartroom door jerking open, the gangway watchman apologising to the captain, and the reporters announcing their newspapers. He slipped quietly along the alleyway, pressed himself flat against the bulkhead outside the partly open chartroom door, and listened. There were indistinct murmurings – complaints from the captain, apologies from the reporters – and then this: 'What do you say, Captain Lord, about this statement from your carpenter that it was your ship the *Titanic* saw?'

Stone leaned closer to the door. A statement from the ship's *carpenter*? Mr McGregor? The good and loyal carpenter, who kept himself to himself and always took off his cap when Stone spoke to him? The captain, too, must have been surprised, because he asked the pressmen twice for confirmation that the carpenter was their source. The men confirmed that he was. Stone closed his eyes. He tried not to breathe.

The captain's voice was at a higher pitch than usual and his words were stretched tight. His denials were driven by barely suppressed rage. Sailors would say anything when they were ashore; the whole thing was an outrage; the captain had known nothing whatsoever of the *Titanic*'s plight until the next morning. All of which was true enough, Stone thought, but what about the rockets? 'You can tell lies by telling the truth,' Stone's mother had once told him.

He could, he thought, stride into the room – right now – and tell the real truth: that he had seen the rockets and he had told the captain. He could say he was sorry, that he'd had no idea it was the *Titanic* and that she was sinking, and that he should have done more. He could do it now; he could end this whole sorry business once and for all.

A reporter said, 'If your wireless had been working, you may have heard the distress call?'

'Indeed,' Stone heard the captain say, as if it were nothing of consequence.

'And you would have gone?'

'Of course.'

'And everyone might have been saved?'

'Very possibly. I only wish that I had known the *Titanic* was in danger. I would have been glad of the opportunity to go to her assistance just as fast as I possibly could.'

Stone drew in a breath. What sort of man could give such an

answer? 'I only wish that I had known . . .' Stone felt like crying out, But you did know! I told you!

Behind him in the alleyway a man cleared his throat. Stone turned sharply and saw it was another reporter – thin, handsome, with tired eyes and a mop of shiny black hair. Stone recognised him as one of the men in the chartroom on the morning the *Californian* arrived in Boston.

The man smiled and shook his hand. 'Forgive me sneaking up on you,' he whispered.

Stone, embarrassed, moved away from the chartroom door, mumbling something about being on his way to his cabin.

'Your cabin is . . . here?' the man asked, walking a few steps along the alleyway. Stone noticed a softness in his voice, a kindness in his eyes. His tone was respectful, his manner sympathetic.

'I'm not allowed to speak to the press. You should talk to the captain.'

'I will, I will. But I thought it might help *you* to talk to someone.'

'No, thank you,' Stone said, moving towards his cabin door.

'If you tell me what happened,' said the man, 'I will write your story exactly as you say it. People will know the truth.'

'Thank you, but no,' said Stone, stepping into his cabin and pulling closed the door.

But the reporter quickly put his foot out to stop it. 'Wait,' he said. 'If you change your mind, come and see me. Today, tomorrow – whenever you like. I will listen.' He took from his pocket a small card, wrote some words on it, and pushed it into Stone's hand. 'Any time,' he repeated, then turned and walked towards the chartroom.

Later that night, as Stone sat at his desk writing to his wife, he thought much about the man in the alleyway. There was something delicate about him – a sadness, a sensitivity. Perhaps he'd done something wrong in his own life. It had been the briefest of meetings, but Stone, for the first time since the disaster, sensed an offer of understanding, of sympathy. 'I will listen,' the man had said. 'It might help ...'

In the soft light of the desk lamp he looked again at the card the man had given him. 'John Steadman,' it said in plain type, '*Boston American*,' and below that an address and telephone number. At the bottom of the card Mr Steadman had written in neat handwriting three simple words: 'Not your fault.'

When Stone took his usual brief walk ashore the following morning he was surprised to see that the report in *The Boston Post* was sympathetic to the captain. LEYLAND LINER GOT NO SIGNALS was the headline, and the story reported that the captain had given a 'stout denial' of the carpenter's claims, and had said most definitely that his ship saw no rockets or other signals of distress.

'You see, Mr Stone,' the captain said to him at luncheon, 'even in Boston the newspapers take no notice of silliness. Sailors are liars, and they know it. You need not worry about the carpenter.'

Stone took note of the word 'you'. 'No,' he said, 'perhaps I don't.'

But he could not make himself believe it. The carpenter's story may have flared and died away quickly, like a struck match, but he knew the glow of it remained out there in the world – tiny, but red-hot. It would flare again, and the city's pressmen would come once more across the water to probe and discover.

So when, late in the afternoon as Stone strolled along the wharf to check the fore and aft drafts, Charlie Groves came running towards him, leaping bollards and dodging longshoremen, he knew what was coming.

'Something's happened,' Groves panted. 'Ernie Gill has gone to a newspaper. He's sworn an affidavit saying he saw the rockets.'

Stone felt a strange calm. 'Did he go to the *Boston American*?'

Groves stared. 'How did you know?'

'Just a guess.'

'He's on his way to Washington, right now – to testify at the inquiry! He's taken his gear with him.'

Stone turned away and looked along the wharf to the harbour. The sun was now low behind the city, and the buildings were becoming dark against the brilliant reds and yellows that lay along the horizon. He imagined Gill out there amid those fiery colours, flying south on the Washington express, preparing to tell the senators all about the rockets.

'The captain is furious,' Groves went on, shifting his weight from foot to foot. When Stone turned back to look at him, at his large, round, perfectly smooth face, it appeared in the early twilight to be that of a child's. The third officer was young, but he was wise too. Stone wished they were still close; he was sorry that this thing had come between them, that he had done something to make Charlie Groves ashamed of him.

'You know,' Groves said, 'it's my duty, I think, to tell you: I believe him. Gill, I mean. I think he did see the rockets. And I think he's done the right thing in telling. It isn't the sort of thing that should be kept secret.' He paused, nodding slowly. 'Yes. It's my duty to say that. But, you know, he doesn't mean it against *you*. You do know that, don't you? He said to Sparks over and over again: "I don't mean this against the second. I don't mean it against the second."'

Stone smiled indulgently, feeling as a parent might towards a child who'd said a silly but endearing thing. He knew that Groves thought he was doomed, and that he was saying goodbye.

'Anyway,' Groves said, taking Stone's hand and shaking it solemnly, 'good luck, my friend.' And a moment later he was gone.

Stone headed back to the ship's gangway. The longshoremen, at work all around him, ignored him. He could, he thought, keep walking along the wharf and out the gate and no one would stop him. He envied Gill – on that train, fleeing south, away from this ugly ship. Gill had simply packed his kit and left; he, Stone, could do the same. He could drift down to New York or Philadelphia and look for work. He could write to his wife and ask her to join him. Or he could go to Nantucket and find a job on a whaler, just like Ishmael. He could keep walking now and be free. But he trudged up the gangway and headed for his cabin. There he would rewrite his letter to the captain. It would be his final version, and this time every word of it would be true.

In the alleyway outside his cabin Groves intercepted him. He looked flustered. 'The captain wants to see you,' he said, 'in the saloon.'

'Of course he does,' said Stone.

The electric lights in the saloon had been switched on and the oak panelling glowed. Chief officer Stewart sat at a dining table; Captain Lord, dressed in his full uniform, paced before it. His forehead was shiny with sweat, his cheeks flushed red, and a vein pulsed in his temple. By heaven, Stone quoted silently to himself, we are turned round and round in this world, like yonder windlass, and Fate is the handspike.

'Thank you, Mr Stone, for joining us,' the captain said as Stone took a chair at the table with the chief. 'Gentlemen,' he went on, stopping his pacing and turning to face them, 'Mr Gill the donkeyman has gone to a newspaper and sworn some sort of document. It is full of lies but it makes things difficult for us. Mr Thomas from Leyland will be here shortly and so will the men of the press. Mr Thomas insists that we speak to them, and so we shall. I have assured Mr Thomas that what Mr Gill says is nonsense, all of it, and that we will be saying so. Mr Stone here has said to me – and written it – that whatever he saw that night, they were not distress rockets. Of course, if he had seen distress rockets he would have come and pulled me out. But he saw no such thing. He has said it, and now we all must say it.'

'I do not wish to speak to them,' Stone said.

Spittle had formed at the corners of the captain's mouth. 'It is very nice, Mr Stone, that you wish things and don't wish things, but you *will* speak. Mr Thomas represents the owners of this ship – he knows that you were the officer of the watch when the *Titanic* met her end, being a clever man with facts and times. He insists you say something.'

Stone sat silently.

'Mr Stone. You will be asked what you saw, and I must know what you will say.'

Stone tried to think.

'You have told me you did not see distress rockets,' the captain continued. 'Now you must say it to the men of the press. Will you say it?'

Again Stone said nothing. He was thinking of the letter he'd been about to write to his captain. *I saw them . . .*

'Mr Stone,' the captain pressed, 'I must know: will you say it?'

Captain Lord's gaze did not waver. Stone stared back at him. The man's face, always as hard and impenetrable as polished armour, now showed subtleties of expression Stone had never seen before. The eyebrows were raised and drawn together; the wide, almost wild, eyes told him there was something other than rage in the captain. Stone was puzzled, but then, slowly, he understood: this was the moment he had imagined when he first went to sea, and for which he had waited ever since. His captain was asking his help – asking Stone to stand against the carpenter and the donkeyman, just as Ahab had asked

Starbuck to stand with him against the whale. Close! Captain Lord was wordlessly pleading. Will you stand close to me, Mr Stone? Will you grapple with them, and from hell's heart stab at them? Will you, for hate's sake, spit your last breath at them?

Stone felt that he must say no, that he had thrown his copy of *Moby-Dick* overboard, that it was lost forever in the sea. But then a vision of Starbuck came to him, weeping on his cross of starlight, radiant and pure, and he heard Starbuck whisper to him: 'Your soul is more than matched; she's overmanned; and by a madman!'

Stone drew in breath to speak. But before he could give the captain his answer there was a loud knocking at the door, which opened to admit Mr Thomas, the ship's agent. The large blubbery man heaved himself into the room blustering and smiling and wiping his hands on his dirty white suit.

'Hello, old boys,' he said, rolling a fat tongue around his red lips. 'Now, just what has been going on in this odd little ship of yours?'

CHAPTER 13

I held Ernest Gill's affidavit tightly in my hand as I stood in the shelter-deck alleyway waiting for Jack Thomas to emerge from the dining saloon. He was showing Captain Lord a copy of the affidavit. I could hear muffled murmurings.

It was early Wednesday evening and my story was still alive. That morning only one newspaper in Boston had run with the carpenter's story – the *Post* – and that paper had dismissed the carpenter and stated its belief in the captain. I was pleased. It meant that a bigger hammer would be needed to crack the nut, and I would be the one to wield it. I was certain Gill's affidavit was true, at least in essence, so what would his captain say when confronted with it? Would he now concede that rockets had been seen and reported to him? I thought that he must, and once he did, I would put to him my question: 'Then why didn't you go?' But even if he did not concede, I had a strategy. I would press the second officer. Both times I'd seen him he seemed to me trapped, panicky and furtive. He wanted to tell the truth, I was sure of it. He only needed a gentle push.

So I'd persuaded Krupp to give me one more day to file the story. We'd paid for Gill's affidavit, I reasoned, so we should use it.

I was not alone in the alleyway. Drunken Frank from the *Globe* had caught the ferry over with me and was now pressing his ear up against the door of the saloon. The old man had an uncanny nose for news; he could be counted on to be snooping around at inconvenient times. He said he was just following up the *Clinton Daily Item* story – the rumours from the carpenter – but I knew he had somehow found out about Gill's affidavit.

'Hear anything?' I asked.

'Nothing,' he said.

In his affidavit, Gill had sworn, 'I had been on deck about ten minutes when I saw a white rocket about ten miles away on the starboard side. I thought it must be a shooting star. In seven or eight minutes I saw distinctly a second rocket in the same place, and I said to myself, That must be a vessel in distress.'

I imagined Lord reading those words, and thought how loud they must ring in his brain. And tomorrow they would be published for the world to see. 'The captain had been notified . . . Mr Stone, the second navigating officer, was on the bridge at the time . . .' Every sentence was fired through with truth and indignation. 'I have no ill will towards the captain . . . I am actuated by the desire that no captain who refuses or neglects to give aid to a vessel in distress should be able to hush up the men.'

The document had a formal, almost pompous tone, yet every word had been chosen by Gill himself. And Gill was right. The men should not be hushed up. I wondered what Lord would say about it all.

I had not long to wait. The door was pulled open and fat Jack Thomas pushed into the alleyway, closing the door behind him. I could see he'd had a long day. There were dark patches under the arms of his suit, his lips were stained purple by something he'd eaten, and he had rubbed a red substance of some kind into his cheeks. He surprised me by launching into a lengthy and energetic tirade against the affidavit and its deponent. He waved a copy of the document in the air, he gasped and spluttered, he said it was all rubbish! Perfectly absurd! Ridiculous!

'Yes, yes, but can we go in?' asked old Frank, blowing his nose into a loose scrap of paper.

Thomas gave a snort; his face was alight. He sucked in air and drew himself up. 'You people,' he said, wiping spit from his mouth with a damp handkerchief, 'you snoop around, always looking for your mud – bribing poor young boys who know no better. You should be ashamed of yourselves.'

'I am very ashamed,' said Frank, taking some refreshment from a narrow flask. 'But can we go in now? Some of us have homes to go to.'

I was not at all sure that Frank did have a home to go to, but Thomas obliged his request, easing himself backwards against the saloon door. It opened; we shoved forward. The room was gracefully appointed – polished boards, splendid wood panels, electric lights with red and yellow glass shades – but I paid little attention to that: I was transfixed by the four men at its centre. The captain and his officers stood stiffly in their uniforms, just as they had when I first saw them. They seemed to fill the chartroom then, but now, in this larger room, they seemed small. As soon as I saw Lord – the stony coldness of his anger, the ramrod straightness of his back – I knew. He was going to deny it all.

'Gentlemen,' he began, without waiting for introductions or niceties. 'This document from Mr Gill is bosh – utter bosh. I have already told you fellows: sailors will say anything when they are ashore.'

And so will captains, I thought.

Lord then spoke authoritatively of latitudes, longitudes, speeds, distances and times. He told us of the international rules relating to the visual range of navigation lights. He invited us to make calculations. Frank and I wrote down numbers and the captain drew for us the inevitable conclusion: his ship could not have seen the *Titanic*, and Mr Gill's affidavit was 'poppycock'.

But I was ready for all this. I asked the captain no questions, but turned instead to his second officer, who stood silently on one side.

'What about you, Mr Stone?' I asked, deliberately using his name. 'Did you see any rockets during your watch?'

There was a loud silence. Frank stopped writing and looked up. We both waited.

'Mr Stone?' I prompted. 'Did you see any distress rockets?'

The length of the silence became embarrassing. I thought, This man cannot lie. He will not lie for his captain. Herbert Stone simply stared straight ahead.

'*I* was on watch at the time, and I saw no distress rockets.'

It was the chief officer who'd spoken. For a short, thin man his voice had a penetrating resonance. The saloon's electric lamps lit up his cavernous sunken cheeks with a fiery glow and seemed to give him a threatening power. He stared directly at me, as if daring me to challenge him. He was not a man who was often contradicted, I guessed.

So I contradicted him. 'Mr Gill swears in his affidavit that Mr Stone was on the bridge at the time.'

The chief officer did not waver. 'Mr Gill may say what he likes. *I* was on the bridge.' He exchanged a brief glance with the captain and then stared straight at me again.

'Mr Gill has sworn on oath. He will go to prison if he is lying.'

'Then let him go to prison.'

'Very well,' I said. But I did not for one minute believe him.

The chief officer went on to speak of waking the wireless operator at dawn, of receiving the message that the *Titanic* was sinking, of the *Virginian* confirming the position at six o'clock. I had heard it all before.

'And then,' I said, 'I suppose you steamed towards the position for all you were worth?'

'Yes. For all we were worth.'

'Racing to the rescue?'

'Racing to the rescue.'

'Thank you,' I said, giving him a weak smile.

'You are very welcome.'

'The captain still denies it?'

'He does.'

'So it's donkeyman versus captain?'

'It is.'

'And you're going with the donkeyman?'

'I am.'

I remembered the Boston pilot telling me I must have made a mistake – that I was missing something, and had set my dogs barking up the wrong tree. No English officer would ignore distress rockets, he'd said. I remembered how Gill's face had lit up when I offered to pay him five hundred dollars for his story. He had never in his life seen so much money, and most likely never would again. He would probably sign just about anything to get it. I remembered the boldness of the captain's denials: Bosh! Poppycock! We saw no signals!

I didn't have one piece of evidence – a document, a photograph – that clinched the matter. But I knew: the captain was lying. I knew

because he was tricky with his words. I knew because he was trying
to overwhelm us with numbers and technical details. I knew because
those closest to him were lying too.

And most of all I knew because, as I've said, I'm a good reader
of faces. In the captain's eyes I'd seen a quiet rage that made his lies
inevitable. I did not think he was a bad man. He was, Thomas had told
me, one of Leyland's best skippers, a man who'd landed a thousand
men on Essex beaches during military manoeuvres – at night, and
with their horses. He had never lost a ship, never run aground, never
had a collision. He had brought his cargoes to port on time and in
good condition. He was known in Liverpool not as a coward, but as
a brave and decent man. But somehow, on this voyage, the sea had
tricked him – I did not yet know how – so that he had let those rockets
go unanswered. And now, fifteen hundred dead! It was an outrage, and
his anger, I thought, was as righteous as it was passionate. His mistake,
whatever it was, could not deserve such perversely disproportionate
consequences. It was his wrath that drove his lies; it had the power,
almost, to make them true.

'The captain's lying,' I said. 'I just know it.'

Krupp looked at me long and hard. 'You'd better be right,' he said,
and he sent my handwritten copy downstairs to the typesetters and
their linotype machines.

Overnight, hundreds of gallons of ink would be pressed onto
virgin newsprint, and in the morning two hundred thousand Hearst
newspapers would be sent out into the world proclaiming that this
unassuming, polite British sea captain had left fifteen hundred people
for dead. For the first time in this whole sad business I felt sorry
for him.

The story ran with the headline SAYS HE SAW THE *TITANIC*'S ROCKETS, followed by an explanatory passage with strong verbs worthy of Bumpton – 'rushed', 'tore', 'exclaimed'. I gave readers a straightforward and dramatic account of events. 'The *Californian* of the Leyland Line was the ship which was sighted by the *Titanic* but which refused to respond to her signals of distress.' Gill's affidavit was set out in full. The report was simple and damning.

Krupp, I thought, could not help but be pleased. But when I was seated opposite him and he stared at me with his small black eyes, his face seemed narrower and more disapproving than ever. He wore the same stale white shirt he'd worn the day before, with his tie loose, so that long, wiry tufts of red hair sprouted from behind its knot. He was eating bread and pickles for breakfast.

'We are not running it in the afternoon edition.'

I thought for a moment he was teasing me. But he wasn't. 'It's a good story,' I said, wondering what it would take to please this man. 'You won't get better.'

'It *is* a good story. But it's not an *exclusive*. That drunk over at the *Globe* has got the scoop on you.' He slid a newspaper across the desk to me. DENIAL ON THE *CALIFORNIAN* was the headline, followed by a piece that reiterated details from the *Clinton Daily Item* story and went on to report the refutations of Jack Thomas and Captain Lord. 'The *Herald* has it too,' Krupp said, 'down in New York.'

'But they're just relying on the carpenter's story,' I said. 'They don't have the Gill affidavit, and Gill saw the rockets *himself*.'

'It doesn't matter who saw what. The story's the same. The ship saw rockets and didn't go. Even I'm beginning to tire of it.' Krupp ate another pickle. For what seemed a very long time he looked at me in silence. He was, I think, wondering what do with me. I decided to help him along.

'Shall I pack up my things?'

Krupp gave a sharp, snorting laugh. 'How dramatic!' he said. 'John, my friend, you underestimate yourself. I'm not going to sack you. I'm going to reward you.'

I waited.

'I want you to go back to doing what you do best. I want you to go to Halifax to meet the *Mackay-Bennett*. She's due any day now, and she has hundreds of bodies aboard. I want you to go up there and take a look at them.'

'I don't want to go to Halifax.'

Krupp dropped a piece of pickled bread on the floor. 'Yes you do. Look at this.' He passed me another newspaper. 'That – there. See? Read that.'

The headline was LINER *BREMEN* SIGHTS 100 OR MORE BODIES, and two or three paragraphs had been circled in red ink. The passenger ship, in mid-Atlantic on her way to New York less than a week after the disaster, had chanced upon the wreckage, and as she drew closer it became apparent that 'the black objects bobbing up and down on the water and mixing with the wreckage were bodies of the victims'.

'You see?' said Krupp. 'Your bodies make an appearance at last.'

I read on. The *Bremen*'s passengers had seen a man in formal evening dress lashed to a door; a young man lying on a steamer chair; a girl tied to a wooden grating. Men and women clung to each other, others were still holding onto children. 'The sight was an awful one to gaze upon,' said one passenger. 'I saw the body of a woman with a life preserver strapped to her waist and the bodies of two little children clasped in her arms.' What must it have been like for these people, I wondered, in those dark minutes after the *Titanic* left them?

I pushed the newspaper away.

'Strange,' said Krupp, 'don't you think? With hundreds and

hundreds of bodies floating about, your man found none of them?'

I could only agree. It was a mystery.

'Anyway,' he said, 'they've turned up now. Halifax is perfect for you. The *Mackay-Bennett*'s got Astor and Straus and maybe Butt too. We'll get you a special pass.'

I sat for a moment. I remembered how, only days earlier, I had searched the *Californian*'s holds, desperate to find these men. But now I did not care about Astor and Straus and Butt. The newspapers of Boston and New York had been filled with nothing else: tributes and double-page spreads and memorial services and toasts in university halls. The whole of America was in grief for them. But *this* story – of what the *Bremen* had seen – was the first I'd read of the dispossessed, the poor, the children. And now they were in the hold of a cableship on its way to Halifax. In a day or so I could see them, if I wanted, laid out on the piers for identification and collection, just like the Shirtwaist girls.

'Very well,' I said. 'I'll go.'

'Good,' said Krupp, taking another pickle.

'But not today.'

He frowned.

'Nor tomorrow, either,' I said, rising to leave. 'The *Californian* has two days left in Boston. I must try again – I need to know what happened.'

'Oh John, enough about that ship! Why are you bothering yourself with it? You've written your piece and the captain has shut up like a clam. You'll get nothing more from him.'

He may have been right, but I wasn't thinking of the captain. I was thinking of the second officer, with his wide eyes and honest face. I had seen, the night before, that he was unable to lie. The chief officer had been forced to lie for him. If I could get to him alone, he would tell me what happened. He would answer my question: why didn't they go?

I could not leave Boston now. Not while that strange and tantalising ship lay so close across the harbour. She was, in a way, the cause of all that lashing and tying and clasping of children in arms. To tell their story, I needed first to understand the *Californian*'s.

'I'll go on Sunday, but not before,' I said, leaving Krupp to his pickles and walking out into the Boston sunshine.

Harriet was at home alone when I visited in the early afternoon. She threw her arms around me with such power my hat was knocked to the floor. When she picked it up, she put it on her own head at a jaunty angle.

'Come,' she said, leading me into the parlour, 'look at *mine*.' She took an old derby from a nearby table and held it up for my admiration. I saw that she had sewn onto its front – a little crookedly – white, purple and green spangles in the shape of the letter V.

'V for ...?'

'The vote, of course.'

'Of course.'

'And victory!'

Her hair was a blaze of fiery red. Around her neck hung a necklace of fresh flowers. She was very beautiful, but when I looked upon her more closely, I was surprised to see that her crisp white shirtwaist was tucked into a pair of *pants* – oversized pants seemingly made of some type of rubberised canvas.

'They're pit brow pants,' she said, extending a leg stylishly. 'English girls wear them when they work in the mines. Did you know English girls work in coalmines? Well, they do. They tuck their skirts in, here – see – so they don't get caught in the wheels of coal wagons. Skirts are forever pulling women to their deaths in English coalmines. So, I'm going to wear them in the New York parade. I don't care what anybody says. Better to wear clothes that save our lives rather than make us pretty – that's what my outfit will say.'

My daughter really was a wonder. But when we sat together on the sofa I sensed that something troubled her, and it did not take me long to find out what. Olive, it seemed, would not allow her to wear her pit brow pants in the parade. 'She says it's enough that we leave off our corset covers,' Harriet explained, 'so the men can see the threads and seams of our bondage.'

'But you want to go further.'

'Yes. And I told Mother I was going to wear my pants anyway, no matter what she says.'

'That's a courageous stance.'

'Yes, it is. But now she hates me.'

'You and me both,' I said, putting an arm around her shoulder.

It is a feature of young women that they can switch moods without warning, and Harriet now drew away and turned to me stern-faced, as if she had just remembered something.

'Your story – this morning in the newspaper.'

'You liked it?'

'Of course. I like all your stories. But Papa, *why* didn't the captain come up to see the rockets? You didn't explain it. You didn't say *why*.'

'I don't know why,' I said.

'Then you should find out. Write a longer piece. Get beneath his skin, deep down into his psyche – find out what sort of man he is, and then tell us why he didn't go.'

'Psyche?'

'Yes. You know, his subconscious mind, something in his past, a suppressed memory.'

Harriet, at seventeen years old, was mistress of all the latest notions. But, I thought, perhaps she was right, and for the next few minutes I let the idea settle and grow. It would make a nice Boston story, this exploration of the 'psyche' – a subtle, Henry Jamesian tale, perhaps, of secret, shifting motivations. *What Lord Knew* . . .

My thoughts were interrupted by a sharp knock at the door. It was a messenger boy from my office, breathless from running. He handed me a piece of paper. 'Go to the ship now,' it said. 'Captain Lord is about to be arrested. File something tonight.' This last word was double-underlined.

At last, I thought as Harriet helped me with my hat and coat, Gill's affidavit was beginning to do its work.

It was dark by the time I got to the ship, but the pier was lit by large electric working lights. Gasoline generators hummed and sputtered, longshoremen hauled sacks of grain. The *Californian* seemed smaller than I remembered her, but as I drew closer I saw it was because she was now sitting much lower in the water. Her main deck was barely above the wharf's timber fenders and the shore gangway sat almost horizontally. Loading was nearly complete. In two days the *Californian* would haul her cargo out into the Atlantic, and I would go to Halifax.

The watchman at the gangway waved me on without question and once again I climbed the internal stairs to the chartroom. I stood at the doorway. The room was full of men. Lord sat upright at the far end of the settee with his arms folded across his chest. Next to him stood a tall, muscular man who seemed far too large for this small space. He was young – American-young, with white teeth and eager eyes. His jacket bore on its lapel a six-pointed silver star and handcuffs hung from his belt. Three pressmen leaned against the chart table, including old Frank from the *Globe*. No one spoke.

I beckoned Frank to come out into the alleyway. As he walked towards me I could see he was drunker than usual; he steadied himself by holding my arm. I drew him away from the door a little and asked him whether the captain was going to jail.

'Jail? Oh no. Worse. Washington!' Frank giggled. 'The marshal's got a warrant. He says the captain and the wireless man have got to go to Washington tonight and if they don't go the marshal will put the handcuffs on. But the captain says it'll delay the ship, and it's a British ship, and he won't go unless the company says so. So your fat girlfriend's gone ashore to try to sort it out on the telephone.'

'My girlfriend?'

'Fat Jack. The captain's in a sulk. Won't say a word till Fat Jack gets back.'

We didn't have to wait long. I heard heavy breathing and felt a movement of air. Thomas appeared at the top of the stairs, swaying and sweating.

'I thought you'd turn up,' he said when he saw me. He squeezed past into the chartroom and Frank and I followed. 'You've got to go,' he said to Lord, trying to get his breath. 'Tonight. Franklin says so. There's nothing I can do about it.'

Lord stood up. 'Very well,' he said, turning his back to the marshal, 'if the company wishes it, then I am perfectly willing to go. Perfectly willing.' Franklin's permission seemed to empower him. 'I will go to Washington and tell the good senators how I had stopped my ship while the *Titanic* was rushing along under full speed. *That* is what I will tell them.' He emphasised key words with a dramatic point of his finger, but he seemed to be addressing an audience in his own mind, for he made no eye contact with anyone. 'And Mr Evans will say how we warned the *Titanic* of the ice with the wireless equipment, how we told her, "There is ice all around!" – and how she ignored us.' Lord stopped for a moment, then gazed at me, Frank, and the two other reporters who were there. 'That,' he said, softening his voice in conclusion, 'is why we have been subpoenaed, and that's what we will say. I expect it will take us about ten minutes.'

No one in the room moved. I looked at Frank, he looked at me, and the two pressmen at the chart table looked at each other. Thomas's breathing remained loud and gaspy. Lord had, I think, surprised us all.

Thomas spoke first. 'Right then, gentlemen,' he said, trying to usher us towards the door with a sweep of his hand. Still no one moved.

'But what about the rockets?' It was old Frank who spoke now, with sudden clarity. 'Do you deny what this engineman says?' It was only then that I noticed he was holding a folded page from the *Boston American* – my story setting out Gill's affidavit – which he now held up for the captain.

'I have absolutely nothing more to say about that,' Lord said. There was the hard edge of anger in his voice. 'I told you fellows my story the other day – here, in this very room – but now you are all putting stock in what that fellow says.' He gestured dismissively towards the newspaper page. 'It is all lies and I will not say one more word about it.'

'But do you *deny* it, Captain?' asked Frank, shaking the page. Liquor was giving some heat to his frustration.

'It denies itself! I don't know why this fellow would tell such a story – I don't know why he would admit such unsailorlike deeds. He says he saw the rockets but didn't tell anyone. Do you suppose that any man – of any race whatsoever – would see signals of distress and not report them to the bridge? Every officer and every man of my crew is an Englishman and a white man, and I tell you, none of them would stand by and see anybody in distress without trying to help. I have heard he received five hundred dollars for his story. Five hundred dollars! There is your answer. That is the reason he is talking such poppycock.'

Once again I had a sense of the irresistible will of the man and of his unassailable belief in the force of his own words. For him, to say something was enough to make it so.

'Captain Lord,' I asked, 'may we put some questions to your second officer?'

Lord turned to me. 'You may not,' he said. 'I have said all that needs to be said.'

'But,' I persisted, glancing at Thomas to try to enlist his aid, 'wasn't it your second officer who was on watch at the time? Can't we ask him what he saw?'

'You may ask *me* what we saw, and *I* will tell you.'

'But the second officer was on the bridge. Did he report rockets to you, Captain?'

'I have told you —'

He stopped suddenly. He was no longer looking at me, but beyond me. I saw him give a slight shake of his head. I turned and saw, framed in the open door of the chartroom, the second officer. The alleyway behind him was dark, and he must have been standing there listening. But now, as he stepped forward, the light from the chartroom fell full on him so that he had a strange luminescence. He seemed almost angelic. I was struck again by his prettiness; he had such high cheekbones and such dark, knowing eyes. He looked at us calmly; he was not the darting, nervous man I'd seen days earlier eavesdropping in the alleyway. I thought, He has resolved to do something noble.

We fell silent and waited.

'I will answer, if you like, Captain,' Stone said, in a voice soft but sure.

Lord stared straight ahead – a hard, crystalline stare. One hand, held palm outwards, pushed slowly at the air. 'There is no need, Mr Stone,' he said.

But Stone did not retreat. 'Truly, Captain. I will answer their questions.'

The other reporters held their pencils still. They were looking to me and waiting, as if they understood: this was my story, this man was my discovery, and it was only right that I should ask the question.

So I asked it. 'Mr Stone, did you see any rockets during your watch and report them to your captain?'

The question was simply put and simply answered.

'I did not.'

I gaped at him. I had not thought he had the courage for such a lie. Indeed, so innocently and convincingly did he speak that I thought I might, after all, have been mistaken. Perhaps he hadn't seen any rockets. The rumours from the carpenter might be false. Gill might be lying. Perhaps the pilot was right. I tried to read Stone's face. He appeared serene. Years at sea had not roughened his skin; it was as white and smooth as a woman's. His eyes were steady. He seemed to radiate the truth.

'Are you quite certain?' I asked.

'I am,' he said. 'I did not notify the captain of any rockets, because I did not see any. Nobody on our ship saw any.'

My next question was impertinent, but I felt honour-bound to put it. 'Mr Stone, has the captain made you say these things?'

Stone did not hesitate. 'No,' he said, 'he has not made me say them. He hasn't made me do anything. He is a good captain.'

Such loyalty! I paused. I could not think what else to ask him. Thomas moved quickly to the centre of the room, clapped his hands and said, 'That's that, then. Everything's resolved. Thank you, gentlemen.'

Herbert Stone disappeared down the alleyway, and Lord walked into his cabin and closed the door behind him. The marshal said he would wait where he was and the two other reporters rushed off to file their stories. Old Frank ambled along after them down the alleyway, muttering to himself.

Jack Thomas surprised me by inviting me for a drink in the ship's dining saloon while he waited for Lord. 'You see, old boy?' he said, generously pouring bourbon into my glass. 'The captain is telling the truth after all. His second officer says so. You've been misled by that grubby boy from the engine room.'

'That grubby boy,' I said, 'is on his way to Washington as we speak, and tomorrow he will tell Senator Smith all he knows. Under oath.'

'He knows nothing.'

'He knows enough. And I wonder what the captain will say about the rockets when *he* is under oath.'

'John, old boy, Smith doesn't care about the rockets! He cares only that brave Captain Lord and his wireless man tried to warn the *Titanic* and the *Titanic* ignored them. Franklin tells me Smith was in a rage about it. Furious! That's why subpoenas were issued, and that, old boy, is what our captain will tell the world. Under oath.'

Perhaps Thomas was right. After all, Stone, the watcher of the rockets, hadn't been called to Washington. 'We shall see,' I said.

Thomas looked at me across the table and finished his drink in one long, aerated slurp. 'You know, John,' he said, 'I am trying my very best to forgive you. But you do make it difficult.'

'Thank you,' I said, likewise draining my bourbon in a single gulp, and holding it out for a refill. 'Now, tell me. What train did you say the captain was catching?'

'The midnight special.' Thomas eyed me closely. 'The marshal will take him along to the station. Why do you ask?'

'No reason,' I said, slowly stirring my bourbon with a pencil.

Part Two

CHAPTER 14

I had not forgotten Krupp's demand that I file a story that night, but he'd been expecting Lord to be carted off to jail, not sent triumphant to the nation's capital by luxury train. So I didn't file, but instead made my way to South Station and followed the captain onto the midnight train to Washington. That, surely, was what Krupp would have wanted.

I have always known just how easy it is to fool people with a simple disguise. Wear a starched blue shirt and pin a polished silver star to your chest and you can direct traffic at the busiest intersection in Boston. Hobble on a walking stick and courteous folk will open doors for you. So I always kept in my satchel a pair of plain-glass spectacles, a woollen cap, and a false moustache and beard, and once I was aboard the train I put them on. Bourbon had made me brave. I felt like getting into the cage with the lion.

Jack Thomas had booked Lord a sleeper berth, but the midnight service offered a late supper and I found him sitting alone in the dining car. Cyril Evans was nowhere to be seen. When I took the seat opposite the captain, he showed no sign of recognising me so I stroked my beard, ordered a drink and offered to buy him one too. He refused. 'I never drink,' he said, 'except for a port wine at Christmas. One glass.'

'If you spent Christmas with my wife's family,' I said in my best Texan accent, 'as I am compelled to do, you'd need more than one glass to get through, yes sir!'

Lord gave a polite smile but then begged my pardon and turned to the window. He was tired, he said, so must be excused from conversation. I apologised profusely.

'My wife,' I added, 'says it is my very worst sin, the way I just prattle on and on, with no one wantin' to listen!' I said that of course he must be silent and restful and ignore me altogether.

Some time passed.

'Although,' I said, 'I can hear an accent, and am mighty curious about what might have brought a man such as y'self to this part of the world at this hour.'

'I am a sea captain,' Lord said. 'From England.'

'What a grand thing!' I said. 'A very grand thing.'

Lord turned towards me a little. I thought he might ask me again to be quiet, but my jovial talk and the gentle swaying of the train seemed to open him up a little. He listened and nodded when I said that my father was a yachtsman, that I was heading south to spend some days with him on the Chesapeake. 'But I know nothing of the water, no sir,' I said. 'Not like you, sir.'

'I do know something of it,' Lord said.

I bubbled and frothed as a woman might, asking him what it was like to be in a storm, what exotic places he had visited, and by slow gradations this reserved British captain began to talk to me. He was, as he claimed, tired, and there were periods of long silence, but on his topics of interest he became voluble, even warm. His supper arrived, and as he ate he told me something of growing up amid the vast cotton mills of Lancashire, of proving to his father that he could be as brave as his four older brothers, of his mother's cold and bony hands gripping his own every morning to give strength to his prayers. His brothers went into textiles, but at thirteen he went to sea as a midshipman on sailing ships. He told me about Cape Horn storms and how, in calmer weather, he would lie flat on the yards and listen to the sails snap and crack beneath him. It was God's workplace, he said. He was sitting upright in his seat, his starched collar buttoned stiffly and his hat in his lap. From this close distance I saw just how noble was his face, with its angular structure, piercing eyes and large forehead rising to a bald crown.

For a while, he seemed to forget I was there. He spoke as if addressing a far-off audience – his mother and father, perhaps, or their sacred memory. He spoke of his mother's bible, and told me how, when the other midshipmen went ashore in Chile's Talcahuano Bay to visit honey-skinned women, he would use it to keep himself strong. When the boys came back to the ship drunk and boasting of sinful things he would take it with him to the open deck above, look up at the masts and yards, and think about the majesty of the wind and sea.

'But things are not now as they were under sail,' he said, his face lit by the electric flashes of passing signals. 'Sail bred *discipline*. One wrong move on a yard and things were over for you. Steam has brought with it a certain . . . laxity. It's hard these days to get good officers.' He spoke softly, as if voicing a profound inner knowledge. 'Yes,' he said, 'steam makes men soft.'

He told me that he sailed as second officer when he was only nineteen, that he obtained his First Mate's Certificate when he was twenty. He was appointed to his first command when he was only twenty-eight years old. 'Most uncommon, you know,' he said, 'to get command so young.'

Lord asked me no questions about my own life. I was glad. I was too tired myself to invent tales of sailing on the Chesapeake. Moreover our train was hurtling onwards and Lord must soon retire for the night, so I tried to guide him to more revealing topics.

I asked about his family. His wife was wonderful and grand, he said, but – and here his face gave a little grimace – his young son was sickly. He turned the subject to golf. When home, he played every Thursday afternoon at the Wallasey golf course. 'For the game, you understand, not for the social side.' Wallasey, he explained, was across the river from Liverpool.

I ordered more bourbon and asked more questions. I felt I was getting nearer to him, that I was following well enough my daughter's advice to 'find out what sort of man he is'. Behind the cover of my disguise I began to feel the full power of his charm. How different this man was to that trapped, defiant figure in the *Californian*'s chartroom! Attack him and he hardens, I thought; flatter him gently and he opens up like one of those giant exotic plants that turn their fronds ever so slowly to the sun.

I drank my drink and dabbed at my lips, wondering how I might bring him round to talking about his officers. In what ways had steam made them soft? Did he have anyone in particular in mind? But then I looked with horror at my napkin. Sitting in it was my moustache. I tried quickly to replace it but I was too late. Lord reached forward and took off my glasses.

'You are the newspaper man!' he said. 'From Boston.'

I nodded, peeling away my false beard. I was embarrassed, but also a little relieved.

'I ought to have known,' he said tiredly. 'You Americans have no manners and no honour. None at all.'

I met his gaze and waited. I tried to see what was *beneath*. He seemed, suddenly, to be young. I thought for a moment that he might say something more; that he wanted, perhaps, to tell me everything. 'I can help you, you know,' I said as gently as I could. 'I will write whatever you want me to write.'

He leaned closer. His hand moved a little, as if to reach out to shake mine. His eyes were red. I don't think he'd slept for days. 'I do not know whose interests you serve,' he said in a harsh whisper, 'or why you hound me as you do, but I will say not one more word to you.' He stood up, his supper half finished, and walked away down the aisle.

The train rattled and swayed, and as Lord closed the carriage door behind him, I thought for some reason of the *Bremen* and all that she had seen, and I felt a soft glow of anger. I may be an American, without manners or honour, but I knew exactly whose interests I served.

For a time, as I sipped bourbon and watched the silvery landscape slip by outside, I wondered why Lord hadn't found any bodies. In my indignant mood I wondered whether he'd searched for them at all. He said he had, but was he lying about that too, just as he was lying about the rockets? It was a conundrum, but the solution came as I sat alone in that dining car rattling south to Washington. Knowing I wouldn't sleep, I gathered up some newspapers from the central vestibule and surrounding seats. I read about the evidence given so far in the inquiry, including Mr Boxhall's account of his firing of rockets. They 'go right up into the air and they throw stars,' he'd said. But it was a small article buried deep that gave me the clue I needed. A bedroom steward had told the senators in Washington how, after the *Titanic* sank, the passengers in his lifeboat rowed towards the lights of a ship. 'We kept pulling and pulling until daybreak,' he explained. 'Then we saw the *Carpathia* coming up, and we turned around and came back to her.' I soon found similar reports in other papers: lifeboats trying to reach a light during the night hours, and turning around only when the *Carpathia* arrived at dawn.

I ought to have thought of it earlier: once the *Titanic* sank, her lifeboats had rowed towards the *Californian*, so that stroke by stroke a gap opened up between them and the silent, floating dead. At dawn, the *Carpathia* made her way to these lifeboats, and the *Californian* made her way to the *Carpathia*. Lord saw no bodies because he was never at the wreck site. It was simple, really. And when I checked my notes of what Cyril Evans had told me, I saw that the wreckage he described – an oar, a lifejacket, a shawl – could easily have come from the lifeboats, not the ship.

But even if I knew why Lord had not found the *Titanic's* dead, I was no closer to knowing why he hadn't gone to them while they were yet living. This, I hoped as the new day approached, was just what the Washington senators would find out.

I worried a little for Lord when he said that we Americans have no manners and no honour. I hoped he wouldn't say such things to the grand senators of Washington.

The British had, after all, set the city alight during the War of 1812 – an act of monstrous petulance – and every Washington school-child knew the cry of the invading British commander: 'I will make a cow pasture of these Yankee Capitol grounds!' It might have all been a hundred years ago, but the ashes of the White House, the Capitol Building and the Treasury could still be tasted on the wind from time to time. And now this: a British ship with a British captain driven recklessly to her doom so that Washington's best men were drowned. Clarence Moore, master of the Chevy Chase hunt, was dead, and President Taft's sorrow for Archibald Butt was that of a bereaved brother. He was said to wander the White House in tears, asking to be left alone.

The *Titanic*'s officers had been spat upon when they got off the train at Union Station. None of them had come voluntarily – they had all been subpoenaed. They pushed out their chests, clenched their fists and fought back. 'We welcome this inquiry,' fifth officer Harry Lowe had said, 'but you Americans got up against us, and now we Britishers are up against you, and we shall see how it comes out!' I laughed when I read this in the newspapers. Mr Lowe seemed intent on making a cow pasture of the Capitol grounds all over again.

But Washington is an unyielding, indestructible sort of place – all that marble, all those hard, bright edges, all that whiteness – and as I say, I worried a little for Captain Lord. He seemed vulnerable as he stood in the main hall of Union Station in the late morning, dressed in a plain blue day suit, staring straight ahead. Tall as he was, he was still dwarfed by the great white arches that soared a hundred feet above him. Their inlaid gold octagons shone down on him like a thousand suns.

Cyril Evans stood two or three yards behind him, pasting down his hair with the back of his hands like a cat cleaning itself. Soon, under oath, he would at last have his chance to tell the world how, on the morning the *Titanic* sank, he'd had precedence. Certainly Jack Binns had never spoken at such an auspicious venue.

I watched the two men from a distance. Jack Thomas had told them that a Washington representative of IMM would meet them from the train, but there was not yet any sign of him. Lord and Evans were alone.

I waited, but when no one came I decided to wait no longer. I stepped outside into the bright sunshine and struck out on foot for the Capitol.

I arrived at the Senate Office Building on Constitution Avenue just before one o'clock. The building was new and enormous, with towering columns and lofty facades of polished marble and limestone. Inside, an usher showed me to the Committee on Territories room, where the inquiry was being held, but told me I couldn't go in yet – the room was full. The luncheon adjournment was only a few minutes away and I could try my luck in the afternoon session.

I sat on one of the polished cedar benches of the anteroom. I could hear muffled voices engaged in the steady rhythm of question and answer. The questioner, I knew, was Senator Smith of Michigan, but in time I began also to recognise the singsong lilt of Ernie Gill. Soon the questioning stopped, the door was flung open and Gill hurried out with the crowd, weaving through clumps of strolling women. I followed him as he slipped along the wide corridors to the top of the steps leading down to the avenue. He paused, taking in the grand vista that lay before him. When I called to him he turned, smiled, and held out his hand to shake mine. His face was flushed; he was triumphant. He told me Senator Smith had read out his affidavit to everyone in the room, and he, Ernie Gill of Liverpool, had sworn that every word of it was true.

'Do you know the captain is on his way here now?' I asked.

'Yes. Mr Franklin has been giving evidence about it.'

'Aren't you going to stay and hear what he says?'

'I don't need to. I saw the rockets. He didn't.' Gill smoothed his great shaggy moustache with his forefinger and thumb. What a strange world it was, I thought, that this small man from the engine room of a British tramp steamer should find himself addressing senators of the United States Congress. I remembered Gill telling me that he'd been good at public speaking at school, that he'd learned the Rule of Three, and that the other boys had listened to him. Today he could not have hoped for a more esteemed audience. The giant dome of Capitol building loomed close, and behind him, in the middle distance, the Washington Monument shone white and glorious in the vibrant light of early afternoon. We stood at the centre of the nation.

Gill lit a cigarette. At the curb below an automobile drew up and three passengers alighted, two of whom, I saw, were Stanley Lord and Cyril Evans in their suits and bowler hats. The third was no doubt the IMM man. They began to walk up the stairs, and in moments would be at the place where Gill and I stood.

I thought Gill might step away – there was still time – but he kept his position, smoking his cigarette, until he stood face to face with his captain. Lord, if he was surprised to see us, did not show it. Evans and the IMM man held back, but Lord was only a yard or so away. None of us spoke. We stood in a triangle, waiting, as if we were the last remaining pieces in a chess game. I wondered whether, in England, some rule of etiquette required a man's accusers to speak first.

I remembered what Gill had told me his ironmonger father once said: apply enough heat and anything will bend. For Lord there must have been some heat in Gill's presence, but there he stood, unbendable as granite. And it was Lord, at last, who spoke first.

'Smoking above decks again, donkeyman?'

I saw a flicker of confusion, almost panic, in Gill's face. The captain addressing him this way seemed at a stroke to re-establish the natural order of things. Gill was back down in the engine room once more, amid the filthy coal and smouldering clinkers.

'I came, I saw them, and . . .' Gill seemed to choke on his words. He repeated them, as if trying to recall a third and clinching phrase to trump his captain.

But Lord would not be trumped. He did something I hadn't seen him do before: he laughed. 'And what, donkeyman? You conquered?'

He laughed again and stepped past us both towards the building's great double doors. Evans and the IMM man followed him, leaving Gill and me alone. Gill was blinking and frowning. I took his hand and shook it.

'Goodbye,' I said. 'You've done well.'

I didn't know whether Gill was Caesar triumphant or Brutus holding a bloodied knife, but either way he was already skipping down the stairs to a large motor car that had drawn up to the curb. I could see the soft green gloves of the chauffer as he held open the door for the donkeyman from Sheffield. Ernie Gill's father might once have told him that his life would be a tough one, and that he would never be far from hell, but here he was, riding a luxury Oldsmobile Limited up the vast boulevard of Constitution Avenue in sunshine so bright it hurt my eyes.

At a quarter to three, the doors to the Committee on Territories conference room were hooked open and people began to drift in. I and ten or so other men of the press found seats on spindly chairs along the eastern wall. Women fought for position in small, roped-off galleries. They flounced and pushed and stamped their feet; a black velvet hat fell to the floor; the plumes of another blocked the view and were plucked out. One lady accused someone of taking her seat. A corpulent woman unable to find space in the galleries asked me to stand. I refused – I could not take down transcript if I was standing, I explained. She rustled away, her skirts hissing like snakes.

On the opposite side of the room, in chairs set aside for witnesses, were Lord and Evans. Lord held his ship's large logbook in his lap.

At exactly three o'clock there was a sudden hush as the committee of four senators took their places at the great mahogany table. Senator

Smith read a short message for the record and then looked up. 'Is the captain here?' he asked. 'Captain Lord?'

Lord stood silently.

'Very well. If you will come up here and take this chair, I will swear you in.' Lord walked forward and took his seat, and Senator Smith passed him a bible. 'Do you swear to tell the truth, the whole truth, and nothing but the truth, so help you God?' asked the senator.

'I do,' said the captain without the slightest hesitation. He had come to Washington to tell his story, and I now brought my pencil to my notebook to write every word of it down.

I knew something of Senator William Alden Smith, the man charged with inquiring into the loss of the *Titanic* on behalf of the American people. I knew that he had grown up wretchedly poor in Michigan and had made money by selling popcorn on the street. I also knew he was descended from the revolutionary war generals Putnam and Alden, so he knew in his veins how to fight the British. It was Smith who had issued subpoenas commanding Bruce Ismay and the *Titanic*'s officers and crew to come to Washington. They complained bitterly, and London's newspapers called him an ignorant fool and his inquiry a preposterous outrage. Smith didn't care. It was British arrogance and pride that had killed some of America's finest, and here before him was the man who could prove it.

'Did you attempt,' Smith now asked Lord, adjusting his red, white and blue necktie, 'to communicate with the vessel *Titanic* on the Sunday, April 14th?'

'Yes, sir,' replied the captain. On the seat in front of me, a woman was sketching him in large, bold pencil strokes.

'What was that communication?'

'We told them we were stopped and surrounded by ice.'

'Did the *Titanic* acknowledge that message?'

'Yes, sir. I believe he told the operator he had read it, and told him to shut up, or stand by, or something; that he was busy.' There was a murmur of excitement in the room. Hands went to mouths, a gasp was heard, someone made a tut-tutting sound with their tongue.

'Told him to shut up!' The senator, always with an ear for the dramatic, paused after repeating Lord's statement. I sensed the room's collective imagining: the mighty *Titanic* racing at full speed through the black night only minutes from her iceberg, brushing off the little man trying to warn her.

Smith looked at Senator Bourne, his colleague from Oregon, who accepted the invitation and asked, 'That was the *Titanic*'s reply?'

'Yes, sir.' Lord's tone had an edge. He seemed to share the room's indignation. I imagined him thinking, Yes, if you wish to find a villain in all of this, look to that ship, not mine.

Senator Smith rounded off the topic. 'And did you have further communication with the *Titanic*?'

'Not at all, sir.'

'Did the *Titanic* have further communication with you?'

Lord's reply came quickly. 'No, sir.'

'Did you see the ship on Sunday?' Smith asked.

'No, sir.'

Smith now drifted to questions about times, speeds and distances, which Lord willingly answered, threading his words and numbers together into a seamless fabric of navigational detail. It was, I thought, all very puzzling: less than two hours earlier the senators had heard Ernest Gill swear under oath that this witness had been told of distress rockets and done nothing about them. Yet Smith seemed not at all concerned with that. Having put his questions about the warning given by the *Californian* to the *Titanic*, he seemed to lose interest. He asked about steam whistles and ice, he asked whether a blind man ought to be employed as a ship's lookout, he asked about the colour of icebergs.

'Do they usually show white when the sun shines on them?'

'When the sun shines on them, they show white, usually, yes.'

How pretty, I thought, but what about the rockets?

Smith shuffled his papers. 'Do any of the other senators desire to ask questions?' he said, pushing his notes away and sitting back in his chair. He looked at his three colleagues; they looked at each other.

Senator Bourne asked whether Lord thought it might be better for ships to have two wireless operators, instead of one.

'It would be much nicer,' Lord said. 'You would never miss a message then.'

Senator Burton asked a question about binoculars. Senator Fletcher asked whether Lord could have gone to the *Titanic*'s relief if he had picked up her wireless distress message.

'Most certainly,' said Lord.

'You could have gone?'

'We could have gone, yes.'

And then, after one or two more questions about nothing much, Senator Fletcher pushed his notes away too. No more questions came. Pressmen began to rise; there was soft talking in the galleries. Lord stood up, gathered his logbook, and began to walk back to his seat. I was astounded. In my notebook I drew a large question mark, and then traced it over again. I could not think why he was being allowed to escape.

But as I watched the captain, a theory began to form itself in my mind. To blame this man would not fit the story Senator Smith wanted to tell his nation. America had lost her heroes and she needed villains to punish, not this tall, careful man who had stopped his ship when he saw the ice, who had waited, and been patient, and whose ship was a medium-sized tramp steamer with cotton gins and corn bales in rusty holds. The *Californian* was no *Titanic*, and it was only the *Titanic* that could properly represent the great Edwardian hubris of her makers. Washington didn't want to pick on the weak man.

As Lord walked back to his seat he was smiling. There was the light of victory in his eyes. He had done just what he said he would; he had told a powerful tale of two ships: a proud, reckless one and a careful, humble one.

But my analysis, fast and clever as it was, was shown in the next minutes to be wholly wrong. I ought to have focused less on Senator Smith's sense of national pride and more on his reputation for distracting witnesses with elaborate red herrings, all the while preparing to come in for the kill. His stumbling and bumbling was nothing but a cover.

'Wait, Captain Lord,' he said, 'there *is* one more thing.'

Lord, not yet having reached his seat, stopped. I thought I saw in his face the briefest flicker of anger. He turned where he was to face the senator.

'If you please,' said Smith, gesturing towards the witness chair.

For some reason, Lord did not seem surprised. He walked back and sat, replacing the logbook on the table and opening it. In its pages was a loose sheet of notepaper, which he now drew towards himself. He's preparing to read a statement, I thought. He knows what's coming.

'Captain,' said Smith, his smile growing warmer, 'did you see any distress signals on Sunday night, either rockets or the Morse signals?'

Perhaps it had truly only just now occurred to the senator to ask about the rockets, but I did not think so. I thought it more likely he'd held back deliberately, to see what Lord would offer up voluntarily. Either way, Captain Lord's moment had come. The question had been put directly to him, and now – before these senators and the American nation, and before God – he must admit or deny.

Lord looked straight ahead and took a breath. 'No, sir,' he said. 'I did not.'

I sat in suspense. Although this statement was true – it was not Lord himself who'd seen the rockets – it was not the whole truth. The room waited in silence.

'The officer on watch saw some signals,' the captain went on softly, 'but he said they were not distress signals.'

'They were not distress signals?' Smith checked.

'They were *not* distress signals,' Lord confirmed.

'But he reported them?'

Captain Lord, still staring straight ahead, swallowed hard. Perhaps the next two words were the most difficult he had ever had to say in his life. 'To me,' he said.

For a while nobody spoke. Perhaps the whole room was thinking what I was.

'I think you had better let me tell you that story,' the captain said.

'I wish you would,' Smith said, leaning back a little in his chair to listen.

And so the captain began. He told us of a ship that steamed up and stopped to the south of them just before midnight. This ship took no notice of the *Californian*'s Morse lamp. 'When the second officer came on the bridge at twelve o'clock,' Lord said, glancing at his page of notes, 'or ten minutes past twelve, I told him to watch that steamer and I pointed out the ice to him. I told him we were surrounded by ice and to make sure the steamer did not get any closer to us. At twenty minutes to one I whistled up the speaking tube and asked him if she was getting any nearer. He said, "No. She is not taking any notice of us." So I said, "I will go and lie down a bit." At a quarter past he said, "I think she has fired a rocket." He said, "She did not answer the Morse

lamp and she has commenced to go away from us." I said, "Call her up
and let me know at once what her name is." So he put the whistle back
and, apparently, he was calling. I could hear him ticking over my head.
Then I went to sleep.'

And that was that. I had taken down his words verbatim, as best I
could, and in the brief pause that followed I scanned what I'd written.
Lord had tried to hurry over the most important sentence: 'At a
quarter past he said, "I think she has fired a rocket."' It was easy to
miss, it referred to only one rocket and it was uncertain – 'I think'– but
it was the first time I'd heard the word 'rocket' come from his lips, and
it shone like a diamond in the sand. I knew from Ernie Gill that more
than one rocket had been seen and reported, but no matter: to have
been told of one rocket was to have been told of them all. In any event,
even in Lord's own statement of things, one soon became several.

'You heard nothing more about it?' Senator Smith asked.

'Nothing more until sometime between then and half past four.
I have a faint recollection of the apprentice opening the door, opening
it and shutting it. I said, "What is it?" He did not answer and I went
to sleep again. I believe the boy came down to deliver me the message
that this steamer had steamed away from us to the southwest, showing
several of these flashes or white rockets. Yes, she steamed away to the
southwest.'

At last. A cracking of the nut. Lord had conceded that his second
officer had seen white rockets, plural, and had reported them to him.
His admission was mired in convolutions and qualifications, but it was
enough. It would be tomorrow's headlines.

I began to think of Captain Lord as a man being reluctantly dragged
up the high mountain of truth, clutching at roots and boulders as

he went, at every stage saying, 'No higher, please.' At first, he'd said nothing whatsoever about the *Titanic* – to his employers, to the press, to anyone. Were it not for a chance reference to the *Californian* in a message from the *Carpathia*, no one would ever have known Lord had been anywhere near the *Titanic*. Jack Thomas had led him a little further up the mountain by forcing him to tell of his dash to the wreck site, but he would not go as far as mentioning the rockets. 'Poppycock!' he had said in Boston. 'We saw no signals!' But here in Washington, Gill's affidavit and Senator Smith's questions had at last brought him to a high ledge.

But it was still only a ledge. It was not the peak. His ship may have seen rockets but, he now said, these rockets were most definitely not from the *Titanic*. They were from some other ship stopped nearby. In the bright airy sunlight of the conference room, Senator Smith seemed doubtful.

'Regarding this ship that stopped by you on Sunday night,' he said.

'Yes, sir?'

'Have you any idea what steamer that was?'

'Not the faintest.'

Another ship steaming up from the southeast and stopping just as the *Titanic* did? Then firing rockets just as the *Titanic* did? Then disappearing just as the *Titanic* did? And this ship never being heard of or sighted by anyone else? None of it made sense, of course, but the captain's voice seemed to command us all to believe it. There was something about the angle of his body, too, and the steady focus of his eyes, that made me think *he* believed it.

Just in front of me, the woman who was sketching the captain had caught his Roman nose with its high bridge in two bold lines; in two narrow marks she had his eyes, and in fast single strokes she dashed off the long bones of his fingers. As I sat watching her I wondered how I might sketch Lord with words, how I might portray his unusual brand of pride. There was something of steel in this man, but how to convey what was in his face when he asked us all to believe that it was not the *Titanic* his ship had seen?

Once again I felt sorry for him, and at that moment I didn't want him to be dragged any further up the mountain. If mystery ships between his and the *Titanic* were what Lord needed to be rid of the terrible guilt for all those deaths, then let him invent a hundred. What else could he do? To deny that those white rockets had come from the *Titanic*, and to deny it absolutely, I now understood, was his only defence. And perhaps the senators understood this too, because they asked not one more question about them.

Washington may have been in the mood for a fight, but in the end Senator Smith and his colleagues treated Lord as if he were a guest at their country club. 'Now,' Smith said to the captain, showing him a warm smile, 'from the log which you hold in your hand, and from your own knowledge, is there anything you can say further which will assist the committee in its inquiry as to the causes of this disaster?'

'No, sir,' said Lord, 'there is nothing. Only that it was a very deceiving night. That is all I can say about it.'

Yes indeed, I thought.

There was a short adjournment. I followed Lord into the anteroom and stood at a distance. I saw Philip Franklin there, waiting patiently for the captain. I had last seen him sobbing at his press conference in New York, and I would have liked to step over and shake his hand. But instead I hung back in an alcove, listening as he took up conversation with the captain. Lord was smiling again; once more he seemed pleased with himself. I couldn't make out everything he was saying, but I heard the words 'agreeable' and 'friendly' – and some odder words, too: 'convivial', 'confab', 'swimmingly'. He spoke as if the *Titanic* might yet come steaming into New York Harbor in the spring sunshine, afloat and happy, never having seen an iceberg or fired a single rocket.

But on Franklin's face I saw a kind of horror. His eyes were wide open beneath lowered eyebrows and from time to time he rubbed his temples with his knuckles. This could not be easy for him, I thought. What Franklin thought of the captain I couldn't know, but I did know that if he, Franklin, had been accused of abandoning so many people, the weight of shame would have broken him. And yet Lord's head was upright; he seemed to bear no weight at all.

I knew what Cyril Evans would tell the senators after the adjournment: that Jack Phillips on the *Titanic* had told him to shut up, that he'd gone to bed and been woken in the morning with news of rockets, and that he'd had precedence on the wireless. I owed it to him to listen, but there was time first for some refreshment to help clarify my thoughts. I found a restaurant on the second floor with marble pillars and silver chandeliers, but I settled for a basement café that was smaller, darker and dirtier. I ordered coffee and added a shot of bourbon from a flask I kept in my satchel. Newspapers lay in a pile on a side shelf, left behind by visitors; I gathered some up and sat at a corner table to read awhile.

The disaster had ignited Washington's moral fervour. There was much to learn, and holy men applied their wisdom to the people like heat to clay. Reverend Muir lectured on 'Lessons of the *Titanic*', Reverend Howlett pondered the 'Teachings of a Tragedy', Reverend Montgomery explained how 'In a World Full of Sorrows God Can Still Be Good', and Reverend Gray exulted in the courage of 'Washington, Our Unshaken City'.

The bourbon had ignited my own fervour. I searched through the papers, my fingers drifting down the columns to speed my reading. I wanted to find somewhere, in all this newsprint, the name of one third-class person who died; or, failing that, a single reference to the fifty-three dead children. For half an hour I searched. I found not one word. Then, finally, I saw this: 'The disease-bitten child, whose life at best is less than worthless, goes to safety with the rest of the steerage riff-raff, while the handler of great affairs, the men who direct the destinies of hundreds of thousands of workers . . . stand unprotestingly aside.'

I pushed the paper away. A drunken woman sat down opposite me. She had seen me use my flask and asked for a shot. She had no teeth and dried blood had caked in one ear. When I refused, she spat at me and staggered away.

I poured another shot into my coffee – a double – and blamed the world for making me do it.

I was about to return to the inquiry when I noticed a small headline: LORD MERSEY HEADS ENGLAND'S INQUIRY. That a British inquiry would be held had not occurred to me. I suppose it ought to have: the *Titanic* was, after all, a British-registered ship. I read on. Lord Mersey, the article said, was a highly respected admiralty judge who would be helped by a panel of expert nautical assessors. England's finest barristers would represent the interested parties. Together, these men would find the truth behind the disaster. The inquiry would be focused, diligent and thorough – in short, superior to the American inquiry in every way. And it would all begin, I read, in one week's time.

My father had once had dealings with London barristers, so I knew something of their ways. They were gentlemen, of course – unfailingly polite, speaking always in perfectly formed sentences – but their gentleness was all on the surface. Underneath they were all tricks and horror. Being questioned by a London barrister, my father said, was like drinking afternoon champagne from dainty glasses: very pleasant at first, but you soon become befuddled, and by the end of it all you feel decidedly ill.

I was certain there would be no 'convivial confab' in London. Captain Lord would be kept on the stand until he explained once and for all why he had not gone to the aid of a ship in distress. He would be dragged up the mountain of truth to the clear, bright air of its summit.

I sat back down, poured another shot and thought about things. I resolved not to stay to hear Evans; nor would I go to Halifax to see the bodies. Instead I would return at once to Boston, give my daughter a hug, then board a fast steamer for England. The *Californian* was leaving for Liverpool tomorrow morning. I wanted to be there when she arrived.

CHAPTER 15

During the voyage across, the weather was calm but cold. I settled myself in the ship's library, organised my notes and papers, and started to write about Captain Lord. His admissions in Washington had, as I expected, made headlines – SAW ROCKETS AS *TITANIC* SANK, CAPTAIN ADMITS – but no paper attempted to explain why he didn't respond to the rockets, or whether he truly believed they weren't from the *Titanic*. They had not got down into his psyche, as Harriet would have put it; that was my task. I wandered the ship from keel to bridge, talking to sailors and learning the terminology; I scribbled notes and sketched diagrams. I tried to see things as Lord would see them. I began to work up a draft manuscript, but the more I wrote, the further the captain seemed to recede from me. He was like a pond covered with thick ice that I could not get beneath.

In the faces of both Max Blanck, owner of the Shirtwaist factory, and Bruce Ismay, owner of the *Titanic*, I'd seen a secret knowledge: the knowledge that they had done wrong. Blanck had climbed a ladder to safety and left his girl-workers to burn; Ismay had got into a lifeboat. 'There was a space in the lifeboat and I got into it,' Ismay said, as if it were the simplest thing in the world. But his face showed that he knew it wasn't that simple. In Lord's face I saw no such knowledge, no tormented conflict, no hints of a troubled conscience. I saw only a flatness, a polished, hard nothingness.

I pushed my manuscript aside. Perhaps, I thought, when I died my daughter could throw it into my coffin with me, and I could finish it in heaven, or in hell.

Then one night I asked the ship's second officer to let me stand awhile with him on the open bridge during his watch. I braced myself against the cold and watched ships' lights appear and disappear as they passed us by. I saw how deceptive they could be: a vessel that seemed small and close often turned out to be large and distant. I learned how vast and black the night was, how cold and hard starlight could be. I felt alone in space, sometimes drifting into strange reveries, imagining that the sea was bewitching me, trying to overwhelm my will, tempting me to jump in. When I shared my thoughts with the second officer he said, 'Men do, you know, during this very watch. They slip into a sort of daze – and over they go.'

The midnight watch: a time of loneliness, demons and trances. I was fascinated. So I took up my pen and paper once again. But this time I began to write not about Lord, but about Stone – the man who stood the watch. What would my story be, I wondered, if it left Lord in the shadows and lit up instead the shimmering, delicate mechanism of Herbert Stone?

When the ship was safely berthed in the River Mersey after our nine-day crossing, a letter was brought aboard for me by the ship's agent. It was from Harriet, and must have come across on a faster steamer. As I read it, I could hear her breathless voice. My daughter never did have much use for punctuation.

Dear Papa,

I am so very pleased you have followed that captain to the ends of the earth to sort it all out but you really did miss the most wonderful suffrage parade in New York and after all you did sign a parade slip and you did promise you would march by my side but never mind I wore my pit brow pants and Mama dispensed with her corset cover although not the corset altogether because you know how vain she is. We were led along by women on horseback and one was dressed as Joan of Arc!

But Papa I want to tell you the most important thing of all about the march and that is that at 9ᵗʰ Street all the industrial women joined us and there was a very special banner among them – all black with white letters saying 'We Want the Vote for Protection' – and it was carried by the mothers and sisters and friends of all the poor Triangle Shirtwaist girls who died. I called out three cheers to them and I thought of all you wrote about those young girls and how kind you were to them.

Papa, speaking of sad things, all your belongings from your newspaper office have been delivered here – boxes and papers and books and your photograph of Mama and me – and although Mama says we ought just throw it all out I don't think she really means it because she has stored everything very carefully in a room upstairs and hasn't even told Vivienne about it. You know what Vivienne would say about keeping your things here. It is very sad that you are not working for that paper any more but I think what you are doing now is much better and don't forget you will always have me to look after you. If you cable me your address as soon as you arrive I will write you a letter every single day because I know how much you like to hear from me.

Your loving daughter,
Harriet
PS: I have included a newspaper clipping of the funeral of poor Mr Astor which took place on the same day as the parade. I think you knew they found his body, didn't you?

I put down the letter with tears in my eyes. It made me think again that this century would definitely belong to the women. And it reminded me, too, that in following the *Californian* to England I had given up more than the suffragettes' parade, more than the *Titanic* bodies in Halifax, more than my job. For the time being, at least, I had given up my daughter.

I walked down the gangway and hailed a cab to take me to Scotland Road, where I knew Liverpool had its cheapest hotels.

I was surprised, as I wandered around Liverpool on a grey Saturday morning, at just what a grand and sombre place it was. St George's Hall was one of the largest buildings I'd ever seen. Its towering walls and columns seemed of a geological scale. The perfectly circular Picton Reading Room looked more like it might contain the city's gas supply than books. The hall beneath, I was told, was carved out of solid rock. Next door stood the great William Brown Library with its facades of rectangles, squares and triangles. I had never seen so many geometrical shapes – not even in New York. This wasn't London with its frivolous theatres and operas and tourists and its great folly of a bridge at the Tower. This was a city that manufactured things and shipped them out, that made its wealth from a thousand factories, mills and mines.

It was a place of ships. The River Mersey ebbed and flowed with them; there was no other port like it in the world. Men built ships here, and White Star and Cunard had their headquarters here; this was the port of registration of the *Mauretania*, the *Lusitania*, the *Olympic* and the *Titanic*. So when I took a seat in the atrium of the Picton Reading Room and flicked through newspapers from the past weeks, I wasn't surprised to find that the city had received a terrific wound. I traced the disaster from the early vague concerns about the vessel's safety – CONSTERNATION IN LIVERPOOL – through to the anguished shock when the worst was known: DEATH ROLL OF OVER 1,500. There were photographs of the ship, poems, diagrams, reports, sermons, lists of survivors and messages of sympathy. Some local people were known to have survived, but many others were missing. It was noted that a hundred members of the crew were from Liverpool. As in my own country's newspapers, much was said about the heroism of brave men – most notably that of Captain Smith and my old favourite, the craven-shooter Major Butt. The major's brother, it turned out, was a citizen of Liverpool.

In the interstices of this main story was another, small at first, but persistent. It was there from beginning to end: the early reports that the *Californian* had recovered bodies, the mystery ship seen from the *Titanic*, Captain Lord's tragic tale of a wireless not working, of no signals being seen, and finally Ernie Gill's affidavit about the rockets sighted and ignored. The papers reported Lord's 'sweeping denials' with gusto, and seemed to believe him, but when he admitted in Washington that his ship did see rockets after all, their tone became muted and doubtful. I thought I detected a note of shame, too, because Lord was one of their own. And when they reported his assertion that the rockets were not the *Titanic*'s, they raised a question that my own country's newspapers never had: but shouldn't he have gone anyway?

One article included a photograph, taken from an earlier, happier voyage, of the captain with his three officers on the deck of their ship. Stewart smiles beneath his enormous moustache, Groves gives a cheeky grin, and even Lord has half a smile. But Herbert Stone, the most handsome of the men, standing shoulder to shoulder with his captain, looks into the lens with troubled eyes, as if he can see the future. I perceived a delicate sensitivity and an extraordinary shyness. Why had this man ever gone to sea?

But the most interesting information of all was tucked away towards the back of a local newspaper, in the Shipping Movements section. It was in the very smallest of type and easy to miss. It said the *Californian* had arrived in Liverpool the previous afternoon, berthing in the Huskisson Dock. It had been a long, slow voyage from Boston, but Captain Lord and his men were home at last.

Bootle was only a few miles north of the city centre, but I was told it never had been and never would be part of Liverpool. 'It's an independent sort of place,' said the red-haired toothless landlady of my hotel as she served up stew and bread, 'and you best be careful going up there – with your strange accent an' all.' My stew began to cool and congeal, but the landlady continued to stand opposite me, watching and talking. 'There was Maggie Donoghue, brains bashed out by a fireman, and little Tommy Foy, chopped up at the age of six.'

'I'll be careful,' I said, stabbing at a potato with my fork.

'And those poor prostitutes – so many of 'em! Teapot Murders they was called, on account of the street where they happened being Lyons Street.'

'Lyons?'

'The tea. They call it the street which died o' shame, and you probably best keep clear of it.'

I arrived in Bootle in the late afternoon. An overcast sky threw a dull grey light onto things. There were soot-covered civic buildings made of stone, and rows of narrow, cramped terraces whose front steps opened directly onto the street. It was one of the most washed-out places I'd ever seen: there was no colour at all, no trees, no grass, no flowers, just black and grey stone. The mighty Mersey was close. I could hear its busy docks – the trundling of the elevated electric railway, the blowing of steam whistles and the clanging of metal. Black smoke belched from distant chimneys.

I soon reached my destination: a small terrace house crammed between its neighbours on Wadham Road. I knocked on a glossy black door and waited.

The young woman who opened it was perhaps in her early twenties, and quite beautiful. There was an eagerness about her, and a softness, that seemed at odds with her surroundings. Her hair, parted in the centre, swept down in two great side curls that sat just above her ears. She wore a white, collared blouse to which she had pinned a blue flower of some sort. It was the first bit of colour I'd seen that day.

'Yes?' she said.

I had, of course, prepared a ruse – a lie designed to persuade her to let me in – but something about her made me drop it. I simply told her my name and said that I'd come from America, which, of course, was no explanation at all of why I stood at her door.

Nonetheless she smiled. She seemed almost to be expecting me. 'Mr Steadman from America? Then you must be here to see my husband.' Her voice had a wonderful lilting music.

'I am,' I said.

'He came back only last night.'

'Yes,' I said. 'I know.'

'You'd better come through,' she said. 'We're having tea outside.' She led me down a narrow hall to an enclosed garden at the rear. A small table was laid with a teapot and cups, and seated at it, in a blue woollen sweater most probably knitted by his wife, was the man I had been trying so hard to speak to for so many weeks.

He was naturally surprised to see me. He stood quickly, looking from me to his wife and back again. The whites of his eyes were washed with pink; I thought, perhaps, he had been crying. I extended my hand. He hesitated, but then shook it.

'Hello, Mr Stone,' I said.

The last time I'd seen him was in the chartroom of his ship, in Boston, when he was defending his captain. Today he seemed tired: there were pouches of soft skin under his eyes and a tiny cluster of broken capillaries in the centre of one cheek. But he had still a strange beauty.

When I asked if he remembered me, he said of course he did. 'I'm not allowed to speak to pressmen,' he said. 'The captain has forbidden it. The company has forbidden it.'

'But I'm not a pressman any more,' I said. 'My newspaper fired me.'

'Then what are you?' he asked.

'Must I be something, other than a friend?'

Mrs Stone had brought up a chair for me, but he did not yet invite me to sit. The three of us stood facing each other around the table. 'The captain said, in Boston, that I must never speak to you – I mean, *especially* to you.'

'But is he your captain while you're here, in your own garden?'

Stone looked to his wife again, as if asking her what to do. 'Let's sit,' she said. 'If Mr Steadman has come all the way from America, then we must at least give him tea.'

But Stone did not sit. 'Captain Lord says you were the one who printed Ernie Gill's story.'

'I am.' I waited. Perhaps he expected me to apologise. 'It was the right thing to do,' I said. I hoped he remembered what I'd written on the card I gave him when we spoke outside his chartroom: 'Not your fault.'

At last we sat, but for some time no one spoke. The garden was a peaceful, private place – even in the weak grey light the flowers glowed, as if lit from within. Mrs Stone, to break the silence, began to give me their names. 'Hyacinths,' she said as I reached down to caress their unfamiliar blue petals. 'And over there – tulips, daffodils and bluebells. We sit out here to catch the last of the light,' she went on. 'It's only a small garden, but I do love it. All these little splashes of life. It gives me something to care for while Herbert's away.'

Yes, I thought, it would be lonely in this hard city without him.

She held towards me a cup of tea. I would have preferred gin, which I'd been told the English drank from teacups, but I accepted the milky brown liquid. Mrs Stone laughed politely at me as I picked up the cup by its rim, rather than its dainty handle.

She asked me about myself – about America, my voyage across, my impressions of England. Her disarming gentleness drew me out. I spoke of Boston, of my daughter, of the suffragettes' parade in New York, of how times were changing. She nodded and smiled and said the vote must come eventually, although she did not approve of the window-smashing in London. That, she said, was a step too far.

'Sometimes you need to be brave,' I said. 'It's an extraordinary sort of courage.'

'Perhaps. But that's a sort I do not have, or want.'

All the while I studied her face for any hint of shame. The Liverpool newspapers had, after all, over the past weeks been filled with stories of the *Titanic*'s rockets being seen and ignored by her husband. But I saw only solicitude and courtesy. The three of us, taking tea around the table in the garden, were like passengers in a little boat safely moored at the dock.

I decided to push the boat out a bit. I told her how grief-stricken the American nation was about the *Titanic*. Mrs Stone did not flinch or hesitate at this first mention of the disaster. No cloud passed across her face; her brows did not furrow. She said, simply, that it was a very tragic thing, but that the ship's captain should never have been going at that speed – at night, with ice about.

Herbert Stone, tapping his teeth with his fingers, said nothing.

I pushed the boat out a little further. I spoke of my interest in the children who died. I said that there'd been barely a mention of them in the papers, either in America or here; that it was hard to find out anything about them. You could read column after column about Mr Astor or Mr Guggenheim, I said, but nothing about the children. 'There were fifty-three of them left behind,' I added, sipping my weak tea. 'But no one seems to care much about them.'

Mrs Stone stirred her tea.

'Or even know about them,' I continued.

Her spoon touched gently the rim of her cup. 'We have no children,' she said, as if that fact alone made all children irrelevant. She looked away.

I tried to lighten the mood. I laughed about how Senator Smith in America had asked a *Titanic* officer what icebergs were made of.

Herbert Stone had all the while been sitting still and silent, but now he spoke. 'It's not such a silly question,' he said. 'Icebergs can have rocks, earth, and there can be air, too, trapped in them.'

'I didn't know that,' I said.

'They can be beautiful,' he went on. 'I saw three that very afternoon, when I was taking my sights – great tall things they were, with high cliffs and flat tops. I'd never seen anything like them.'

Here was my chance. 'And you also saw some the next morning, I think?'

He poured himself some more tea but did not offer me any. 'Why are you here, Mr Steadman?'

'I've come to observe the London inquiry. I want to write about it.'

'No. I mean *here* – right here, in my house, with us, now.'

I couldn't tell whether his question was defensive or aggressive or pleading. 'I wanted,' I began, 'to talk to you in Boston – in private. Mr Thomas had allowed it. He was to organise our meeting, but the business with the marshal, and Washington, intervened.' For a moment I saw again the pained, shy eyes I'd seen on the *Californian*. 'I wondered then,' I continued, 'and I wonder now, whether there's some way I might help you.'

'Help me?' Stone gave a short, dismissive laugh. 'When you said in Boston that you would help me, you were all the while arranging to publish the story of Mr Gill. That's how you helped me then. Heaven knows how you plan to help me now.'

'I do remember, Mr Stone, what I said, but I also remember what you said – that you saw no signals that night.' I paused. Mrs Stone put down her cup. 'But now, here in England, will you admit what you saw?'

Stone stood up and extended his hand. 'Goodbye, Mr Steadman. I'm sorry if you've wasted your time.'

'Perhaps,' I said, standing slowly and taking his hand, 'publishing Mr Gill's affidavit might, in the end, help you very much.'

Mrs Stone showed me out. At the door I thanked her and asked where I might find a nearby public house. She gave me some directions and then held my cold hands in her own. 'I'm sorry,' she said, 'that you have to leave so soon.'

'You have absolutely nothing to be sorry for,' I said.

I had not been drinking for more than ten minutes in the local tavern – a dark, squat building lying low among the odorous vapours of the Mersey – when I was interrupted by none other than Mrs Stone herself. She strode into the small room and drew up a chair at my table, panting a little. 'You were able to follow my directions, then,' she said. 'I'm glad I found you.'

I stood and bowed and said the pleasure was all mine.

'I had to come,' she said, dabbing her face with a handkerchief, 'to tell you that you are wrong.'

'I often am,' I said, smiling.

'About the children, I mean,' she went on. 'The *Titanic* children. When you said that nobody knew or cared about them, you were wrong.'

She produced from her handbag a folded newspaper clipping and slid it across the table to me. NORFOLK FAMILY OF ELEVEN WHO WERE WIPED OUT IN THE *TITANIC* DISASTER ran the headline above a photograph. 'The first photograph published of the Sage family,' the caption read, 'all the eleven members of which went down in the *Titanic*. The group shows the father and mother with their five boys and four girls.' Every one of the children's names was set out, and the piece went on: 'Mr and Mrs Sage kept an inn at Gaywood, near King's Lynn, on the main road to Sandringham, and afterward moved to Peterborough, where they had a business in Gladstone Street. Some time ago Mr Sage decided to emigrate to Jacksonville, Florida, where he intended to start fruit-farming, and the family were on the way to the land of their adoption.'

I had not so far, in all of the hundreds of pages of newsprint I'd read about the disaster, seen a single image of any of the children who died. But now, in my hands, I saw nine of them. And they were all from the one family.

'You see, we do care,' Mrs Stone said. I didn't know who she meant by 'we' – she and her husband? Liverpool? England? humanity? – but it didn't matter. I studied the photograph. The Sage family had positioned themselves stiffly and formally in front of their large, perfectly square brick house. The shot had been taken from a distance but I could see the children clearly enough: a girl sulking near a window, a boy standing with his little sister and looking dreamily into the middle distance, two children sitting precariously on a wall, a handsome young man in a doorway, and the eldest son sitting on a horse. The father was leaning nervously near a window, his arms crossed. The mother, straight-backed and tight-corsetted, sat with a little boy on her lap. And there, in the centre of the photograph, the eldest daughter stood tall in her bleached-white shirtwaist, her hair high and wild.

I slid the clipping back across the table and Mrs Stone replaced it in her handbag. 'He knows their names,' she said. 'Every one. He has memorised them.'

I drained my ale. 'It's very sad,' I said, 'to think of all those children drowning.'

'But they didn't drown,' she said. 'I know that's what the newspaper says, but please don't think they drowned. My husband told me – they had lifejackets on, and the water would have taken the heat from their little bodies very quickly. Soon they would have stopped shivering and by the end they'd have felt quite warm.'

'Quite warm?' I smiled. 'Among the icebergs?'

'Yes,' she said, without a trace of doubt or irony. 'Quite, quite warm.'

It was an odd phrase, and I took out my notebook and wrote it down. *Quite, quite warm.* I tried to imagine the children floating in their lifejackets in that black and forbidding water feeling quite, quite warm. There was comfort in the idea – it was much better than thinking of them struggling for breath – and if it was comforting for me, I supposed it must be a hundred times so for Mrs Stone's husband.

For a time we did not speak. Mrs Stone seemed nervous, as if she were building up courage to tell me something. Her eyes darted about and she ran her fingers through her great sweeping side curls. She adjusted and readjusted her green and white necktie, which reminded me of a schoolboy's. Hard Merseyside men stared at her – she was the only woman in the tavern. 'Would you mind terribly,' she asked, 'if we went somewhere else?'

'Of course not,' I said. 'Wherever you like.'

I followed her from the tavern to the street outside. The sun had set long ago but the twilight lingered. We climbed some narrow stairs and walked along a series of laneways between cavernous brick buildings. We crossed a footbridge above a freight railway, then climbed more stairs and arrived at a wrought-iron bench set in a patch of grass not much bigger than the bench itself. We sat and caught our breath.

Behind us, somewhere, was 'the street that died o' shame' and the ghosts of Maggie Donoghue and Tommy Foy. In front of us lay the great yards, warehouses and cranes of the Merseyside wharves. Gulls swooped and soared and the shouts of men drifted up from the piers. Through narrow gaps between buildings I could see the flat grey sheet of the river moving bodily and silently.

Mrs Stone told me that her husband's ship was down there

somewhere, being unloaded. 'He's a good man, you know.'

'Yes,' I said. 'I do know.'

She frowned a little. I did not think she'd expected such a quick and compliant response. She had been preparing herself for debate. 'Do you think the people in London – at the inquiry – will see that he is?'

'If he speaks the truth, I think they will.' I leaned back a little and lit a cigarette.

'When you said,' Mrs Stone continued after a time, 'this afternoon, in our garden, that you could help him, what did you mean?'

'I could write his side of the story,' I said. 'I could explain it all.'

She looked at me awhile, thinking. 'You could show people that he's a good man?'

'I could try,' I said.

'How would you do it?'

'I could describe you,' I said, smiling. 'Perhaps that would be enough.'

Mrs Stone laughed. This higher space seemed to calm her, to open her out, and she began to tell me about her husband's voyage to Boston, and how difficult it had all been. She told me of his childhood – of a sensitive boy who loved books growing up among the granite and limestone of Devon, of a cruel father who stuffed rags in his mouth and told him not to cry. Herbert's father had once drowned kittens in a bag and forced his son to watch.

'His father was an odd man,' Mrs Stone said. 'When I first met him he made me hold his hands so I could feel how rough they were. Then he gripped me tighter and tighter, and when I cried out he just laughed. "A little princess," he said. "Herbert's got himself a little princess . . ."' She winced at the memory.

'Was Herbert scared of him?'

'A little. He always tried to please him, but never could.'

She told me how hard Herbert had worked to get his First Mate's Certificate and to obtain his position as second officer on the *Californian*. He'd looked forward to working with Captain Lord, whom he knew to be one of Leyland's best skippers. But he'd been disappointed: for some reason, the captain seemed not to like him. Herbert had made some mistakes – small ones, but the captain never forgot them. 'My husband is a shy man,' Mrs Stone said. 'The captain need only have encouraged him a little.'

Life at sea was difficult, but Herbert had made a go of it. The encouragement he did not get from his captain he found in his books. He loved the American novel *Moby-Dick* most of all, and hoped always to be as loyal to his captain as Starbuck was to Ahab.

'Even unto death?' I asked.

'Unto death,' she said, again without doubt or irony.

Mrs Stone looked at me with beautiful eyes. A delicate wetness had formed at their edges and in one there was a single tear. 'Please do write his story,' she said. 'I would be grateful.'

'I will write it,' I said, 'and I will do it justice.'

'Do you promise?'

'I do.'

She took from her handbag the photograph of the Sage family and handed it to me. 'Then you must keep this,' she said. 'I have a spare. And remember: he knows their names. Every single one.'

I had three days before the *Californian* witnesses were due to give their evidence in London, so the following morning, Sunday, I said goodbye to Liverpool and took a train to Peterborough in Cambridgeshire. The journey lasted more than four hours but I was glad I took the trouble. The air flowed more freely through this town than through Liverpool. Parks sparkled with the moisture of spring and lace curtains swayed gently in open windows. I ate a boiled egg and drank some gin at the station bar then walked the short distance to Gladstone Street. On the corner of Hankey Street I stopped before a small bakery nestled up against a long row of broad, two-storey brick terraces.

Outside, withered flowers were piled in an empty bread crate. When I stepped closer I saw an assortment of cards among them. 'God Bless You John and Annie, and your dear, dear children. How sad we are for you.' 'For Fred, Gone to a Better Place, from Management, Lane Brickworks.' I saw one note in a child's handwriting: 'To my Freind Connie who Sleeps with the Angels.' This last was accompanied by a small drawing in light, feathery strokes of a stick-like figure lying back on what may have been wings, or otherwise the petals of a flower.

I knocked on the door of the bakery but there was no answer. An elderly woman emerged from the adjoining house to tell me that the family – the new family – were away for the day on a picnic. I asked her if she had known the Sages.

'Of course,' she said. 'They were my neighbours.'

I asked if she might be so kind as to tell me a little about them. 'Whatever you like,' she said, holding her door open for me. She showed me to a seat in her front parlour and brought tea and cakes. She was an ample woman, with teeth as brown as wood and a surprising cluster of jewels at her throat. Her name, she said, spreading herself on the sofa, was Mrs Goddard, with no children and a husband long dead.

She spoke freely, as if I were an old friend. The Sages, she explained, had bought the bakery next door two or three years ago. They'd lived in rooms above and behind it. In one corner of the large yard was a deep well, in which one of the girls, young Dolly, had nearly drowned. 'After that,' Mrs Goddard said, sucking crumbs from her fingers, 'Annie had the well filled in and swore that her girls would never go near water again. Never. And now – just think of it! – they've *all* drowned.'

I thought about telling her that they'd died of cold, not drowning, but Mrs Goddard had already moved on. She told me that the town of Peterborough was so terribly sad about what had happened. Nobody could bear to take the flowers away. 'We will never forget them,' she said, dabbing at her eyes with the loose sleeve of her blouse. She told me of John Sage, the father, an adventurer who dragged his family hither and thither in search of fortune. The children, she said, were high-spirited. The middle boys, Doug and Fred, played rugby and bounced their chests together like seals; one of them had done some bricklaying. The youngest boy, Tom, not much more than a baby, had golden curls, and the youngest girl was an excellent mimic. Eleven-year-old William dreamt his days away and was forever getting lost. He cried once when he saw a caterpillar eaten by a sparrow. 'The mother was too soft with that boy,' Mrs Goddard said. 'I don't know why. Somehow his gentle ways mesmerised her. He was her favourite.'

But the most impressive of all the children, she said, was Stella, the eldest daughter. She was an excellent dressmaker, but in recent months had put away her sewing machine and collected signatures in support of the London window-smashers instead. She was only nineteen but had spoken at the town hall through a speaking trumpet and travelled alone to London, in defiance of her mother and father. 'Such spirit that girl had,' Mrs Goddard said, standing up to take a folded newspaper from the drawer of a side table. She opened the paper to a double-page spread of thirty or so inch-square images of people lost on the *Titanic*. 'There,' she said, pointing to one of them, 'that's her.'

I was astounded by what I saw: the high spirits, the wilfulness, the playfulness. Stella Sage was not smiling, but she seemed to be on the verge of an explosion of laughter. There was such mischief in her eyes that I nearly laughed myself. I saw in that picture a girl with an inexhaustible fund of strength and an unstoppable drive for life. In short, I saw my own daughter.

'She never wanted to go,' said Mrs Goddard. 'Her work was in London, not the farms of Florida.' She took back the clipping and looked again at Stella's photograph. 'I liked her most of all.'

'I'm sure she was extraordinary,' I said.

As I accepted one more of Mrs Goddard's little cakes, I wondered how it was that this young woman who'd given public speeches and travelled to London by herself had been unable to find her way into a lifeboat. And how could it be that not one of her brothers and sisters had been saved?

CHAPTER 16

Samuel Johnson said that if you are tired of London you are tired of life. I must have been tired of life. It was the midst of the London Season and as I walked along I was buffeted by men in top hats and women clutching theatre programs. It was warm – so warm that people sweated and grunted on the underground train and complained that it was as hot as midsummer. On the streets trams rang their bells, automobiles broke down and horses fought for space. I smelled gasoline, spring flowers and excrement all at once. The newspapers advertised matinées and evening performances at a hundred theatres. The hotels were full; I found no lodgings until I drifted south across Waterloo Bridge and took a room in a cramped hotel in the shadow of the railway station. The station, the desk clerk told me, was being rebuilt – during the day there would be dust and noise, which was why the rate was so reasonable.

I laughed when I saw the room: a narrow bed, a thin cupboard and a desk squeezed into a space no more than two yards across. But the hotel was within walking distance of Buckingham Gate, where the *Titanic* inquiry was being held, so I signed the register and wired my new address to my daughter. I then lay on my bed and drank myself to sleep.

The next morning I woke early. I wanted to be sure of a good seat at the inquiry. The day was overcast but still warm and as I walked across Westminster Bridge swampy vapours drifted up from the river. The grass in St James's Park was lush with a heavy wetness and the flowers along Buckingham Gate sagged with the weight of bumblebees.

At half past nine I arrived at the Scottish Drill Hall. It was a vast place with three or four hundred folding chairs on the main floor and in two galleries above. There were towering walls, acres of oak panelling, and floorboards polished by years of soldiers' marching boots. At the front of the hall was a raised chair for Lord Mersey, the Commissioner, and to the left and right were lower chairs for his assisting assessors. Before them were rows of desks for the barristers and solicitors. The witness stand – a small, flimsy desk on a raised platform surrounded by a thin rail – was an exposed, vulnerable place. Mounted behind it was a model of the *Titanic*'s starboard side, perhaps twenty feet in length, and a large chart of the North Atlantic. A little further along, hanging from an upper gallery, was an enormous cross-section of the ship's interior.

It was wise of me to arrive early. Very soon there was a crowd of people bustling to find seats, and by ten o'clock the hall was full. Feathered hats bobbed impatiently and there was much tut-tutting. People grumbled about the acoustics, about the insects, about the uncomfortable chairs: there ought to be someone to show you where to sit; it was too hot and the curtains made it hotter; it was impossible to hear anything from such a distance. The reason the hall was so full, I learned from a newspaperman sitting next to me, was that two famous survivors of the disaster were due to give evidence that morning. Sir Cosmo Duff-Gordon was said to have bribed the crewmen of his lifeboat not to row back for survivors, and Lady Duff-Gordon, his wife, was said to have complained about the loss of her secretary's beautiful new nightdress. London society had turned out to hear how this couple might defend themselves.

Just before half past ten there was a hush. An usher called for us to stand and be silent, and in swept Lord Mersey and his five nautical assessors. They sat, and a barrister stood up and began to speak. My pressman neighbour told me the speaker was Sir Rufus Isaacs, KC, the Attorney-General. I struggled to understand what he was saying – his back was to us and he spoke quickly in a soft drone, as if already bored – but I could tell that something was wrong. A murmur sprang up in the watching crowd. Chair legs scraped on the floor. Soon Lord Mersey announced that the *Lusitania* had been delayed on its voyage from New York. The Duff-Gordons would not be appearing today.

There was rustling and whispering in the hall and some people got up to leave. The usher asked for silence. He was ignored, but through the noise I could hear fragments of what the Attorney-General was saying to the Commissioner. There were 'some other witnesses' due to give evidence today and he proposed to call them now. This was followed by unhappy mumbling from Lord Mersey, but Isaacs went on. 'The reason, as your lordship will appreciate, is that we cannot always get them here. They are here today and I think it will be convenient to examine them now.'

Seated in the very front row of the public part of the hall, neatly dressed and huddled together, were the men of the *Californian*. I was behind them and many yards distant but I could see them clearly enough: Lord, Stewart, Groves, Gibson and Evans. Stone sat alone, separated from the other men by an empty seat. He was looking down at his lap, nodding his head gently and mouthing words silently to himself.

Isaacs, turning towards these men, gave a quick nod and Captain Lord stood up. The audience fell silent. I sensed their puzzlement: no one knew who he was. They saw only a tall man in a dark blue suit with a shiny bald head. In a moment he was at the witness desk.

'This,' said Isaacs to Lord Mersey, 'is the master of the Leyland steamship *Californian* of Liverpool.'

Slowly Isaacs turned to Lord, and as if to double-check his facts asked, '*Are* you the master of the SS *Californian* of Liverpool?'

In Boston, in his chartroom, Lord had seemed monumental – in his square black uniform with its golden epaulettes that shone like beacons – but here, in his civilian suit, in this grand hall, he looked small.

'Yes, I am,' he said quietly, staring straight back at his questioner. Neither the Commissioner nor the Attorney-General, I noticed, had done him the courtesy of using his name.

No matter. I knew it. He was Stanley Lord – Lord of the *Californian* – preparing for one last time to tell his story.

It took two days for the *Californian* witnesses to give their evidence. At times they threw their words into the hall with defiance and clarity, even pride; at others they looked at their feet and mumbled sulkily, as might petulant schoolboys in a headmaster's office. The Commissioner listened carefully throughout, encouraging, reprimanding, cajoling, and trying to make sense of the events being described to him. He seemed perplexed. Eight rockets fired by the *Titanic* and eight rockets seen by the *Californian*: what other conclusion could there be? When the round-faced, bright-eyed Groves was asked whether he thought the ship they saw was the *Titanic*, he said, 'Most decidedly I do.'

Stewart and Stone, on oath under the penetrating gaze of the Commissioner, no longer had the courage for the blatant lies they'd told in Boston. Who was on the bridge at the relevant time? 'Mr Stone was on watch,' Stewart conceded, rather meekly. 'I turned in about half past nine.' And were any signals seen? 'I saw white rockets bursting in the sky,' Stone admitted. 'I informed the master.'

Yet Lord, for hour after hour, denied absolutely that it was the *Titanic* they'd seen. Staring straight ahead with unwavering eyes, he spoke of company signals, of rockets answering Morse lamps, of rockets fired by a ship that was definitely not the *Titanic*. He said these things and seemed to believe them. His hands were never clenched and never in his pockets. There was the light of the sincere about him, and the wise. At times he seemed to smile inwardly, like a priest in possession of profound knowledge that others could not share.

'What is in my brain at the present time is this,' said the Commissioner, addressing Isaacs but looking directly at Lord. 'What they saw was the *Titanic*. That is what is in my brain.'

'I know,' said Isaacs, turning towards Lord to see what effect the Commissioner's words might have. 'I know.'

Lord did not flinch. He made no response at all. He simply stared into the middle distance like a man who, with his head in a noose, sees through to some greater truth beyond this world.

At the end of the second day, when it was all over, I followed the *Californian* witnesses out into the street. Stewart gathered them together and kept them away from the press. Even in this broad public place hundreds of miles from their ship, the men did what they were bidden. Lord was not among them. I was told he'd returned already to Liverpool; he needed to get back to his ship. But that evening I saw a photograph of him in a newspaper, standing alone in his immaculate double-breasted suit. His bowler hat, starched collar and long umbrella gave him the look of a London gentleman. The nobility of his face was clear, with its sharp lines, powerful jaw and high cheekbones. But due to some fault in the printing process his eyes appeared as blank white circles, without pupils, like a ghost's, or a demon's.

For days afterwards I sat in my room in the Waterloo hotel, going through my notes. I had a promise to keep, but how to do so with such confusing material? I had thought I'd return to Boston after the *Californian* witnesses had made their appearance at the inquiry, but my writing about Herbert Stone had become something of a mania. I sketched scenes of his childhood and youth – his father's workroom, his father drowning kittens, his early days at sea – and tried to convey something of his nervous shyness. 'Herbert Stone,' I wrote at the beginning of my manuscript, 'tapped his teeth with his fingers as if playing a small piano.' I bought and read as much as I could of the novel *Moby-Dick* so that I might better understand his dreams and motivations.

But I had not been able to push my storyline past the moment when, in the chartroom of his ship, Stone lied for his captain. It had been loyal – Starbuck-loyal – but it also disabled him. I remembered it well: as Stone spoke he'd taken on something of the glazed exterior of his captain and retreated deep into himself. His lie had conveyed him far away from who he was, and by the time he appeared before the inquiry in London he seemed to have disappeared completely. He'd stood on the witness stand, grasping its thin rail for support, and given answers of a peculiar emptiness.

So I wrote to Mrs Stone and asked for her help. She had not spoken to me at the inquiry, at her husband's request, but I thought she might do so now. What, I asked, had she thought of Herbert's testimony? Did she think he might agree to see me? She replied at once: her husband was now back at sea on the *Californian*, and as for his answers in London, all she could say was that he'd done his very best.

But she also told me a third thing: although her husband had rejoined the *Californian*, Captain Lord had not. The Leyland Line had suspended him. It was, Mrs Stone wrote, all so very sad: the captain had removed his belongings from the ship without saying a word to anyone. He would not even let the apprentice help him. 'But Herbert was the most upset of all,' she wrote, and added one final detail: when the captain walked with his bags from his cabin for the last time, Herbert said, 'I'm sorry, Captain,' and extended his hand to say goodbye. But the captain had not taken it. He just turned away, saying, 'Yes, I am sure you are.'

CHAPTER 17

In late May, when the days grew long and young women in green trousers took to the Serpentine in rowboats, I received a letter from Harriet begging me to come home. Her mother had become impossible in the summer heat; something had gone wrong in a séance and Vivienne was angry about it. But still I stayed in England. For the time being, my daughter was on her own.

A few days later I received a surprising transatlantic telegram from my old friend Jack Thomas. 'To John Steadman and his engine man,' it read, 'my hearty thanks for nothing.' I didn't know what he meant, until I saw in the London papers that Senator Smith had delivered his findings. Large sections of his speech and report to the Senate were published verbatim, and what I read shocked me. 'It is not a pleasant duty to criticise the conduct or comment upon the shortcomings of others,' Smith had said to the United States Senate, 'but the plain truth should be told.' And that plain truth was that Captain Lord had been informed of the *Titanic*'s distress rockets and done nothing. Had he gone to them, 'there is a very strong probability that every human life that was sacrificed through this disaster could have been saved'.

Every human life. I drank more gin and loosened my shirt.

Smith demanded 'drastic action' by the government of England against not only Captain Lord, but the owners of his ship, which were, Smith pointed out, also the owners of the *Titanic*. He offered a devastating comparison: 'Contrast, if you will, the conduct of the captain of the *Carpathia* in this emergency . . . By his utter self-effacement and his own indifference to peril, by his promptness and his knightly sympathy, he rendered a great service to humanity. He should be made to realise the debt of gratitude this nation owes to him!'

What must Jack Thomas have made of it all? He had asked me to write him a hero, and instead, here on the public record forever, was a statement that Cunard was a company of action and 'knightly sympathy', while the International Mercantile Marine was a company of inaction and indifference. Captain Smith of the IMM sank the *Titanic* and Captain Lord of the IMM left her passengers to die.

And what effect must these words have had on Lord himself? Senator Smith's speech had been published in every newspaper across America and England. There could be no wider audience. Just how could his convivial chitchat with the folksy American senators have yielded such poisonous results?

More was to come. At the end of July, in London's high summer, I sat among the hushed men and women of the Scottish Drill Hall to hear Lord Mersey deliver his sombre, measured report on the disaster. He began reading just after ten o'clock, and just before noon he reached the part of his findings dealing with the *Californian*. His words had a hypnotic monotony as he described the eight rockets fired by the *Titanic* and the eight rockets seen by the *Californian*.

'It was suggested that the rockets seen by the *Californian* were from some other ship, not the *Titanic*,' he said. 'But no other ship to fit this theory has ever been heard of.' He read on with the steady rhythm of a pendulum clock, as if he were intoning a liturgy. 'When she first saw the rockets, the *Californian* could have pushed through the ice to the open water without any serious risk and so have come to the assistance of the *Titanic*.' His final words echoed Senator Smith's and were shocking in their simplicity: 'Had she done so she might have saved many if not all of the lives that were lost.'

Every person in the hall was silent. They had registered something astonishing in Lord Mersey's flat words. Newspapermen rushed out to write their merciless headlines. 'This portion of the report,' *The Daily Telegraph* declared the next day, 'stands out as a thing apart – a horror which in the days to come will wound the human instinct of the race wherever the story of the *Titanic* is recounted.'

I had once suspected that this story would disgrace a nation, and I was right.

For a time I remained sitting in the hall. I thought about Liverpool's monolithic buildings and its proud, serious men. Captain Lord could not stay there, I thought. He must take himself away, to an island, a cave, a mountain top – any place where the surging sea crashing onto rocks, or the jagged cries of swooping gulls might drown out the memory of what his own country had said about him.

But two weeks later, an acquaintance of mine at a London newspaper told me he'd heard from a source within the Board of Trade that the board had received a letter from Captain Lord. The captain wasn't hiding in a cave, then, or on an island, but sitting in his parlour writing letters. What, I wondered, did he have to say?

I secured an interview with Sydney Buxton, the President of the

Board. His office, in a narrow brick building squeezed between the granite masterpieces of Whitehall, was cramped and hot. Buxton sat behind a large mahogany desk too big for the room. He was thin and wiry, perhaps sixty years old, with an overhanging upper lip and a small tuft of hair that sat on top of his head like the feathers of an exotic bird. He had poured me a drink – a very fine whisky – which I sipped as he read the letter of introduction I'd given him. In his usual overblown style, Senator William Alden Smith of Michigan asked Mr Buxton to render me every assistance in relation to the *Titanic* disaster, and in particular the conduct of the *Californian*. 'If he could give such assistance,' Smith went on, 'he would be owed a very great debt by the entirety of the American Nation, which was desirous of seeing that justice be done.' The letter was written on the striking blue letterhead of the United States Senate, and I need hardly say that I had written every word of it myself.

Buxton accepted the letter unquestioningly – perhaps because Senator Smith had made it so very clear to the world that the American people expected 'drastic action' in relation to Captain Lord. The Leyland Line had done its duty; Lord had been sacked. Now it was the turn of the British government.

'Very well, then,' Buxton said, turning his face into the breeze of an electric fan that had been placed on a nearby table. The fan whirred loudly in an irregular way; I wondered whether it generated more heat than air. 'What does your senator want us to do?'

'Captain Lord, I think, has written to you?' I asked.

'He has.'

'Perhaps I could see that correspondence?'

Buxton pushed across to me a large brown envelope, from which I withdrew two thin sheets of paper. The handwriting was precise, the slope of the letters perfectly parallel. Lord asked, in short, that the board overturn the London inquiry's findings in relation to the *Californian*. The Commissioner, Lord wrote, had got it all wrong. The ship they saw that night could not possibly have been the *Titanic*: her lights were too dim, and she moved. The *Titanic* had bright lights and was stopped. Lord wrote of times, positions and bearings.

I had heard all this before. But then, at the end of the letter, I read: 'If you consider there was any laxity aboard the *Californian* the night in question, I respectfully draw your attention to the information given here, which was given in evidence, which proves that any laxity was not on my part.' And: 'I fail to see why I should have to put up with all the public odium, through no fault or neglect on my part.'

This admission of laxity was entirely new. He had made no such concession in Washington or London. But it came with a sting in its tail: the laxity was not on his part, and of course there was only one other candidate. I didn't like it. I have never liked it when a strong man tries to blame a weak one.

'He has lost his position, of course, with Leyland,' Buxton said when I'd finished reading. 'He's on the beach – and will be for a long time.' The board president was perhaps hinting that this was punishment enough. 'It's a bad business,' he continued, pinching his nose. 'A bad, bad business.'

'Yes,' I said. 'It is.'

'Does your man,' Buxton went on, holding up the senator's letter, 'want us to send the captain to prison? We could, of course.'

I hesitated. Lord's letter had made me angry. It contained not one particle of regret or remorse. I did not a see a man planning to retreat from the world, only a man making excuses for himself and blaming others. I thought about what Mrs Stone had told me of her husband: how he had trusted his captain; how he had, in a way, loved him; how he'd hoped to be as loyal to him as Starbuck had to Ahab, unto death.

I remembered Stone bravely telling his lies in Boston because Lord had told him to. Herbert Stone deserved more from his captain, I thought, than this nasty little letter.

'It would be better,' I said at last, 'for Lord to stand up and take it on the chin, to admit to his mistake and say sorry.'

Buxton narrowed his face and breathed hard through his nose, making a soft whistling sound. He seemed to be a man perpetually short of air. 'But it's rather a lot, isn't it,' he said, 'to take on the chin? I mean, all those people – dead.'

Both of us sat quietly for a moment. I was sweating just a little. Buxton poured me another drink, and one for himself. 'Tell me, then,' he pressed, standing now to look out of the window, 'tell me – because I will take note of it – what does your man in Washington want me to do?'

I looked again at Lord's letter lying on the desk before me. I made a mental note of the address written neatly at the top of the page: 10 Ormond Street, Liscard. I imagined him sitting in his house, 'on the beach', waiting, thinking. I thought, too, of his wife and son.

'The senator says,' I replied after a while, 'only that he wants justice to be done – you can see it there in his letter.'

'Yes, yes, I can see that. But what *is* justice, in this case?' Buxton turned away from the window and looked at me over the top of his spectacles.

'Perhaps,' I offered, 'only that the captain be at last made to tell the truth?'

Buxton's puzzled look developed into a smile and then a short, swallowed laugh. 'Make him tell the truth?' he echoed. 'Oh, you Americans really are wonderful!'

I did not think myself so very wonderful, nor my idea of getting Lord to tell the truth so very silly, so the next day, a warm Thursday in mid-August, I took an early train north.

Liscard was a pretty village in the newly formed borough of Wallasey, located, as Lord himself had told me, on the Wirral Peninsula, across the River Mersey from Liverpool. On my map I saw parks, woodlands and walking trails, and places with such names as Port Sunlight and Woodchurch. It was all very pleasant and when I alighted from the electric train at Wallasey village I noticed at once the soft quality of the light. The green of the parks and trees was tinged with gold as if sunset were near, although it was just before noon. There were three or four automobiles on the street and a horse or two, but people seemed mostly to walk. This was not Bootle. There were no ghosts of murdered children or butchered prostitutes roaming these streets, only boys with clean white collars and girls with skipping ropes hung casually over their shoulders.

I dropped off my suitcase at a guesthouse in the village and then strolled north along the main road. I bore left at a junction, walked past a large stone church, and soon arrived at the low hills and white sand traps of the Wallasey golf course. There was a clubhouse of red brick with high, decorated gables, and inside the proprietor showed me to a lounge with a great vaulted ceiling and tall windows. There was no bar, but I was told I might order drinks by ringing a small bell that he handed me.

I sat at a secluded corner table and waited, ringing as often as I dared, until in the late afternoon I heard the laughter and talk of a group of golfers returning from their game. When they appeared in the lounge – well-fed men with stomachs straining at the buttons of colourful shirts – a waitress brought a round of ales to their table.

And there he was, off to one side, taller than the others, standing quietly in crisp white trousers and a red-check sweater. He did not see me. He stood while the others sat, and smoked his pipe while they drank. He said things from time to time, in that deep voice of his, but there was something wooden in his exchanges. He spoke of the weather, and made a joke about the state of the fairways, but the laughter of the men was strained. They responded to him with a studied politeness.

'I play every Thursday,' Lord had told me on the train to Washington. 'For the game, you understand, not the social side.' And true to his word, when the men rang their bell for a second round of ales, Lord did not stay. He took his leave and I quickly paid for my drinks and followed him.

Waiting outside was a woman I assumed to be his wife – tall, strong and severe – pushing a perambulator holding a large, round-faced boy. The boy looked to be three or four years old – too old, I thought, to be in a pram. Lord perhaps thought the same, because as soon as he'd embraced his wife he lifted the child out so that the boy might trot along with them as they walked. But the son did not walk for long. Even from a distance I could hear his complaining – there was a stone in his shoe, an insect in his hair – and eventually his mother lifted him back into the pram. There his whining continued, and his father strode ahead – to be out of earshot, I supposed.

Lord never once looked around. We walked for a mile or so: the main road back to Wallasey village, a road towards the east, a small path across a sports field. Soon enough, the Lords arrived at their home and opened the front door.

I thought about calling out to them before they disappeared inside, but there was no need. Mrs Lord unexpectedly turned and came towards me. A moment later she stood before me, a forbidding, corsetted woman in black. From her hat hung a heavy veil, which she now lifted.

'My husband asks,' she said without introduction or niceties, 'whether you might, in the name of humanity and all that is honourable, see your way clear to leaving him alone.'

I was so surprised by her tone, her appearance and her formal syntax that I couldn't think what to say. She waited.

'I had hoped,' I said at last, 'to ask him a question.'

'Why would he allow you to ask him questions when you pay no heed to his answers? You listen to that labourer from the engine room and you publish his lies, but you ignore what my husband says. Has he not suffered enough to satisfy you?'

'It is not my wish to make him suffer.'

'In which case, I ask again that you please leave him alone, because he suffers by your presence.'

Twenty yards or so behind her, the captain entirely ignored me. He jiggled his child's pram, trying to free a wheel that had caught on the doorframe. The boy was still sitting in it, sniffling and grizzling. For a brief moment, in the half-light of the late sun, I saw the captain's face. It showed the same straight lines and sharp angles I had seen in his chartroom, in the Senate chamber in Washington and in the Drill Hall in London, but it also showed something new. I tried to read it, but Mrs Lord had moved to block my view.

'Doesn't he suffer,' I asked her, 'by his own guilt?'

She stared at me as if I had uttered a profanity. 'Guilt? You insist on misunderstanding things, Mr Steadman. There is no guilt to suffer. My husband has already taken steps to clear his name, and soon all this silliness will be behind him. You should look to your own soul. Search out the blackness there; find your own guilt for what you have done to us.'

'Do you know,' I asked, 'that your husband seeks to blame his second officer for what happened?'

Mrs Lord's expression hardened yet further: an attack on her husband was an attack on her. Her words came at me with cold contempt. 'My husband has done all he can for that man.'

This angered me. I knew exactly what Captain Lord had done for his second officer, and none of it was noble. 'But,' I said before I could stop myself, 'your husband did not do the one thing he should have done for that man, and that is come up to the bridge when he was called. That is what he should have done, and that is why I am here: to ask him why he didn't. Please let me ask him: why didn't he go up to the bridge when Mr Stone told him of the rockets? Or if you won't allow me to speak to him, then let me ask you: why did your husband leave all those people for dead?'

There was a blur of movement, a stinging flash of burning on my cheek, a sharp intake of my own breath. Mrs Lord had struck me hard across the face with an open, ungloved hand. She stood perfectly still, locking her gaze to mine as if daring me to strike her back.

Perhaps I had deserved it. Perhaps Mrs Lord was right to say I should examine my own soul. Perhaps I'd sacrificed a good man's livelihood and reputation only to enhance my own. But it did not take me long, as I stood face to face with Mrs Lord, to remind myself of the real reason why I'd done what I had. It wasn't for my career, or my newspaper, or Herbert Stone – or even for the truth. It was in the service of those who died. Lord *should* have gone to them, and even the most loyal and determined of defences from his wife could not change that simple fact. In all this dreadful business, it was the one moral absolute.

The stinging on my cheek cooled. 'Thank you, Mrs Lord, for your time,' I said. 'I shall take up no more of it. You may tell your husband I will not bother him again.'

Mrs Lord made no reply. Instead she drew down the veil of her hat over her face and walked to her husband, who waited for her at their house. They went inside and pulled the door closed behind them.

I knew I had lost my chance, that I would not be back, that Lord was gone from me forever. After all this time I had not got from him a confession or an explanation. Perhaps Sydney Buxton at the Board of Trade was right to laugh at my American naivety. Stanley Lord would never tell the truth.

Mrs Lord's hard words made me more determined than ever to keep my promise to Herbert Stone's wife. So on the evening of my return from Liscard, still smarting from Mrs Lord's blow, and her words still sounding in my brain, I got to work. I arranged my papers on the narrow desk of my hotel room, drank whisky straight from the bottle, and tried to push through to new territory in my account of Stone and his motivations. I needed to give sympathetic colour to his answers in London.

But again I struggled. Late in the evening I turned to the pages of *Moby-Dick* for inspiration. I read for an hour, and then another. As I was putting the book aside I looked again at the photograph of the Sage family, which I'd been using as a bookmark. I passed the image to and fro behind the distorting glass of the whisky bottle, magnifying this face and then that. One by one the Sage children stared back at me: the young man on the horse, the children sitting on the wall, the others. I drifted into an indignant mood; I felt once more the wrong committed against these children who seemed to cry out to me from their flimsy photograph.

Then I heard Mrs Stone's voice. 'Remember,' she said. 'He knows their names. Every single one.' And with the startling, revelatory clarity that whisky sometimes brings, I understood how to tell the story of Herbert Stone.

The transcript of the British inquiry was available for purchase from His Majesty's Stationery Office, in the form of one slender paper volume for each day of the hearing, and the following morning I bought a complete set: thirty-six volumes, a thousand pages, twenty-six thousand questions. For a week I read the closely typed pages day and night, making notes in the margins and underlining sections with coloured pencils. I read much about navigation, lifeboats and icebergs, about Mr Ismay, the Astors and the Duff-Gordons, but I could find nothing about the Sages. Not one third-class passenger had been called to give evidence.

Nonetheless, as I read carefully the evidence of others – *Titanic* crew members, third-class stewards, first-class passengers – the Sages began slowly to emerge in my mind, like figures moving behind a screen. I drank whisky and let its warm spirit conjure scenes on the sinking ship as clearly as if I'd been there. And when I put pen to page my words at last flowed quickly and freely. I hardly slept.

'Eight White Rockets' appeared in a number of small journals on both sides of the Atlantic, was serialised in one newspaper, and received some warm reviews. One London commentator called it a 'provocative piece'.

On the copy I sent to Mrs Stone I included a brief inscription: 'Now everyone will know their names.'

In mid-September, I received by post an envelope containing a short note. It was not a reply from Mrs Stone, but a message from my wife. There was no greeting, only a few words in pale blue ink on a white card: 'I know who Stella and Will are. I mean, I know who they *really* are, and I see what you have done. Thank you.'

It was time for me to return to Boston.

Eight
White Rockets

AN ACCOUNT OF THE SEA TRAGEDY
OF THE *TITANIC* AND THE SAGE FAMILY

By John Steadman, an American journalist

———

Dedicated to my wife Olive, my daughter Harriet,
and my dear little boy. 'There is a better way.'

The first rocket

The tremor is low and rumbling and does not last for long but it's enough to wake Stella Sage, always a light sleeper. In the dark she can smell the closeness of her four youngest siblings. She wonders if her mother and sister in the cabin next door, and her father and three brothers hundreds of yards away in the ship's bow, have felt the shudder too.

The family of eleven are on their way to Florida to start over. Nineteen-year-old Stella, a dressmaker who hadn't wanted to make this voyage, tries to go back to sleep. But soon she hears footsteps outside the cabin door, and women calling to each other in a language she can't understand. And now four-year-old Tom and seven-year-old Connie, head to toe in the bunk below hers, are awake, talking and giggling. 'Go back to sleep, little ones,' Stella whispers. 'Be quiet now.' The children fall silent. Stella lies awake and listens.

Something doesn't seem right. The footsteps and voices outside have grown louder and there are new sounds – escaping steam, slamming doors. But what strikes her most is the lack of vibration from the engines. After five days of their gentle rhythm, the stillness is stark.

Now she notices something else: it is easier to roll over one way in her bunk than the other. The cabin is tilting. She gets up and turns on the light. All four children are awake now – Will, Ada, Connie and little Tom.

'Get up,' she tells them, 'and get dressed. Don't leave this cabin. Especially you, Willy-boy.' Eleven-year-old Will is something of a wanderer. Stella throws a coat over her nightclothes, steps into the alleyway and knocks on the cabin next door. Her mother appears, half asleep; behind her, Dolly – fourteen years old and difficult – lies in her bunk. 'There's something wrong with the ship,' Stella says. 'We must get dressed and go up on deck.'

Her mother says they should wait in their cabins so they don't miss Mr Hart, their steward, when he comes to tell them whatever it is that's happening. Stella, never good at waiting, disagrees. She says she'll find out herself what's happening and be back in five minutes. Before her mother can stop her she is hurrying forward along the E-deck alleyway. There are other people wandering around, mostly women, but some men too, who have come up from the men's quarters in the forward part of the ship.

At the third-class stairwell Stella finds a group of twenty or thirty people. Some are still in nightclothes, others are fully dressed and some have put on lifejackets. When Stella asks what's wrong, people tell her different things: a lost propeller blade, an iceberg, a problem with the ship's plumbing.

She runs further forward and looks down Scotland Road, a broad, white-walled alleyway that runs unimpeded the full length of the ship. It's crowded with men and luggage, and stewards handing out lifejackets. The jackets are cumbersome things, large cork panels sewn into white canvas with tangled straps dangling low to the floor, and most of the men, already struggling with heavy luggage, don't take them. So the stewards stack them instead in neat piles along the alleyway wall.

Stella thinks of going to find her father and brothers but decides against it. Instead she gathers up two lifejackets and runs aft again to her mother's cabin. She tells her what she has seen and insists they put on their warmest clothes and the lifejackets: there are more beneath the bottom bunks. Leaving her mother and Dolly to help each other, she gets the younger children into jackets. They all gather together in the alleyway. Stella has never seen her family look so odd – the children are like bizarre creatures in a school play. Tom doesn't want to wear his jacket; it's too big for him, the cork panels pressing up under his chin so that he cannot move his arms freely. He's clutching his favourite blue blanket, which has sewn onto it the image of a yellow giraffe.

'Jimmy Giraffe wants you to wear it,' she says, and Tom seems satisfied. He's fascinated by giraffes and tends to do what Jimmy tells him.

Stella leads them forward and up the stairs to the third-class reception foyer on D deck. There are now perhaps a hundred people jostling and shoving around the central stairway. Most are wearing lifejackets. There is much complaining, but there's laughter too. Stella lines the children up along the portside wall and leaves her mother with them while she goes to find her father and brothers.

But she does not need to: they're pushing their way through the crowd towards her. Her father seems thin and tired, but her brothers – George, eighteen; Doug, seventeen; Fred, sixteen – are tall and strong, with cloth caps at jaunty angles and cheeky smiles. Dolly rushes up to them.

'Look at me,' she says, doing a turn in her lifejacket. 'Stella made me wear it. I think it's ugly.'

'Come now,' Stella says, giving her father a quick hug, 'surely it's better to wear clothes that save our lives than make us pretty?' Her sister pouts a little, but Stella cheers her with a wink. Dolly once nearly drowned in a backyard well, and the family have indulged her ever since.

Stella sees that her father's and brothers' legs are wet. Her mother kneels to feel the bottom of their trousers then stands again. 'There was water in our cabin,' her father apologises, as if it were his fault. 'We might have to bunk in up here for the rest of the trip.'

Stella glances at her brothers: their lifejackets have squared up their shoulders so that they look like powerful rugby players, and they're staring at the ladies all around. 'That would put the foxes in the chicken coop,' she says, laughing.

Ada, ten years old and prone to whining, says she's tired and wants to go back to bed. Will wants to go upstairs to look outside. Stella tells Ada to be quiet and Will to stay right where he is. From now on they need to keep together.

A young man runs into the foyer carrying a large chunk of ice in his gloved hands. 'It's from the berg!' he says. 'There's tons of it up the front!'

The children gather round to look in wonder at its strange translucence. Will is captivated. He presses the tips of his warm fingers against the ice until they melt tiny indents in the surface.

Stella can hear patches of lively ragtime music drifting down from somewhere above. She thinks how odd it is that a band should be playing so late. It is well after midnight.

Mr Hart appears and announces that the women and children are to go topside. 'There's no occasion for alarm,' he says, 'it's only a precaution. You'll be taken up in groups.'

The Sages are not in the first group and when Stella complains, Mr Hart says again that there's no occasion to worry. Either he or another steward will be back down shortly to get them.

When he's gone, taking twenty or so women with him, Connie sways her hips and copies his high-pitched, singsong voice. 'There's no occasion, there's no occasion . . .' Although only seven, she's an excellent mimic and Stella can't help but laugh. Soon Doug and Fred join in the fun, saying the words in as many different voices as they can.

Minutes pass. Even though the doors to the welldeck above are open, the room is warm; someone has opened all the radiator cocks. All around, people are waiting, some standing in groups, some sitting on their luggage, others smoking.

Then there's a distant roaring sound – escaping steam, Stella thinks – followed by a single pop, like a cork being pulled from a bottle. A moment later, a young stewardess runs down the stairs towards them. Her lifejacket makes her movements awkward; she looks as if she will fall. Her eyes are alight.

'A rocket!' the stewardess says. 'They've just fired a rocket, I saw it – it went right up into the sky and then exploded.'

People who have been sitting stand up and there's murmuring and whispering among the crowd. Everyone knows what a rocket at sea means.

Stella looks to her father, willing him to lead them all up to the open deck. 'Don't you see?' she asks him. 'This ship is in trouble. We must go up.'

Her mother steps closer to her husband and slips her arm through his. Stella can see her father is trying to decide what to do. She turns to her eldest brother. 'George, please tell him. We've got to go.'

When George is silent she looks again to her father. She knows she's his favourite – he's always loved her wild curls, her playful energy – and she can persuade him to do almost anything. But now he surprises her with his resolve.

'No,' he says. 'This isn't one of your rallies. We'll do what we're told. We will wait for Mr Hart.'

On the SS *Californian*, Herbert Stone, the 24-year-old second officer, is standing the midnight watch on the cold, open bridge. His ship is stopped and he's looking at the lights of a distant steamer. He has been trying to contact her with the Morse lamp, but to no avail. Then, just after half past twelve, he sees a small white light climb into the air above her and burst into stars. The cluster drifts slowly downwards.

A few weeks later, in the warm spring air of the Scottish Drill Hall in London, he describes what he saw to a polite and attentive audience. 'I was walking up and down the bridge,' he tells them, 'and I saw one white flash in the sky immediately above this other steamer. I did not know what it was; I thought it might be a shooting star.'

There is a gasp in the ladies' gallery and excited whispers. A shooting star! Behind the flimsy witness stand, Stone begins to fidget.

'*What* did you think it was?' asks Mr Butler Aspinall, KC, appearing for the Board of Trade and on behalf of the British public.

Stone shrugs. 'It was just a white flash in the sky.' He pauses, then adds, 'It might have been anything.' He looks up at the gallery, as if its occupants are just as likely as he to know what the flash might have been.

Aspinall is not satisfied. He tries to narrow down the possibilities. 'But what did it suggest to your mind? What did you say to yourself? What did you think it was?'

Stone, wide-eyed, shifting left and right, is throwing nervous half-smiles this way and that. He appears to be thinking hard about what he'd thought on that night, and at last he answers, 'I thought nothing.'

So, on the *Californian*, Herbert Stone, officer of the watch, eight years at sea, sees a white flash and thinks nothing; but he does bring the binoculars to his eyes so he can study the steamer more intently. 'Watch that steamer,' the captain had said, and Stone is doing what he was told.

Meanwhile, below and behind him, standing at the starboard rail of the shelter deck smoking a cigarette, Ernie Gill is thinking many things: that the fourth engineer has no right to talk to him in the way he does, that it wasn't his fault the pump broke, that he didn't mean to drop the spanner. He has a mind to go to the chief engineer about it. He ought to, because he's not just a fireman or a greaser but the assistant donkeyman, and he knows his rights.

He draws hard on his cigarette and its tip glows bright red. The smoke gathers and thickens because there is absolutely no wind. Then, on the horizon, he sees a white light.

'I had pretty nearly finished my smoke and was looking around and I saw what I took to be a falling star,' he explains later to the enthralled spectators in the Drill Hall. He has never had such a large audience in his life. 'It descended and then disappeared. That is how a star does fall …'

A falling star. On the *Californian*'s shelter deck, Ernie Gill makes a wish. It involves the fourth engineer getting what's coming to him.

The second rocket

Stella is worried. Mr Hart has not yet come back and the third-class reception area has become dangerously crowded. More men have arrived, bringing their luggage with them, and there's not much room to move around. Mr Kieran, the chief third-class steward, has taken up a position at the top of the stairs and will let no one pass.

Another steward smiles at Stella's father and says he ought to take his family down to F deck to wait in the dining room, where it's warmer and there's more space.

'No, thank you very much,' says Stella, placing herself between the steward and her father. 'We want to go up, not down.'

The man wanders off and Stella places her coat over Connie and Ada, who've fallen asleep on the floor in their lifejackets. She reties the laces of Dolly's boots – never in her life has Dolly been able to keep her laces tied – and slides young Tom's golden curls behind his ears. When Fred and Doug begin to bounce their chests together like fighting seals, she says they should stop their tomfoolery but can't help laughing.

Her mother stands with her father, talking softly in his ear. She's always been his support. When he took up work as a corn grinder she learned to make cornbread; when he became landlord of a public house in Norfolk she waitressed at tables; when he bought the bakery at Peterborough she woke at four every morning to stoke the ovens. And when he announced that he was taking the whole family to Florida to grow oranges, it was her mother who persuaded Stella that she must come too. 'You have a special strength,' her mother said, 'that your father needs.'

Stella has always thought of her father as a man of action, and admired his various schemes, but the emergency on this ship seems to have overwhelmed him. Normally a fast thinker, he's become slow and passive. He wants to wait rather than act, and speaks only of doing what he's told. Stella wonders whether something has broken inside him.

Just then she hears again the distant popping sound. It is another rocket. If her mother is right and she has a special strength, then now is the time to use it.

The *Californian* is swinging imperceptibly anticlockwise, bringing her bow around to the south. Alone on the bridge, Herbert Stone is wondering what to do. The more he thinks about it, the more it seems that it was only a flash he saw, something in his peripheral vision, hardly anything really, and if he'd been looking the other way he wouldn't have seen it at all. His eyes linger on the speaking tube leading to the captain's cabin. If he were to call down, what would he say? That he'd seen a shooting star?

He wishes Gibson, the apprentice, would come back from below decks so he could talk to him about it.

Three or four minutes pass and then – there, above the steamer – another flash of white light. This time he's looking through the binoculars when it happens and what he sees is very clearly a rocket, streaking skyward and bursting into white stars.

He knows the regulations about distress signals. He learned them verbatim for his First Mate's Certificate, memorising them from crib cards he'd written up in neat capitals. Rockets throwing stars are a signal of distress. But when he studies the ship closely there doesn't seem to be anything wrong with her. She's been sitting there stationary and silent for an hour. Why, all of a sudden, start firing rockets? Stone isn't sure what to do. If he wakes the captain, what would the captain do anyway? He wouldn't steam anywhere tonight – not with so much ice about, not in this darkness. And if he wakes him for nothing the captain will think him a fool. 'It will be an easy watch,' the captain had said, 'with nothing much to do.'

Stone decides to wait just a little longer and see what happens. If there's another rocket, *then* he will call the captain.

Ernie Gill, meanwhile, stands aft on the shelter deck. 'I threw my cigarette away,' he later tells the audience in the Drill Hall, 'and looked over, and I could see from the water's edge – what appeared to be the water's edge – a great distance away, well, it was unmistakably a rocket. You could make no mistake about it.'

He watches for a few more minutes. Over his shoulder he can see the shadowy outline of his own ship's bridge, silent and dark.

'It was not my business to notify the bridge, but they could not have helped but see it,' he explains to his sorrowful listeners in London. They are spellbound, and he tries to look each of them in the eye. He knows they understand. He can't do every job on the ship. Others should do their job properly, just as he does his. 'I am not a sailor,' he says, his voice heavy with regret: if only he *had* been a sailor, this whole sad business might have turned out differently. 'I do not know anything about latitude or longitude. My compass is the steam gauge.'

So he goes below and slides back into his bunk.

The third rocket

The slope of the deck beneath her feet is increasing; Stella has to lean a little to keep her balance. There are rumours that wireless messages have been sent out asking for help and that the first-class passengers are being put into boats. And Mr Kieran, at the top of the stairs, now has two more stewards, with broad chests and thick arms, standing with him.

Most of the people crowded into the reception area are women and children. Stella wonders where the rest of the third-class men are.

Her father has said there were hundreds quartered with him and the boys in the ship's bow, but there are only about twenty here.

At last Mr Hart returns, out of breath, and says that he will now take another group up to the boat deck. There's a surge of people towards him, and Stella pushes through and reminds him of his promise. When Mr Hart agrees to take them, Stella tells her brothers and sisters to join hands, youngest to oldest, and not to let go no matter what. Her father picks up his suitcase and the older boys their satchels.

'Leave the luggage,' she calls, pulling the satchels from her brothers.

But her father doesn't want to leave his suitcase. It has in it family letters and photographs and the papers relating to the Jacksonville farm. Stella takes it gently from him and places it against the wall. 'We'll come back for it,' she says. 'Later.'

Mr Hart leads them up the stairs, but when they reach the top Mr Kieran puts out his arm to stop her father.

'No men,' Mr Kieran says.

'But we are nine children,' Stella says. 'Of course our father must come with us.'

Mr Kieran insists: women and children only. His two assistants step forward, arms crossed on their chests. 'The men stay,' Mr Kieran says, turning to Stella's father, 'or you all do.'

Stella sees her mother slip her hand into her father's. It's her way of saying she will not go without him. But he kisses her and tells her she must, for the sake of the children.

'Not them either,' says Mr Kieran, pulling George, Doug, Fred and Will from the line by their shoulders. 'The baby may go, but not the others.'

'I am not a baby!' shouts Tom. 'I'm four!'

Mr Hart is becoming agitated. If they delay further he will go without them; he has the other women in the group to think of. Stella pushes Will forward. 'This one must come with us,' she says, stepping closer to Mr Kieran as if daring him to say otherwise. 'He's only eleven.'

'He seems older,' Mr Kieran says.

'Well, he's not,' says Stella. 'Look at him!'

Will's face is translucent; he is angelic. Mr Kieran hesitates, then nods him through.

Stella's mother embraces her husband and sons, and Stella follows, hugging them hard one by one. 'I will put Mother and the little ones in a boat,' she says, 'then I'll come back for you.'

Her father kneels to Tom, who still clutches his blue blanket with its yellow giraffe, and tells him he's a brave boy. 'It's cold now, but think how warm it will be when we get to Jacksonville. Remember what I told you? About the oranges? And the giraffes? But for now, make sure you take good care of your mother and sisters.'

Mr Hart is leading the group outside onto the open welldeck. Stella pauses to watch her father and brothers walk back down the stairwell. When George slips his arm tenderly around his father's shoulders, she has to stop herself running after them. She whispers her promise to herself: she will come back for them. Then she turns and follows Mr Hart and the others across the deck.

There is no wind and she can hear voices and ragtime music drifting down from the forward decks. The moon isn't up but the stars blaze as brightly as she's ever seen them. For a moment she holds the rail and looks out into the dark. She can't see the horizon, but as her eyes slowly adjust she makes out, in the blackness, a light. It's faint and dim, but she can see white with a tinge of red. A ship! But in this strange, depthless darkness, she cannot tell how far away it is.

And then: an angry hissing sound. It's the sound she's heard before, a sound like escaping steam, but here on the open deck it's much louder. She looks forward and sees the rocket rushing skyward. It explodes with a loud echoing clap, and for a moment its stars light the whole ship. The crowds on the deck crane their necks to look up. She notices that the little wooden boats hanging from ropes down the side of the ship are filled with people – she can make out the bobbing feathers of extravagant hats.

Stella Sage doesn't know much about ships, but she does know that rich women would not get into such flimsy boats unless something was terribly wrong.

When he sees the third silent white rocket above the steamer, Stone grips his binoculars tight. He'd promised himself he would call the captain if he saw another one, but still he wavers. He wonders where the apprentice has got to.

'What did you think they meant?'

In the Scottish Drill Hall Mr Butler Aspinall, KC asks him the question yet again. The room has become very quiet. Newspaper reporters have stopped writing and ladies are holding their fans still in their laps. The great musty curtains that have been hung to improve the acoustics seem at last to be working: people imagine they can hear the witness breathing. The audience watch him move from side to side like an animal in a zoo. They feel sorry for him. They can tell he is a good man, kind and gentle, who is doing his best. But they want to shake him by the neck, too. The sharp-faced Commissioner offers him water and reminds him to speak up.

'I thought . . .' There's a catch in Stone's voice and it seems possible he might cry. He casts his eyes about the hall, as if looking for help, then drifts into incoherent mumbling.

Lord Mersey, high on his central dais, is growing impatient.

'Come on, man, come on!'

'I thought, perhaps, the ship was in communication with some other ship. Or possibly she was signalling to tell us she had big icebergs around her.'

Aspinall is not looking at the witness. His thumbs are hooked into his waistcoat, his head is craned backwards and his eyes are closed, as if he is trying to visualise for himself this strange scene on the North Atlantic. How could rockets bursting in the sky convey such a message? 'Possibly,' he says slowly. 'What else?'

Stone – furtive, fidgeting, fussing – develops another idea. 'Perhaps,' he says, 'she was communicating with some other steamer at a greater distance than ourselves.' He looks pleased with himself.

But now the Commissioner huffs and puffs, leans forward and takes off his glasses. 'What,' he asks, 'was she communicating?'

'I don't know.'

'Is that the way in which steamers communicate with each other?'

'No,' Herbert Stone has to admit.

'Then you cannot have thought that.'

A gentle twitter of laughter rises in the Drill Hall and quickly subsides. The audience sits perfectly still, perplexed by a shared knowledge: everybody knows what rockets at sea mean.

The fourth rocket

Little Tom is having trouble keeping up as Mr Hart leads the group along a wide alleyway of ivory-white panelling. When he tries to run he trips on the front panels of his lifejacket and Connie lets go of his hand. He's almost in tears. Stella wishes George or her father were here to carry him.

'You take his hand,' says her mother, 'and I'll look after the girls.'

This arrangement works better. Stella holds onto Tom, lifting him whenever he trips, and Dolly, Ada and Connie form a chain behind their mother, like ducklings. Stella keeps a close eye on young Will, who trots along by himself and runs ahead from time to time. The children are frightened, but Stella reassures them by singing songs and talking of Florida sunshine.

They climb another staircase and come upon the foyer of a little restaurant. There's a knot of first-class passengers ahead; Mr Hart says they'll have to wait a moment. The restaurant door is open and Stella sees beautiful wall panels of walnut inlaid with gold, and a ceiling of moulded flowers and garlands. The tables have been set for the next day with glittering silverware and lamps with pink silk shades.

The children wander in and stare in wonder: never have they seen such a place. Tom kneels to sink his hands in the soft carpet. Connic traces with her finger the roses in the tapestry upholstery of the chairs. Will stands silently before the coloured patterns of the stained-glass windows. But what enthrals them most are the crystal bowls of fresh fruit laid out on the carved buffet tables. They step nearer and gaze at the green grapes and red apples and the plump, glossy oranges. 'Just like Daddy's farm in Jacksonville!' Tom says.

As Ada extends a hand towards one of the bowls, Stella, watching from the door, calls out to her, 'No. They're not ours to take.'

'Just one?' Ada asks.

'To show Daddy?' adds little Tom.

'No. Not even one.'

'Oh *please?*' insists Ada. She's a stubborn girl, and seems on the verge of a tantrum, but Stella sweeps in and takes both her and Tom by the hand. 'Come along,' she says, cutting off any further complaints. 'It's time to go.'

'Don't worry, young lady,' Mr Hart says to Ada as they pass into the alleyway. 'There'll be more oranges up ahead – you'll see.' Ada seems unconvinced; Stella hears her mutter something about not liking oranges anyway.

Mr Hart hurries them along another corridor that eventually opens out into a vast atrium filled with light: the Grand Staircase, he says. Stella has heard of it but never seen it. She moves further in to look: the staircase seems to run from the very bottom of the ship to the top, and is crowned by a great dome of iron and frosted glass lit from behind. The steps sweep up in graceful symmetrical curves to foyers at each deck; the balustrades are inlaid with delicate swirls of iron and little bronze flowers. Mr Hart leads them up – B deck, A deck, and then, at the very top, standing just beneath the enormous glass dome, he weaves his way through a cluster of first-class passengers and opens a door to the boat deck. They follow him through into the freezing night air.

Stella, holding tight to Tom, is last to step out. She is astounded by what she sees. They are standing at the base of the ship's second funnel, and from this close it's impossibly tall. The electric floodlights at its base make it look like a giant tower of gold. The deck itself is hundreds of feet long; Stella would never have thought a ship could have so much open, uncluttered space. Electric lamps and ornate windows throw their light onto the deck, but beyond the ship's rail Stella can see only blackness. It's as if she were standing on a lit stage. At the forward and aft ends of the deck some lifeboats have been lowered to deck level. Others have already gone. In their place, ropes dangle loosely down the ship's side.

The first-class passengers stand around in quiet groups. Stella almost laughs: she has never seen such beautiful clothes – silk, lace and feathers abound, as at a grand ball, and diamonds – but all this finery is crushed beneath bulky cork lifejackets. And here at last is the ship's band, playing their instruments – three violins, two cellos and a double bass – just outside the entrance to the Grand Staircase. The six men wear white jackets with green facing and fancy piping, and sway to the music as they play.

Officers and sailors work at the lifeboats. They help wealthy ladies step across the gap into the boats, they ease ropes through bollards and pulleys, they call out orders and instructions. People are calm; they speak in soft tones. The proceedings have the air of a strange, secret ceremony. There is no rushing or pushing. Mr Hart looks up and down the deck, trying to find a lifeboat that might take his group. No one comes to help them.

A man wearing a ridiculously tall top hat and a long, thin waxed moustache of the pompous kind steps away from his group and appears before Stella. She instantly dislikes him.

'Ladies,' he says, with a flourish of his hand, 'welcome to our little party on the promenade.' When he turns back to his wife, Stella overhears her say with a sneer, 'The whole ship must have been invited.'

Stella feels the insult and wants to say something, but two things happen in quick succession. The first: a shout from an officer at the very forward end of the boat deck, near the ship's bridge. 'Stand clear!' he yells, pulling a lanyard attached to a tube secured to the rail. There's a rush of sound and a great flash of light as a rocket soars up, leaving a faint white trail, and explodes into stars. Everyone looks up; there are gasps. 'Another one!' someone says. And the second thing: the frantic voice of her mother begging Mr Hart and anyone else to help. 'Will is missing,' she says, hunting about, calling his name. 'Stella, Will is missing!'

The white stars of the rocket still light the children's faces. But

William Sage, eleven years old, is nowhere to be seen, and Stella knows her mother would not dream of getting into a lifeboat without him.

During his ordeal in the Scottish Drill Hall, Herbert Stone seems, in a moment of lucidity, to share the common knowledge of what rockets at sea mean. 'Naturally,' he says, as if it were the most ordinary thought in the world, 'the first thing that crossed my mind was that the ship might be in trouble.' But though the kindly London barristers had led him to a concession of trouble, not once could they take him as far as admitting distress.

'You knew, did you not, that those rockets were signals of distress?'

'No!' says Stone, most emphatically.

Of course they could not have been: he has just watched three of them without doing anything. Distress, after all, means a ship sinking; trouble might be something less: a damaged propeller or rudder, a blown boiler, a man overboard, a fractured crankshaft. But even as Stone wonders what the trouble might be, another rocket climbs slowly skyward, bursting into stars that fill the lenses of his binoculars with their white light.

It is the fourth, and now his anxiety is almost unbearable. It can only be relieved in one way. He pulls the stopper from the speaking tube and prepares to blow down. The captain, he knows, is asleep in the chartroom below. But once more he pauses.

The ship to the south looks just as she always has: calm and still and perfectly all right. The rockets, for now, have stopped. Soon it will be time for his mid-watch coffee, and Gibson will bring up bread and butter from the galley.

'Did you obtain a certificate from the Board of Trade as a mate?' he is asked by Mr Thomas Scanlan, MP, representing the interests of the hundreds of sailors and firemen who died on the *Titanic*.

'As a first mate in steamships, yes.'

'Was that certificate given to you after examination?'

Stone knows where this is leading. 'Yes,' he says, looking very much like he wants to say no.

'I suppose before you sat for that examination you read something about signals?'

'I learned them.'

'Now, do you mean to tell his lordship that you did not know that –' and here Scanlan reads from the printed regulation itself, which he clutches in his thick-fingered hands – '"rockets or shells, throwing stars of any colour or description, fired one at a time at short intervals" is the proper method for signalling distress at night?'

'Yes, that is the way it's always done, as far as I know.'

'And you knew that perfectly well on the night of the 14th of April?'

Once more the Drill Hall falls still and quiet. Even the traffic outside on Buckingham Gate seems to have paused. The giant cross-section of the *Titanic* suspended beneath the ladies' gallery by slender ropes undulates slowly in the warm air.

'Yes,' Stone says. He did know it perfectly well on the night of the 14th of April.

When the ladies close their eyes, they are there with this strange man on his dark bridge, looking over his shoulder, trying to see what he sees.

Lord Mersey intervenes. 'And is not that exactly what was happening?'

Stone looks at his feet. He seems to have forgotten what was asked. Lord Mersey waits, but still Stone says nothing. The spring pollen makes someone sneeze. Scanlan, feeling perhaps the dismay of the ghosts he represents but also sympathy for the downtrodden, guides Stone gently along.

'Now,' he says quietly, as if coaxing a schoolchild to tell the truth about missing sweets, 'you have heard my lord put that question?'

Stone nods.

'Well, you must answer it. That was what was happening?'

'Yes.'

Both Lord Mersey and Scanlan stare hard at him. 'The *very thing* was happening,' says Lord Mersey, less gently than Scanlan, 'that *you knew* indicated distress?'

'If that steamer had stayed on the same bearing after showing these rockets —'

'No, no.' Lord Mersey holds up a hand to stop him. 'Do not give a long answer of that kind. Is it not the fact that the *very thing* was happening which you had been taught indicated distress?'

'Yes.'

Scanlan presses. 'You knew it meant distress?'

'I knew that rockets shown at short intervals, one at a time, meant distress signals, yes.'

'Do not speak generally. On that very night – think of it – when you saw those rockets being sent up you knew, did you not, that those rockets were signals of distress?'

Everybody waits. Some ladies do not realise they have moved forward on their seats – to the very edge. Finally, it comes.

'No.'

It is an affront to logic, and the whole hall feels it. It is too much for Lord Mersey. 'Now, do think about what you are saying!' he cries out, as if in pain.

A hushed murmuring runs around the hall. There's rustling of dresses in the gallery; a man is pushing past knees to get out to the aisle. Stone is again casting his eyes about, searching, more frantically this time. Something is at work in him, something more powerful than truth and dignity. It's as if a puzzling drama were being enacted in the hall, one that needs the grand entrance of its main player to make sense of it all.

The fifth rocket

Will Sage has always been a special child. Stella remembers him crying once because he saw a caterpillar being eaten by a sparrow. Another time he fell asleep in the fork of a tree and could not be found for hours. There's something in the soft texture of his being that delights his mother and makes him her favourite; her love for him is absolute. Stella has seen the pair of them sitting for hours in the long grass of their backyard, watching bumblebees and looking for dragons in rain clouds. Will is an innocent; when he makes daisy bracelets to give to his sisters he doesn't know that his brothers laugh at him. There is something other-worldly about him; his spirit seems to come from far off.

So now Stella is angry at herself. She should have watched him always, she should have held his hand. 'I'll go and find him, Mother,' she says. 'I'm faster than you are, so you stay here with the others and I'll go down.'

Connie rubs her mother's dress against her cheek. 'Don't worry, Mummy,' she says, placing her open hand on her chest as she's seen Mr Hart do. 'There's no occasion.'

Stella laughs in spite of herself. 'Very good, Connie,' she says, 'very good.' She takes her mother by both hands. 'Connie's right. There's no occasion to worry. Wait here. I'll bring him to you.'

She pushes past the first-class passengers back into the Grand Staircase foyer and runs down the stairs, weaving in and out of people who mill about and get in her way. They whisper and tut-tut but she does not care. On the B-deck landing she looks about, calling Will's name loudly, but cannot see him. She wonders whether he has gone lower, perhaps all the way to his father and brothers.

'You looking for a boy, Miss?'

Stella turns to see four bellboys, perhaps thirteen or fourteen years old, standing to one side of the electric lifts in their bright green, brass-buttoned suits. They have matching green caps adorned with the emblem of the ship's line: a white star on a red background. They're smoking cigarettes.

'I am,' Stella says, hurrying over to them. 'My brother. Have you seen him? A skinny boy of eleven?'

'Grey knickers and striped shirt?' asks one.

'That's him.'

'We saw him, Miss,' says the bellboy. 'Down there.' He points to the same alleyway Mr Hart brought Stella and her family along earlier. 'He went aft.'

Then he *is* going to his father and brothers, Stella thinks. She thanks the bellboys and runs off down the alleyway, but she's perplexed. Will has always preferred being with his mother rather than his father. What, she wonders, could he be going to him for?

At the foyer of the fancy restaurant she pauses to catch her breath. Glancing in, she sees that many of the lamps with pink silk shades have fallen over. The slope of the deck is increasing. She can see men climbing up the outside of the bay windows.

And then she sees Will, standing near the buffet tables. He's taking the polished brass rings off the napkins and putting them in his pocket.

'Will!' she calls, running to him and taking him by the arm. 'What are you doing?'

'Nothing,' he says.

'Why are you taking those?'

'Because I want them.'

'Oh, you silly, silly boy!' says Stella, tightening her grip on his arm and leading him from the restaurant. 'They're not yours to take. And Mother is beside herself with worry. Come along.'

'But I'm not finished yet.'

'I said come *along*!'

Back on the boat deck, Stella finds her mother and sisters standing with their group, just a little further forward from where she left them. Her mother falls on Will, pushing her face into the cloth of his cap, but he wriggles free and turns to Ada. He takes from his pocket a large, bright orange, holds it to his nose and breathes in its scent. It seems to soothe him.

'This is for you,' he says, holding out the fruit on his open palm as if it were the most solemn of offerings. 'That's why I went back. This is what we'll grow in America.'

Ada, speechless, kisses her brother on his soft cheek. Turning back to his mother, Will says, 'And this is for you.' He reaches into his pocket again and hands her a brass napkin ring. 'I polished it especially.' She takes the ring from him and kisses it, her face serene. Stella wonders what she is thinking. It has never been easy to tell, and she marvels at how, amid all this drama, her mother can be so calm.

But now is a time for action, not tranquillity. Stella looks around for Mr Hart but cannot see him. He has gone, Dolly explains, to look for a lifeboat. It seems there aren't many left with space enough for all the women in the group. They are to stay here until he returns. Stella helps her mother usher the children into a nearby alcove where they can huddle against the cold.

A ship's officer is giving orders further forward along the deck. He must be a senior officer, Stella thinks when she catches sight of him: he has no lifejacket, but wears a greatcoat instead, with golden rings on the cuffs. Every now and then he talks to his men with an odd politeness: 'Steady there, if you please. Belay that, gentlemen. Hold fast there, if you wouldn't mind.' He is attending to a boat, smaller than the others, which has been lowered to sit level with the boat deck. Eight or so first-class passengers have gathered there, including, Stella sees, the man with the top hat and waxed moustache who spoke to her so sarcastically. His wife is rearranging the fur around her shoulders, adjusting the ostrich feathers in her hat, and giving instructions to a woman Stella assumes is her maid. One by one the officer helps the women step across the narrow gap between the ship's side and the flimsy boat.

Stella is astonished by what she sees next. The woman with the ostrich feathers reaches her hand back to her husband, who says to the officer, 'May I go with my wife?' He takes care always to keep his top hat straight.

'Oh, certainly do,' says the officer. 'Please do.'

The man steps daintily into the boat, and other men follow. A moment later the officer gives an order and the boat begins its descent to the sea. Stella counts twelve people in it. Half of them are men. And there are seats for at least thirty more. Why in the name of God are her father and brothers being held below in the crowded third-class foyer when these men are being let into half-empty boats with a 'certainly do' and a 'please do'?

Even as she watches them, another rocket is fired. Stella has been keeping track: this is the fifth. It's so close the hissing and explosion shock her, and by its white light she sees something that, for the first time, brings real fear. The black seawater is only a few feet below the forward welldeck.

'Mother,' she calls, 'they're letting men into the boats! There are plenty of spaces for Father and the boys. I'm going to get them.'

Her mother instantly protests but Stella takes her by both shoulders. 'I'm going, Mother, there's no point trying to stop me.' She speaks with as much force as she can muster. 'And you must give me your promise, here and now, swearing on all that is sacred, that when Mr Hart comes back, you and the children will get into the next boat. Do *not* wait for me. I'll get in a boat with Father and the boys.'

Her mother refuses. 'I cannot go without you, Stella. I will not!'

'You will,' insists Stella. 'You *must* – for the children. For Will.'

Her mother is silent.

'Promise me: when the time comes you and the children will get in a boat. I must have your promise.'

And at last, as the stars of the fifth rocket die out, her mother gives it.

Captain Stanley Lord, fully clothed, sleeps deeply on the chartroom settee. His cap is drawn down over his face to shield his eyes from the light of the chart table lamp. The whistle of the speaking tube, when he at last hears it, is piercing and insistent. It drags him from the depths of sleep. Disoriented, he struggles to remember where he is as the whistle sounds again. He turns over and buries his face in the softness of a cushion, then hears it yet again, angry now at whoever is blowing it. He forces himself up and walks slowly to his cabin next door. The whistle stopper is at the end of his bunk; he removes it just as it begins to wail once more.

It is the second officer calling from the bridge above. Mr Stone sounds distant, uncertain, hesitant.

'What is it?' Lord asks into the speaking tube.

'That steamer, sir. She's firing white rockets.'

Lord pauses, still not quite awake. 'What steamer?'

'The one you pointed out to me.'

Now Lord remembers the vessel he saw: a small steamer, stopped by the icefield, waiting for dawn.

'Any colour in them?' he asks.

'No, sir. They're white, just white.'

'Are they company signals?'

'They're white rockets.'

'What does she want?'

'I don't know, Captain.'

'Well, you had better Morse her and find out, hadn't you?'

'I *have* been Morsing her,' Stone says, 'but she isn't answering.'

Lord hears the petulance amid the distortions of the speaking tube. He knows the second officer wants him to come up – and he will, he will – but first, Mr Stone needs to do some work himself. That is why he is paid.

'Try again, Mr Stone,' Lord says. 'Try again. Find out what she wants and then send the apprentice down to tell me.' He waits, but all he hears is the soft hush of air in the tube. The second officer has not replaced the stopper; he must still be standing there.

Lord squeezes the whistle stopper back into the tube and returns to the chartroom, still not quite awake. The light of the room hurts his eyes. He lies down on the settee and replaces his cap over his face, listening for the tapping of the Morse lamp. There it is – click-click, click, click-click. He closes his eyes and waits for the apprentice to come down and relay whatever interesting information the diligent second officer finds out.

In less than a minute he's asleep once more.

'What do you think it was firing rockets for?'

When the question is asked of him in London, for the first time, Captain Lord stares directly ahead. His face shines like polished bronze, his eyes are deep blue. Although he is not in uniform – he wears a blue suit and a crisp white shirt with a starched collar buttoned high and tight on his neck – the ladies and gentlemen of the galleries know what they are looking at: a captain of the British Merchant Marine, loyal, courageous and true.

Obvious as it is, the question was never put to him by the American senators. Here in the Drill Hall it hangs heavy in the air while the occupants sit in silent awe at what they think is its simple answer. But this captain before them on the stand, with all his lived experience of the sea and its ways, must see in the question a very great complexity which they do not appreciate, for he does not answer it.

The question has been asked by Sir Rufus Isaacs, KC, the Attorney-General. As he waits for a reply he reaches up instinctively to adjust his wig, then remembers he's not wearing one and runs his hand through his hair instead. These are executive proceedings, not judicial. There are no wigs or gowns.

Isaacs' voice is more beautiful than might be expected of a man who grew up in East London, the son of a Jewish fruit merchant, and who left school at fourteen and was sent off to sea at sixteen. Its modulations are subtle and sweet. There's a cadence and pace to his words and never a hesitation, as if he is reading from a script he can see in his mind.

At last Captain Lord answers. 'When?' he says. 'When? I never knew anything about these rockets until seven o'clock the next morning.'

It is forthright, but it is not an answer to the question, and Isaacs knows it is not honest. He has read the witness proofs: he knows that chief officer Stewart told Captain Lord of the rockets when he woke him at half past four in the morning; he knows too that Herbert Stone told him of them much earlier.

But Isaacs says nothing. He waits. He has the measure of the man; he knows he will correct himself.

'Wait,' the captain says, 'I did hear of one rocket.'

'And did you remain in the chartroom when you were told that vessel was firing a rocket?'

'I remained in the chartroom when he told me this vessel had fired a rocket.'

The captain seems to think this an answer of clarity and courage, but for Isaacs it is perplexing and unfathomable. 'I do not understand you,' he says, with the tone of a man used to understanding things. He pauses. He seems, almost, to slouch. Onlookers in the galleries think he has given up. He turns away from his notes, away from the witness, and stares hard into the lofty ceiling for inspiration. 'You knew, of course, there was danger to steamers in this field of ice?'

'To a steamer steaming, yes.'

Isaacs turns his gaze back to the witness and raises his eyebrows. 'I do not understand,' he says again. 'It may be my fault.' He starts from the beginning once more. 'What did you think this vessel was firing rockets for?'

'I asked the second officer,' Lord replies, emphasising each word as if explaining a complex maritime idea to a landlubber. 'I said, "Is that a company signal?" and he said he did not know.'

Isaacs thinks again how that is not an answer to his question. 'Then that did not satisfy you?'

'No, it did not.'

Isaacs sits down. In the ladies' gallery there is accord: he *has* given up. There is an extended silence. The machinery of the inquiry seems to have temporarily seized, until eventually the Commissioner himself takes up the questioning. He starts exactly where Isaacs had.

'What did you think the rocket was sent up for?'

'Well, we had been trying to communicate with this steamer by Morse lamp from half past eleven, and she would not reply.'

Again, it is not an answer. Lord Mersey puts the question a fourth time. 'What did you think she was sending up a rocket *for*?'

'I thought it was acknowledging our signals, our Morse lamp. A good many steamers do not use the Morse lamp.'

It is an answer but it is not credible. 'Have you ever said that before?'

'That has been my story right through.'

Lord Mersey does not believe him. Nowhere in his proofs of evidence does it say that rockets are used to answer Morse lamps. And Isaacs, who knows the sea, does not believe him either, because he is rising from his chair, slowly, like a cobra. His balance is perfect, his voice lilts and floats, he achieves a seesawing rhythm between question and answer, as if in a courtly dance.

'If it was not a company signal, must it not have been a distress signal?'

'If it had been a distress signal the officer on watch would have told me.'

'*I say again*: if it was not a company signal, must it not have been a distress signal?'

'Well, I do not know of any other signals but distress signals that are used at sea.'

'You have told me already, some few minutes ago, that you were not satisfied it was a company signal. You did not think it was a company signal?'

'I inquired, *was it* a company signal.'

'But you had been told that he did not know?'

'He said he did not know.'

'Very well. That did not satisfy you?'

'It did not satisfy me.'

'Then if it was not that, it might have been a distress signal?'

There is a silence. The courtly dance has come to a stop. Isaacs looks down at his notes and waits. Lord is so still he seems not to be breathing. Then, at last, he speaks.

'It might have been.'

At the back of the hall someone can be heard gently sobbing.

'And you remained in the chartroom?' presses Isaacs.

'I remained in the chartroom.'

The light climbs higher in the tall windows and the hall fills with a lazy warmth. Fifty lawyers, twenty clergyman, sixty pressmen and hundreds of ladies and gentlemen in the public galleries stare in wonder at this tall, straight-backed man. They begin to see him not in his civilian suit behind a bare and spindly desk, but in his square bridge-blazer with its polished brass buttons and its sleeve-ends dipped in gold, sitting in his cabin at the very centre of his ship. They see him talking to the second officer above about rockets exploding silently in the dark night, rockets which *might have been* distress signals. They see him *remaining in his chartroom*, not seeing the rockets, and not hearing, either, the sharp tolls of the bridge bell ringing out the hours of the midnight watch, loud and clear and pure.

The sixth rocket

Stella rushes back down the Grand Staircase for the second time, knowing she cannot rely on her father. She's the parent now, and must lead him and her brothers up to the boat deck, encouraging them all the way. I have a special strength, she says to herself, that my father needs.

And she must get them into a lifeboat, of that she is now certain. She has seen the black sea rising towards the forward welldeck and now, inside the ship, she can see green water swirling at the bottom of the Grand Staircase.

The ship is sinking.

She runs along first-class corridors, pushing through little knots of passengers with her broad shoulders, not caring about upsetting rich people. She ignores a group of third-class girls walking the other way – friends she's made during the voyage, who beg her to turn around and come with them to the boat deck. She strides straight through a crowd of young men on the aft welldeck who whistle at her as she passes, and slips by Mr Kieran and his thuggish helpers when they try to stop her at the top of the stairs. But when she gets to the third-class entrance foyer it's almost empty. She cannot see her father or her brothers. Their luggage, too, has gone.

She calls out for them, describes them to the few remaining people, opens doors and looks down alleyways. No one remembers seeing them leave the foyer. Stella runs back up the stairs and asks Mr Kieran whether he's seen them. He says he has not.

'You should have let them come up with us!' she says. 'You lied to us. They *are* letting men into the boats.'

Mr Kieran shrugs his shoulders, smiles, and tells her she ought to beware of becoming hysterical. Stella says that he ought to beware of being thrown overboard.

She searches the third-class common room, a large, open space in the raised stern housing, where at least a hundred people are gathered, mostly women. There are babies and toddlers too, with drooping eyelids. Stella wonders why they are still here. She can see ten, twenty, thirty children. And where are the men? The ship's bow must now be completely under water, and hundreds of men slept there. Where are her father and brothers?

Now she remembers something that chills her: the comment a steward made to her father as they waited in the reception foyer. 'Why not go down to the dining room on F deck?' he'd said with a honey-like voice and cloying smile, 'where it's warmer and there's more space?'

'Surely not,' Stella whispers. 'Surely not.'

She runs back down the stairs to the foyer, through the starboard-side door to Scotland Road. At the forward end she can see seawater, but halfway along, the companionway down to F deck is still dry. She takes the stairs two at a time and pushes open the double doors of the dining room.

And this is where all the men are. The room – the largest third-class space on the ship – is filled with them. The warm air is thick with their smell; most would not have bathed since leaving England. How still and quiet they are, thinks Stella. They sit at tables or on piles of luggage; they stand in groups, smoke cigarettes and drink tea. Some are drying their clothes on the backs of chairs. But why are they here? Many of them are young and strong and if they rose up together nothing could stop them. Yet they've stayed in this room like animals waiting to be fed by their keeper.

But what most dismays her – and frightens her – are the people she sees on their knees, bowing their heads in prayer. There are two groups forward and one aft, being led by men in black gowns and high collars. Above the general murmur of the room she can hear their silly mutterings.

And there, in the aft group, are her father and brothers. Her father's head is bowed low and close to the minister's gown, like a child trying to hide in his mother's skirt. Just behind him, George prays with his father, but Doug and Fred are looking about with nervous eyes. All of them, she notices, have taken off their lifejackets and placed them on the floor to kneel upon.

Herbert Stone had thought the captain, on being told about the rockets, would come at once to the bridge. Instead he asked about company signals. It was the first time that night – as Stone stood watching the steamer, and Morsing her, and sipping his coffee, and pacing the deck, and now, at last, talking to his captain – that the notion of company signals had entered his mind.

'You were an onlooker, paying careful attention,' Mr Butler Aspinall, KC puts to him in London, in that way barristers have of delivering profound truths in flat statements, 'keeping those lights under observation, and then this question comes from the master. What do you think he meant by such a question?'

'I do not know, except that he had the thought in his mind that they may have been company signals of some sort.'

Aspinall eyes him above his spectacles. 'Was it in yours?'

Stone hesitates. 'That they were company signals?'

'Yes.'

'No.'

Company signals were not in his mind, because he knows what company signals are: coloured flares or balls or Roman candles, used in complex patterns to indicate which company a ship belongs to. And he knows that what he saw were not these. He saw white rockets, pure and simple.

Aspinall presses the point. 'You did not believe they were company signals?'

'I had never seen company signals like them before.'

'Then what did you think they were?'

'I did not think what they were intended for; white rockets is what I saw them as.'

'Wait. You did not think they were company signals?'

'No.'

'What did you think?'

'I just thought they were white rockets. That is all.'

White rockets, that is all. In the Drill Hall men and women turn sorrowful faces to each other.

But Stone has done his duty. He has told the captain and the captain has ordered him back to the Morse lamp. When he walks over to the tapper he's calmer. He sends a message out into the night without making a single mistake: 'We are the *Californian* stuck in ice who are you?'

He cannot make out a response. He sends again.

'Who are you?'

There is flickering, which he tries to read, but Gibson is at last back, mumbling about how long it took to find the key to the store, and how the rotator for the patent log wasn't where it was supposed to be, and how he was worried he'd wake the chief officer himself with all his clattering and banging.

Stone interrupts him. 'That ship has been firing rockets. I've just told the captain.'

'What do you mean?'

'She's been firing rockets. The captain asked me to contact her with the lamp.'

Gibson takes up the binoculars and trains them on the ship. 'She has a strange glare of light on her after deck,' he says. 'Heavens! I just saw a flash – on her deck.'

It's another rocket. Stone watches the faint streak towards the sky and the burst of white stars. It's the sixth he has seen, but it's Gibson's first.

'You say you told the captain?' the apprentice asks.

'I told him.'

'Shouldn't he come up?'

'He said to find out what she wants, and then you're to go down and tell him.' Stone feels Gibson's eyes on him. 'He thinks they might be company signals,' he explains.

The apprentice looks baffled. 'But it was a rocket.'

'Yes.'

'A *white* rocket.'

'I know.'

Stone can hear the apprentice breathing and feel the warmth from his body. He senses a doubting, a mistrust. 'You have a go at Morsing her,' he says. 'Try to get her.'

Gibson moves to the lamp tapper and Stone lifts the binoculars tight to his eyes. The silence presses in.

The seventh rocket

'We were *told* to come down here to wait,' says Stella's father. 'Mr Kieran said a ship is coming to pick us all up and this is the best place to be.'

'It is the very *worst* place,' says Stella, surveying the hundreds of men crammed into the room. With the ever-increasing slope of the deck the floor creaks as if it's being stretched on a rack. Stella half expects the polished boards to splinter. George stands close to his father while Fred and Doug look at her expectantly, holding their lifejackets limply at their side. Fred, sixteen, picked up some work this year as a bricklayer and Stella had marvelled at his broadening chest and thickening shoulders. But now he looks like he's about to cry as he slips his hand gently into hers, just as he used to do when he was a small boy. 'What are we going to do, Sis?' he asks.

'We have to go up,' she says, pulling him towards the door.

'No,' says her father. 'There's a ship coming, we must wait here.' He is a thin man; he has never stood still long enough to get fat. But now he won't move.

Time is short. Stella, exasperated, persuades him to come with her to a porthole and look through it. Can he see a ship coming? she asks. Can he see anything at all? Her father, cupping his hands tight around his eyes to keep out the light of the dining room, admits that he sees only the black sky.

'It's not the sky,' Stella says, 'it's the sea. This whole room is under water!'

Her father jumps back from the porthole. When he looks at her, she sees something new in his eyes and she knows she has him now. 'Let's go,' she says.

She leads them out of the dining room, up the companionway and aft to the reception foyer. Mr Kieran and his stewards still keep guard at the top of the stairs, but as another group of men push forward Stella and her father and brothers slip through with them. On the welldeck a seaman is trying to stretch a rope barrier across to keep the men back, but they cannot be stopped. The seaman is thrown to the deck and his rope cast aside.

They take the same route Mr Hart took, past the second-class library, up the aft staircase to the fancy restaurant, and forward along the first-class corridors to the Grand Staircase, where this time no one lingers. The green water is only two decks below.

When they reach the boat deck, Stella sees at once that most of the lifeboats have gone. There are hundreds of people here now, pushing, crying, waving farewell, begging to be told where to go. There are first-class passengers in hats and gowns, but there are engine-room labourers too, some with coal-blackened faces, and sailors and stewards, and third-class men in scuffed boots and wet trousers. People move awkwardly in their lifejackets, and little clouds of mist form at their mouths as they breathe and talk. Further aft, the band is still playing its lively music.

Her father and brothers stare open-mouthed at all this activity, but Stella is more interested in what she sees in the darkness beyond the ship's bridge: the lights of the other ship are still there, ethereal, formless, suspended in blackness. This is the ship Mr Kieran says will come to them, but her lights are immobile. She seems to have moved no closer.

Aft along the sloping deck, she finds a boat being lowered. Full of people, it jerks awkwardly down, foot by foot, bumping along the ship's hull plates. The water at this end of the ship is still a long way down.

There's the rush of yet another rocket soaring skyward, and once again the light of the explosion reveals something that brings her fear. In the lifeboat sit Mr Hart and the women and girls he led up here, but nowhere in it does she see her mother or her siblings.

'Where is my mother?' she shouts down to Mr Hart, but he does not respond, perhaps because he cannot hear her over the shouting of sailors, but more likely, she thinks, because he is ashamed. He has gotten into a lifeboat knowing there are still hundreds of women and children on the ship.

But she doesn't need him to tell her where her mother and siblings are after all. When she turns away from the rail, they are there before her. Her mother is embracing her father and next to her, holding hands

dutifully in a chain, are Dolly, Ada, Connie, Will and Tom. Little Tom
lets go of Connie's hand and rushes forward. His eyes are alight with
the excitement of adventure. He holds tight to his blue blanket; his
golden curls sit on the shoulder panels of his lifejacket.

'Stella!' he cries. 'We waited for you. We didn't get in the boat.'

And as Stella stares hard at her mother, trying to hate her for her
breach of promise, she can already feel Tom's cold little hand slipping
into hers.

When Stone, looking into the night, sees another rocket he says softly
to Gibson, as if thinking aloud, 'A ship isn't going to fire rockets at sea
for nothing.' He walks again to the Morse lamp key. 'There must be
something the matter with her.'

Gibson says, 'We should wake Sparks.' As Stone hesitates, the
apprentice presses. 'We should wake him up and get him to send a
message.'

Stone is unsure. It isn't up to the apprentice to order the waking of
the wireless operator, it's up to the captain. 'The captain told us to use
the Morse lamp,' he says, taking to the key again. 'He didn't say anything about wireless.'

In London, Mr Thomas Scanlan, MP asks Captain Lord why he
didn't give such a command. 'When you were in doubt as to the name
of this ship and the meaning of her sending up a rocket, could you not
have ascertained definitely by calling in the assistance of your Marconi
operator?'

Lord's response is immediate, and he seems to think it a complete
answer to the question. 'When? At one o'clock in the morning?'

Scanlan, round-faced, thick-set, swelling with Irish bluster, says
simply, 'Yes.'

'I did not think anything about it,' Lord says. 'I was not at all concerned about the steamer.'

'Had this steamer which you saw, and which you say was at all events about the same size as your own, had a Marconi installation, and had you obtained the assistance of your operator, you could have got into direct communication with her, whoever she was?'

'If she had had a Marconi, of course we could have got into communication.'

'You had the Marconi?'

'Yes, we had.'

'Would not it have been quite a simple thing for you at that time to have wakened your Marconi operator and asked him to speak to this ship?'

'It would if it had worried me a great deal, but it did not worry me. I was still thinking of the company signal.'

'At all events, now, in the light of your experience, would it not have been a prudent thing to do?'

'Well, we would have got the *Titanic*'s signals if we had done.'

'As a matter of mere precaution, when you were in doubt and left word that someone was to come down to your cabin and give you a message, would not it have been a proper thing to have tried the experiment?'

'I was waiting for further information. I had a responsible officer on the bridge who was finding things out for me.'

He is right. On the bridge his second officer is diligently finding things out for him – looking through binoculars, operating the Morse tapper, and taking bearings – while the wireless operator sleeps peacefully below. As Herbert Stone goes about this work, carefully and conscientiously, the bridge bell tolls three times, once for each half-hour of the watch. It is half past one.

The eighth rocket

As Stella Sage leans over the rail and watches the seamen disconnect Mr Hart's boat from the falls and push it gently away from the ship, another rocket is fired. The explosion no longer surprises people. Most do not even look up.

The lights of the other ship are still no closer. She wonders why it is not coming to them. 'You should have got into the lifeboat,' she says to her mother.

'I thought it best that we stay together,' her mother replies. 'No matter what happens.'

There's a resignation in her tone, but Stella remains determined. She will somehow get the family into a lifeboat. Nothing will stop her, even though the world has become perverse. The deck slopes ever more steeply forward, the lights burn a dim orange-red, and the band has stopped playing ragtime. The sad music of hymns now floats in the frigid air.

The rearmost boat is being loaded at the very aft end of the ship, supervised by the same senior officer she saw earlier politely inviting men to get in. He has a kind look to his face. This will be their boat, Stella decides, and she hustles the family to it.

But there are problems. The senior officer is being assisted by a junior who does not have a kind look to his face. The young man shouts and curses and waves a gun in the air. A large crowd is surging and pushing, and because the ship is listing, the lifeboat hangs away from the ship's side. A three-foot gap has opened up, with nothing but the black sea beneath.

'Let the little ones through!' Stella shouts. 'Let them through!'

At the aft end of the lifeboat a plank has been laid down and women are being helped across it one by one. Stella positions her family at the forward end and then jumps quickly into the boat. A woman on board shouts at her. 'Get out! There's no more room!' But Stella ignores her and calls to her sisters to jump too. Dolly and Ada leap across. Connie hesitates; the gap is too wide. She starts to cry. George lifts her under the arms and swings her into the boat. He passes little Tom in next and then helps his mother.

There are already some forty people in the boat and it is filling fast, but Stella at least has her mother, sisters and youngest brother aboard.

Then things begin to go wrong. People who've seen the Sages jump begin to do the same. A young woman leaps over, a baby is thrown and caught by a passenger, a child lands awkwardly on a steel rowlock and howls in pain. An older boy jumps in, at which point the junior officer leaps after him and tries to pull him out. There's a struggle; the officer threatens the youth with the gun; women beg him not to shoot. When the boy at last gets out of the boat, another young woman tries to jump in. She catches her foot on the lip of the ship's side and trips. As she clutches the rim of the lifeboat, her legs flailing in empty space, Stella thinks she must surely fall into the water. But two men standing on the promenade deck below take hold of her legs and pull her screaming back aboard the ship.

Stella begins to feel strangely distant from the events around her. She senses she is losing control. Ada and Dolly are both crying now, the crowd is pushing forward harder. Then comes a deafening explosion as the junior officer fires his gun into the air. Some men drift away but Stella can still see her father. George has put his arm around him to shield him from the shoving of other men.

Someone is shouting and Stella is surprised to find it's her own voice, calling Will to get into the boat. But the junior officer blocks him. 'There will be no more men in the boat!' he says, holding the gun flat in his hand, ready to strike anyone who might try to get past him. Will is placid; he seems almost to smile.

Her mother, teetering beside her, begs for Will to be let on board. 'He's only eleven,' she says. But still the officer refuses. Two more women step across the plank into the boat. One is holding a baby in her arms.

The ship, it seems, has righted itself a little, because the lifeboat now hangs closer to the ship's side. But no one else gets in. The boat jerks and sways. The lowering has begun.

Stella, standing upright in the boat, turns to her mother and takes hold of both her hands. She knows what is about to happen, and she must try to stop it. 'You have a special strength too, Mother,' she says. 'Be strong now. Let them go. Let *him* go.'

For a moment the world drifts away. All Stella can see is her mother enfolding her, kissing her on the cheek – so gently! – and saying, 'You're right, my dear daughter. I have a special strength.' And before Stella can say anything more, her mother has slipped herself free and stepped out of the lifeboat as daintily as if she were leaving an omnibus. Ada and Dolly scramble out after her.

The lowering of the boat stops. The junior officer, standing a few feet above, looks at Stella. 'You too?' he asks.

She's still holding the hands of Connie and Tom. Connie is sobbing for her mother and Tom repeats to himself in a high-pitched voice, 'There's no occasion! There's no occasion!' Their little hands tighten on hers.

On the deck, Ada and Dolly have joined their brothers, and her mother clutches Will. Stella sees her father behind George, being buffeted by men. He holds out his arms and calls to her. 'There's another boat,' he says, 'on the other side, big enough to take us all.'

Stella looks at her father: his narrow, anguished face, his fear, his love. 'Of course there is,' she says softly to herself. 'Another boat, big enough to take us all.'

She steps out of the lifeboat into the warmth of his embrace.

On the *Californian*'s bridge Stone stands in silence with Gibson, transfixed by the strange ship in the distance. She has fired another rocket, the eighth that Stone has seen. It is twenty minutes to two.

The atmosphere is odd. The air is perfectly clear, but seems to quiver with an unearthly energy. It makes Stone think of the ether between the stars, which can be neither seen nor felt, which has neither weight nor substance, and which, a teacher once told him, allows heavenly bodies to fly through it without the slightest hindrance. He waves a hand in front of his face. He wants to make sure the air is there; he wants to feel a breeze. The dead calm agitates him.

'Look at her now, Jim,' he says to the apprentice, his voice rising in pitch. 'She looks queer, don't you think? She looks very queer out of the water. There's a funny change of her lights.'

Gibson peers through his binoculars. 'She seems to have a big side out of the water,' he says.

'Yes, her lights look peculiar. Unnatural, somehow – as if some are being shut in and others opened out.'

'They don't look the same as they did before.'

'No,' Stone says, 'they don't.'

The lights seem to pulse and flare, like someone blowing on an ember. Stone waits for more rockets. Four bells comes and goes – two o'clock, halfway through the watch – and now he notices that the ship's lights are fading. He turns to Gibson. 'Go down, wake him up and tell him,' he says, suddenly firm.

Gibson hesitates. 'Tell him what?'

'That we couldn't get her with the lamp, that we tried again but couldn't, that she's fired eight rockets altogether and now she's disappearing in the southwest. Make sure you wake him. *Make sure.*'

When Gibson is gone, Stone leans forward over the bridge rail towards the ship, as if by being a little closer he might solve her riddles. When he'd first seen the ship, with Captain Lord standing by his side at the rail outside the chartroom, her masthead light and red sidelight were beautifully clear and steady. Now all he can see is the yellowish, indistinct glare of deck lights.

He doesn't hear Gibson come back, and gives a little cry of surprise when he finds him standing at his elbow.

'Sorry, Second,' the apprentice says.

'Is he coming up?' Stone asks, turning inboard from the rail.

'No.'

'Why not?'

Gibson shrugs.

'Well, what did he say?'

'He asked me if they had any colour in them.'

'And?'

'I said they were white, all white.'

'What else?'

'I said she was disappearing in the southwest, just like you said. Then he said, "Very well," and we are to let him know if anything is wanted.'

'If anything is wanted,' Stone repeats slowly. 'So he's not coming up?'

'No.'

Stone, left alone with his thoughts and his decisions, turns slowly to the steamer once again. Her lights – the queer, glowing, changing lights – dim further.

In London, Mr Butler Aspinall, KC tries one last time to understand. 'What did you think, at the time, the rockets meant?'

Stone stares straight ahead, keeping his body still. 'I knew they were signals of some sort.'

'I know that – of course – they are signals. But signals *of what sort*, did you think?'

'I did not know at the time,' Stone says.

Aspinall feels as if he is clutching at mist. There is something strange about this witness. He seems able to suspend his own thinking, like an animal that can stop its breathing when it senses danger.

Even the Commissioner seems unnerved by the vacuum of Stone's answers. 'Now, do try to be frank!' he implores.

'I am,' Stone says.

'If you try, you will succeed. What did you think these rockets were going up at intervals of three or four minutes for?'

'I just took them as white rockets, and informed the captain and left him to judge.'

The ladies in the gallery look on in fascinated horror. They put aside their opera glasses. What they see is plain enough to the naked eye: a man who reported the rockets to his captain but who now desperately wishes he had done more. Herbert Stone is sorry. They can see it in his anguished eyes now welling with tears, in his clutching of the flimsy rail of the witness stand. Let him go, they think. He is a good man. He has been tortured enough.

But the Commissioner, a man who has built his career on judging, deciding and thinking, does not let him go. He is appalled by the blind faith the witness has in his captain, as pitiful and absolute as the trust an infant son might have in his father. 'You mean to say,' Lord Mersey says, his hands resting in clenched fists before him on his great desk, 'that you did not think for yourself?'

Stone is silent.

'You know, you do not make a good impression upon me at present,' Lord Mersey tells him.

Aspinall tries to help the witness. 'You know they were not being sent up for fun, were they?'

'No.'

'Did you think that they were distress signals?'

'No.'

But for Stone on his freezing bridge, in the depths of night, whether the steamer has been sending up her rockets for fun, or distress, or some other reason, matters no longer, for at twenty past two, her lights disappear altogether.

Stone walks to the rear bulkhead, picks up the speaking tube and blows into its mouthpiece. Moments later he hears the captain's weary voice.

'What is it?'

'The ship firing the rockets has disappeared, bearing southwest by west.'

Stone can hear the captain breathing at the other end of the tube.

'There was no colour in them?'

'No, Captain, they were all white rockets. All white.'

'Very well. Put it in the log.'

Stone hears the stopper being replaced in the tube. He takes the scrap log from its small cupboard and writes an entry in it by the light of the compass binnacle. He describes the rockets and notes the times he whistled down to Captain Lord, and the time he sent down the apprentice. He has informed the master, as was his duty. Now the troublesome steamer has gone, and there is peace at last on the bridge of the *Californian*.

When Stella feels the deck beneath her feet rise suddenly she almost falls, but steadies herself. A low groan comes from deep in the ship and the deck lights glow red. Ahead of her the seawater has reached the forward end of the boat deck. It creeps along, swirling in menacing currents around the feet of desperate men trying to right an upturned boat. One of them kicks at the water as if it were a dog biting his heels. Another, standing nearby in a splendid military uniform, shouts at people in an American accent and waves a gun at a poor cowering boy with dark skin. But it's all in vain: the boat floats uselessly upside down in the deepening water. Stella can see no other lifeboats.

A man in evening dress is trying to lash himself to a wooden door. Another ties steamer chairs together to form a raft, but the chairs keep sliding away from him. A woman has strapped her lifejacket around her waist rather than placing it over her shoulders, and it looks like an outlandish girdle. She's struggling to carry two children – a baby in a sling and a sleeping toddler propped over one shoulder. She cries out for help but no one comes.

Stella would like to go to her aid, but she must think of her own family. If Doug and Fred could hunt about for chairs, or anything made of wood, perhaps they could lash together a raft big enough to hold them all.

But it's so difficult to stand up. The deck is too steep to walk any further aft. Stella keeps her balance by leaning against the wall of a small deckhouse. Her father is squatting on his haunches to bring his face level with little Tom's. She can hear him talking of the ship that is coming to take them all to Jacksonville, but Tom doesn't care any more. His eyelids droop with exhaustion and he holds his blanket to his face. He's had enough of the adventure now, he wants to go to bed.

Will has run off again. Her mother is calling out for him, but there's nothing that can be done. The water is only a few feet away.

Doug chases three dogs that have come loping along. The animals are skittish and nervous. Stella is grateful that someone has at least thought to free them from their kennels. When Doug tries to loop a rope through their collars she asks why. 'So they won't be alone,' he says.

Fred comes to her and once again takes her hand. He doesn't say a word, but squeezes her hand in nervous little pulses. Dolly comes to her too, crying and saying she's scared of drowning.

'Don't be silly,' Stella says, 'you can't drown with a lifejacket on.'

Connie is holding onto Dolly's dress with both hands and will not let go, even when Dolly tries to push her away, but George, smoking a cigarette, picks Connie up and tells her there's nothing to worry about.

Stella can still see the lights of the ship in the distance and thinks there might yet be a way through; if they can all stay together in the water, it must surely come to them eventually. They can keep each other warm with their bodies in the meantime. Yes, she thinks, there might yet be a way through.

Now the ship lurches and the water runs up along the deck towards them. It all happens more quickly than Stella expects, but also more gently. The sea surges and gurgles about her legs, then her waist, then lifts her delicately away from the deck altogether. Yards quickly open up between her and the ship. Her lifejacket keeps her floating high in the water; she does not even get her hair wet.

She looks around for her family but just then the cold comes to her, all at once and without mercy. She has no thoughts, just the sensation that she is burning. She tries to cry out but can make no sound. She cannot draw in enough air. She stutters and gasps and feels her body burst into spasms of shivering.

Now she sees her father in the water. He is nearby, reaching instinctively upwards, as if by clutching at handfuls of air he might somehow drag himself out of the ocean. George, too, is near and she sees some of the others. She at last finds her voice. 'Keep together!' she cries. 'You bigger children make a ring, with the little ones inside. Make a ring. Hold onto each other.'

There are grinding, roaring sounds behind her and people are screaming. She does not turn around to look but searches instead for the rest of her siblings. Her father, she sees, has little Tom, and her mother is pushing Connie towards them with the backs of her hands. 'In the middle,' says Stella, 'yes, that's it – it's warmer there. The little ones inside.' George and Fred and Doug are trying to grasp the arms of their sisters, but the girls are drifting away. Dolly holds her hands up to the sky, as if trying to warm them against the distant stars. Ada has dropped into the water the orange given her by Will and is trying to pick it up again.

But where is Will? Her mother is near her now, calling his name. Stella calls out for him too, but there's no answer. The ship has gone altogether and there is an engulfing darkness.

The children have almost formed a ring but now it falls apart completely. In this bitterly cold water their little hands cannot hold on. They are drifting away. Her father is crying out, 'Please help us, we have children here!' But Stella knows that no one will come. There are hundreds of people in this black water. She can hear their cries and groans flying unheeded to heaven.

Connie drifts near and asks her if she may close her eyes while she waits.

'No,' says Stella. 'You must not close your eyes.' But her voice is a thin whisper and Connie can't have heard, because her eyes are now closed. Ada has closed hers too, and Dolly, and Doug. She gives up trying to stop them. The children float high in their lifejackets and the water is calm; it won't splash into their mouths as they sleep. And the water is not, after all, so very cold. She realises she has stopped shivering.

Fred and George are splashing about, trying to do something with rope and a deck chair, but they soon give up. They too close their eyes and rest.

The children's faces are lit by starlight. They look like sleeping angels. Wisps of mist lie on the water and gather about their necks in scarves of gossamer. Stella still cannot see Will. Perhaps someone has reached down and pulled him into a lifeboat. In this silvery light people will have looked at him in the water and seen that he is not a man, as the officer with the gun had said, but just a little boy, with a face more beautiful than any on earth and eyes that shimmer like a dragonfly's wings in summer. They will have pulled him aboard and women with feathers in their hats and fur round their necks will have covered him with blankets and blessed his white cheeks with kisses.

Here's little Tom now, floating next to her. His eyes are wide open, staring straight ahead into the mystery of things. With the back of a gentle finger Stella slides his eyelids shut and leans forward to kiss him. 'Goodnight,' she says, 'my dear little brother.'

The reddish-white light of the mystery ship is hanging steady beneath the North Star. All our exploding rockets, she thinks, and it never did come. But there's no point waiting any more.

She turns away from the cold light in the north, and from her sleeping family, and begins swimming south towards Jacksonville, where the water will be warmer. This is a journey she must make alone.

Stella can feel the powerful stride of her arms and already she begins to feel warm – quite, quite warm.

EPILOGUE

The *Titanic* gradually disappeared from the newspapers. The Great War came, and then the Second World War, and the industrial slaughter of so many people seemed to erase the public memory of all that had gone before. The loss of fifteen hundred in one night hardly seemed to matter any more. People forgot about the disaster altogether, or otherwise knew of it only vaguely.

I made a mediocre living doing what I did best: searching out the truth and giving voice to the dead. I discovered cruelty and recklessness in army generals and wrote biographies of men vaporised during bombing missions. After the war I put aside my typewriter and surprised myself by turning seventy. I had always thought growing old was something other people did.

My daughter, meanwhile, flourished. In 1920 she voted in her first Massachusetts election, and celebrated by hosting a party in which she and her female friends wore men's evening suits and held cigars in their mouths. They had joined the enfranchised at last, my daughter said in a short speech, but they still had a long way to go. A year or so later she married a military man, but she promised me he was no Archibald Butt. He'd never once shot a craven and never would. I grew to like him very much. When he died of cancer after the war, Harriet said, as simply as if she were stating a mathematical truth, that she would never marry again. She had no children, and when she invited me to share her bright and airy house in South Boston, I agreed. The move made Olive and Vivienne angry at first, but in time they grew used to the idea and would visit on Sundays to drink sherry and play cards.

My manuscript about the *Californian* affair languished in a bottom drawer. But then, one freezing January morning in 1959, when I was eighty-three years old, Harriet took me to see a new British film about the *Titanic* disaster. The cinema was crowded, and there were gasps and cries as the ship reared before us on an enormous screen. The *Californian* was shown stopped nearby in the icefield, with Captain Lord sleeping below and Stone and Gibson on the bridge above. I laughed a little: Stone was portrayed as a self-assured officer of perhaps forty years of age – nothing like the baby-faced, timid man in his early twenties I had met. Lord was shown asleep in his cabin bunk in his pyjamas, rather than fully clothed on the chartroom settee; he was overweight and in his fifties, not a lean and bronzed 34-year-old.

But the movie, inaccurate though it was, brought back memories, and later, at home, I took from my drawer my manuscript. 'Do you think,' I asked my daughter, 'that you might seek to have this published after I'm gone, to set the record straight?'

'Gladly, Papa,' she said. Harriet knew something of the book business, having worked at Beacon Press for a short time after the war.

'But it's not quite finished.'

'No, it's not.'

'Do you think, after all this time, he might agree to see me?'

'If you ask him nicely,' she said, sliding closer to me on the couch and leaning her head against mine, 'I don't see why not.'

What is it about some women that makes them age so well? Why did I know as soon as I saw Mrs Stone that she'd been able to float above those earthly things that had dragged the rest of us down? She reminded me of a seabird carried aloft by air currents rather than by the flapping of wings; she had the sort of strength men never have. We become such ponderous, sullen things, we men, but Mrs Stone was light – oh, so light.

It was a misty afternoon in late November in that same year of 1959 when she welcomed Harriet and me to her home in Bootle. It was a smaller house than that in which I'd seen her almost fifty years earlier, but it was all she could afford, she said, so there was no use complaining. She had raised three children since we last met, two sons and a daughter, who were now raising children of their own.

We sat in the front parlour and spoke of jet travel, television, supermarkets and *Sputnik*. Mrs Stone made us tea, and when the afternoon light began to fade she turned on a small electric radiator. In its soft orange glow the three of us looked almost young again. For a while no one spoke, and in our little cocoon of warmth time seemed to slow.

'We were so very sorry,' Harriet said at last, 'to hear about your husband.'

'Thank you,' Mrs Stone replied. 'Herbert was the gentlest of men. I miss him very much.'

He had died, she said, quite suddenly, during his usual morning walk to work. A brain haemorrhage. He had been a storeman at the nearby docks, still able to lift heavy boxes even at the age of seventy-two. He stayed at sea for more than twenty years after the *Titanic* but he was never very happy. He never got his own command. He went missing once, from his ship in London, and was eventually found sitting alone on a pier in Devon. He didn't return to sea again after that. 'He much preferred his work in the warehouse,' she said. 'He loved it.'

I wondered what it had been like for him – all those years in that warehouse to think and remember. And I wondered what it had been like for this gracious woman who sat before me with pretty flowers pinned to her blouse. I felt sorry for her: when Harriet and I took our leave she would again be alone in this house. I was grateful for my splendid, devoted daughter, with me always, more important than air.

'Why are you here?' Mrs Stone asked softly, and I recalled that once her husband had asked me the very same thing.

'I'm on my way to see Stanley Lord,' I said, 'and it would hardly have been polite not to call in on you, would it?' I waited a little, smiled, then added, 'And you never did tell me what you thought of my story – of the eight rockets.'

'Didn't I?'

'No, you didn't.'

'Well, I thought it was very sad.'

Again we fell to silence. A wireless crackled softly in an adjacent room, and I could hear someone picking out a tune on a neighbour's piano. Children laughed in the far distance. Mrs Stone seemed to be listening for something specific in these sounds, angling her head one way and then the other, but I could not tell what.

'Did Mr Lord,' she asked, closing her eyes in thought, 'ever tell you what *he* thought of your story?'

'I doubt he would have bought a copy.'

'My husband sent him one.'

'Then I doubt he would have read it.'

Mrs Stone seemed to ponder this carefully. Then, without speaking, she rose and left the room. I wondered whether we had been dismissed, but a moment later she returned with a thin brown envelope. 'If you're going to see Mr Lord,' she said, 'then please do give him this.' She took from the envelope a small sheet of yellowed paper on which words had been scrawled in pencil.

I knew at once what it was, even though so many years had passed. My memory clarified, like images resolving on photographic paper: the *Californian*'s bridge; a small, unlocked cupboard; the ship's scrap log; the stubs of torn-out pages, one stub showing that a particular page had been cut out with meticulous care.

Mrs Stone handed me that page now as reverently as if it were a sacred parchment, and in the soft light I read Herbert Stone's tentative, pencilled words. 'One Bell: Ship – southwest – fired white rocket. Four more rockets – Informed Master by speaking tube. Two Bells: Morsed ship as per captain's orders. Two more rockets. Strange glare of light. Three Bells: One more rocket. Eight in total. Informed Master by apprentice. Five Bells: Ship disappeared in southwest. Informed Master by speaking tube.' The words were faded and smudged, yet they were enough to drag that little piece of history through time and space to appear vividly before me once again.

'Your husband cut this page out?' I asked.

'No. Not my husband.' She gave a little laugh. 'Mr Stewart did. Do you remember him? The chief officer. A strange man. He sent this page just before the war, to return it to its rightful owner.' Mrs Stone paused, then added, 'He cut it out to protect the captain, you see.'

I did see. The words 'Informed Master' appeared three times on the page. In this whole sorry business, those two words were for Herbert Stone the most important of all.

'Herbert wrote to Mr Lord many times over the years,' Mrs Stone said. 'He pleaded with him. As I say, he even sent him a copy of your story. But he never heard back.'

As I looked around the room, the years seemed to blend away and make vivid my sadness. There were framed photographs of Herbert on the walls – with his children, with his grandchildren – but images came to me of him facing the men of the Boston press in the cramped chartroom of his ship. He had been fearful then, a trapped animal, and his eyes had looked to me for help. I'd given him my card and asked him to talk to me, but I should have done more.

'Make sure he reads it,' Mrs Stone said with a new firmness. 'Make him read that page and make him understand: my husband called him, and he should have gone up. It's simple, really. If he can accept that, then at last, at long, long last, this thing will be over.'

I gave my promise: I would deliver to Lord the scrap log page and I would make him read it. And perhaps I would get from him, finally, an admission.

Shortly afterwards Harriet and I took our seats in a taxi. As we drove away I looked back and glimpsed Mrs Stone standing in her doorway, framed by golden light as if already in heaven.

That night, in our Liverpool hotel room, with Harriet mixing gin cocktails, I couldn't stop thinking about what Mrs Stone had told us. I had a vision of Herbert writing letter after letter to Lord and never getting a reply. I imagined the pencils, the erasers, the discarded drafts, and wondered what words he'd used. I wondered what I would have written, had I been Herbert Stone writing to Stanley Lord.

From somewhere deep in my memory came the words of one of my countrymen, which I had learned by rote as a schoolboy. 'O Captain!

my Captain! our fearful trip is done . . . O Captain! my Captain! rise up and hear the bells; Rise up – for you the flag is flung – for you the bugle trills . . .'

'Hello, hello! I am pleased that you have come,' said Stanley Lord when he opened his door to Harriet and me two days later. The old captain's home – a two-storey, pebble-stone terrace house with large bay windows – was only half a mile or so north of the house he'd lived in when I last saw him.

'Thank you for agreeing to see me,' I said. 'This is my daughter, Harriet.'

Lord gave a low bow. He was now very thin, with sunken pits at his temples and cloudy white spots in his eyes. I was not sure how well he could see us. But even in the infirmity of old age there was something tough and unyielding about this man: the sags and folds of his face seemed only to emphasise the strong, hard bone of his skull underneath.

He led us into a warm, open living room with a large armchair, two couches and a gramophone. Small stained-glass panels glowed behind the lace curtains of the bay window; vases of flowers sat on its sill.

A puffy man of about fifty stood nervously by the window. He closed his hands into little fists, which he held beneath his chin, and smiled at me through lips drawn tight around two prominent front teeth. I knew at once who he was. He had his father's baldness, and had pulled strands across his head and smoothed them down with hair cream.

Lord introduced the man as Tutty, his only child. 'He is named Tutton,' Lord said, 'my wife's maiden name.' He spoke in slow, measured sentences, as if his son's presence required a special explanation. Mrs Lord died two years earlier, Lord told us, but Tutty had never married and still lived at home, and so was able to care for him just as capably as his wife had. Nor had Tutty gone to the war; he would not have lasted long abroad, Lord said. It was much better that he stay put at home, where he could look after the garden and listen to opera on the gramophone.

'Do you like the opera?' Lord asked me.

'As a matter of fact,' I said, 'I don't much care for it.'

'Neither do I,' Lord replied with a chuckle, 'but Tutty does, don't you Tutty?'

Tutty said nothing, but hung up our hats and coats and led his father by the arm to the large chair. Harriet and I sat on one of the couches, Tutty went to make tea. Here, too, the walls around us bore framed photographs: Lord in full captain's uniform on the bridge of a ship; Lord with his wife and Tutty on a beach promenade; Lord, Tutty and another man in a touring car.

I was a retired Harvard professor, Lord believed from the letter I'd sent him, researching a history of the nitrate trade, and by the time Tutty returned with the tea, Lord was speaking expansively about his years as a commander in the Nitrate Producers' Steamship Company. He told us of the ships, the ports, the officers he'd sailed with. It was a special breed of men, he said, who worked in the trade: proud Englishmen with courage and initiative. He showed us a polished silver frame containing a reference from his employer. 'We regard him as one of the most capable Commanders we have ever had,' it read.

Harriet was charming. She listened, she praised, she asked questions. I marvelled at her storytelling. It was a perfect blend of fact and fiction; her transitions were so seamless that even I became confused. In one moment she joked about Harvard being located in a suburb called Cambridge, in another she awarded me the Beacon

Hill Prize for Historical Writing. By her openness she encouraged
Lord to be open; by her flattery she made his aged skin flush pink. She
was an elixir, and he was young again. He spoke of the first war, when
he'd almost sunk a German submarine, and of how he had become an
expert in transporting horses. He sent Tutty out to find for us letters of
commendation from the governments of America, France, and other
places.

A large grandfather clock chimed away the quarter-hours. It was
a pleasant scene: one old man sharing his memories with another, two
dutiful children patiently listening. It was, as Lord himself might have
described it, most convivial. But it was time for me to bring things into
sharper focus.

'You were also, I think, captain of the *Californian*?'

It was inelegant, and Lord turned sharply. He blinked and opened
wide his cloudy eyes, and I had again the sense that perhaps he could
not see me, that my daughter and I for him were only blurs and
shadows.

'I was,' he said. 'And what of it?'

I had to be careful. The scrap log page lay in my pocket, and I
needed to find a way to make him read it. 'I wondered only whether,
perhaps, you'd kept up with any of the men you sailed with on that
ship?'

'No,' said Lord. 'None of them. I saw Mr Groves once – in
Australia, I think it was – and Mr Stewart I saw some years ago in
Liverpool.' He sat thinking for a while. 'The whole business was an
outrage, of course.'

'What business do you mean?'

'The *Titanic*.' He still pronounced the name in his own strange
way, *Ti*-tar-*nic*. From his mouth it sounded like the name of a caustic
chemical.

'So Lord Mersey got it wrong?'

'Of course he did. He wanted a bloody goat, and I was it. The whole thing is a damned shame.'

Lord now spoke freely and quickly: about how he'd been portrayed in the recent movie, how someone at the Mercantile Marine Service Association in Liverpool had helped him to lodge a formal complaint, how his name would soon be cleared once and for all. He didn't need Lord Mersey or anyone else to tell him about the *Californian* and what she saw. He had *been* there, on the spot, and he knew they didn't see any *Titanic*. A ship like that at sea was an utter impossibility to mistake.

His voice had grown in power and volume. Its deep timbre seemed to infuse every particle of air in the room with its vibration. He still had an uncanny power to possess a space. I was reminded of the way he'd enthralled the Boston pressmen with his lilting voice that flowed around us like a warm breeze. He seemed now as he did then: trustworthy, persuasive, believable. He was animated by his innocence.

'But what about the rockets?' I asked.

He turned to me slowly, as if he'd forgotten I was there. Tutty stood up, as a warning to me, perhaps, not to go too far.

'The rockets?' Lord repeated.

'Yes,' I said. 'The rockets seen by your ship.'

'They were from another ship,' he said. 'Another ship firing rockets. My man at the association has worked it all out.'

I waited a moment to let his point settle. 'And the ship seen by the *Titanic* – that was not you?'

'Oh no.'

'There were two ships, then, between you and the *Titanic*?'

'Two ships.'

'So, four ships altogether?'

'Yes. Four ships!'

He was triumphant. He was looking over my head in his old way, as if addressing an audience in the middle distance. Harriet and I glanced at each other. She was as surprised, I think, as I was: we had expected anger from this man, or a refusal to speak at all about the *Titanic*, not this energy. Lord was in a heightened state; he seemed almost thrilled. There was not one sign of remorse, not a hint of regret, not a single note of sadness. There was still no admission that he'd done wrong, only a very great certainty that he was right.

Now, I thought, was the time to do what I'd promised Mrs Stone. But Tutty had moved to take up a position behind his father's chair, and before I could reach into my pocket, he announced it was time for his father's walk.

Tutty bustled us into his father's old Austin and drove us to New Brighton, at the mouth of the Mersey. People of the Wirral, Tutty said, came here to breathe the sea air and be revived by the spirit of the great river. The water was vast and grey, but the lowering sun threw warm colours generously onto the opposite bank. We strolled slowly along a wide promenade. Harriet took the old captain's arm to guide him gently, leaning her head into his shoulder from time to time. Tutty and I walked a few paces behind. His father's eyesight was failing, Tutty said, and he had other problems too – his heart, his kidneys – but his legs were still strong.

Tutty told me he'd been so very annoyed when his father took himself off on the ferry to Liverpool to complain to the marine association about the *Titanic* movie. The young man at the association had taken the case up with such gusto that his father now spent his days gathering documents, swearing affidavits and writing letters. The project animated him, but it exhausted Tutty. He wondered when it would all end. 'If Mother were here,' he said, 'she would have told Father to leave it well alone. She never spoke of it, you know. Not once, in all those years.' He paused a moment then added, 'And nor did I.'

A mile or so behind us was the silhouette of an amusement park with rides that Tutty had heard of, he told me, but never ridden – the Big Dipper, Helter Skelter, the Big Wheel – but they were all quiet now. The season was long over. Ahead, in the river itself, was a low granite battlement linked to the shore by a platform of glistening green stone, which was exposed by the low tide. 'It's called the Rock Battery,' Tutty said, blowing his nose into a red silk handkerchief.

We arrived at a wooden bench with a commanding view of the battery and Liverpool Bay beyond. I was getting very tired. The light was fading, but the twilight would last an hour yet. Gulls swooped and soared; men shouted from distant boats. Children still played on the rocks, poking sticks into crevices and collecting muddy shells in woollen hats. Tutty helped his father onto the bench and I sat next to him. Lord struck his walking stick twice on the ground and called for Tutty to get us all some tea from a vendor in a motor van. Harriet offered to walk with him, and the two set off together.

And so, forty-seven years after I first met this stern British captain and began to seek out his story, we sat alone together and stared out to the sea that had tricked him so cruelly.

We chatted quietly for a while. He replied to me sometimes in odd ways, so that my words seemed like stones dropped down a dark well. I never knew quite where they went, or when I might hear a splash.

'Funny,' I said to him, 'things seem smaller to me now. I find, at our age, only the important things resonate. All the rest . . . is nothing.'

'I can't see the river any more,' he said, 'but I can hear it. I know it is ebbing, just by the sound.'

When I looked closely I saw that he was right: the vast grey surface of the river was moving almost imperceptibly seaward. But what, I wondered, could he hear? The water was perfectly calm. No ships or ferries disturbed the surface and there was no wind to whip up wavelets. Even the gulls had settled.

'It is kind of you, Captain Lord, to talk to me, but I wonder whether you know who I really am? Do you know that I'm John Steadman, the man who published the donkeyman's affidavit against you, all those years ago?'

He waved a hand impatiently. 'Oh yes, yes, of course,' he said, but I didn't think at all that he did know. I pressed him further. 'And do you know that Mr Stone, your second officer, has died?'

He seemed puzzled by the question. 'I don't know anything about him.'

'He has, I think, been sending you letters?'

Lord hesitated. 'I have never read any letters from that man. None at all.'

The page from the scrap log still lay in my pocket, thin and fragile as rice paper. I thought of Herbert Stone's tentative, pencilled words – 'Informed Master by speaking tube' – and wondered if now was the time to produce them, but Lord suddenly asked, 'Do you know your Bible, Mr Steadman?'

'I'm from Boston,' I said in answer.

'Blessed are the meek, for they shall inherit the Earth. They got rid of me from that ship, Mr Steadman, but Mr Stone stayed on.'

I turned to him. His eyebrows were raised and his clouded eyes stared blankly at me. He held his hands out, palms up, inviting me to ponder one of the great mysteries of the world.

We were at the nub of the matter. As I sat there on the bench with him, watching Tutty in the distance struggle with cardboard teacups, I thought back to the time all those years ago when Lord had struggled to push his son's pram through the doorway of his home. I'd seen then an expression on his face that I'd not quite been able to read – a contortion of his sharp nose, a drawing-down of his eyebrows, a grim tightening of his lips. But now, as my memory returned, I suddenly knew what I'd seen. It was a deep and abiding disgust at his coddled, whimpering son, and all the weak creatures of God's earth.

All his life Lord had despised the weakness of others – the apprentices who'd drunk wine and slept with Chilean prostitutes; the officers who'd trained in steam, not sail; the dithering, timid Mr Stone. Yet Mr Stone had kept his place, while he, the capable commander, had been sacrificed.

I saw it clearly. When Stone called down on the speaking tube that night, talking of rockets in a tentative, feeble voice, Lord heard weakness. He may have thought of his son, who would not walk by himself, who wanted always to be pushed in his pram, who clung to his mother and turned away from his father. In those moments in his cabin, not knowing anything about the *Titanic* or her fate, not knowing he had only minutes to act, he wanted Stone to do what an officer of the watch should do: use his initiative and find out what was wrong.

And on that freezing bridge above, Herbert Stone heard his captain's gruff annoyance and did not want to anger him further. Perhaps he heard in Lord's voice something of his own overbearing father, who'd stuffed rags in his mouth and made him watch kittens drown in a bag. He was worried about the rockets, but he'd told Lord about them, and that was enough.

So responsibility for action fell like a snowflake from the sky, landing gently between them, touching neither. And in this con-centrated moment in history, nothing was done.

Those rockets! Unanswered then and unanswerable ever after.

A moist air drifted up to keep Lord and me warm. Sharp edges gave way to gentle shades of green and grey and blue. Somewhere far out to sea were thunderstorms; I could see lightning dancing and flickering on the horizon. From the deep past a thought came to me: There is energy all around. And perhaps it came to Harriet too, because I could see her in the distance – still beautiful and radiant in her sixties – with her back to us, standing still and looking out to the horizon's lively light.

The captain and I sat quietly for a moment. The dusk was deepening, the twilight almost over. Out in the bay a haze had developed, hanging low over the outgoing tide. Lord turned to me and I saw again the cloudy opacity of his eyes. Their pupils were flaring open, as if trying to adjust to the fading light.

'You say you have someone helping you,' I asked, 'at the mercantile association?'

'Oh yes. A young man. He has figured it all out. It was not the *Titanic* we saw.'

I paused. 'No,' I said. 'Of course it wasn't. Absolutely it could not have been. As you say, a ship like that, at night, could never be mistaken.'

Lord lowered his eyebrows and blinked quickly, as if suddenly confused. Was I mocking him? I reached out and took both his hands in mine. His skin was loose and papery beneath my touch, but I could feel the iron strength of the bones beneath. I thought he might withdraw his hands, but he did not. I held them for a full minute, and then another.

And they were as I expected: warm – quite, quite warm.

A Note on the Writing of *The Midnight Watch*

The Midnight Watch is a work of fiction based on true events. Much of what is described in the novel is the result of careful research and represents my best guess as to what actually happened during the *Californian*'s voyage and afterwards. Other parts of the novel are pure invention, and some parts are a blend of fact and fiction.

John Steadman is entirely my own creation. The *Boston American*, however, was a real newspaper and was the paper that broke the *Californian* story by publishing Ernest Gill's affidavit. All quoted newspaper stories and headlines are true, and much of what is said in the novel's various press encounters is taken directly from contemporaneous newspaper reports. I have based my portraits of Philip Franklin, Senator Smith, Sydney Buxton, Lord Mersey, Sir Rufus Isaacs and other minor figures on historical sources, but the IMM Boston agent Jack Thomas is entirely a product of my imagination.

John and Annie Sage and their nine children were a real family who died in the *Titanic* disaster. Little is known about what happened to them, but what I offer is a likely scenario based on the few facts we have and a close reading of inquiry transcripts.

Captain Lord, Herbert Stone and the other members of the *Californian* crew were real people. I have tried to offer authentic representations of them, but have added colour and depth with my own imagining of their thoughts and emotions and some elements of their backstories. Their evidence before the American and British inquiries I have taken verbatim from the transcript, with occasional minor alterations for clarity. One liberty I have taken is to attribute to Herbert Stone a fascination with illustrations of *Moby-Dick* that were not in fact published until 1930. I did this because I love the way these images so powerfully convey the 'heartless voids and immensities of the universe', and the tragedy of a man who did his very best to remain loyal to a flawed skipper.

I encourage readers interested in learning more about 'The *Californian* Incident' to visit my website (daviddyer.com.au).

Acknowledgements

An early version of this novel was written as part of a doctorate in creative arts at the University of Technology, Sydney, and I would like to acknowledge the invaluable instruction and guidance of my supervisors Delia Falconer and Debra Adelaide. I am grateful too for the wonderful assistance and astute advice of my agent Gaby Naher. My particular thanks go to George Witte and his team at St. Martin's Press for so enthusiastically embracing this novel, and to Meredith Rose for her meticulous editing and unfailing good humour. I must also thank my dear friends John Borrow, Rita Mallia, Heinz Schweers, Colan Leach and Jenny Wells for reading early manuscripts, and the lovely staff and students of Kambala school for their warm support during the writing of this book.

Finally, I thank my mother and father for their patient indulgence of my many years of *Titanic* obsession.